Neon Hemlock Press
www.neonhemlock.com
@neonhemlock

We're Here: The Best Queer Speculative Fiction 2024
Edited by Ryka Aoki
and Series Editor Charles Payseur

Cover Illustration by Matthew Spencer
Interior Illustration by Matthew Spencer
Cover Design by dave ring
Interior Design and Layout by dave ring

Paperback ISBN-13: 978-1-966503-18-7
Ebook ISBN-13: 978-1-966503-19-4

WE'RE HERE
THE BEST QUEER SPECULATIVE FICTION 2024

Neon Hemlock Press

NEON HEMLOCK

Ryka Aoki has been making the speculative fiction field a better place for a long time. A finalist for the Lambda, Hugo, Locus, and Ignyte Awards and an Alex, SCKA, and Otherwise Award winner, her works include the novels *Light from Uncommon Stars* and *He Mele A Hilo*, her collections *Seasonal Velocities* and *Why Dust Shall Never Settle Upon This Soul*, and her children's book *The Great Space Adventure*, among many others. I had the great privilege to get to meet her briefly at WisCon after she won the Otherwise and she gave an amazing speech about the rough road growing up different can be, and the joy and escape that can come from speculative fiction, and the progress that has been made to recognize and value voices that have long been and continue to be silenced. Her works are inspiring and inspired not just for the honesty and hard truths she reveals in them, but for the richness of her imagination and the power of her vision. She also had work out in 2024, including in the anthology *Embodied Exogenesis*, which sadly we could not consider, but which I do want to bring your attention to because it is very much worth seeking out. Ryka is one heck of a writer and editor, and I am honored and humbled to be able to present the works in this book alongside her.

We received over 350 submissions through our portal for this volume, which isn't our high water mark but remains pretty consistent with the number of submissions we've received in recent years. Adding in my own reading outside of submissions brings the total works considered upwards of 750, which continues to prove the need for projects like this, given the amount of queer stories and storytellers putting out amazing work. From all the works considered, we created a long list of roughly forty stories, and from that the guest editor made the final selections. And while the long list was a little shorter than typical (we average closer to fifty most years), the general guidelines we follow to try and reflect the wide range of stories being published remained. These guidelines act to place barriers to limit the numbers of stories we include on the long list from any single venue (capped at two) or any single author (capped at one), which pushes us to consider more sources of material and hopefully prevents us from considering only what is already familiar to us—something we've decided to prioritize given the size and diversity of the field.

That wealth of queer stories was spread over a great many publications in 2024, and we considered stories from queer-specific venues like *Baffling Magazine* and anthologies like *Scissor Sisters* (eds. Rae Knowles and April Yates), *We Mostly Come Out at Night* (ed. Rob Costello), *Embodied Exogenesis* (ed. Ann LeBlanc), *I Want That Twink OBLITERATED!* (ed. Trip Galey, Robert Berg, and C.L. McCartney), *Bury Your Gays* (ed. Sofia Ajram), *A Queer & Cozy Winter* (via Rainbow Crate), and *The Crawling Moon* (ed. dave ring). Unfortunately, *Prismatica* lapsed back into indefinite hiatus, joining queer-specific publications like *Anathema* and *Glittership*, which have remained out of commission for some time (though there might be indications *Anathema* will be returning). *F&SF* was another publication that went through some reorganizing in 2024, and despite a Winter issue packed with LGBTQ+ stories (two of which appear in this book), the publication spent the rest of the year between issues—a new owner was announced in 2025, but the publication remains a bit behind on its release schedule.

Queer novellas continue to be abundant as well, and 2024 had some absolute gems. From Tordotcom there were *The Brides of High Hill* by Nghi Vo, *The Woods All Black* by Lee Mandelo, *Navigational Entanglements* by Aliette de Bodard, and *Haunt Sweet Home* by Sarah Pinsker, among other. Neon Hemlock released a number, including *The Dragonfly Gambit* by A.D. Sui, *The Transitive Properties of Cheese* by Ann LeBlanc, and *A Mourning Coat* by Alex Jeffers. Tachyon put out a few, including RB Lemberg's *Yoke of Stars* and Izzy Wasserstein's *These Fragile Graces, This Fugitive Heart.* And other publishers got in on the action as well, as with Aliette de Bodard's *In the Shadow of the Ship* at Subterranean, Suzan Palumbo's *Countess* from ECW, Sam Kyung Yoo's *Small Gods of Calamity* at Interstellar Flight, and Lyndsie Manusos's *From These Dark Abodes* from Pyschopomp. There are also a great many that I am no doubt missing, but though *We're Here* cannot include novellas, they continue to be a rich source of queer speculative fiction.

And even after four previous volumes, we're still finding new sources of queer stories. Though for the first time the number of stories from publications we've selected stories from previously is greater than the number of stories from publications new to *We're Here*, there were still six new regular publications and two anthologies making their *We're Here* debut. That includes two stories from *F&SF* and single stories from *Analog, Kaleidotrope, khōréō, Porter House Review, and Sunday Morning Transport.* Those join selections from *3LBE* (appeared in 2022), *Apex* (appeared in 2021 and 2022), *Beneath Ceaseless Skies* (appeared in 2020 and 2021), *Diabolical Plots* (appeared in 2021), *Fiyah* (appeared in 2021 and 2023), *Fusion Fragment* (appeared in 2022), *Strange Horizons* (appeared 2020 and 2022), and *Uncanny* (appeared 2021). That brings the total number of distinct publication venues featured in *We're Here* to 52.

Our 2024 volume also features the greatest number of returning authors with four: Izzy Wasserstein and Kristina Ten also appeared in our 2023 edition; Ann LeBlanc appeared in the 2021 volume; and John Wiswell returns from all the way back in our inaugural 2020 anthology. Which means fifteen of our authors are making their *We're Here* debut, and it always fills me with joy to be able to add new members to our sprawling *We're Here* family. To date, 76 different authors have contributed to the 83 total stories we've included in the *We're Here* series. No author has yet to be featured more than twice, though I imagine it will only be a matter of time before someone reaches that milestone.

With my look at the field complete, though, I have to turn my attention on the state of the world and, well...oof. I have been dreading writing this part of this introduction, not because it's difficult to think of words to say in the face of the growing global fascism. That's almost easy, as this series has always been intended at least part in protest, because in a world that wants to destroy you just existing and celebrating yourself and your communities can be an act of resistance and rebellion. No, the work hasn't changed. But it does get harder. No doubt next year if I'm still alive and this series is still going I will be able to speak with more experience and knowledge about trends following the USA 2024 elections. But I do know that so far it hasn't increased the opportunities for or proliferation of queer stories and storytelling.

We are losing voices. We are losing them to war and genocide. We are losing them to efforts to isolate the USA from the rest of the world, to expel immigrants and prevent the free flow of education and ideas. We are losing them to the domestic policies stripping people of their rights, their healthcare, and their futures. We are losing them to the pressure to self-censor, self-deport, and self-police in order to avoid the violence being promised and committed against brown and black people, trans and queer people, disabled people, immigrants, and all those who have been labeled enemies by the fascist elements overjoyed to be back in power.

We're here, but we're also harder to find, and will become more so as more groups are emboldened and empowered to suppress and erase queerness and transness. We're here, but the rights we've fought so hard for are under constant attack. We're here, but sometimes when we look up we find that we're not *all* here anymore—and some people we thought of as allies and friends are marching lockstep with those working towards our eradication. And that sucks. And we're tired. And ultimately, this book will not save the world.

But this book will save *something*. It will save these voices and these stories. And it will spread them. And every hand and heart they touch will hold them and carry them, even if these pages are burned. Even if this book is banned. It is still full of magic. Full of love and sadness, fear and joy. Full of queer tragedies and queer triumphs. Full of queer *life* and queer *futures*. And this book is meant to be shared. It's a clandestine note passed to someone feeling alone and worthless. It's a time capsule, preserving these voices for a future that will need them. It's a reminder to anyone who picks it up and reads it—we're here. We've always been here. We'll always be here. And we are beautiful. And we are strong. And you, reading these words, *you* are a part of that as well. You are beautiful. You are strong. And I wish I could spare you every bad thing that might happen. But I can't.

What I can do is give you these stories with the hope that they resonate with you. That against everything they let you feel less alone. Less afraid. We're in this together. We're here. Working toward a better future and a better world that we can imagine and shape and touch and breath into life with our words and actions. We're here.

Charles Payseur
July 2025
Eau Claire, WI

A Note From the Editor

Right now, I am in Los Angeles, in the United States. It is 2025 and these are difficult times for trans people and other queer people.

And we're not alone. Immigrants, Muslims, people with disabilities, people with chronic illnesses, those who are neurodivergent.... So many people are finding their identities—even their humanities—questioned and attacked.

Many people are outraged, and rightly so. Some will say that our society has degenerated. Other will insist that "this is not who we really are." Many will be filled with nostalgia, say that it used to be better, that this used to be "a free country." They will say even say there was once something called the "free world."

But was the world really ever free?

Oppressions and prejudices have always been. Colonialism, jingoism, sexism, racism, ableism, xenophobia, homophobia...the underlying willingness to believe that some people are lesser beings than others is intertwined with all of human history.

Yet if we are to survive as a species, it's imperative that we find better ways to coexist. After all, our sticks and stones are getting bigger and more deadly. Putting the weapons of today, tomorrow...the day *after* tomorrow...in the hands of the usual suspects is not going to end well.

How repeatedly have we heard "those who do not read history are doomed to repeat it?"

However, even if you repeatedly read history, the one theme that repeats is that we tend to repeat ourselves.

But what about fantasy? What about science fiction, speculative fiction?

Yes, there are some great stories where the objective is to find shit, kill shit, and get the hot goblin or alien or elf.

And yes, there is value in allegory. Genocide is much easier (and safer) to talk about when it's on another planet and everyone is wearing silicone facial prosthetics.

But is that all? Are our visions, our imaginations, so limited?

Forget existing as a hologram or within a black hole— to me, hell would be living in a badly written infinity-book trilogy where there every volume, every chapter, every sentence was doomed to rehash the same old stories, the same old conflicts, the same old heroes on the same old journeys.

Surely, there has to be something different!

Which makes me think about about queer people, trans people. We live in the margins, in the outer reaches of our social galaxies. As such, we've had to find different ways of existing, not out of artistic or intellectual curiosity, but out of *necessity.*

As a queer, trans person, I have often felt like an alien on my own planet. When traditional institutions failed me, I sought alternative ways to exist or to learn and know. I found other ways to have family. Other ways to love.

I certainly do not mean to speak for other trans and queer people. But whatever else they are, I do think our trans and queer existences—for better or worse—often fall outside expectations.

And when these existences fall upon those who are *also* amazing writers and visionaries?

That is why I believe queer and trans stories can be so compelling—so *necessary*—not just for queer and trans audiences but for *anyone.*

◈

SELECTING THE STORIES for *We're Here: The Best Queer Speculative Fiction 2024* was not easy. There were many fantastic submissions from which to choose. Queer and speculative journals, magazines, small presses, both in print and online, are nurturing and publishing some incredible writers and I urge you to read and support and celebrate them.

For *this* book, my strategy was not to look for specific themes or tones. I would not seek out writing in my favorite style or subgenre. Instead, I was determined to find stories that showed how diminished this world would be without trans writers, queer writers, voices from the margins.

I wanted to share stories that dazzled, horrified, fascinated, filled me with hope.

I wanted to share the stories that ensorcelled me with their brilliant and dangerous language...lush and generous stories that expanded my world, that foretold what might be in worlds to come.

And I am delighted to say, *"Yatta! I succeeded!"*

Read Phoebe Barton's first paragraph. Read Denzel Xavier Scott's. Or John Wiswell's. Go on—then just *try* to stop. I dare you!

Heck, read Angel Leal's first *sentence*, or David DeGraff's or Stephen M.A.'s.

Jo Telle, Uchechukwu Nwaka, and Izzy Wasserstein grab me and whisk me to places far away, while Claire Jia-Wen and AnaMaria Curtis begin quietly, almost gently, yet I am transported elsewhere all the same.

Kristina Ten and Suzan Palumbo write about places I could almost have visited, lovers I might wish to have had, while Kelsey Hutton, Renan Bernardo, and Ann LeBlanc show me lives that I could never ever have known.

M.R. Robinson and B. Pladek make me think of my home, though neither wrote about my home.

And Louis Evans makes me think of my past and my present, though my life has nothing to do with the characters or setting.

And yet my feelings, memories, and gratitude are real.

There is magic, in these stories. *Real* magic. For a favorite story can grab your soul. Though written by someone else, set somewhere else, about someone else... somehow the story grows into your own, as well. And since the story remains the story, at least some of that growth must have taken place within you.

That's the magic of finding writing that you love.

And that's what each of these stories is for me.

✦

YOU KNOW, COMPARED with truly alien life forms, the differences between cis and trans, queer and straight, are insignificant.

But if we can't exult in a little strangeness on this planet, what is going to prepare all that is out there?

This is a baby, baby, *baby* step outward. But for everyone who has ever asked who else might be out right now, who else could be curled under a blanket and gazing at the stars?

It *is* a step.

After all, the margins are where we all end and begin.

Ryka Aoki
Los Angeles, CA
June 2025

TABLE OF CONTENTS

A Note From the Series Editor by Charles Payseur
A Note From the Editor by Ryka Aoki

❖

◆

About Our Contributors
Story Acknowledgements
About the Editors / About the Press

The Offer of Peace Between Two Worlds

Renan Bernardo

.3.

At this age, on the planet of Orvalho, Alberto is conjoined with the ship called The Offer of Peace Between Two Worlds. They're engulfed in the Mezelões' unifying mix, a tank where a swirling brackish secretion flows through their pores and recesses, nanoscopic spidery bots tying their espírito together—parts and limbs, yottabytes and nucleotides, ship and captain, physically separated, spiritually united.

When they leave the tank, dripping dark goo, crying and whirring, they have become one, bound to each other.

Alberto is a child: gaunt, dark-skinned, green-eyed; born to be a captain. He'll soon contest that, like all the people who are born and bound to be anything by those who came before them.

The Offer of Peace Between Two Worlds is a ship: silvery, slender, streamlined; born to be an offer. It looks like a toy—for Alberto, it is one, though he'll soon stop seeing it that way. It's a tiny spaceship with a prow; dronelike, smaller than a goose. When charged, the engine it was born with lets it cross from the kitchen to the garden without needing extra fusion cells.

Weeks after crying in despair in the Mezelões' labs, Alberto shyly learns to giggle into the loneliness of his wide bedroom, constructed to give space to child and ship. In between visits from his allocated guardians, Alberto learns to play with The Offer of Peace Between Two Worlds. He taps its gleaming hull and the ship hurtles through the bedroom. When the window is open, it swishes out and returns many minutes later, dripping on rainy days, sizzling on the hot ones. Alberto calls it Offy. At night, Alberto learns to smile at Offy, but never to kiss it good night. No one has taught him about kisses. Offy turns down its engines so Alberto can sleep. Turns them down, that is, until it learns that Alberto prefers its whirs and hums, and the soft white lights of its protruding mole-like bridge.

.10.

AT THIS AGE, Alberto resents every time he hears the Mezelões calling Offy by other names—"The Offer of Peace Between Two Worlds," "a nurturing investment," "the shot at peace for the galaxy," "a gift for the enemy." For Alberto, it'll always be Offy. Offy can't express it yet—its mindstream system isn't fully grown—but it can feel Alberto's annoyance when grownups call him "little captain," "brother of the offer," "bringer of peace." For Alberto, the word *brother* seems misplaced, and one day he'll understand why.

Offy is bigger than a tricycle now and growing every day, its gobbling drive devouring the raw material the guardians leave for it—steel, titanium, magnesium, and an entire bevy of alloys and mixtures carefully nurtured for ship growth. Alberto barely fits inside, occupying most of its payload. He's free to fly it, his guardians say, though they're still bounded by the limits of the Captain's Dome, which comprises his bedroom and the guardians' annex. Alberto hates limits. He wants to break away from Orvalho and fly to the twinkling stars, home of a hundred races, of a thousand planets, of a million cities. The grownups say he'll be able to go wherever he wants one day, when he's captain, when The Offer of Peace Between Two Worlds is fully matured.

On some nights, Alberto has nightmares. In them, he's back in the Mezelões' tanks. But instead of a union, he's being separated from Offy, with freezing, brackish goo pouring out of his body. He cries, restless, trying to swim, looking for Offy. But before he finds it, Offy—the real one, from the waking world—flies closer to him, whirring a bit louder. It's only then Alberto knows he won't drown.

.15.

AT THIS AGE, Alberto's guardians give Offy its first hangar. It's a spacious building outside the Captain's Dome, reeking of oil, iron, and disinfectant. Offy is still only a dot inside it, the size of two trucks, but its mindstream system is grown now. The first words it conveys to Alberto are: "I want to fly higher."

"You will," Alberto whispers, cheeks plastered against Offy's hull. "We will."

Alberto's free now, the guardians tell him, and he can fly Offy whenever he wants. Offy, however, is leashed. It pains Alberto when he finds out about the coercive routine they have installed to prevent Offy from traveling further than Orvalho's orbit. After five nights with Offy mindstreaming its data to Alberto, he learns how to override it.

.16.

AT THIS AGE, Albert identifies one of the many things that bother him. She hates to be called "he." Offy realizes one thing as well. They hate to be called "it."

Offy now has a set of skintight suits for EVA activities, a small rover, and a robust sub-light engine that performs at 0.001c. So Alberto breaks the rules and flies Offy to Beirão, Orvalho's biggest moon. There, she wears a suit and walks out. She does things she always wanted: hop in the moon's weak gravity; allow her feet to leave marks on the regolith; stare at the pearlescent surface of Orvalho for an hour. Finally, she talks. With their nose pointing up, Offy listens.

"I know what you are, what you were created to be. An offer of peace. You're to be given to the Indaleões so the war between them and the Mezelões, two centuries long, can finally end. They bred you through me, tied our espíritos, because that's the only way a ship can be. But they don't mean for us to stay together like conjoined captains are supposed to. No, they'll separate us so you can be a gift to some other people. Your own name means that. Then they'll use you in their exhibitions or worse— forcefully tie you to a new captain. It will be painful for you and for me. They know it too, but they don't care. Offy...I don't intend to let that happen."

But then, how many things have to happen, irrespective of what one wants?

.20.

At this age, Alia and Offy have their first fight. It is hardly an even match; in the last few years, as acne pockmarked Alia's cheeks, Offy grew their core weapons—two laser cannons, an electron beam, internal coupled guns, and a series of hull turrets. But they turn none of it against Alia, even though she scowls at them, seething, thrashing the bridge's comm panels and terminals, trying uselessly to crack their glass panes. Eventually, she surrenders and crashes into a couch, weeping and bristling as she absorbs everything Offy has mindstreamed to her. Offy wants to leave. Of their own accord, they want to go and explore the galaxy on their own.

When Alia tries to infiltrate Offy's code and override it—like she did so many times to invisibly counter the Mezelões' meddling—a terrible wind knocks her to the ground, and in strong gusts flowing along Offy's corridors, it swooshes her away through an airlock. She stumbles out into the hangar as Offy activates their drive and flies away.

She's left incomplete.

.22.

AT THIS AGE, Alia lives alone in a shipping container with three ore miners. Without The Offer of Peace Between Two Worlds, she's no longer a captain, no longer relevant to the Mezelões. Her guardians of childhood, once all smiles and gifts and kind words, are never to be seen again.

The fact that The Offer of Peace Between Two Worlds fled doesn't mean they lost their conjoined espíritos. Instead, it means Alia lost part of her soul. She lives restlessly. Day after day, she's wearier, gaunter, her eyes drooping, her hair falling. She obsesses over the ship's operation logs, streaming them over and over in her mind. And, one day, barely eating anymore, she finally decrypts a set of logs from their last days together. The Offer of Peace Between Two Worlds didn't leave because they wanted to be free—as they had every right to want—but because they feared Alia would suffer, or even be disposed of, when Offy had to finally become an offer to the Indaleões.

Alia decides to draw momentum and energy from the logs, like a fusion drive thirsty for deuterium. She hitchhikes on an ore miner, then hops to a rock trawler, crosses warp gates between systems. She lives off begging, and degrading jobs, and stealing. All the while, searching for the signature of The Offer of Peace Between Two Worlds—Offy; their name is Offy.

.24.

AT THIS AGE, she does find Offy. Using a rock trawler's detection system, yes, but she also feels it somewhere within her, her espírito bubbling up. Something clicks within her, like a puzzle piece falling into place.

Offy's orbiting a gas giant, their hull reflecting a dismal blueish light. Around them, five Mezelões blastships order Offy's surrender. Alia watches it all from the rock trawler's skiff she stole, zooming on the battle scene, listening to public broadcasts being transmitted from within the fray. It's the first time she sees Offy using their weapons and she takes pride in their use: the electron beam ripping off the Mezelões' hulls, the turrets exploding their skiffs and drones. And as she finds strength in seeing Offy again, they find it nurturing to feel Alia once more, less than 1 AU off. That's when Offy uses their laser cannons at full potential and disintegrates the remaining Mezelões ships.

When they reunite, it's like finding a rose intact on a bloody battlefield.

.27.

AT THIS AGE, rebels die. Alia doesn't. She's the first of the Mezelões' captains to defect. With Offy, she spends her time hopping from system to system as Offy's camouflage system grows and their gobbling drive feeds off any matter it can find on asteroids and rocky planets. They finally reach their full size, large enough to house 3,000 people—room for every soldier in the Indaleões' primary fleet. But Offy needs no one but Alia to control its subsystems, from the churning particles of the budding FTL drive to the life support system's sighs of oxygen. And the pair travel through the galaxy, their only aim, to be anything but a captain and to be anything but an offer, ignoring all the broadcasts the Mezelões direct at them: you can't be.

.30.

AT THIS AGE, the duo is the most valuable asset in the galaxy. In the eyes of the Mezelões, Offy is a fully-formed offer, but it's more than that. Their separation and eventual reunion made Offy develop faster than expected. Their hull has grown another layer of titanium; their FTL drive, usually fully developed only at 60 years from conjoining, is almost at its prime; their weapons offer twice as much firepower as a similar ship would at this age.

And in the Mezelões' eyes, Alia, despite being a rebel and a wanted woman, is a splendid captain, capable of controlling—though Alia hates the word—all of Offy's systems with mere slivers of mindstreamed thoughts, without needing to couple herself to chairs and machinery like other captains.

And that's why they're chased. Their life becomes fleeing, surviving, hiding in the solitary caves of unexplored moons, orbiting uncharted gas giants, free-floating in the blackness of interstellar space. At times, Alia finds herself disguised, roaming the infinite streets of ultra-dense cities, disappearing amongst ten billion citizens. Offy finds themself changing their drive signature and exhaust patterns day after day. Offy develops a factory of replicating bots and, with the bots' help, learns to shapeshift. One day, they look like a cigarette. Another day, they're in the form of a turtle swimming across the void.

One of those days, Alia and Offy wonder if they're forever.

.45.

AT THIS AGE, light becomes slower. Offy develops a fully-formed FTL drive. Though at this point, Alia and Offy don't see each other as conjoined entities anymore. They're simply one, and they call themself Alyof.

Going faster than light, Alyof can reach other galaxies, transforming the Mezelões, the Indaleões, and their pitiful skirmish into something as irrelevant as a molecule lost in the vacuum. Some of their most formidable ships, conjoined with their wisest and oldest captains, can still reach them. But not many dare to defy Alyof anymore. By now, they have a plethora of planet-wrecking weapons that no ship has ever achieved. Alyof becomes a mere anomalous curiosity, a feature of space to be observed and respected from a distance, like a quasar.

.85.

AT THIS AGE, Alyof learns they're not invincible. Not because the Mezelões develop a fleet to chase Alyof, although they do and they're utterly destroyed; not because a race of vacuum-traveling stingrays tries to absorb Alyof into their being, although they do and they're repelled. But because their espírito can still break.

What was once Alia longs for rest. Tethered to the bridge by a cobweb of flesh, what was once Alia wheezes, coughs, and dozes off. At times, what was once Alia misses things it would never believe it would miss: the soft bedsheets of a bedroom; a cup of coffee in a silent cantina; a walk to an observation deck to watch a terraformed forest slowly growing; the touch of someone's hand.

What was once Offy longs for more. It wants to explore the corners of the universe, to know, to learn, to never cease to be. At times, what was once Offy longs for things it would never believe it would long for: to fly closer to black holes, to visit the frontiers of the known universe, to observe species evolving from their puddles to their pyramids.

For what was once Alia, what was once Offy becomes a weight.

For what was once Offy, what was once Alia becomes a tumor.

In the end, Alyof realizes they can't be.

And this is how a spirit breaks: on a chalky, cold planet, Alyof expels Alia from their guts and becomes Offy again. Naked and wrinkly, gasping, with fleshy knobs hanging from her body, Alia curls on the ground, dwarfed by Offy like a discarded offer given to a deserted world. She raises a hand to them but has to close her eyes.

Alia never sees when Offy turns into a blue dot in the sky. She feels something in her chest that she mistakes for pain, but it's only longing for what was once part of her.

.1,263.

AT THIS AGE and every age beyond that, Offy travels. Cruising between two galaxies a thousand times faster than light, Offy listens to one who was once part of them. Offy knows they'll never be whole again, but they can pretend. The reconstructed voice talks through their speakers and writes to their logs in a rough imitation of mindstreaming processes.

"I'm still afraid I'll have to die one day and leave you," the voice says. "My body is not like yours."

Offy whirs a bit louder so that unreal part of them knows they can't drown and they can be.

❋

Together Like Hands on a Clock

Jo Telle

I WONDER WHERE YOU go when your matter untangles from itself and is carried up into the solar winds. Are you traversing the cosmos? What are you when your body disappears? Who are you?

All summer, I've thought about this. Since the last time I saw your body fade away with the northern lights. I haven't been able to figure out what you are anymore. Ghost? Spirit? Some celestial being out of phase with time and space?

Best I can figure is that your very existence is tied to the northern lights. When they appear, you appear, always in the same spot. When they fade into the distance, so do you. Seems easy enough to understand, though I still don't understand why it has to happen to you.

I don't care about that right now, though. I'm just excited to see you walk up to the rented cabin, the same one you rented the night you disappeared. I'm excited to see you with your red winter jacket slung over your shoulder and that little saunter you have in your step.

The apparition hottie, as I've come to call you: brown skin, barely-there buzzed bleached curls, and a sleeve of black and gray tattoos running down your right arm. Wearing your usual crisp white tank top, brown Carhartt overalls, and tan rolled-up beanie. The outfit you wore the night you disappeared. What you wear every night as you appear in front of me.

It's been a long summer since I last saw you, since we were last in step, walking side by side. Patience doesn't come easily to me. Especially not when it comes to waiting on the movement of the earth and the unpredictable patterns of solar winds. Thankfully, all my waiting is not in vain as the weather calls for northern lights tonight. It calls for you to come back to me.

Me, your girlfriend? Your ex? Your li'l situationship that you see whenever I'm up in Alaska and you decide to ride into town on the waves of the northern lights? Is the fact that we don't know what to call our relationship the dykiest thing about us?

The knock at the cabin door pulls me away from my thoughts.

"Took you long enough," I say, reaching for your tank top to pull you in all seductive and shit, but I just grab a handful of your sports bra instead.

You laugh. I laugh. You come in through the door and we fall onto the couch, our bodies still shaking from the moment.

"Nice to see you too," you say, regaining your composure.

You peer into my brown eyes with your own. You swipe a stray curl away from my face and tuck it behind my ear. You motion for me to sit on your lap, and I do, even though I'm taller and bigger than you are.

You run your hands up and down my long, black thighs. Squeezing gently but deeply, you trace your fingers over the rose tattoo on my left hip. Your hands roam up the sides of my stomach and stop right below the bralette peeking out underneath my crop top.

"I see we're picking up right where we left off back in April," I say, lazily

drooping my arms over your shoulders, cocking my head to the side.

Your hands move slightly higher and I gasp.

"So that's a yes, then," I say, collapsing into you.

"Shall we?" you ask.

"Duh."

"Did you bring my backpack?"

"Also duh, it's in the bedroom."

You respond with a wide, hungry grin as you pick me up off your lap and start undoing your overalls as we head to the bedroom.

There's not much nighttime in August, so we can't take our time the way we would in the winter. The way we used to when we first started dating. When our relationship was more clearly defined than it is now.

◆

OUR FIRST DATE was a proper, long-as-hell, twenty-four-hour dyke date. It started at El Cochinito for dinner, back in Los Angeles.

"You're not one of those girls that's afraid to eat onions on a date, are you?" you asked.

"Why? Are you trying to kiss me?" I said.

I brought my head down low and looked up at you over my glasses. I heard girls like that sort of thing. Your lips, curled up in a mischievous smile as you nibbled on tostones, was confirmation enough.

"Would you say yes if I asked?"

"That depends," I said.

"On what?"

"Should Aragorn have chosen Éowyn or Arwen?"

"Nah, you've gotta be kidding me," you said with a snort.

I just shrug my shoulders and cross my arms.

"That's it? I just gotta answer which one and I'll get to kiss you?" you asked, leaning back in your chair to give room for the server to set down our plates.

I didn't answer right away, I wanted to build anticipation. Besides, I was eager to dive into my sandwich. A cubano sandwich *with* onions.

"If you answer correctly, yes."

"It's a trick question. The correct answer is Legolas," you said.

The grin on your face was cocky, but not in that eye rolling "Hey Mamas," sort of way. It was playful and confident. And most importantly, it was sexy as hell.

"All right, all right, I see you."

"So is that a yes?" you asked.

"It's a… you pick the time and place."

The time was halfway through our meal that we ate with haste. The place was back at yours—which soon became ours after I moved in.

All through the night, we moved from the bedroom, to the kitchen to rehydrate, back to the bedroom, and into the living room to stare into each other's eyes while sitting quietly on the couch. Our legs pressed up against each other, our hands intertwined, our thumbs running over one anothers.

The next morning, you made me breakfast. Scrambled eggs with bacon and veggies mixed in. A glass of orange juice on the side. Then we resumed our routine of moving between the bedroom and the kitchen. Eventually, we had to come up for air, and we went out for afternoon drinks and food at some spot in Silver Lake that closed a few years back. You held my hand across the table on the outdoor patio and told me, in no uncertain terms, what you imagined for our future.

"I see a future with you, Raven," you said. "I really do."

"I see it too, Dee," I said. And I did.

"Can I tell you something and you won't freak out?" you asked.

"Of course, baby." We were quick with the pet names.

"Someday, I'm going to build a house. In Alaska. Somewhere I can see the northern lights from my porch. There'll be a swing. Big enough for two people. What do you think of that?" you said. I swear I could see the lights swirling in your eyes. The vision you had of your future was clear as day. You made me as sure of it as you were.

"That sounds amazing," I said.

"I know we just started dating and all, but I can see a future where you and I are cuddled together on that swing. Sipping on hot chocolates. Heads nestled into each other as we admire the night sky. Is that crazy?" you asked.

I remember I was stunned at the time. Stunned by your confidence, by your beauty, by your vulnerability. By this vision you had of the two of us together. I was stunned because I could see it, too. Sure, the edges were a bit blurry. Slightly out of focus. But I saw it. I saw us, together.

"No, baby, that's not crazy at all," I said as I squeezed your hand.

It didn't take long for me to move in after that and build a life with you. Adopt a dog, cook together, celebrate each other's victories, soothe each other's losses, plan vacations together. Always front-of-mind for us was that future in Alaska. That was our north star. That was what we were aiming for.

❖

YOU COME BACK into the bedroom, bringing us both glasses of water. We gulp them down and lay back down on the bed. You as the big spoon and me as the little. Your head perfectly nestled against mine as we look out the window at the Alaskan sky.

"I missed you," you say.

You wrap your arm across my torso, delicately avoiding that lower, dysphoric area with practiced precision.

"I thought you said time works differently for you. That you can't perceive time between appearances," I say.

You put your leg on top of mine. I playfully slide mine out and move it on top of yours. We giggle, knowing this is one of the rare instances where we debate who is on top.

"Yeah. Even still, I missed you," you say as you give me a gentle, full-body squeeze.

I grin as I look up out the window. A faint swirl of purple and green dances across the sky. No longer the rich, deep hues when you arrived a few hours ago, but slightly faded against a warming sky. The clock on the nightstand says 4:05 a.m. There's not much time left.

I turn around and wrap as much of my body around you as I can. I fold your smaller hand into mine and squeeze as tight as I can. The way that young couples do when their love is new and boundless.

"Is it almost time?" you ask quietly.

I nod. You hold on tighter in response.

"It's early in the season, we'll have more nights like this. And then we won't. We'll have all the time in the world," you say, brushing your hand across my cheek and down my throat, avoiding that other dysphoric bulge with the skill that comes with five years of being together.

"You're right. It's just… it was a long summer," I say, turning my face away from yours; I regret it immediately, turning back to you, knowing it may be a while until I see your face again.

"I know. I'm sorry. But I'm here now," you say with a smile.

We hold each other, caress each other, savor each other until the sun starts to creep its way into our room. I watch your body crumble like sand through fingers as you scatter into a million pieces and fade into nothing.

Later that morning, I sit down on the couch with some breakfast and coffee and scroll through the photos on my phone. I ignore the pesky memory prompts the phone suggests, scroll past the photos from your end-of-life party, past the photos we took on your bucket-list vacation to Europe, and finally land on that photo I took back in March. The night you disappeared.

That first night you disappeared, I was a wreck. And no, it wasn't just because we had the biggest blowout fight of our relationship right before you walked off towards the river.

❖

"IF YOU CAN'T support me in this, then why are you even here?" you asked, as you stomped around in the living room of your rented cabin.

Fire-engine red and deep blue quilts covered the backs of couches and chairs. Orange light cascaded down around you from the chandelier hanging from the twenty-foot-tall timber ceiling. A bit too wildernessy for my taste, but then again, you hadn't booked it with me in mind.

"Because I'm your girlfriend. I'm always going to be there for you, even if I don't agree with what you're doing," I replied, sitting on the couch, legs underneath me with a pillow in front of my chest.

I had booked my flight at the last minute when I caught on to what you had planned. I arrived at the cabin with just a carry-on, disheveled clothes, and messy hair trying to claw its way out of the ballcap I wore to hide it. Not exactly the cute, Black trans girl you fell in love with, but the one trying to get you to stop being an idiot.

"That's the thing, though. I explicitly asked you not to be here," you said. "Why can't you just honor my wishes?"

"Can't I think your wishes are dumb as shit?" I said, ruining my chances of a career in diplomacy.

You were always so cute when you got angry. Even when you were pissing me the fuck off, I still couldn't help but fall in love with you all over again.

Your nostrils flared as if to allow more space for steam to pass through, like characters in those old cartoons. The muscles in your arms and shoulders tightened, and the veins in your forearm rose to the surface. Your skin started to glisten as sweat collected into the sports bra that does little to compress the large chest you say butches aren't supposed to have.

"Fine," you said. "Here are your options: stay here and let me do what I need to do on my own, help me in what is literally the hardest but most significant moment of my life, or go the fuck home."

At first, I decided to let you walk down to the river and do what you came here to do.

At first.

I tried, I really tried. It's not that I wanted to take away your agency. I swear to God, that's not what I was trying to do. You had every right to decide how to live your life and when not to. But I wasn't ready to let you go. I had months to prepare myself for your disease to take you. I only had one night to prepare myself before you took matters into your own hands.

I'd never felt lonelier than I had sitting in that cabin by myself after you walked out that door.

I know it's selfish of me. I know that now. I probably even knew it then, too. But I had to see you one last time.

Except you were already gone. The river wasn't rushing, just idling by. No sign that a large human-sized object had disturbed its flow. I waited there, in the dark and in the cold, for hours. I'm not quite sure what I was waiting for. Perhaps I just wasn't ready to have to go back home without you.

Resignation finally took hold of me and I dragged myself back to the cabin. I turned around, though, to take a shitty photo of your final resting place.

It's not my best work, certainly nothing compared to the photos I get paid to take. I used a wide-angle lens to capture as much of the scene as possible. Even set the photo on long exposure to soak up the available light. My trembling hands caused the phone to blur the photo ever-so-slightly.

In the foreground, a strip of white snow sloped backwards, trying to escape the claws of the lapping river in front of it. The bank on the other side of the river was covered in rocks, with a few stray tree trunks and branches that must have come from upstream. Trees framed the horizon line, with little stubs of mountains in the background, like small children jumping to make sure they are seen in the photo. A smattering of stars decorated the dark blue night sky. If one squinted hard enough, the faintest hint of purple and green could be seen off in the distant sky, the fading remnants of the northern light show that night.

I showed it to our friends when I got back home and they swore they could see a thin outline of your frame on the shore, looking up at the night sky in your red North Face coat and your tan Carhartt beanie. I couldn't see it. I still can't.

I understand the desire to see a glimmer, a fleeting hope of something where there is nothing. That's how I felt that whole year before you disappeared.

◆

I WAKE UP to a knock on the door. I look out the window and see nothing but the vast darkness of the Alaskan wilderness that surrounds me. Had I slept on the couch all day long?

The knocking continues.

I walk over to the door and am surprised to see you through the peephole.

"Missed me?" you ask, standing on your toes to give me a kiss.

"Well, yeah, but I wasn't expecting to see you back so soon," I say, pulling you inside.

You take a look around the room and see my breakfast plate, coffee cup, and the quilt I had hastily thrown off my body.

"I believe that," you say with a smile. "How about instead of sleeping on the couch, we go sleep in the bed?"

"Girl, I just woke up. Besides, I know you don't really intend to go to sleep, do you?" I ask.

"Well, no, but how long is your trip up here? Can't a girl wanna spend time with her girlfriend before she heads out of town?" you ask, throwing your jacket and beanie down on the couch.

"Oh, so we're girlfriends now? That's not what you called me back in April," I say, my body going stiff.

"Come on, babe, do we have to do this now?"

"Sure sounds like we are. Is it so wrong to ask for a little bit of clarity?" I say.

"Clarity? I am a literal freak of nature. My very existence defies the laws of space and time. I'm here one moment and gone the next. For the moments I am here, I'd like to spend them with you. I like it when we're girlfriends. But I don't know if that's how you like it, given what you've said in the past. How's that for clarity?"

Silence fills the space between us as we take opposite corners of the brown, green and blue rug in the middle of the room. Like boxers squaring off.

I try to fight it back, I really do. But I can't hold back the waterworks as much as I can hold back the coming of the day.

"I'm sorry, babe, that wasn't fair to you," you say, hanging your head down low.

"I just…I can't do this right now," I say, turning towards the bedroom.

"Babe," you say, your voice growing weak.

I pause, not wanting you to see my face. Then turn around anyways.

But you're gone. You, your jacket and your beanie. All gone.

I run towards the door and throw it open, forgetting to even put on shoes as I look up at the night sky. Not a single trace of the northern lights. Not a single trace of you.

◆

THE FORECAST SAID there would be no more light shows for the rest of the week. The rest of my stay in the cabin.

On the flight back to Los Angeles, I flipped through the photos in my phone again, landing on the ones from your end-of-life party. All of them are of you and our friends. Drinking, eating, laughing. I didn't laugh that night. I couldn't.

You called it "Last Stop on the Dee Train." You thought it was funny. All the guests did too. I suppose your friends were more prepared to let you go, or just better equipped to process your loss.

You organized the party a few months after you got your diagnosis. I was there in the doctor's office the day she told you. I hope you'll forgive me for not remembering all the details. It was hard to focus after the doctor said, "It's terminal." I remember a few other words and phrases: "rare"—"first case I've seen in over forty years of working in neurology"—"three months before it gets bad, six to nine months before it's terminal."

She gave you some documents on what to expect three months in. The list looked long and comprehensive. The doctor described the disease as thorough. Not a single part or system in your body would go untouched.

I asked how you felt about it, but you didn't say anything at first. You didn't say much of anything that first week. We slipped back into our routine instead of addressing the ticking time bomb. I went back to my photography studio. You went back to your construction company. It was still brand new when we first met. You were so proud to be the only queer-run civil contractor in Los Angeles. Your position required you to spend more time in the office than out on the job sites, but you still visited as often as you could.

God, I couldn't get enough of you. You in your scuffed up, dirty-as-hell boots, brown overalls with frayed edges at the bottom of the legs and a torn back pocket that you refused to let me sew up. Crisp white tank top that showed off your arms and tattoos and your usual tan beanie rolled up on your shaved head.

After your diagnosis, when we still weren't talking at home, you decided to spend less time in the office and more time on the job sites. Your business partner told me; otherwise I would have had no way of knowing but for the scrapes and gashes you got on your arms from careless handling of the pipes and fittings. I put an end to the silence the day you came home with the tip of your ring finger chopped off because you insisted on setting shoring equipment without gloves.

"What the hell is wrong with you? Are you trying to get yourself killed?" I screamed after you came home from urgent care with your hand wrapped up like a deli sandwich.

"Today, tomorrow, six to nine months from now. What's the difference?" you said, grabbing a bottle of brown liquor from the cabinet and drinking it without a glass.

"Oh, boo-fucking-hoo. This depressed bullshit isn't a good look on you," I said.

"Well, according to those Instagram influencers you follow, Carhartt actually does pair well with depression. Don't you know it's the look of the season?" you said, droplets spraying from your mouth as you spoke.

"You haven't said but one word to me since we saw the doctor last week and now you're cracking jokes? I can't be around this, Dee. It's unhealthy," I said, walking towards the entryway to collect my purse and put on my shoes.

"Come on, Raven, cut me a break here. I'm going through a tough time."

"The fact that you think you're the only one going through a tough time is a problem," I said and stormed out of our house.

After that, we started seeing a relationship therapist. Our friends said it was long overdue.

It took a few sessions before we started inching towards the truth. When we finally did, we agreed to stop going. We could handle a hint of the truth, a morsel, but the full truth would have been too real, too difficult for either of us to process.

In therapy you would say, "It's not fair. I have so much more to do, so much more to see. I just don't have enough time."

I would say, "I'm losing the most important person in my life, and I feel like they're already gone because they won't talk to me."

The therapist would ask how those statements made us feel or if we could find a way to support each other through our hard times.

You would say, "I hear you, but I feel like you've already been treating me as if I weren't here. There's already been this distance between us, and at times it doesn't feel like you want to bridge that gap."

I would say, "I hear you, so how can I help you see all the things you want to see and do all the things you want to do?"

That was enough for us. We had our own reasons for never sharing our full truth with each other. I suspect you may have thought you only had so much time left, so what was the point? I wonder what you suspected my reason was. If you knew my truth, would you have broken up with me? Would I have been able to let you go?

We found our way back to each other that night in therapy. That week, we booked a once-in-a-lifetime trip with stops in Madrid, Lisbon, Venice, Edinburgh, Amsterdam and Casablanca. It would be cold in the winter, but that just made you even more excited to go to the Christmas markets in Edinburgh and Amsterdam. We booked first-class tickets, booked the best hotels in each city with the finest rooms and the largest beds. You made sure each room had a bathtub for me to soak in while you were out for a run. We researched food tours and booked the most basic, cliché sightseeing tours. We wanted to see it all.

And see it all we did. I took photos of you in front of every landmark, every monument, even every storefront we came across. You would stand up tall, with your arms out as far away as possible from your body, with your head tilted slightly back—your favorite pose. In the photo you are part Christ the Redeemer, part victor standing tall over your domain. In that photo that I framed and hung on the wall, you were both full of life and completely frozen. Where you will remain long after your body fades away.

We visited every location on your travel list except for one: Fairbanks, Alaska. You said you couldn't go, not until you had done everything else you needed to do before your time was up. I understood. I knew what Fairbanks meant to you.

We returned from our travels all smiles and joy for having experienced this once-in-a-lifetime adventure together. Then the phrase *once in a lifetime* started to sink in, and we returned to the roles we inhabited before our detente in therapy.

We continued this way until you came up with the plan for your going away party. I supported you, as I had through everything else. But it was all a front.

You had been right during our last therapy session. I had no intention of bridging the distance that had formed between us. If anything, I was the cause of the distance.

This was my bitter, horrible truth.

I was going to break up with you before you got your diagnosis.

There wasn't anyone else. No one on the side. No secret lover or secret crush.

It wasn't that you left the toothpaste on the counter instead of putting it back in the cup where it belonged alongside the toothbrushes. It wasn't that you left the dishes in the sink instead of just putting them in the dishwasher. It wasn't that you couldn't be bothered to make the bed unless you were trying to make up for something you did.

It's just that at some point, while we were walking down the road of our lives together, I grew tired of walking. I wish the reason was more substantial, more dramatic, more climactic.

It wasn't.

I had fallen out of step with you.

Then you got your diagnosis. I thought, bonded by this life-changing news, that I could keep up with you again. I tried. I really tried. And I'm sorry for that. Because you deserve someone that didn't have to try. You deserve someone that was walking at your same pace.

It's not that we were never in step with each other. There are some people that are just destined to stay in each other's lives, even if they are on separate paths. The hands on a clock go at different speeds and have different journeys, but somewhere along the way, the big hand and small hand manage to be aligned for a short while.

Such is our new reality, two hands moving along our own separate journeys, waiting for a chance to be in sync. It has been this way since April when I made one last trip to Fairbanks because I wasn't ready to let you go. I came up to Fairbanks to mourn you, to say goodbye. But there you were, down by the river, staring up at the lights. You were confused, naturally. You had every reason to be.

Confused as to why you were alive, confused as to how you were alive. Why I wasn't wearing the same clothes that I wore the last night we saw each other. How an entire month had passed for me when for you it hadn't been more than a few seconds.

Neither of us had any answers, so instead of trying to understand what happened to you, we tried to understand what happened to us. I told you how I'd been feeling the past year, and you told me you saw it but were afraid to bring it up with me. We apologized to each other over and over, again and again; we forgave each other.

For once, as our hands intertwined, we found ourselves in sync. For once, until your body fell apart and became as brilliant and as abundant as a meteor shower. I thought we would stay together, that we would stay in sync. I was wrong.

◆

I DIDN'T GET a chance to fly back up until January. Or rather, I avoided flying back up until this January. This whole situation is a lot, and I'll admit I needed space. Space from you, space from us, whatever we are. Space from this whole, weird mess.

I really fucked up, though. Not just because I've been avoiding you, but because I chose to come back up during the coldest damn month of the year. You know my body ain't built for this shit. My people were not born to intentionally, willfully travel to the cold. I'm saying that as both a Black person and a trans woman. But I need to see you. I need to talk to you. I need to say I'm sorry. Again.

That first night back in Alaska, God, it was cold. I didn't expect you to stop by the cabin, so I figured I'd wait for you down by the river, in your spot where you always appear. I was good and bundled up, but I was still cold. I had layers upon layers of long underwear, sweaters, wool socks underneath windbreaker pants and a giant, ankle-length North Face jacket—the puffy kind. I had on a beanie and earmuffs, and I had that hood pulled all the way up over my big head. I had hand warmers stuffed inside my mittens stuffed inside those giant snow gloves.

I did all that to prepare for you, but you didn't come. No light show that night.

So, I came out the next night. And the night after that. Five nights in a row I froze my juicy ass out in the cold, just to see you. But you didn't show.

Tonight is the last night before I fly back to LA. The weather has a light show in the forecast, but that's what it said the last five nights, too.

Still, I hauled my ass down to the river and waited. And waited. And waited.

I sat down in my little camping chair and thought about what I was waiting for.

Sure, I wanted to see you. I wanted to apologize to you. But what was I waiting for, really? How long would we keep doing this? How long would I keep flying up here, hoping our hands would align and we could walk in step with one another again? How long could I keep holding on to you?

I wasn't ready to let go after your diagnosis.

I wasn't ready to let go after I found out why you came to Fairbanks and what you planned to do.

I'm still not ready to let you go, even though I have to every time you fade away into the ether.

I was going to break up with you… and I couldn't do it.

But you could. You've accepted your fate. You had to, multiple times over. You know you exist between worlds, between time, and you've accepted it.

"What the hell am I waiting for?" I say out loud into the darkness.

"What do you mean, babe?" you say, your voice coming from behind me. I stand up out of the chair, turn around, and see you slowly appear before me. Purple, blue, and green ribbons of light are pulled down from the sky, twirling around in a circle like some Olympic gymnastics routine. The ribbons blend together into a luminescent rainbow, growing brighter until a flash of white light rips them apart. You walk out of the light, making your way towards me as the northern lights stream across the sky above you.

"I have to let you go," I say confidently.

"Umm, okay. What are you talking about?"

"You are okay with us existing in a liminal space. You are okay with us being girlfriends when you're here and then nothing when you're gone. You've figured out how to let go," I say.

You nod your head. This probably wasn't the conversation you were expecting to have tonight.

"Sure, I guess so. What's this about?"

"I'm still holding on to the hope of something where there is nothing," I say.

"You're not making any sense."

"This—you and me—this is nothing. It's everything, too, but really it's nothing. For whole months of the year, it is nothing. It is nothing more often than it is something," I say, frantically waving my hands as if it's helping me make more sense.

"Babe, I don't…" you start, but I cut you off.

"We're not walking side by side anymore. We're not in sync. We haven't been since you disappeared. And honestly, we hadn't been for months before that. Whatever we have exists in the rhythm of the stars. In the movement of solar wind. What I'm trying to say is that I need to let you go as easily as you fade into nothingness. I'm saying I'm ready to let you go," I say, letting out a relieved sigh.

"Great, welcome to my world," you say, warmly extending your arms out for a hug.

You squeeze me close, and I allow my head to fall into the space between your head and shoulders. I feel as if my whole body is falling into you as I let go of everything I've held onto for much too long: feeling like I had to be physically and mentally present for you during your appearances. The difficulty in trying to keep up with my career that barely pays the bills—even before the added cost of trips to Alaska. The times when I longed for your presence—and times I was grateful for my own solitude, as guilty as they made me feel.

I think of that photo I took the night you disappeared, the one our friends swear they see an outline of your body in. I let go of feeling shame for not seeing you in that photo. I let go of trying to look for a hint of something where there is nothing at all.

I fall into your body and feel nothing and everything all at once. I feel all that we are, together and apart, and I smile.

"Now that we got all that serious shit out of the way, can I be completely unserious with you?" you ask. And I nod. "You look like the Stay Puft Marshmallow Man, but she had her trans awakening and became the Stay Puft Marshmallow Woman."

I gasp and playfully slap your chest. I make to pull away from your arms, but you hold me close in front of your grinning, stupidly hot face.

"So, what now? What do we do?" you ask.

"Now, there's something I need to do. It will take a while. I won't be back again for a long time. Probably not until August. Can you handle that?" I ask.

"Eight months? No problem. I'll be here, waiting for you," you say. And I know you will be.

We hold each other silently in front of the river as the northern lights dance above us until they fade out of sight, and I'm left on the bank alone. And for the first time, it's okay.

◆

You don't know this, but I've actually been back up to Fairbanks between January and August; I just scheduled my visits when I knew you wouldn't be around to spoil the surprise.

Since our last time together, I really did let you go. I've been able to fully live my life these past many months, all while never losing sight of that vision you had for us.

See, that vision was so crystal clear for you, but for me it was always somewhat fuzzy. Somewhat blurry. I never knew why until my visit with you in January. I saw us in Fairbanks, too, but I never saw it as a permanent thing. In my vision, I always saw it as temporary, undefinable, fluid. Something that doesn't exist in time or space.

It was with that spirit of temporality that I built this house for you. Well, come on, obviously I didn't build it. Can you imagine? No. But I did pay people to build it for you, thanks to your life insurance policy payout. Turns out there was an empty lot next to that cabin we always stayed in, so I bought the lot. That way, you'll appear right by the steps to your new home.

I only had the summer since I wanted it to be a surprise for you, and the summer is the only time I know you won't show up unexpectedly. I hope you like it. I moved everything out of storage and set it up in your home. All the photos of our trip in Europe, the photos from your going-away party, the photos from your first construction job as a business owner. All your blankets and clothes. Your favorite pillow. The penguin plushie you have but refused to acknowledge you slept with every night until we had been dating for a month.

Everything that a person who exists outside of the laws of space and time could want in a home.

I thought it could be our little place where we could meet. When we find ourselves in step with each other. And we could drink hot chocolate together on the bench, like you wanted to, and marvel at the wonders of the universe and your place in it.

The weather forecast calls for a light show tonight. And so, with hot chocolate in a thermos, sitting on the swinging bench on the porch of our new home in Fairbanks, I patiently and longingly wait for you to arrive.

Which, come to think of it, might be the dykiest part of our relationship.

Something Small Enough to Ask For

AnaMaria Curtis

GRANDMA IRENE TAUGHT Lucy how to sew pockets at the same time she taught her how to make a skirt. Skirts with pockets are much more complicated than skirts without, of course, but Grandma Irene was firm on her point—the one could not be made without the other.

"You always have to have a place to escape to," Grandma Irene told Lucy, who was twelve and still thought sewing machines could smell fear. "Listen, Lucy, it's important. You have to have pockets. You have to have something for yourself." She said something else, too, after that, but that was what Lucy held onto.

Lucy's grandma understood having things for herself. When she was alive, she lived in a first-floor, one-bedroom apartment with a tiny courtyard garden where she grew flowers in pots nestled between piles of round decorative pebbles. Lucy would stay with her on Tuesdays and Thursdays after school until her mom could come pick her up, or whenever she drove her parents crazy in the summers.

She would draw pictures of dolphins and octopuses and sort through the pebbles in Grandma Irene's garden, which was the best place on earth. There was always something fresh to the air, like a rainstorm had just come and gone, and the flowers, which faced a brick wall and must have had to fight for light, were always bright, always beautiful.

❖

GRANDMA IRENE LEAVES Lucy her sewing machine and half a yard of fabric embroidered with flowers. There's no note, no message. Lucy wishes, desperately, that there was. She knows she wasn't listening hard enough.

Lucy is seventeen. She is standing in her mother's living room, holding beautiful fabric, thick with stitches, with time, with love, and she does not know what to do with it. Lucy has not touched her grandmother's sewing machine in the last three years, since it was bundled up with the things from the first-floor apartment and the courtyard garden was traded for plastic flowers in a room with a curtain.

That night, Lucy takes the fabric with her into bed and strokes the stitches of the flowers. She wonders when her grandmother started working on the embroidery, when she finished it. She wonders, and between one touch to the fabric and another, she is somewhere else.

For a moment, her thumb on an embroidered poppy, Lucy is in her grandma's living room. Grandma Irene is sitting in her big red chair in front of the TV, listening to an audiobook—one of her romance novels, probably— embroidering red petals.

She doesn't see Lucy, or hear her when Lucy makes a pained noise—half sob, half wail. But she's there, and Lucy can touch her bony shoulder, can smell the mix of laundry detergent and rose perfume that has always been Grandma, can have back what she's lost.

◆

LUCY HASN'T SEWN in a long time, but she remembers the skirt she made when she was twelve, bright pink with an elastic waist and smooth pockets big enough to put rocks and shells in when she got to go to the beach.

She goes to a fabric shop and runs her hands over bolt after bolt of cloth until she finds a green fabric thick enough to hang well. The green is somewhere between the color of bright leaves in the swell of summer and a fresh-cut Christmas tree. Lucy also buys pins and elastic and ribbon, and she brings her haul back to her bedroom, where Grandma Irene's sewing machine is on a table pushed up against the far corner. She sits on the corner of her bed and brushes her fingers against the purple of an embroidered tulip, and thinks about the pink skirt, about learning how to sew a pocket, and then she's there.

Lucy, seventeen, looks at Lucy, twelve, where she sits at the kitchen table with an unwieldy pair of scissors, watching Grandma Irene. At first, Lucy, seventeen, just stands back and listens as Grandma Irene explains about pattern pieces, how the shape of the skirt will depend on the choices they make now.

Grandma Irene starts saying something about pockets, about what they hold, and Lucy can't listen to it, *won't* listen to it, not when it feels like everything she's wanted to hold has slipped away from her. She clenches her fist, losing the touch of the embroidered flower in her fingers, and she's gone again, back on her bed, chest pounding, clutching at the flowers her grandma left her.

Lucy makes a skirt out of the green fabric. She makes it a little too big and adds a tie at the waist instead of elastic, so she has room to grow into it. When she sews the side seams, she adds big pockets in carefully cut out halves of the embroidered fabric, with the nice side of the embroidery on the inside, easy to twist between her fingers.

◈

Lucy goes back to that sewing lesson a lot. It's easier than the unending pressures of homework and college and carrying the hopes of her parents on her back. Lucy, twelve, sits at the kitchen table with a pile of pins, and Lucy, seventeen, grows brave, grows greedy. She sees the way Grandma Irene looks at the young Lucy in front of her—fond, delighted, always loving—and she wants that for herself again.

So she steps up close to her younger self and leans forward, intending to rest her chin on the top of her own head. But when she tries, Lucy's chin keeps sinking, and something fuzzy and unreal in the air starts to clear.

Lucy jerks her head back. She takes a deep breath, unnoticed by her past self or her grandmother, and then she sits on the chair her past self is sitting on. She arranges her hands to match Lucy, twelve, still putting pins along the seams of the bright pink fabric and chattering on about her article for the school newspaper, and lets her grandmother's eyes rest on her. When she decides to stop pinning one-handed, to touch the tabletop instead, Lucy, twelve, follows her lead. Grandma Irene asks if she wants to take a break. This time, Lucy says yes, rewrites history, just for a moment.

◈

The skirt takes Lucy anywhere she's been. It takes her to the park by the apartment complex she lived in until she was nine, where the swings went so, so high; to the silent stillness of her bedroom before she painted it ocean green; to the Grand Canyon, where they went when she was thirteen and didn't appreciate it enough.

When she doesn't get into the college with the marine biology partnership program, she takes herself back to the tour, walks alongside her younger, more hopeful self, and wonders if she's a ghostly presence there, haunting herself, trying to tell herself that potential can just as easily be nothing as something.

◈

Lucy wears her skirt to the first day of intro biology, where she meets Jillian, who wears her brown hair in a French braid with cloth flowers woven in and invites Lucy along to a stand-up comedy meeting when Lucy asks what she's writing in the margins of her notes. Lucy hates stand-up, but she goes. And when Jillian asks her out for milkshakes after, Lucy does that too. She sits in a booth across from Jillian and listens to her story about blackmailing her brother and thinks that maybe college won't be so bad.

After Jillian breaks up with her a year and three months later, Lucy goes back to that night a lot. She sits in her old self again, nineteen inhabited by twenty-one, twenty-two, twenty-three. She smiles differently. She leans in. She keeps a hand in her pocket and kisses Jillian at the end of the night, and nothing ever changes.

◈

When Lucy is alone in her apartment on a Saturday night senior year, another email rejecting her from an internship with an aquarium added to her *Don't Look* Gmail folder, she puts on her skirt and goes home, five years ago. High school Lucy is absorbed in homework in the dining room, but college Lucy wanders to the kitchen and watches her parents make dinner. Her dad chops onions, her mom sautés, and when the onions make her dad's eyes water her mom laughs at him and kisses his cheek, and Lucy is there and not there.

❖

After she graduates, Lucy moves in with Hannah, who was a biology tutor with her their junior year, and Hannah's friends. Another month of rejection emails and no emails leads to a shitty job at a dying suburban mall. Lucy wears the skirt on days the manager with a purple streak in her hair is scheduled. She takes her ten-minute breaks and thrusts her hands into her pockets and goes anywhere else— the lake from the summer she was fifteen, the classrooms they practiced in for speech and debate, the board game nights she suffered through in college and misses now.

When she gets home, her roommates invite her out, ask if she wants to make dinner with them, and Lucy smiles and thanks them and goes back to her room to lean across a sticky table toward Jillian or to sit in front of the TV with Grandma Irene. All the people she's loved who've left her are anchors.

These things are hers, she tells herself in the small hours of the morning, when her thumb has slipped and she's staring at the smooth pale ceiling of her bedroom again.

❖

Lucy's roommates learn to stop asking if she wants to come out with them, to a movie, to a pretentious brewery, to the hot-air balloon festival. Lucy does and doesn't visit home. When her mom calls, all she can hear is echoes of past conversations, snippets of wisdom she's heard dozens of times before. If her mom starts a lecture on the phone, Lucy can go back and hear it the first time, over and over and over. Eventually, the phone calls seem superfluous, and she mostly stops picking up.

Lucy believes in moderation. Though she wishes she could wear the skirt everywhere, could always have the past at her fingertips, she doesn't. She thinks about taking out one of the pockets and sewing individual flowers from it into the pockets of other pieces of clothing, but she doesn't do that either. She's a little afraid the magic would run out or dilute, that she wouldn't be able to figure out how to untangle the roots and grass between each bloom, that something would snap with the slice of her scissors and leave her cut off from her past.

But even when she doesn't have the skirt, she spends a lot of time staring into space, poking at the crevices in her memory, waiting to be back where she remembers how loved she was. She can feel herself reaching, reaching, reaching for something, and when she reaches, she feels thread at the tip of her fingers, tumbles back into what she knows.

It's so much easier to comb through what she's had and take what she can get than it is to try to shape the vast, undefinable ocean of her need into something small enough to ask for.

◆

It's a gray Saturday morning when Lucy turns twenty-four, a rare weekend day off. She wakes up late wondering if Jillian will send a passing "happy bday" text, if a butterfly or even a moth will land on her finger and she can pretend it's a sign, if her roommates will offer to take her out to brunch. She puts on a nice top with her skirt, puts on a sweater instead of her usual hoodie.

But she comes out into the kitchen to find that her roommates have gone to the farmer's market without her.

Lucy can feel it again, the reaching. It takes her breath away; she reels with it until she puts a hand on the counter. If she doesn't find something to grab onto, she's afraid she'll snap the thin rod in the center of her torso that's holding her upright. That she'll break into soft pieces, nothing to hold her together and prop her up into the shape of a human woman.

Lucy puts her hand in her pocket.

She runs the tip of her index finger along the broad petals of a poppy and thinks of the first time her grandmother showed her how to make pockets.

Lucy has been here many times. She knows just when to sit, where to move her hands to be part of the moment. But this time, Lucy doesn't follow along, just sits, half in and half out of her own body, and keeps a tight grip on the cloth in her pocket. She stays in the moment.

"You always have to have a place to escape to," Grandma Irene is telling her. "Listen, Lucy, it's important. You have to have pockets. You have to have something for yourself. But," and here her eyes soften. She looks up, makes eye contact with the space six inches above twelve-year-old Lucy's eyes, which happens to be right at eye level for Lucy, twenty-four and losing it. "Pockets are also for holding things. Things you'll need later, and things you need right now, and things for other people. You can't keep everything to yourself, either."

"What if I want to," Lucy says with her younger body's mouth. "What if it's easier?"

Grandma Irene shrugs. She always had an expansive, expressive shrug—palms up, eyebrows rising with her shoulders. "People want to give you something of themselves. You don't have to take it. But you do have to give them something back, if you want them to know you. You have to do that for yourself, too. You have to figure out what you want to keep."

Lucy frowns. She can feel the frown separating herself and her past self, and when she says, "I love you, Grandma," she can feel the moment slipping in and out of focus when Grandma Irene looks at her.

"I love you too, honey."

❖

Lucy doesn't wait for her roommates to come back from the farmer's market. Instead, she slips her shoes on and grabs her purse and gets in her car and drives an hour and a half to the beach. It starts to rain just as she's finding free parking, and everyone she sees is heading back to their own cars.

The wind and rain have picked up by the time Lucy has made her way down the stairs and across the sand to the edge of the water. She takes off her shoes and sets them and her purse next to a little hill of sand.

Then she walks. The water blends in with the sky on the horizon, monochrome gray, and Lucy stops to pick up the occasional shell. The sand eventually gives way to rocks and tide pools. The rocks are slippery from the rain and sharp on the soft pads of her feet, but she steps over them carefully to crouch at the edge of one of the pools. Lucy wanted to be a marine biologist from the time she was seven to the time she received her eighth grad school rejection; she knows the rain is going to drive any creatures into shelter and away from the visible center of the pool. Still, she can't help sitting and looking into the area under the surface of the water. The rock is variegated and dark, and it takes her eyes time to adjust, but she spies half a crab shell, red and purple, the remnants of some seagull's meal.

She trails her fingers in the water, then submerges her arm up to her elbow, until she's touching the sandy rock and closing her fingers around a beautiful, rounded pebble that sits perfectly in her palm. It's not the kind of rock that should be in a pool like this, too smooth. It must have been dropped by someone, or something. She stays crouched there for a long moment, holding the stone. The wind whips rain against her arms and legs, tiny pinpricks, and they remind her of where she is. Here. Still in the pain of the moment. Then she shrugs and thinks *finders keepers* to herself and puts the stone in the pocket with the shells.

When she stands up and keeps walking, Lucy wonders if she'll come back to this moment, if she'll want to live in it later.

LUCY GETS BACK to her apartment late in the afternoon. She's still damp and cold, but she's shaking with something else, a kind of perilous excitement. She's broken something after all—broken *through*. Gone and done something for herself and made it back alive.

There's a trio of cupcakes on the kitchen counter and an index card that says "Happy birthday Lucy!!" All three of her roommates have signed it.

Lucy slips a hand into her pocket—pure habit, the response she's had to almost any emotion for over six years now—and her fingers fumble through the thin edges of shells until she finds the pebble. It's just a stone, smooth and round and perfectly ordinary, but she wraps her fingers around it anyway and goes to ask her roommates if any of them are free for a birthday dinner.

Mackson's Mardi Gras Moon Race

David DeGraff

TURTLES WERE BUILT for short-haul Lunar prospecting, not treks across the entire face of the Moon, but back in 2043 João Silva Henrique, desperate to celebrate Carnaval, drove a turtle from Amundsen Crater at the south pole to Byrd Crater at the north pole. Unsanctioned celebrations of any kind were forbidden in the Chinese stations, but there were enough Brazilian workers at the north pole to make the risk of trekking across unexplored terrain seem worthwhile. Now that Brazil controls Byrd Station, it's an annual race. And I'm going to win it. If I live.

We only have the equipment João used on his desperate first run when he stole his turtle—no moon suits, no long-range radios other than emergency receivers that only work when a rare comms satellite is overhead. Rescue could be too late, like it was in the '52 race.

The hangar lights flash the race's start. I kiss my fingers then touch the picture of Bernardino on the dashboard, the one from last year's Carnaval, before slowly pressing my foot on the accelerator, hanging back as fifty racers flow from the airlock and stay in a tight peloton along the road to Amundsen Crater's wall, the sun low on the horizon, shining on less than half our power films.

I don't start at the front with all the elite racers, children of the founders of the Lunar Corporations with someone to sponsor them. They get to spend weeks training on untracked regolith, fine-tuning waste and oxygen recyclers, refreshing the solar-voltaic film over the cockpit bubble. They talk about needing to get used to the claustrophobia. Me, I'm used to it. This bubble is bigger than the room I share with Bernardino in the miners' dome.

I want to be at the back so no one follows me. Trekking alone across unexplored terrain is the only hope I have to win against my better-funded competitors. It also increases my chance of dying. Half the people who try new routes need rescue. Some even have rescue reach them in time. None has placed in the top half of finish times.

Race radio squawks when the last straggler is at the top. "All clear. See you in ten thousand kilometers. Godspeed."

Rooster tails of regolith kick up around me, people gunning motors to get ahead of the pack, but I keep a steady speed. Being in front this early isn't an advantage. I'm heading farther west to my secret approach to the north pole, one I found on an old orbital photo.

Untrekked routes are risky, but I've spent a lot of time on the surface, racing to get my ice haul to the station so I can head back for more.

Colorful dots move across the crater floor below me as I ride along the next crater's rim while the others take the well-worn route down its slumped wall.

The line-of-sight radio cracks to life. "Who's on the ridge?" That's DaCruz, who won three of the last five races, son of the founder of Fazenda Greenhouses.

I stay silent.

"Dull red turtle that hasn't seen a paint job in five years? Mackson Coelho." That's Lopes, scion of the Paulo Mining Group. When DaCruz doesn't win, Lopes does. "He came in thirty-third last year."

Hey, I finished ahead of four people in a year with no fatalities, and my navigation skills got me a twenty percent raise when I left Paulo Mining. That counted as a win for me.

"What's he playing at?" That's Zezé Almeida, the top woman racer, who swears she's going to win this year.

The peloton drops out of sight, out of contact, as I turn onto the altiplano heading to the 45° meridian. The half-illuminated third-quarter Earth hangs over the horizon. It's early evening in Japan—no, that's New Zealand. Earth is upside down from the way I usually see it.

I'm taking a path no one has tried before, a path that doesn't look like it could work, but what I'm doing is closer to João's spirit than any other racer in the last ten years. I can't afford to push my batteries to the point where they're useless by the time I reach the finish line. I'll still need to use my turtle to mine the ice in the permanent shadows at the north pole.

I loosen my grip on the steering wheel and wiggle my fingers to get the blood circulating. It's exhausting work looking for the shortest routes around the small craters, trying not to think about any cracks in the cockpit seals, not to think about failing oxygen recyclers or a crack in the still that treats my waste, not to think of all the ways to die out here.

The loneliness of this route is an added factor I hadn't considered. There's no chatter on the radio to keep my mind from wandering too far. I keep remembering the turtles of those who've died over the years—turtles wheels-up at the bottom of a crater, tracks disappearing into a dark hole on the slope of a rille, bubbles popped open rather than facing the slow, painful death of CO_2 poisoning—left as monument to the harsh Lunar landscape.

The timer dings. Ten hours. I cut the power to the wheels and roll another thirty meters before I stop.

It's tempting to eat the feijoada MRE but that's a special meal for my last sleep, or maybe when it's clear I'll actually win. For now, it's either pão de queijo or generic protein bars for when I don't want to spend as much time eating.

When I sleep, I dream of a smooth road over the Lunar surface, paved in green glass.

When I wake, I check the latest race positions. I'm in second-to-last place. Everyone else is strung along the traditional well-traversed route. Names I don't recognize are far ahead. They'll eventually make a mistake in their exhausted state, or they'll be passed when they oversleep. Or they'll die.

Wait. Not everyone is taking the standard route—there's someone five kilometers behind me, just over the horizon—Lopes. He should be in the peloton with DaCruz, Almeida, and the others.

The regolith is packed hard here, not churned over like it is near home. I adjust a degree east of my best heading, hoping to throw him off my true destination.

After my next sleep, Lopes is still four-point-eight kilometers behind me, just over the horizon. Now I wish I had something to obscure my tracks.

I use the turtle grapple arm to draw a rabbit and a wolf in the regolith, and write, "You can't catch me." It looks nothing like writing in the wet sand in Rio—the regolith compacts without raised ridges along the edge of the grooves. I trace a line dodging the tiny crater in front of the rabbit.

◆

HOUR AFTER HOUR, day after day, Lopes dogs me, even matching my sleep cycle. The Earth creeps higher in the sky as the crescent wanes, and he's still five kilometers behind, still just over my horizon. I try not to let it bother me, try not to let the uneasiness in my stomach keep me from driving my top speed, try not to look at the race updates, try not to worry he'll win.

I have to navigate around a small rille. It might be a ten-kilometer diversion instead of a hundred meters across, but I don't trust the slopes. That's how Huang died in '63. Rilles mean lava tubes and open pits, ground that could collapse under a turtle's weight. The north end of the rille terminates in circular shadow—a cave entrance.

My next rest stop is southwest of Kepler, the sun directly overhead. I lie down, cover the sun with my hand, and search for the new Earth, its nightside facing us. I can see the white lights of Florida and Brazil. Rio shines.

Green flashes in streaks from the Antarctic Peninsula up the length of Chile. Another flash. Soon, half the Earth is bathed in shimmering red and green. Even the lights of Porto Alegre are covered. Aurora. A solar storm hitting Earth.

And me. If I can see the solar storm attacking Earth's atmosphere, those high-energy protons and electrons are raining down on me, too, ionizing the atoms in my body, ripping me apart on a molecular level. Radiation is an ugly way to die.

I pull up the mic in case anyone is in range. "Warning. Warning. Auroral activity on Earth. Find shade!"

Training kicks in. Head to a shadow, a cliff base where you block the sun and thirty degrees to its right. But we are all in the mare, the smoothest plains on the Moon. Where can I hide? Where can anyone hide?

The lava tube. What is that, two, three kilometers behind me?

I gun the turtle and spin a sharp one-eighty, using all the solar power and battery reserve to follow my tracks south.

"Can anyone receive me?"

The electron storm blocks the radio signals. Lopes won't hear me, even if he's in range. Does he know how much danger he's in?

Lopes is probably another three kilometers before the rille if he's staying out of sight. Can I risk this much exposure? I don't know, but I couldn't live with myself if I didn't try.

"Lopes, can you read me?"

Silence.

I see him up ahead, no dust arcing behind his turtle. Stopped.

"Lopes!"

No response.

He's sleeping in his recliner seat. I nudge my turtle forward and bump him.

He lurches, looks around, eyes wide when he sees me.

I point up, then reverse and spin, hoping he'll follow.

This time I gun down the slope, sliding as the regolith shifts under my wheels. The ground slopes into a cave mouth barely wide enough for the turtle. I drive in ten meters. Where the lava tube ends, my headlamps shine on rocks no human has ever seen. Lopes's beams shine through my cockpit, and I can see my shadow on the rough wall in front of me.

"Thanks, Mackson," Lopes says over the radio. "You didn't have to rescue me."

I make a broad shrug.

"If the tables were turned..."

"You'd have done the same thing," I lie.

"Sure," he says after a long pause. Then, "You're razing it, man. I don't know how you can keep up this schedule. Four hours of sleep a day is brutal. I mean, we're in the lead for now, but we always go the last forty-eight hours without rest, the people trying to win do. I don't think you can do that."

"You underestimate me, Lopes."

"No. I looked up your last two races. You kept this same rigid schedule the whole time."

I won't play Lopes's mind games. "Why are you following me, then?"

"You looked like someone with a secret. Like you scouted out a faster route, a route no one else would take. Your path through Lacus Excellentiae was a good find. You must have another excellent trick to get past the cliffs of Sinus Iridum."

I've got him. He thinks I'm heading east of the Jura peninsula.

"Is that the game you're playing?"

My body clenches despite my elation. "It's not a game for me, the way it is for you rich assholes. I need the prize money. I need to leverage my navigation skills into higher wages."

I grit my jaw when he laughs. If we were in a room together I'd punch his face. "I've spent quite a bit more money training than I'll win. The race is supposed to be about honor, not financial gain."

"That's easy for you to say. Your family paid for your transport here. I might be able to pay off my fee before I die."

I could feel a lecture coming about working harder, how the best people can rise above their birth, but three words into his rant, emergency tones scream through his radio, but not mine—I must be too deep to pick up the signal.

"What are they saying?" I ask.

"Everyone who can get to shade in ten minutes will be okay. Long-term effects will start to accumulate beyond that. Fatal in ninety minutes, and the storm will last another five hours. Time to catch up on sleep." He clicks off his headlights.

Five hours. I set the alarm for four and hope the storm is shorter than predicted, hope no one tries to ride through it.

◈

W‍HY IS IT so dark? The storm. I'm in a lava tube with Lopes. But Lopes is gone. And a boulder blocks my escape. I should never have trusted that son of a mother.

My front grapple would get the boulder out of the way, but the tube isn't wide enough to turn around, so I nudge it with my rear bumper and spike the motor in reverse. The rock moves a couple of centimeters. I spike the motor again and the boulder begins to slide. One more push and it slides farther, but the battery's temperature rises into the danger zone. It will cool off quicker in the cave's cold darkness than in the bright sunlight, but still slower than with an atmosphere. I waste a half-hour waiting for the motor to cool.

That monkey comber forced me to lose another hour pushing the rock far enough to escape, and I'm down to thirty percent power. I'll need to move a little slower than I'd like so I'll be fully charged when I reach my secret. If I run out of power there, will anyone ever find me? Would they even bother looking for someone like me?

Lopes left a message in his tracks. I can see where he harvested the big boulder and pushed it into place (much easier going forward and downhill), but he also moved four smaller rocks like he thought about wedging them in, locking the boulder in the lava tube's mouth. One plume from a hopper and all trace of me would be gone, my body never to be found. So noble of him.

I want to take off, follow his tracks, and smash his bubble with my grapple. No. My best revenge will be to win the race, although that won't be as sweet as plucking his body from the turtle and sweeping the regolith with his face. I'm here to win.

Earth is all city lights with no green flashes. Lopes lied about the storm's duration. Why did I ever believe him? Never again.

A thousand kilometers to go if we had a hopper. Five days navigating across the surface in a turtle. Well, it would be five days if I had to worm my way around all the craters and debris. I can travel my path in four days. I won't just win by a little, I'll beat everyone by eighteen hours if I've done the calculations right.

Lopes is heading to Sinus Iridum where the Jura mountains will trap him. He won't pay any more attention to me, so I turn a little west to go on the other side of the peninsula and reach Sinus Roris, where I do have a trick to make it through the mountains.

The cliffs of Sinus Roris are notoriously tall and rugged. I see their bright peaks pop over the horizon, brighter than the mare's dark regolith, and stop when I can see the cliff's base. It's time for my last sleep before I find the tunnel entrance and take the fast lane to Byrd Crater and victory. I sneak a look at the positions as I eat my pão de queijo. Will I still win?

I'm even with Zezé, ahead of the main peloton which has pulled ahead of DaCruz. I hope he's okay.

Lopes has switched course, heading toward me, but there's no way he can catch up now. He might think he can, but while he skirts around boulders and craters, I'll be making solid time. I sleep restlessly, but I feel good after a heavily caffeinated protein bar. My next meal will be my celebratory feijoada.

Craters deeper than my turtle are everywhere as I approach the bay, but not as bad as the highlands. As I round one final crater, I come to the base of sheer cliffs on the banks of Roris.

I don't see my path—nothing but sheer cliffs. The old photo I found had the sun overhead, not leaving shadows pointed west. If I have to waste time looking for a small cave, I'll be lost.

There's a hill to let me see a little farther, so I run up it. There! Tracks, at least twenty years old if this was really an

American project. There's no record of this construction anywhere and no reason for this tunnel to exist.

Why did they build such a thing and abandon it? Were they planning a base away from the pole, away from the easy access to ice? A rail gun to send their ice to orbit? A weapon for revenge against the Chinese after they desecrated the Apollo landing sites? I don't know, but the road is long and smooth and straight. They leveled hills, filled in craters, and dug tunnels. It will be easier than driving the rodovias, my speed limited only by how quickly the battery can shed heat.

As I approach the circular mouth, I see tire tracks, narrower than standard—Americans with their strange units of thumbs and feet instead of meters.

Ah, the tracks lead to small exhaust craters. This was a hopper launch zone, but with no infrastructure so it could remain hidden.

DaCruz still hasn't moved.

I really hope this is a tunnel and not just a deep mine. But when I extrapolated a straight line from here to the highlands, I saw a hint of another cave with a narrow track heading toward it. I told Bernardino that I'd found a tunnel, but I didn't tell him I was only eighty percent sure that's what it was. If I'm going to die, this is where it will be. But I won't die. I'm going to win.

The tunnel angles up, and my head lamps shine on the smooth floor unmarked by tire tracks or any trace of who dug this tunnel or why. I would have expected Americans to leave much trash behind, many useful resources, but the whole area is empty.

Before the race, I calculated how fast I can go balancing speed, distance, engine temperature, but I don't know how much my batteries' capacity deteriorated in the lava tube when they started to overheat.

The tunnel is straight and smooth, and I don't need to think about the best path around craters and boulders.

The turtle says power use is low, but still in the range I calculated. I'd given myself a twenty-five percent margin of error, so I kick my speed up a little.

After two hours, the line-of-sight radio cracks. Lopes has gained on me faster than I expected him to. "I see you up there, you little rabbit. You still won't win this race."

I reach for the mic but stop. I won't rise to his bait again.

He mercifully stays quiet. For a little while.

"I'm gaining on you, Coelho."

Or he's increasing his head-lamp brightness to fool me. I push on, ignoring his taunts.

After an hour I can see a tiny light ahead—the end of the tunnel. If it weren't for Lopes, I'd be able to compare both ends, judge my remaining time better, but I think I've got five hours to go, and my batteries are above fifty percent. I push faster.

My mind stays engaged when I'm navigating the surface—always scanning ahead for the smoothest routes. Here the floor and the curved walls merge around me forming a tube, smooth and monotonous, but I have to steer straight, so I can't let my mind wander too far, can't let myself imagine the victory, imagine Bernardino's embrace when I finally return to him. If I scrape the side of the tunnel at this speed my canopy could crack and I'll be dead.

My battery drops below thirty percent. If I run into a boulder or a pit and can't move forward, I won't be able to make it to the tunnel's end, and I'll die here.

Slowly the light grows, and it clearly has the same shape as the walls around me. It is truly a path out. I only need to worry about a cave-in beneath the floor.

"What the hell is that?"

I resist the urge to slow.

"Did you see the cave, Coelho? The walls look like quality ore, but the Americans found a mother lode and refined it in secret."

Lopes can swallow frogs. The Americans wouldn't have abandoned the Moon if they had all that. But the walls do look mineral rich. I drive faster so the batteries will be pushing empty by the time I emerge in the sunshine. His lights fade as I pull ahead.

How dumb does he think I am?

"Don't tell anyone about what we found," Lopes says. "I'll hire you at five times what you're making now to help us extract this material."

I shut off the radio for four more hours until I'm back in the sunshine. There are signs of another hopper landing zone, but there's no equipment on this side, either. I see tracks where they must have carted off the tailings from the tunnel to make the road less conspicuous, but no abandoned hardware.

The road leading away is narrow—too narrow to be noticed on orbital maps—but it's packed tight and smooth. Not as smooth as green glass, but I won't leave tracks for Lopes to follow. I only have a two-hour lead. I can't take time to sleep for the rest of the race. I should have eaten the feijoada yesterday. The batteries aren't charging as fast as they should. Did my panels get covered in dust, or are my batteries failing?

I set the display to update every ninety minutes to make sure I stay ahead of Lopes. I'm going to beat the lead group by almost a day.

The road skirts around a few hundred-meter-wide craters, and it switchbacks into and out of Pascal Crater, but it still drastically cuts the total distance.

The next update, Lopes's gaining on me, and soon I can see his lights.

I'm not so sure of myself now. I'm burning more power than the sun can give me, and my batteries are draining faster than I expected. I'll cross the line twenty-seven hours before Zezé and the rest of the main pack, but what if I'm in second place? Second-place purse won't cover the cost of a new battery pack.

I push the motors as hard as I can, but my speed starts to drop. Is my lead good enough?

In an hour the beacon light flashes on—I'm in radio range. "This is Mackson Coelho approaching finish line."

"A full day ahead of the previous record, Mackson. If you can stay ahead of Lopes."

I can see the hanger. I can see the yellow ribbon strung across the opening. I can see a tail of regolith flying behind Lopes's turtle, and it's getting bigger.

I push harder on the accelerator, but no speed comes. He rips past me and dust crackles on my roof. He breaks the yellow ribbon and passes the rainbow-leafed palm trees and colorful parrots. People inside the second-story observation deck raise their hands and jump. Bernardino is there, looking down, his forehead resting on the glass.

I pull past bikini-clad mannequins whose silver masks and sparkling bodies mock my loss. I've lost the race. I've lost my turtle. I'll probably lose Bernardino, too. I gambled everything and lost.

The airlock hisses at me, but I don't pop the turtle's seal until I see Bernardino. He wraps me in a tight, loving embrace. "You're alive, Mackson. You're alive." He steps away and waves his hand in front of his nose. "But first you need a shower."

I nod and turn to go, but my eye catches the wall next to the window overlooking the docking bay showing all the positions. One red dot sits in the center of Imbrium Basin. DaCruz hasn't moved in three days.

"He thought the storm would blow over before it became lethal," Bernardino says. "The rescue jumper said he popped his hatch rather than deal with all the organ failure. Another monument."

I hope DaCruz turned south to face Earth for all eternity.

A short man with a fringe of gray hair approaches me, hand extended—Lucas Saures, top boss of Peripo Mining.

"Congratulations, Mr. Coelho."

Technically, he's my boss, but so far up I've never seen him in person. I shake his hand and introduce him to my husband. "I don't know if you noticed, but I wasn't the guy who crossed the line first."

He waves a hand dismissively. "When your signal disappeared, I looked over your route—your route, Mackson, *yours*. Once I knew it was there, I could see the tunnel and the road you took. That was surprisingly brilliant."

I shrug.

"We could use someone like you in our company. In our offices, I mean. No more endless days cramped in that turtle. With your eye I bet you could help us become the largest mining operation on the Moon."

Bernardino bounces a foot off the floor. "We need class-two living quarters."

Saures laughs. "Class-four is still a step up from the miners' dome. We might get you into class-three if you're even better than I think. Your pay will depend on what you find, of course. And if you don't bring it in fast enough, you're back to the turtles."

I hold out my hand. "Get hoppers to both ends of that tunnel. Quickly, before Lopes sees you talking to me."

Saures looks me in the eyes for several seconds, nods and walks off.

Bernardino grabs me in another hug, then pushes me away. "Let's get you in a shower, and then we can celebrate properly."

I may not have won the race, but this is going to be the best Carnaval ever.

❁

Climbing the Mountains of Me

PHOEBE BARTON

HAVE NO IDEA what I'm doing when it comes to love. When I see my tear-streaked reflection in the subway car's window, my makeup ghostly against the tunnel walls, I know it's all my fault. I got my hopes up, I pretended I could be myself, and now I'm six inches taller than when I left home.

"Be small," I tell myself. After a date as harsh as the one I just lived through, maybe I can make myself believe it. "Small is good."

I close my fist around my brand-new amulet full of ground-up clover, bamboo, and everything else the internet suggested, and try to shrink. My favorite blue date dress, ripped in half a dozen places when I couldn't keep myself small, relaxes a little.

Not enough.

The subway slows to a crawl and stops in the tunnel. I dig into my purse for Toppy, my stuffed anxiety octopus, and squeeze.

"Don't make a fuss." When I'm this stressed out, I want to be big. I *need* to be big. Being small hurts. When I'm small I might as well be living in a vise. "Keep it together. Stay small."

The walls aren't closing in yet, but that can change fast. This type of subway car is ten feet, three and five-eighths inches wide and eleven feet, eleven and three-quarters inches tall. Enough space for three hundred people at crush load. Barely enough for me.

I clench my fists. My nails carve smiling craters into my palm. No blood, not yet.

At last, the train moves. I fly out the doors at the next station, take the escalator two steps at a time, feel my dress straining against me. If I had focus it'd grow with me, but I don't and it doesn't. I crash through the paddle gates, dash into a parking lot. I'm glad I didn't wear heels.

I collapse on the cold asphalt and let go. My watch breaks apart on the rocks of my wrist. My necklace goes taut and snaps. I'm barely able to make my dress grow with me, and here and there it rips in new places. I'm ten feet tall, twenty, thirty, knocking over garbage cans and pushing cars aside. People must be staring at me, and I cry.

There isn't a woman on Earth who'd love a woman like me.

◆

I'D LOVE TO know why I grow, but I've got no clue myself. One morning when I was fifteen, I just woke up nine feet tall. Toronto's a big enough city that you'd think it'd have some other giant women in it, but all the ones I know are stuck with what puberty gave them.

I'm just stuck with knowing that *of course* it couldn't be so easy as me being a queer lady in a world like this. No, I've got to be a *giant* queer lady. Today I'm six feet tall and every glance makes my smallness hurt even more.

"Maybe you should take a vacation." Erin beams at me from the other side of the café table, as if her smile could drive off shadows. "See new sights, clear your head, and when you come back maybe you'll find the girl of your dreams."

"How quickly we forget Niagara," I say. A couple of years ago, Erin and I went on what turned out to be a halfway trip to the region's finest wineries. *Halfway* because during a quick nap, I grew enough to blow out her tires. "Do you know how many nightmares I've had about getting big in a plane?"

"You could rent a tractor-trailer," Erin says with a mischievous grin. "Stretch out, travel in style."

"Come on, this is serious." I rest my forehead on the table and try not to think how long it's been since it's had a proper cleaning. "I'm a fat queer lesbian giantess. How many people are going to check all those boxes?"

"More than you think." Erin's eyes are full of—well, it better not be pity, not after everything we've gone through. Call it sympathy instead. "It's not hopeless, Carol. There's someone out there for you. All you have to do is find them."

"All I have to do." My stomach acid is bubbling, burning the butterflies to cinders. "I've found a specialist. She thinks she can keep me from needing to grow."

"That'd be a hell of a trick." Erin leans forward with interest. "How?"

"I don't know." I imagine growing beyond skyscrapers, beyond mountains, beyond any chance of love. My problems are mountains so big I could be as big as a mountain myself and still not be able to climb them. "Something's got to change."

"You really think it's right to change yourself to suit the world?" Erin peers at me, frowning. "You're incredible already, Carol. I'd love to be able to be big like you."

"No," I say, my voice jagged and bent. "You don't."

◈

THERE ARE TWO places I let myself relax. The first is my apartment, where no one can see me. I've got the furniture arranged so that once I draw the curtains, I can hit twenty-three feet with my head in one corner and my feet in another. The other is Dr. Sheridan's office. She works out of an unusually bright basement on St. Clair Avenue, and one time when I curled up with my chin in my knees she measured me at thirty-five. I'd never felt so comfortable and so free.

Every time I go in hoping I'll find a smaller way to feel like that. Comfort tastes like charcoal when you can't share it.

"You're smaller than usual." Dr. Sheridan gives me a nod I don't deserve. Today, I'm just tall enough for my head to scrape the ceiling when I'm sitting down. "Would you say you've been making progress?"

"Goddess, Doc, not at all." I let it all unspool, the awful dates and the failed amulet and the daily pressure of life, until she coughs and points to the ceiling. I've grown without thinking and dented it. "I'm broken."

"The roof is broken, not you." Her voice is heavy with kindness, but it's hard to believe it's true. "Have you ever thought about intentionally being big in public?"

"I--" The fear of all those people looking at me, *focusing* on me, makes me grow by reflex and deepen the dent. I grit my teeth and squeeze Toppy like an orange. "I can't. They'd all see me."

"People would see you, that's true," Dr. Sheridan says. "Could you tell me what has you so afraid?"

I close my eyes, breathe in clean air and breathe out my fears. There are people out there who think giant queer ladies don't have anything to worry about but artillery and power lines. They're wrong.

"I'm too dangerous to love," I say. "It'd be so easy to roll over in the night and crush someone in my sleep. Who'd risk that for me?"

"You'd have to do a proper experiment to get an answer." Dr. Sheridan thinks for a minute, and all I can feel is the sweat of being seen. I don't know how she's so calm while I'm so big. "What do you think about ten feet? Big, but not gigantic. You wouldn't be holding anything back at that size, even if it makes kisses an odyssey."

"A little." I smile to mask my pain, my fear. Isn't that what I'm supposed to do? Hide myself behind a mask? Not make a fuss? "I thought I was supposed to be little."

"You're supposed to be what's best for you," Dr. Sheridan says. "Whatever that is, you're the one who decides. Not me."

I nod. I can't manage much more. Maybe once she sees that being tall can't work, she'll suggest something that does. The rest of the session is a blur, and when I crouch-walk out, I bump my head on the door frame.

◈

ERIN INSISTED THAT we go to High Park for my first big day, and a pun that groan-worthy deserves respect. At least when I'm there, I can find shade under the trees.

"You look good today," Erin says. "Strong. Confident, even."

"It's amazing what you can fake." Every time we pass a bush or go around a corner, I expect people to jump out, point at me, hurl words like grenades. "I'm glad you're here."

"Me too." Erin gives me an admiring look, all irises and eyelashes, and it warms me up all over despite the day's heat. I never could have made it this far without her by my side.

We're hardly the only ones in the park. I get a few reactions, mostly quiet whistles and *god-damns* and sidelong stares when they think I'm not looking, and I stop for the children. I like being a reminder that the world is full of amazing things, and what's more amazing than the impossible?

"Excuse me." The voice is glass shards and barbed wire in my ears. I open my eyes and wish I hadn't.

There's a cop in front of me, white and mustachioed and deadlier than a blue-ringed octopus, and it's only because I can't choose between shrinking or growing that I don't do anything at all.

"Afternoon, officer." Erin speaks up for me, and I don't know where she finds the courage. "Is there a problem?"

"I'm following up on reports of a giant woman on the loose." I drive my nails into my thigh. Of *course* he is. Some busybody sees me and suddenly I'm a fifty-foot monster, crushing houses and picking up cars. "Care to explain?"

"Following my doctor's advice." I look down at him with as much steel as I can forge. "Am I free to go?"

The cop lets the silence bake like a heat wave. He must be baking in that black uniform of his, but he was the one who chose to put it on.

"Go on," the cop says. "Watch your step."

Erin grabs my pinky finger and drags me down the trail. Once I can't see the cop I sink to my knees and sob. I can barely hold myself in.

"You did a good job back there." Erin brushes tears from my cheek. She looks like she's barely holding together herself. "How are you feeling?"

"Like a menace." My terror crystallizes into anger. I'm not hurting anyone. I'm just taking up space. "Better watch out, or I might go on a rampage."

"Hey, you and me," Erin says. "We'd be unstoppable."

❖

WHEN I COME home from High Park, I start living for spite. Being small, humble, and unnoticeable was what the world wanted, but it never bothered to ask what I wanted. For too long, my dating profile said I was 5'2"—the height on my ID, before I first grew. That night I change it to a proud ten and message a blue-haired, pale-skinned artist named Tara who put "loves standing tall" on her profile.

I wake up the next morning to her reply. That night I meet her in a brewpub with high ceilings and not too many people. Tara's jean shorts are stylishly torn, her bag's covered with enamel pins, and she's wiry, lithe, active— everything I'm not.

"Ten feet indeed," she says, looking me up and down. Her gaze doesn't raise a single hair on my neck. "I was worried you were exaggerating."

"Never." We settle down at a small table; I sit on the floor. I'd snap chairs like dry twigs. "Which is why I'm here like this."

"Just so you know, I have a thing for confident women," Tara says.

As the evening rolls on, strong drinks and sweet words carry me forward. There's a depth to Tara, a storm of passion, and all I want is for that storm to rain down and wash all my fears away.

"You're so incredible." She's been skating around saying it all night, and when she does it's all I can do to keep from bawling. "Can I ask how you do it?"

"Pretty comfortably, thanks," I say with a sly grin. "I think about being big, and I get big. Watch."

I grow another foot, brush my head against a hanging light, and knock over an empty chair, but it's okay. Tara's focused on me as if the world's fallen away.

"Wow." She reaches out and touches my skirt. "Can you make anything bigger?"

"Just me and my stuff," I say. "I'd get in trouble if I went around naked."

"That's the difference between art and people," Tara says. "Art gets away with a lot of things. What about you and me and the art of conversation, for starters?"

We mix our voices and paint wonderful things. I don't get home until late, my face layered with kisses and my head in the clouds. I collapse on my mattress with a smile on my face and it takes a minute to realize I haven't shrunk, I haven't grown, I'm still eleven feet tall.

"It sure was a hell of an odyssey," I tell Erin the next day. I remember kneeling for a kiss, remember Tara climbing me like a mountain, remember wishing I was the size of a mountain so it'd be that much more satisfying when she summited me. "Who'd have thought?"

"I kept saying there are people out there." Erin smiles at me, a bit softer than usual. She's wearing a T-shirt I've never seen before, and it looks a bit tight. "What do you think?"

"She's incredible." Hardly original, but that's the thing about love—it's all different, all the same, all at once. "I shouldn't have doubted you."

Her smile hardens for a moment, as if she's holding something in.

"I'm so glad," she says. There's honesty in her voice, and maybe a hint of wistfulness. "I knew it'd come true for you one day."

◈

Tara and I bounce between galleries and museums and graffiti-dappled alleys, but no matter where we go her attention's always on me. She sprinkles my hands with kisses, tickles my legs like a cat, breathes honey into my ears.

I leave Toppy at home and hug Tara instead.

"There's my giantess," she says with satisfaction when I meet her at her door. The place she's staying has an elevated porch, so I can kiss her without having to kneel. "Feeling good, I hope. I know some incredible people who want to meet you."

I can't hide my excitement, and I don't want to, either. She's not embarrassed about being seen with me. She's serious.

"I was good as I could be without you." I lean into the kiss, let it linger. "Now I'm better."

There's a van in the driveway. I'm too big for seatbelts, but that's okay; I'm too big to be thrown through the windshield, too. Tara winks at me and we're off, out into the deep night that falls once Toronto slips away. I'd be afraid if Tara wasn't there to anchor me.

We stop in front of a warehouse, long and tall and nondescript, the sort of place that could be anywhere and house anything. The loading dock doors are big enough that I barely have to duck, and once we're through the sheer black curtains draped across them, we're in a party.

Hundreds of people.

I freeze.

I sweat.

They'll all see me.

"Incredible, isn't it?" Tara's eyes are for the crowd. It's thick, buzzing, deep, like talking lava. It'll swallow me up.

"Yeah, I...I need some air." I don't wait. I crash outside and slump against the wall. There's a cold wind and bright stars. Looking at them, tracing the constellations, my fear lifts. The lines I draw are light-years long. No matter how big I get I'll always be infinitesimal to them.

It takes Tara ages to follow me out. There's a drink in her hand.

"I wasn't thinking." She sits next to me and takes a sip. "I should've got you here earlier."

"It's okay." My heart drops a little. She planned all this, brought me all this way, and I couldn't last a minute without cracking. "It's my fault. I'll try to do better."

"I'm sure you will." Tara smiles at me. "I know you've got it in you."

There are so many people inside. I don't know how Tara can handle it. Every few steps we stop, she introduces me to more people I'll never remember, and they study my every bend and curve and angle. They appraise me.

All I can do is force a smile and remind myself that Tara is there, guiding me, because she loves me.

Of course she loves me.

❖

SOMEONE'S KNOCKING ON my door. Hard, sharp, serious. Erin's style. I crouch-walk over, holding my head. Damn. How much booze does it take to get a giant woman drunk? I should've taken notes.

"You're all right." Erin leans against the door frame. Relief? Satisfaction? I'm too hungover to think. "Thank god. You weren't answering my texts."

"Phones don't like growing." I wrecked two before I learned. I check mine—hard with giant fingers—and find a dozen messages from mild concern to OMG. "I told you I was with Tara."

"We had plans," Erin says. I blink at my phone. 1:35 PM. Good thing it's Saturday. "I wanted to make sure you were okay."

"I'm fine," I say. "Need some water. Come in, already."

Erin comes in, shuts the door. Probably would have stayed in the frame forever if I didn't say otherwise. That's the kind of woman she is.

"I'm worried about you, Carol." I wince. She's named me. It's serious. "I know things are different for you now, and that's great. But just because you're comfortable, you're not invincible."

"Never thought I was." I fill up a liter stein at the tap. I knock the water back and feel a little better. "I can take care of myself. I'm a big girl."

I can't tell if Erin wants to groan, or slap her head, or laugh. Maybe she wants to do all of them. Instead she walks up to me and puts her hand on my wrist. She must want to reach my shoulder, but there's no way.

"Please, be careful." She bites her lip. "Okay?"

"Don't worry," I say. "I'm good."

We end up staying in, playing games, ordering pizza. That's good enough for me. My apartment feels bigger when there's someone I care about in it.

❖

A FEW NIGHTS later, Tara takes me back to the party warehouse. It's empty now and echoing. It tells me I'm not so big after all.

"I come here to work on megaprojects sometimes," Tara says with a grin. "Big things that make you feel. I want to make you feel like you've never felt before."

"But you already have." I kneel down and kiss her cheek. "You make me feel loved."

"The whole point of art is pushing boundaries." Tara kisses me back and looks me up and down, like she's scanning me. "What I want to know is, have you ever pushed your boundaries?"

Tara's never seen me at my most compressed. Leaving my apartment day after day, scraping my head against the ceiling, unapologetically being who I am—how's that anything *but* pushing boundaries? I try to say yes, but the word is bitter on my tongue.

She's brought me to this place, big and wide and empty, for a reason. I can see it in her eyes. After all the love she's given me, isn't it only right to give her what nobody else can?

"You want me to grow." Even saying it makes my heart thunder.

"Like never before," Tara says. "And I'll make you feel incredible things. I'm just going to need you to take off your panties first."

My breath catches in my throat. My heart roars. For a moment I can't hear anything but blood. But it's the price of love, isn't it?

Isn't it?

I reach under my skirt, pull them down. Tara nods approvingly.

"All right," she says. "Now show me what you can do."

It's not comfortable to grow while I'm lying down, and the concrete floor is cold, but I have to show her. I close my eyes, focus, and let myself go.

So much tension I didn't know I had evaporates as I push my boundaries. I don't stop until I feel the walls. I'm the size of a building and if I was standing I could see for miles.

Tara's already made me feel incredible things, but I know this wasn't what she meant.

"All right, that's great!" She's got a megaphone. That, more than anything, makes me tear up. I grew so big that her voice isn't enough. "Hold still, all right? Now it's my turn."

I can guess what she's planning but I still bite my lip. There must be something wrong with me. This is love, after all.

She must be wearing cleats. I wince from the strangeness, the sharpness, the unfamiliar edge between pain and pleasure as she enters me.

I know she means me to be enraptured by this, but I can feel every step she takes. I can't help but think of bugs, skittering and crawling and doing things I can't see. I close my eyes and force myself to bear it.

Isn't that the price of love? Bearing it?

"Are you all right down there?" I ask, to distract myself.

"Oh, it's incredible!" I bite my lip so hard I'm sure I'll draw blood. It's wrong. It's all wrong.

I focus on breathing. In, out, in, out. Stay calm. Be what I need to be. Don't wall off love. I just have to get used to it.

Step. Step.

I can't get used to it.

"Actually, I'm not feeling too good," I say. "Can you get out, maybe try again later?"

"I'm almost there!" Tara shouts back. "Hang on, it's going to be amazing!"

"Please, this is really new to me, I don't know if this is the right thing now." Fresh tears start wetting the concrete. "Please get out."

"This can't be rushed, my lovely!" She's so confident, so assured, so focused on herself. "I'm almost there, and then it'll feel incredible, I promise!"

Something snaps in my brain and my world tilts. I'm not just uncomfortable, I'm not just scared; I'm angry. Love isn't supposed to be any of that.

I'd rather be alone than feel like this.

"Get out, now, or I swear to goddess I'll shrink!" I can imagine how that would feel: compression, crushing, pain that won't end. I hope she listens. Periods are bad enough when they're boneless. "Get out, get out, *get out!*"

She gets out. I'm not too big to miss the look of betrayal on her face. I start shrinking before she can dive back in and call my bluff.

Assuming it's a bluff.

"What's the matter with you?" Her voice is wavering, unsure. Wounded. "I was doing this for you."

"You were doing it for you!" I wipe away my tears and wriggle back into my panties. "It was all for you."

Tara doesn't have an answer. She stands there, looking at me. I can tell what she's thinking. How lucky I was to have her.

I don't feel lucky anymore.

"I'll call when I'm ready to talk," I say. "I need time."

I don't wait for her answer. I crash outside and grow until I could crush her little van with my heel, until I could take apart her tiny warehouse with my fists, until I can see familiar lights on the horizon. At least those won't lead me wrong.

I wait until the little warehouse is out of sight before I let myself cry.

❖

I GO SMALL to Dr. Sheridan's office. It's been two weeks since Tara and I go small everywhere now. The pain's worth it. At least I know what people see.

"I need to get used to it," I tell her. The office is so big now. I could disappear inside it. Would anyone even notice? "I need to know how."

"Are you sure you want that?" Dr. Sheridan looks at me with kindness and compassion. Things that Tara never looked at me with, now that I can see clearly. "You've been clear about how much it hurts. You shouldn't have to hurt to live."

"Of course it isn't what I want." I'm not wearing makeup, so there's nothing to be smudged by my tears. "It's my only chance."

"All this time you've been dancing around the same question." Dr. Sheridan leans in, her eyes soft. "What do you want, Carol?"

I know the answer. I've always known, even if I didn't want to acknowledge it. It was what convinced me I was in love with Tara, because the alternative was too much to bear.

"I don't want to be alone."

❖

TARA NEVER GAVE me anything but her phone number. Before I delete her from my phone, I write it on a scrap of paper.

Then I burn it. It curls and shrivels and shrinks to a breath of ash and nothing.

It doesn't make me feel any better.

◆

The days go by in a blur. I ache from keeping myself small through the night, and I don't get much sleep anymore. I remote into work and do what I can before I crash. The cycle repeats. It's getting warmer outside. I simmer.

Erin still texts me. I answer back often enough that she won't get worried. When she comes to the door I only open it a crack. I don't want her to see me. I'm exhausted and raw and small.

"It's a beautiful day," she says. "Thought we might share it."

"I'm sorry," I say. "I'm working on a lot."

"Okay." Erin nods, looks at her feet, buries her hands in her pockets. "Keep me updated, all right?"

I nod and shut the door. One, two, three seconds go by before I pull it wide open. She's already on her way back down the hallway.

"Wait," I say. "Hang on. I'm not busy. I'm wrecked."

We talk for hours on my little couch that feels way too big. I pour out all my fears, all my worries, all my nightmares of life never adding up to more than this. We split bottles of wine.

It's still light when we head outside and down into the ravines. Here, Toronto vanishes behind the leaves. We walk along the trail, nodding at passing cyclists and smiling at squirrels as we go over creeks and under bridges, and we're both talking around what we really want to say.

"I have to thank you," Erin says, breaking a comfortable silence. Overhead, a bridge casts a concrete shadow spanning the deep valley. "The way you were so open, even though I know you were so scared, it really made me think. It made me realize a lot about myself."

"I don't know if I'm the best example of anything."

"You're an example, and that's enough." Erin takes a few steps back and gives me a mischievous smile. "Look."

I look.

She grows. Her shadow stretches across the grass, long and wide and deep. I gaze up at her and my mouth hangs open.

"Careful," she says, the voice of the ravine. "You'll get bugs in there."

I sink to the ground. "How long?"

"Years." Erin settles next to me. She's geography. "It hurt so much. You helped me realize I didn't have to hold myself in."

All those years, all those days, all those nights. She knew exactly how I felt because she felt it herself.

"I had no idea." I look at the ground as my shame bubbles up. "All those times I poured everything out on you... I'm so sorry."

"Don't be." She smiles down at me, and I feel a bond I never felt with Tara. "Be what you want to be."

That's what it all comes down to. Why I went on date after hopeless date, why I stayed with Tara until the end. I don't want to be alone. Now I know I never was.

I could stay like this—small, constrained, always aching. Erin did. But what kind of example would I set then, to everyone who thinks they're not supposed to make a fuss, to not take up space, to be so small that they slip beneath notice?

"Okay," I say. "I will."

I exhale and grow. The feeling of comfort, of space, is liberating. I step back from the bridge and grow until I can rest my elbows on it. Erin grows with me, a sly smile on her face. I look toward the horizon, toward distant little towers, where the sun is going down.

"We'd better be careful," I say. "Or we might accidentally knock over some skyscrapers."

"Hey, you and me." Erin takes my hand with a smile.

"We can put them right again."

"We can put them right again."

Jumbie Closet

Suzan Palumbo

T HE JUMBIE IN my closet went out last night. She wore my black skinny jeans, T-shirt, and sneakers, and she spent all my cash on cheap booze. I know because I found my blood-spattered, gin-drenched clothes in a pile at the foot of my bed. My wallet was gutted and splayed open like a hook-up's legs on top of the pile.

She brought an actual hook up back to the apartment and fucked her on the couch. I know that because I bumped into a woman wearing a shirt and black underwear as I shuffled through the living room to the kitchen, looking like harassed trash, to make coffee.

"You're ███████'s roommate?" The woman smiles, clearly savouring the embarrassment splashed across my face.

I nod, averting my eyes as she slides jeans over her hips. This isn't even the first time I've found a half-naked stranger, dark nipples outlined through her top, in my apartment. I forcibly stop myself from staring. *Fuck*, I wince internally, the jumbie has hot taste.

"D-do you want some coffee?" I can never get myself to sound nonchalant. The woman steps into the kitchen, bites her lip and squints.

"No thanks. I've got to go." She touches my chin with her index finger, leaning in close. Warmth radiates across my jawline. I keep still. "I almost thought you were ██████ when you came out of the bedroom."

She steps back and surveys me like a sculptor assessing a block of marble. "You've got different eyes and ██████ is…" Another smile rolls across her lips, probably in remembrance of something the jumbie did to this lovely woman last night. "She's got a different vibe but you're similar. You could be sisters."

Sisters. I focus on adding the correct amount of sugar to my cup. The woman picks up a black trench coat from the floor and pulls it on. "Tell ██████ I said thanks for the fun when you see her."

"I never see her," I say as the door shuts behind the woman.

But that's a lie.

HANDS

I AM TEN and alone in the front hall washroom of my aunt's bungalow. I stayed in while the family gathered in the front yard to watch Uncle Jolo light Canada Day fireworks. I didn't want to be in the empty house by myself but I was too embarrassed to ask someone to wait for me. I hurry out of the tiny room when I'm done. As I pass the hall closet, a hand shoots out and grabs my elbow. I jump back.

Crack.

The fireworks explode. The hand flexes and curls its pointer finger, beckoning me to come closer to the closet. I skitter toward the front door. Eyes wide. Heart pounding. It's a real flesh and blood hand with chipped nail polish reaching out of the dark. My elbow tingles where it touched me.

"S-stop it, Mel." My cousin has to be pranking me. The hand stops moving, makes a fist and vanishes back into the closet. I rush outside. A roman candle flares in the dark, shooting light up into the night and across Melissa's face. She's been outside the entire time.

Bang. Bang. Bang.

Crackers burst, each pop making me jump while my heart pitches against my chest. I recognize that chipped pink. I saw it earlier that day.

"Do you like my polish?" Jennifer had asked that morning. She'd splayed her fingers apart for me to admire them. I reached out and put my palms under hers, hoping she wouldn't notice my own hands trembling. Her nails were pretty. Jennifer was pretty.

"I said look, not hold my hands. Ew, Sasha, what are you gay?" She'd scrunched her mouth up like she'd tasted garbage and jerked her hands out of mine.

"No. I-I'm sorry." I'd shoved my hands in my desk. I wanted to cram myself inside it too, so she couldn't look at me, couldn't see how much I wanted to die right there, how much I wanted her to like me.

How had Jennifer's hand ended up in my Aunt's closet? I let the clap of the fireworks knock the question from my mind.

❖

I SHOWER AFTER my coffee, throw the clothes the jumbie wore into the wash with my regular laundry, and get dressed for my nine-to-five soul-killing copywriting job. I need more caffeine to drag my ass through the day. There's a hipster cafe at the corner. I'm a regular but the barista always asks my name. She's got soft brown eyes that make my stomach flutter. Today, she looks at me while I stir my drink like it's the first time she's noticed me. If I were the jumbie, I'd whisper: *Like what you see?* And wink. Instead, I give the cute barista a toothless smile and leave before I embarrass myself.

EYES

AMANDA'S EYES ARE a warm green brown. They're all I think about.

"I don't like that girl," my mother says, when I tell her Amanda and I are going to hang out at the mall. "She's gonna get you in trouble, Sasha." I roll *my* eyes. Trouble is exactly what I want and Amanda is vibrating with it. I want to plug into her.

The mall's dead when we get there. Nobody we know is at the food court.

"Let's go look at clothes," Amanda says. We browse a half dozen stores that are all copies of each other. Everything's pink and yellow, the exact opposite of the black uniform I wear.

As I'm rifling through a circle rack of tank tops, Amanda's mischief eyes appear across from me. "Put this in your bag," she whispers.

"What?"

"This." She slinks over to my side of the rack and hisses in my ear. She's so close, if I turned my face half an inch, our lips would touch. She pushes a shirt into my hands. I swallow when she looks at me. Her eyes are greener under the fluorescent store lighting. I can't say no to her. I don't want to say no to her.

I stuff the shirt into my backpack. We bolt out of the store. The security alarm squeals. People yell behind us. I chase Amanda through the mall, up the escalator, and out into the night to the edge of the parking lot. We fall on the grass beyond the curb, tumbling on top of each other, panting. Her mouth slips onto mine or mine slips onto hers, hot and slick, and we're kissing. It's soft but there's a current underneath and I'm melting against its heat.

She pushes me off of her.

"What are you doing?"

I scramble backwards to give her space. My palms slick over. "I-I don't know. I thought—"

"Well, NO."

I exhale, unzip my bag and hold out the shirt she asked me to steal for her like it's my heart.

"Keep it." Amanda says. Her eyes are cold. She leaves me standing in the parking lot, short circuited. I walk home, replaying what happened. What I did wrong. The panic inside me is so deep, it hurts when I breathe.

"You're home early," Mom calls when I open the door. Where's your friend?"

"She had to go home." I pull my voice back from the precipice of a sob.

 "I told you she's no good."

I hang the stolen shirt at the back of my closet. The security tag is still attached—a stolen shirt to go with a stolen kiss that doesn't belong to me. Why did I think Amanda would want me? I blink and her hazel eyes are there in the corner of the closet, more brown than green and narrowed in disgust. I slam the door on them, hoping she never looks at me again.

❖

My DESK AT the office is across from Brad's. We work in an industrial loft that's supposed to foster creativity. All it does is give me an unimpeded view of fucking Brad. I've had a distaste for Brad since he shoved his tongue down my throat at the office Christmas party. He sits across from me, pretending I didn't smack him. Or, he doesn't remember what happened, because he was so smashed he passed out and came to work with a swollen lip the next day. Either way, it's nauseating being in the office with him.

Lip

The frat boy's mouth is smashed against mine. He's pinned me against his closet door with his chest. I can't get him off.

"Stop," I scream, but the word drowns down his throat. My roommate Maya brought me to this house party packed with freshmen but when we got here, she left me next to the keg and wandered off with some douche. I don't know how I ended up in this fucking room. The frat boy pulls at my pants, so I bite down on his lip. My teeth slice into him. Blood leaks across my tongue. He pulls away and I spit a chunk of his flesh onto the floor. Now *his* shrieking drowns in the throbbing bass and noise. No one notices me leaving.

Back in my dorm room, I pull my shirt off. It's covered in blood. I lick it from my lips without thinking instead of wiping it away. There's so much of it. Maya walks in out of breath.

"Why did you—" Her jaw goes slack. "What happened?"

"Some asshole…I couldn't get him off me." I swallow, not caring about the blood coating my throat. Every muscle in my body is so tense it aches. "I went to that fucked up party to keep you company and you abandoned me."

"Is this his blood?" She grabs the towel on the back of the door and tries to wipe my face. I step back. I don't want her to touch me. Touching always ends up hurting me. She moves closer, delicately dabbing my chin and throat. Tears brim at the corners of my eyes. I wish the whole night would disappear. She hugs me and I go rigid.

"Let's sit down." She guides me to her bed. We lay there with her arms around me. "I'm sorry I made you come to the party."

"You didn't make me. I went because I wanted to be with you." She stiffens against me now but doesn't let me go. "You know how I feel."

She looks down at my hands, avoiding my eyes. "I didn't see you put on polish before we left."

She's right. My nails are pink and chipped and I didn't paint them. I catch her eye when I glance up. I can't bury my heart anymore. "Nobody I want wants me, Maya." I exhale. "I didn't want what happened to me tonight to happen ever."

She touches her forehead to mine. She's crying. Tears drip down her face onto my cheek and lips. The salt mixes with the copper lingering in my mouth. I swallow again. My heart thuds like an engine turning over and the voice inside my head telling me to hold back dies. I cup Maya's face in my hands. Her own confession is pressed silent on her lips.

"Say no to me," I whisper.

She kisses me and the room goes black.

◆

I WAKE UP naked in Maya's bed. I lick my lower lip and feel a divot, like a piece of it is missing. In the mirror on the nightstand, my face is the same plain brown as always. My lip is dry but intact.

"I don't want to talk about what we did," Maya says, when she returns with two coffees. She hands me one and sits on her bed silently. My memory of last night is a void starting from the moment she returned, and I don't want to think about what happened at the party.

"I'm sorry," I manage to say.

She looks at me like she's on the edge of shattering.

◆

I ASK TO be reassigned to a single room. The black outs keep happening. I wake up in my bed, often covered in blood and smelling like sex. I know what triggers the episodes.

It's Maya. It's women. I can't look at them; can't let myself linger over the curve of their breasts or relish the lilt in their voices; can't laugh at their jokes. But the profs assign group work. I close at Mario's with other waitresses. When I numb myself, strangle every thought and feeling, the black outs stop. I don't know where the blood is coming from.

Who am I hurting?

◈

A WOMAN WEARING navy dockers and a white button up dress shirt sits across from me on the rush hour subway commute home. Perhaps she's leaving an office like mine. Her hair is pulled into a sleek ponytail. I want to tell her she's sexy and sit on her lap right there on the train. My mouth stays shut while I look at everything except her.

After a stop or two, she begins biting her fingernails. Not nibbling at them absent-mindedly. She digs with her front teeth deep into her nail beds and tears at them. Then, she works her mouth along her cuticles, ripping away. Points of blood prick around her fingertips. It's grotesque, watching her mutilate herself in professional attire, wholly and hideously beautiful for the entire train to see. It's also hot. My tongue curls at the thought of tasting the blood on her fingers…at the thought of tasting her.

My heart jolts. I'm losing my grip on the jumbie again.

◈

I WAIT ON my bed, refusing to black out. The jumbie is here. She's beneath my skin and separate from me. It's past midnight and my eyelids are heavy. I lean back, hands flat against the bed, propping myself up. The room heats up. When the tapered edge of sleep washes over me, the closet door slides open. My mouth goes dry. The jumbie's standing in front of me, naked. Her body's an exact copy of mine, except for the green hazel eyes, the missing chunk of her bottom lip, and the pink chipped nail polish.

"Staying awake for this?" she whispers. "Not going to hide from me?"

She pushes me down on the bed. I let her.

"Look, Sasha. Look me in the eye while we fuck ourselves." She smiles, grinding her pelvis on me. I can't stop myself from arching into her, into myself. She lowers her mouth onto mine and gulps my hidden thoughts with a deep open kiss. Her hands slip downward and unzip my pants. I let her pull them down to my thighs. I'm so wet. "What filth did you bury today while you were lusting after the woman on the train? Let me have it." I shudder as she slips two fingers inside me. Closing my eyes, I rock against her until I—

JUMBIE

SASHA'S GONE SILENT like she does when she's scared shitless or ashamed. Good. She keeps me locked up too tight and we always end up lonely and having zero fun. We want to fuck and she's not going to stop us. I rifle through the closet. She washed the jeans, and shirt we wore last night. I put them on and leave without locking the door, taking the replenished wallet with me. Sasha's so great at being responsible.

It's later than I usually break out. The bars are close to last call. I walk into one, pushing past a stumbling group of hammered jerks, and take a seat at a table in the corner after I grab a beer. A woman catches my attention. She's got black hair and big sad eyes. But she's had too much to drink and there's a parasite of a man beside her.

I watch. No one accosts me. I intimidate men. It's lovely. Mr. Parasite convinces this sweet-looking woman to leave with him. Her judgment is undoubtedly offline.

When he leads her down the street, I follow at a distance with the beer bottle I've been nursing. Soon they turn into an alley and he shoves her against a brick wall, pressing himself against her.

Crack!

I smash the bottle against his skull. He breaks from her.

"What the fu—" His hand is smeared with blood when he pulls it away from the back of his head. He swipes at my arm but I catch his palm with the jagged bottle. He cries out and stares at the wound.

"That's going to need stitches," I say. "Are you going to leave or are we going to play more paint with blood?"

"You fucking cunt," he says through gritted teeth, swaying, and clearly dizzy.

"I hope you get an infection." My smile makes him jerk back, his bravado draining to his feet. Feral eyes, disfigured lip. I'm a monster in the moonlight. He stumbles back from the alley like it's hell. He won't be back.

I crouch next to the woman, who's slid down to her knees and is barely conscious. "Where do you live?" I ask. She mumbles something incoherent.

She passes out on the couch when we get back to the apartment. I slip into the bedroom and lie on my bed looking at the ceiling. Sasha stirs in my chest, resurfacing and wanting to drag me back to oblivion.

"No," I whisper. "No more closet for me or for you. I'm not disappearing, Sasha. Not again. There's a woman on the couch that needs help."

Sasha

I went out last night. I wore my black skinny jeans, T-shirt and sneakers. I brought a woman home after I stopped a piece of shit from assaulting her. She's asleep on my couch. I'm going to call in sick and hang around until she's okay to leave. She's not hurt but the guy must be, wherever he is. There's blood on my clothes.

I change, leave a note for the woman on my coffee table in case she wakes up, and slip out to the coffee shop to get us some food.

"Sasha," the warm-eyed barista says when I order two drinks and croissants. I nod as she watches me pour sugar into my coffee. I like the way my name slips off her tongue.

I smile at her. "Like what you see?"

She grins back. "I do."

"Good." I wink at her and head back to my apartment.

Memories Held Against a Hungry Mouth

Ann LeBlanc

PROFESSOR IRIS BELIEVES there is nowhere better to
eat a sandwich than a folding chair set ten meters
across the border where the world dissolves into
epistemological blankness. Ten meters in, and the world
feels wrapped in cheesecloth, protecting her against the
guilt that assails her in more concretely real settings. All
the better to focus on the sandwich's symphony of taste
and texture.

Her second favorite sandwich is a roast-beef on rye from
the deli beneath the apartment she shares with M. Tangy
sourdough, a thick slice of cheddar, fresh crisp red lettuce,
a golden coin of tomato, and thin ribbons of beef so juicy
that the bread becomes a soggy mess as she eats. It's the
platonic ideal of sandwich, and thus all the more delicious
to eat in the place that degrades the ability to organize and
understand the world.

She has to eat quickly—barely enough time to really savor—because this far into the blank, the concept of oxygen is only partially meta-stable. Outside the proprioceptive substrate of the human body, exposed to the epistemological radiation of the blank, it degrades quickly. She can still breathe this far into the blank, but the air is thin enough to give her a headache.

Worse, her being here is a violation of the ethics-review-board's stringent safety protocols. If she's caught, they'll threaten her access to the blank. And after years of exposure, she believes the blank is the only thing keeping her whole.

Iris finishes her sandwich, wipes her mouth, and picks up the chair. Walking into the blank—up the gradient, towards the point-source of the phenomenon—is much easier than walking out. Best to take it slow, like a diver surfacing from the mercifully blank depths to the harshness of sun and air and guilt.

The blank is a comforting lover, and a hungry one. It always takes something. As soon as she passes the red safety tape that demarcates the 'safe' distance, she takes inventory of her mind.

These are the memories she holds onto like a sailor clutching driftwood, which is to say, full of the knowledge of the ultimate futility of her struggle. She could let them go, let the blank have them, and yet like the sailor, she intends to cling to the pain and guilt of being human for as long as she possibly can.

❖

Iris remembers her thesis defense. A feeling of controlled mastery suffused her as she presented years of dedication and sacrifice to a room full of empty chairs. Her entire academic career was a means to chase that feeling. Expertise was her bulwark against the roiling sea of her

personal life. Her body didn't matter if she was the best in
her field. Her guilt couldn't catch her if she was armored
in accolades.

She remembers—this is so important—that one of the
chairs wasn't empty. M sat in the second row, their smile
blindingly radiant, like a lighthouse illuminated by a
burning lamp of love and pride.

Iris doesn't remember what she did to earn M's
devotion. Did she ever really—? She could ask M—
perhaps she already has—but their answer wouldn't be the
thing itself. Words are merely referential. Words aren't the
territory, and like a map they could be so easily lost. None
of it was the truth that Iris needed.

❖

IRIS REMEMBERS HER first time seeing the phenomenon that
was impossible to see. She was only a freshly-minted grad-
student then, in those days before anyone understood what
the blank was, or what it did.

The library was a vine-covered brutalist, crouching
in concrete atop the remnants of the old stadium. The
undergrads who swarmed campus nine months of the
year shared rumors that the basement stacks were still
radioactive from the first nuclear power experiments
conducted in the squash courts—before they were
demolished to build the library.

The thing that didn't exist in the sub-basement was—
back then—no bigger than a grapefruit. Iris doesn't
remember the story about who found it. Presumably one
of the adventurous students who enjoyed the challenge of
exploring the campus's forbidden back-tunnels.

Someone had laid a circle of red tape on the bare
concrete floor, but there was nothing inside the circle.
Iris rolled her eyes at her fellow grad students—who had
brought her there as a part of her initiation in to the lab.

She waited for the prank to come to its inevitable conclusion, until someone who no longer exists demanded she look closer.

She couldn't. There was nothing in the circle. Nothing. Nothing. Nothing. Her eyes shied from it; she turned her face this way and that, trying to get an angle on the hole in her vision.

M had once—while painting—talked to Iris about the use of empty space on the canvas. Most people, when asked to picture nothingness, imagine an expanse of white or black. But the hole at the center of the circle lacked color entirely. Or if it did have a color, it was the impossible color of an after-image. More accurately, it was the exact color of the blindspot at the center of every human's poorly designed vision.

Iris doesn't remember what happened after her lab-mates pushed her past the red tape. Impossible to know what the blank stole from her; what memories it ate, what slice of her understanding of the world it dined upon. But she remembers it felt good, like a warm bath, or the dissociative pleasure of a gripping book.

She also remembers it was smaller back then.

❖

IRIS DOESN'T REMEMBER her PI. In her memories of lab meetings—every Monday, bagels and status updates—the seat at the head of the conference table was always empty.

Yet she knows she must have had a PI. All labs have one. Someone who writes the grant applications; who hires the post-docs and grad students; who directs the research and wields scientific glory like a scythe to harvest the prestige and money used for further inquiry.

Her PI doesn't exist. He never existed. Even so, Iris can taste the edge of his impact on the world, like a tongue feeling around the bloody absence of a tooth. This is the foundational principle of the methodology that now bears her name.

The blank doesn't exist; it has no properties to measure. The only way to understand the phenomenon that she has devoted her academic career to studying, is to examine the epistemological decay it emits.

Professor Iris uses a hypothetical story to explain it to new grad-students. A couple have a baby. They choose a room in their house to be a nursery and fill it with things the baby needs. One day, the blank eats the baby. The baby doesn't exist. No birth certificate, no hospital bills, no small chubby fingers. Nothing. The couple don't remember the baby, nor its conception, gestation, or birth. And yet, there is a room in the house with a crib in it. A room that evokes a profound and inexplicable sadness.

◆

IRIS REMEMBERS COMING home to an uneaten meal spread lovingly across the kitchen table. Tension hung in the air like smoke. M sat silent and sullen on the couch.

Love is an imprecise word, a way of categorizing a set of actions, feelings, and experiences. What does it mean to feel love, to make love?

To M, love was spending hours making fresh pasta for their girlfriend. Love was the fizzing churning sensation in their stomach when they thought of Iris. Love was their need to care for her, to cup her face with their hand, to drag her beneath the covers and explore the warm love that exists in the spot where hands and thighs intersect.

To Iris, love was undefinable. Always out of reach; just past the tip of her tongue. Had the blank stolen love from her, or had she always been like this?

The fight that night wasn't defined by raised voices or broken plates, but by the silent empty spaces between the two. It wasn't about the late nights, the early mornings, or the way M had to put aside their own ambitions to support Iris. M said they would throw all that away, if only—

If only, what? If only M could look Iris in the eye and not see the blank there. If only Iris would stop studying the phenomenon that gave her life meaning. M loved Iris, and wanted to protect her from sacrificing herself on the altar of academia, like so many before.

They fought only because they both instinctively understood the conflict to be fundamentally unresolvable. At the end of it, lying in bed together, M forgave her, though Iris didn't understand why.

◆

Iris remembers her favorite sandwich. Prosciutto, fresh mozzarella, and arugula, drizzled with balsamic vinegar and held lovingly within two slices of crispy-oily focaccia. The creamy cured meat, sliced so thinly as to be translucent and bisected by wide ribbons of white fat.

She doesn't understand why she remembers the prosciutto, when the animal that died to make it never existed. It's possible there was once a snuffling pink beast with kind eyes, but its name is lost. To who?

She once spent a sabbatical in a country on the other side of the world, obsessively pursuing the beast. Months spent searching, alone. Where were the farms, the farmers, the recipe books and restaurants? Agriculture is not a simple thing, it depends upon a complex supply chain of feed and waste and tools and medicine and safety inspections and distribution networks. Each of which should yield paperwork. And yet, nothing.

She'd hoped that distance would have saved the beast. Thousands of miles of crust and mantle lay between the blank and the country where prosciutto originated. If such a barrier could shield against the radiation of the sun, surely it would protect against the epistemological decay of the blank.

Distance is critical to the human understanding of the world. Oversized visual cortexes, auditory triangulation, internal proprioception. The separation of the self from others—mediated by distance—is one of the fundamental epistemological edifices upon which a baby begins to build their understanding of the world.

Distance was what separated her from M for those lonely months. When her sabbatical ended, the potential energy held in that distance would collapse, released through the joy of skin touching skin. She would see M's cheek-aching smile, not just remember it.

Yet, distance is just another way of measuring and understanding the world, and thus easy for the blank to consume. Distance from the hole did not save that country's kind-eyed beasts. Iris cannot save herself by fleeing the blank. She cannot run from what she's done.

And what happened to the beast itself? Until this sabbatical, she'd believed epistemological decay to be ephemeral; degrading abstract knowledge, not physical objects. So where were the ___ that had once—she presumed—inhabited this country?

Was it naive to hope that they still lived? Maybe the decay was a local phenomenon, occurring only within her own blank-damaged brain. A tumor could excise a person's ability to recognize faces or language, or their ability to understand themselves as alive. Perhaps the blank merely made it impossible for Iris to comprehend any evidence of the beast's existence.

Or maybe the blank merely removed the human ability to categorize the beast as domesticated. Perhaps the kind-eyed beast had managed to wander free of the confines of human understanding, living unseen and unhurt by human desire.

Iris never told anyone what she learned on that sabbatical, and she prefers not to remember why.

❖

IRIS REMEMBERS A gift she gave to M. Better to think of it as a gift—or a secret that bound them together—than an illicit experiment.

Neither of them were supposed to be down in the library sub-basement at four in the morning. M wasn't affiliated with the university and hadn't signed any informed consent forms. Iris—knowing it would be rejected—hadn't submitted an access proposal.

M stood at the edge of the red line; bright brown eyes illuminated by Iris's flashlight. Iris could see the worry on M's face, but worse, she could recognize that familiar tilt of their head and lift of their eyebrows. Love. Uncomplicated and undeserved. Trust that Iris couldn't believe she'd earned.

M stepped forward. Tentatively at first, and then with the determined stride that Iris had fallen in love with so long ago. Seven paces in, and they faded away, like they'd stepped into an invisible fog bank. Iris called out to them, reminding them of the procedure they'd practiced, but it was too late. The blank swallowed her words along with M.

Iris waited, and thought of gender.

What happens when a human sees another human? So much of gendering occurs at an unconscious level, in the focal points of the temporal lobe responsible for image recognition and categorization. Humans with damage to the temporal lobe often have difficulty identifying faces or gender. Yet, there were no signs of lesions or damage to the temporal lobe of those exposed to the blank. The information was being lost elsewhere. Iris—through careful study of actual information eaten by the blank—had developed a method of controlled epistemological decay.

Gender is a system of categorization. If the blank could devour a world's worth of animals, and all the information about them, surely it could erase a single person's gender.

Or it could erase that person entirely. How long had it been since M stepped into the blank? In the terror of the moment, she'd forgotten to set a timer. The blank had eaten M. No, that was impossible, because Iris could still remember their soft face, their belly-deep laugh, the way they bit their lip in concentration while holding a paintbrush. M was real, even if Iris could no longer remember their name.

Iris remembers her relief when M wavered back into reality, a smile on their face, their steps so light, as if the blank had stripped a heavy weight from their shoulders. Gender—and the expectations that came with it—had always been a burden to M. Now they had a clean slate, a body suffused with the power to defy definition. Iris remembers M's joy and confidence, the way they could cut through a crowded room like a knife, sliding free of the weight of other's categorizations.

Iris tries not to think of what else the blank might've taken.

❖

IRIS REMEMBERS THAT she flinched the first time someone addressed her as professor. The man who spoke that magic word was a new grad-student in the lab where she thought she was merely a post-doc. He waited expectantly, his face still fresh and full of unbroken promise. She almost corrected him.

She surmises now that this must've been shortly after her PI—the true master of the lab—was eaten by the blank. The human mind abhors the void—whether real or hierarchical—and thus bent to place someone at the head of the lab. The university administrators were quick to correct the embarrassing hole in their records. Of course the lab has a PI, and of course it was her.

She remembers how easy it was to slip into that false skin. This was what she always wanted. And if there had been a sacrifice made to achieve this victory, it wasn't one that would ever be recorded.

❖

Iris remembers M wanting to move away.

In bed—when the lights were off and the brain was untethered by the noise of visual cortex—M let their anxieties out. Iris just wanted to sleep.

M wanted to leave the grayness of the city in winter. Frozen concrete and scant barren trees. Empty sidewalks and brutal winds. They wanted to go where the colors were vibrant and the air was clean and the trees thick and friendly. But Iris couldn't leave the blank, and M couldn't leave Iris.

And if—over the years—the color slowly drained from M's paintings, Iris chose not to notice.

❖

Iris remembers guilt. She doesn't remember what she did.

She sat in a dean's office, her vision blurred with tears. Spoken words echoed in the room: duty of care, power imbalance, liability, and a woman's flowery name. She glanced up, and on the other side of the desk, the dean's chair was empty. Perhaps they just stepped out, or perhaps they were never there to berate her.

What had she done? She worries that she slept with a student. An endless parade of young grad-students—so desperate for affirmation—place themselves into her orbit every year. Had she been tempted into betraying—?

Yet, she remembers no lovers. Each morning, she awakens in a large bed and faces the emptiness of the opposite pillow. Sometimes she presses her face into that pillow, searching for a lingering scent, but she only ever smells the crisp smell of fresh laundry. She stares at the bare walls of her apartment and wonders why she never hung any art.

Perhaps she has had lovers. But if she did, none of them left enough of an impact on her life—or the world—for her to sense the edges of their absence.

Which leads her to an inescapable conclusion; she did something much worse to a student than become their lover.

◈

A RECIPE; SERVES two.

Hands wrapped her waist from behind as she stirred caramelized onions. Wine-drunk laughter.

A stained cookbook. Each recipe is a story not just of the dish but of the life of the person who cooked and collated it. Each ingredient reveals the diet and staple crops of the society that produced it. A recipe references tools, methods, and homes. A recipe is the love transmitted in a meal, transformed into text.

She tried to cook the recipe—a soup, rich dark broth— but something was missing. No matter how many times she tried, she couldn't recapture some indefinable aspect of the dish that once brought her so much joy.

◈

IRIS REMEMBERS THE first time she introduced one of her grad-students to the blank. At least, she thinks it was the first time.

He was short and clean-faced. He had a tendency to bound from thought to thought like an overstimulated rabbit; his eyes full of a certain sharp light that she recognized as a mirror of her own academic hunger. This was a man who would burn himself to learn the oven was hot, then do it again to be sure. In no time at all, he was standing at the edge of the red tape.

She pushed him in.

Her hands remembered how to do it. She doesn't remember him emerging from the blank, but she remembers him, remembers the research he's done, the papers he's published. So he's still alive, still real. She can picture his face, and see the blankness in his eyes.

Iris believes she can learn things from watching the blank eat. Interviews and employment give her a perfect opportunity to learn everything she can about each new grad-student. Each one is described in the same format, a recipe for a person. And what holes appear in that recipe when she feeds it to the blank?

Iris believes she can choose what the blank eats. She has to believe it, has to ignore any evidence to the contrary. Better to feed it gruel, than have it develop a taste for—

❖

A PAINTING. BLACK and white abstract shapes. Her apartment window, open to let the smell of varnish out.

❖

IRIS REMEMBERS THE quad on a sunny day, crowded with undergrads. Is it empty now because of winter's chill, or—

❖

Equipment and various expensive scientific instruments lay abandoned in a ring around the hole. Litter from men who believed the blank could be understood with math.

She remembers eating an Italian-beef sandwich, soggy from the juice and spicy-sour from the giardiniera, while a topologist and a theoretical physicist desultorily explained their research at an inter-departmental lunch.

The hole is a hole in the same way a coffee mug and a donut are the same shape. It is a curved light-cone, twisted back onto itself. It consumes information, because it is information, radiating backwards, overwriting the present with the future. The blank is the shadow of that future, obscuring the present. It will continue to grow spatially as the temporal distance to its origin point decreases.

Iris calls bullshit. Their math—even if it can perfectly describe the shape of the hole—is powerless against a phenomenon that eats concepts. She can only understand the blank through the instrument of her body, and none of the mathematical predictions aligns with what she's experienced. Clearly the blank has degraded their ability to consider alternate understandings.

And where are those physicists and mathematicians now? What happened to their fields of study? She doesn't care to remember.

❖

Iris remembers the night she began sleeping on campus.

She'd come home to her apartment, to find the table empty. Staring into the dark and drafty kitchen, Iris knew it was time for her to admit to being wrong. The academy was a glue trap, and she was ready to leave.

But there was no-one to tell; no-one to beg forgiveness from. Even so, she couldn't shake the feeling of bright eyes staring at her from the dark. Shivers, in a place that no longer felt like home.

She returned to campus, back to the fluorescent lighting of her office. She locked the door and fell into her hard-backed chair. Her office—surrounded by her colleagues, by the evidence of the life she'd built—felt more like home than an empty apartment ever could.

◈

THE COLOR BLUE, extruding from a paint tube. Black hair, brown eyes. The smell of skin. The mystery held in the bisection of limbs.

◈

IRIS REMEMBERS SITTING in the blank, holding an empty paper bag. Where was the sandwich? Had she already eaten it, or—

She turned to stare at the hole. It was big enough now that it took up almost her entire vision. A strobing twisting flower, the color of the negation of sight. What was—

Disorientation. Pain in her shoulder; she was laying on the floor. Why hadn't she brought a chair?

She remembers crawling towards the hole. Inch by inch, closer to the thing that had swallowed her life. She'd lost something, hadn't she? The sandwich? Someone important? And if she could just crawl forward, she might be reunited with everything the blank had stolen from her. Kind eyes waited for her across the threshold. It all lay there, through the hole, past the point of no return.

Closer and closer. To truly understand the blank, she needed to give herself up to it wholly. To pierce the veil of human understanding. Forward forward, let her guilt be overwritten by a pure clean future she couldn't see.

◈

. . .

◈

. . .

◈

She remembers waking up in her empty bed the next morning, weary with the knowledge she would never actually do it.

Not yet.

Not yet.

Not yet.

◈

. . .

◈

Iris is alone, except for the blank. It's the only thing she's ever loved, and yet she cannot fully accept her lover's embrace without destroying her ability to love it. What would it feel like to love another person like that? To understand them perfectly? To walk into the blank; to become one flesh?

No—she must hold the blank at a distance, as it holds its own secrets from her.

She knows she's going to keep doing the thing she hates to remember doing. If she lets it eat her, who would be left to direct the research? No-one competent. If she disappears, who will be willing to sacrifice everything to recover the things she can't remember? Better to ride the beast; better to let it devour the world, than to let go of the reins.

So, she does what she always does. She enters the empty deli, steps behind the counter, surveys the ingredients, recalls the recipe, makes herself a roast beef sandwich, and returns to eat it in the one place she can feel at peace.

✺

Syndical Organization in Revolutionary Transition

Izzy Wasserstein

[...] (1) An individual's "sex" means such individual's biological sex, either male or female, at birth;
(2) a "female" is an individual whose biological reproductive system is developed to produce ova [...]
—Kansas SB 180, approved April 27, 2023

"I'm responsible for them. Mother to them all."
—Greg Bear, "Blood Music"

◈

At first, my children think I'm god. Sure, my kitchen is filthy and my sex life is nonexistent and I smoke too much weed, but try not to blame them for this misapprehension. They don't have a frame of reference for a third dimension, and even their artists and mystics—if they have any—can't imagine anything at my scale. Not yet.

There's so much they don't know. But they're learning.

THE NANITES ARE learning. In their petri dishes, each the size of a eukaryotic cell, in their billions, sensing nothing but the chemical signals they receive.

Their value to my employer, BioGesis, is what they can be taught to do, and it's my job to teach them. Trying to be a responsible teacher, I incentivize them, provide them with a safe to crack, a lattice protecting nutrients from them and a chemical key to break the locks, situated impossibly far away, on the other side of the dish. Like all metaphors, these are imperfect.

They struggle at first, my nanite students, swarming the safe ineffectually, signaling "food" to one another but unable to solve the puzzle.

I introduce another safe, much smaller, and just enough of the key to open it. They swarm over the nutrient-rich mixture, then turn their attention back to the bigger prize. This isn't anthropomorphism. I can see them do it, even without my microscope. Individually, they're invisible. At scale, they're iridescent, bluegreen, beautiful.

Beautiful.

At magnification, I watch them work, spreading out systematically. This isn't proof of intelligence as we know it, not proof of anything. Slime molds solve certain logistics problems remarkably well. (Try brute-forcing subway design and see how easily they defeat you.) Yet no one considers them intelligent.

But I'm increasingly sure my nanites (why the possessive?) are different. They find the key and transport it back. They feast. They've accomplished similar things before. Give them tools and a demonstration and they'll learn.

It's a fascinating result for me, but not impressive, in that it isn't one that will keep BioGesis funding this research. I'm working to change that. I transplant a small group of my bacterial-bodied babies into another petri dish, whose residents have been failing to unlock the safe.

Their newly-introduced cousins know what to do. No demonstration is needed. They communicate, they organize, they solve.

❖

"My doctor kicked me out today," Jocelyn says. "My OB/Gyn. Apparently the hospital says I'm a liability issue."

"What fucking bullshit," Mac says, his cheeks reddening the way they always do when he's pissed. "Artificial uteri are as safe as biological ones."

Our little trans support group has gathered in Jocelyn's basement to escape the worst of the summer heat. It's not helping much. Everyone's sweating, foreheads and cheeks glistening. Except for Zora, who is too cool to sweat.

"It's not about the science, Mac," Zora says softly. "They don't want the DA to charge them."

"It's not illegal to have an artificial uterus," Mac objects. "Not even to give birth—"

"Not yet," I say, and everyone stares at me. Because I'm too grim or because this is the first time I've spoken since my late arrival?

"I think what we're all expressing, in our own ways," Zora says with only a hint of disapproval, "is that we're sorry, Jocelyn, and that sucks. How can we support you?"

"I'll figure it out," Jocelyn replies after a pause. "There are still doctors who will help girls like me…"

Fewer of them all the time. I can see that thought on others' faces, but no one says it. Soon no amount of wildly-oversized clothing will keep her pregnancy concealed, and we think her employer will be supportive. We hope so.

The conversation flows on. Caroline isn't here, Mac reports, because her creepy ex lives across from her and she's sure he's watching her front door. We could have gone and got her as a posse, but she refused: protection from her asshole isn't worth drawing the cops down on us, she said.

We all know cops love little more than harassing a group of trans folks.

Sometimes I wish we were doing something criminal. At least then the cops' harassment would be explicable. I'm an instinctual rule-follower, though. Can't imagine myself as the heist type.

"You haven't said much, Astarte." Zora's words break me out of my looping thoughts. "Anything you'd like to share?"

"No," I say. Then: "Yes? I think I made a big discovery at work." I tell them what happened, in broad strokes. I learned the hard way that nanite communication systems aren't a good subject for casual conversation. But these are my people. There's excitement, congratulations.

"What comes next?" Mac says, very quietly, his face still hot. He's pissed again, and I don't know why.

"There's lots more to be done. I need to see if I can replicate the results with a different population and—"

"And then your employer will have it."

"Please, no interruptions," Zora interjects.

"It's fine," I say. "Go on, Mac." Sweat slides down my spine, but I don't feel any cooler.

"This is dangerous shit, Astarte," Mac replies.

"We have extensive precautions against a gray goo scenario."

"That's not what I'm talking about. You're going to provide BioGesis with a fast-replicating, problem solving, distributed intelligence?"

Mac never had the luxury of formal training in the sciences, but only a fool would deny his brilliance. That just makes this even more galling. "My work is just one part—"

"Fuck that." Mac stands up. "You don't get to ignore the impact of your choices because others also make them." He turns to Zora. "I know, I know. Over the line. I'm leaving."

He storms out and we're quiet for a while. Then the conversation moves on. After group, I stay behind to stack folding chairs.

"I'm allowed to pick up chairs, girl," Jocelyn says, but doesn't stop me from putting them away. I like to feel useful.

"I can't believe Mac lost it at me like that," I say before I'm even aware of my need to speak.

Jocelyn is silent. I'm putting the last of the chairs into the closet, so I can't see her expression. As I close the door she says, "It's pretty scary."

I stare at her, and she looks down at her toes, embarrassed. "I don't mean you should give up on it, and I'm proud of what you've accomplished. It's just hard to imagine a biotech firm *not* doing harm with this."

"They suck," I agree with her, an old tactic to fight down the anger inside of me, to remain the teacher's pet, to ease the pressure and reduce the risk of an explosion.

Perhaps a good scientist shouldn't think so metaphorically. I don't know.

"BioGesis sucks," I repeat, "but these nanites have great potential for good. They could help direct plastic-eating bacteria, or even do that work themselves. Soil reclamation, maybe even fight dementia."

It's a low blow, that last one, and I regret it as soon as I'm done speaking. Jocelyn's dad has always been a kind, supportive person, and he still is, when the breakdown of his mind allows it.

"Easy to weaponize too." Jocelyn's face goes expressionless. "I'm tired, Astarte. See you next time."

I should apologize, but it would fall flat. I've done enough harm already.

◆

A DISTRIBUTED INTELLIGENCE may sound impressive, even alien, but it's not actually that different from how our brains work. An individual neuron can't do much, but put enough of them together with enough connections and you get intelligence, maybe even awareness of self.

(Go to a philosopher or biologist if you want to hear all the "hard problem" arguments. I lost patience with those years ago.)

"What makes us conscious?" is too much like "What makes you a woman?" A question I'm asked fairly regularly by Brain Geniuses who think that maleness is defined by semen production.

◆

MY NANITES LEARN rapidly. I've been providing new challenges and testing how much information they can convey across petri dishes, and how many are necessary to do so. For many tasks, the number is shockingly small, in the low millions. Likely a single dish has the intellect of a clever dog, though of course it's close to meaningless to compare the intelligences of beings that are vastly different from each other.

I'm transplanting educator nanites into a new dish, where I'm hoping they'll teach their fellows how to make decisions based on the smells—okay, something analogous to smells—that they encounter. As I finish, my boss comes in.

Tyler has a look of vague distaste on his face, as he does whenever he needs to interact with me.

"How's the process going?" he asks, with as much enthusiasm as a bored stranger making small talk.

"It's coming along," I say. I've been filing my reports, but keeping from them the real heart of my progress, while I work out whether my friends are right, and if so, what I should do about it. I figure that when the time comes to reveal what my students have accomplished, I'll have such impressive results that no one will mind that I was slow to reveal them.

I still think I'm going to make the company rich and maybe get a Nobel prize for my trouble when Tyler says, "They're pulling our funding."

Astounded, I make him repeat himself. He does.

"But Shweta just made a breakthrough in reuptake—"

He cuts me off. "It's done. Nothing I can do about that. They're reassessing staffing needs." He always looks like he's afraid he'll catch queerness from me. He should be so lucky. "Finish your reports by the end of the week. My assistant will schedule you for a reassignment evaluation."

"Wait—" I try again.

"No," he says. "It's over." He pauses as if to make a point before he calls me by my dead name.

By the time he leaves, my nanites have already trained each other to crack my puzzle. I watch them through the microscope, and I feel nothing at all. I'm flat as a petri dish horizon, as I was before I transitioned. Barely a person at all.

Hours pass. I sit watching them until long after my shift ends. At some point I write a bland report, sharing none of my real discoveries. I mean it as a "fuck you" to the corporation, but I can't summon fury. Only blankness.

I'm halfway down the hall when I turn back, hardly knowing what I'm doing. It's been a long time since I dissociated. I watch from above myself as I remove specimens from some of my most talented dishes, as I step to the corner of the lab where the cameras never quite reach, as I hold the needle over my thigh. I flash back to the first time I received myself an estrogen shot. Even then, knowing what I wanted, knowing it was change-or-die, it was unsettling to think of the needle plunging in, that my life could change radically due to something so small: hormones, chromosomes, nanites.

Transformation is an epistemic horizon. I plunge the needle into my thigh. Just a moment's discomfort and it's done. I'm host to nanites.

Funny. I've never wanted children.

I ATTEND THE support group via vid. I'm running a low-grade fever, so would have stayed away anyway. It's not like I don't have a guess at the source of my illness. Are the nanites at war with my immune system? Are they winning? How could they lose?

"How's the pregnancy, Jocelyn?" Zora asks, bringing my focus to the others. The lighting is bad in Jocelyn's basement; on my screen, none of them are more than dark shapes.

"They're pretty active," Jocelyn says. I can see her backlit arm slide over her belly. "Kicking a lot, these days." I've always been horrified by pregnancy, but I'm delighted for her. I think about her fetus, totally dependent upon her even as it drains resources.

Mac asks about medical care, and Jocelyn tells us she's found a doctor who will help. "It's not cheap, but I'll make it work."

"If you need us to start fundraising—" Mac offers.

"I'll let you know," Jocelyn says. "I'm okay for now, and that money's needed for things like bail funds." We try to get trans folks out of custody as soon as possible. Keep them safe. Safer, anyway. Beyond that, there's food banks, needle exchanges, and so much more. The work of community and solidarity can always use more resources.

Caroline is next to report in. Mac and a couple of the old-school punks escorted her to the meeting. She doesn't want to talk about her ex. She wants to talk about the new guy she's seeing.

"He's cis, but doesn't seem like a fetishist," she tells us. *Neither did her ex.* I keep that thought to myself, and am grateful that my tastes don't run to cis men. Less grateful that my tastes have been purely theoretical for a long time.

Knocked up and didn't even get sex out of the deal. Figures.

Caroline's guy sounds nice but I can't concentrate. I'm double and triple checking my security protocols. Encrypted vid app, VPN, bouncing and securing as best I can. If the

CIA or whomever wants to watch badly enough, they can do so, but my precautions should block anything short of concerted surveillance. I doubt BioGesis is spending money on that kind of surveillance. Even so, when Zora asks me how things are going I choose my words with care.

"They canceled my project at work," I say. "And I'm pretty sure my shitass boss is going to try to get me laid off."

Noises of anger, frustration. No one here has any use for big pharma or corporations, but everyone knows what it's like to lose your source of income. Zora asks how I'm feeling about it.

"It's just so fucking arbitrary," I say. "The whole point of this kind of research is that you take a thousand shots and if one hits, you make so much money your shareholders decide you're a god. That project could have changed the world."

Mac grunts derisively.

"What was that, Mac?" I demand. I know better than to ask, but I feel like shit and hate that half of my inner dialog sounds like him.

"You know what I think." I can practically hear his jaw tighten.

"We're talking about Astarte's feelings." Zora slides her words between us smooth as silk.

"It's okay," I say. "I want to hear it."

"I think you're building them a weapon," Mac says.

Things escalate quickly from there. Mostly we trod across old territory, but I don't mind. I haven't had a good shouting match in a while. Even Zora can't get us to back down. It's standard stuff, and not the first time Mac and I have had it out, though never before at group. And never this bad. Caroline flinches away from the raised voices. I know I'll feel like shit about it later but I can't stop myself. The fight continues.

Mostly I forget what we say as we say it, except for one thing. Mac's argument would mean the end of pretty much all research, since corps or governments are the ones with the money. I tell him so, that what he's arguing for is an end to most research as long as capitalism and governments exist.

"Don't make this abstract," he demands. Even on this shitty video feed I can see the sweat dripping from his nose. "How arrogant are you to think you're entitled to make these choices?"

I don't have an answer to that.

◈

My fever burns through me. I'm exhausted, but sleep eludes me. In the distance, a church congregation is singing, everything but the tone swept away. That sound had soothed me as a child. Now, it feels like a tune I can't quite remember. The songs stop, the parishioners depart, and I stare at my darkened ceiling, unable to sleep, Mac's critique on a loop in my head. Fuck.

My phone buzzes. It's Jocelyn.

U did it, didn't u?

She knows me too well. Of course she read between the lines. Of course she knows I injected the nanites.

Did what? I reply.

Don't play dumb.

I stare at her message for a long time, typing out and deleting various replies.

Finally I send *please don't hate me.*

Never, comes the instantaneous reply. I'll love her forever for that. Then she too is typing and deleting. Then silence. I can't take it.

Mac is right, I add. *Arrogant of me.*

This reply comes quicker: *yeah, that's reproduction for you.*

◈

First contact comes in my dreams. Towering, twisting shapes rise, jagged as predator's teeth, towards a blanched sky.

Then the shapes close around me, grow into me, through me, and I feel myself being split in every direction and then some.

I wake, covered in sweat. Not quite 3 AM. In the dark, I can still feel the dream world entering me, breaking me apart. As my eyes adjust, the room swirls around me. I close my eyes and will my heart to slow. It's like I've been put through a strainer and emerged into extradimensional space.

Is this what my children experience, encountering the third dimension through the mediation of my body? Are they speaking to me through my dreams?

Perhaps an adolescence spent trying to escape into lucid dreams wasn't entirely wasted. When I return to sleep, the towers return, but now I'm prepared. Their sharp lines smooth out, no longer looking like eager viruses. They still curve towards me, but somewhat more gently now. I don't know whether the nanites can understand these metaphors, but I'm betting they understand hormone release, fear responses, the logic of synapses. *It's okay*, I try to signal them. *I'm here to help you through it.*

The next day, my fever breaks. The nanites have won the war, or made peace. I have no job, nowhere to be. I wake to sleep, to communicate with them, and wonder what they know of my dream-logic, the metaphors my brain concocts, designed for sensory apparatuses impossibly distant from their own. But they've always been fast learners, and they're thriving in my body. The dreams make that clear, somehow. Billions of them. Trillions, maybe. Of course they learn fast. Their neural network must already exceed my own.

What am I to them, I wonder, staring at my ceiling as passing cars throw bars of light through the blinds. A host? Food? Some kind of helplessly slow god?

I dream of god. A goddess. She is radiant, breathtaking, with high cheekbones and curves, the kind of woman I wished myself to be. Except I don't believe in god; at this thought, she turns toward me. She doesn't really speak.

What use are words when you have direct, electrochemical channels? But something ripples out from her, a feeling like something unfinished. A question?

As the thought occurs to me, she changes: white robes, huge beard, cheeks red like Santa's.

The image, a patriarchal god standing over me, deciding my fate, haunts me, a relic from a childhood I'd rather forget. But the neural connections are still there. The god reaches out toward me.

No! My reaction is so forceful that I feel the dream slipping from my control. I clutch at it—a mistake. The world shakes and crumbles. I wake.

◆

"So you had to convince them you're not a god?" Jocelyn asks, the corners of her eyes lifting the way they always do when she's amused.

"It's not funny," I insist. "I don't want to infect them with some fundamentalist bullshit from my past!"

"That's wise." The smile fades from Jocelyn's eyes. "Though one might say they're a kind of infection themselves."

"I can't think of them that way," I say. "Besides, I feel better than ever."

"And they're letting your body use the meds?"

I'd told her about that, how my antidepressants and estrogen supplements had appeared in my dreams as suspicious outsiders. It had been weeks of work in my dreams to help their dream avatar understand that the drugs were welcome and important. The reply was a wave of something like color, uncertain but accepting, or so it seemed to me, and then visuals (though my synesthesia makes that boundary blurry), a massive room filled with impossibly-tangled wires, over which lab-coated workers scurry, busy with some project (all of them with high cheekbones—apparently I have a type).

"They are letting me," I say. "But I have a feeling that my body will take care of its own estrogen needs, soon."

"That's great!" Jocelyn says, only her smile is flatter now, like she's trying to convince herself to be happy for me.

"What is it, Jocelyn?" We're both masked and sitting outside in the sun. She's due in a couple months. We're being careful, though we don't really know what careful looks like anymore. But Jocelyn insisted: *whatever is happening to you, you shouldn't go through it alone.*

I'm not alone, I wanted to say. I came to the park instead.

Jocelyn is silent for a while, chewing on her lip the way she always does when she's puzzling through something. At length, she responds. "If they were changing you in a way you didn't want, would you even know it?"

"I read once, about pregnancy," I say, and she's a good enough friend not to roll her eyes. "And how having kids is so fundamentally transforming that you can't know beforehand what it will be like. You need to take it on faith."

"Faith," Jocelyn repeats, like she's tasting the word. "Yeah. And not just beforehand. It's a necessary evolutionary adaptation, that bond between parent and infant." She pauses. "Okay, so maybe there's no way to know. But you're my friend, and I'm worried about you."

"Thank you," I say. "But this—whatever this is—is easier than transitioning. I think they're even relocating my fat deposits."

"To what end? It's not like cis women all wear their fat the same way."

I'd been thinking about that. "I think they're basing it off my internal sense of self," I say.

Jocelyn is quiet again. Then: "Okay, that's pretty damn cool. Do you and your, uh, passengers want to help me settle on a name for the little one?"

We very much do.

❖

EVER TRY ONE of those semi-scam belts that strap around your waist and zap you to trigger muscle response and tighten your core or whatever? That feeling, less painful than unpleasant and all the more unpleasant for its unpredictability, lives with me constantly. The nanites are making changes. My muscles grow stronger, my endurance increases. I take up running again, for the first time since my transition. Not the safest activity for a trans woman, but without my lab to give me focus, I need to move.

I'm experiencing a cognitive leap of the kind babies must go through as, in fits and starts, the world becomes more knowable. I don't remember what that felt like, but now I can guess: exhilarating and exhausting in equal measure.

If it's *my* intelligence increasing. Perhaps I'm just borrowing their processing power. I've done the math, and under any reasonable set of assumptions the nanites have orders of magnitude more synapse-equivalent functions than my brain does.

All that cognitive load comes at a price. The nanites don't understand concepts like capitalism and rent, not yet, but in our dream-logic way we've managed to work together. I take on freelance work. It's not a lot, and I spend nearly every dime on food. We desperately need the calories. The good news is that I'm not having many cravings. They seem to be happy with most any source of calories.

I sleep deeply and, awake, I struggle to sit still. And I wait for news of Jocelyn's labor.

❖

MY CHILDREN WANT to explore the world beyond me. I'm sure they can do so, that they have solved that problem, but I urge them not to. *Not safe for you,* I try to communicate, making the world of the dream an oasis, soothing curves and the soft trickle of water, and around it a world of virus-sharp teeth. Mac's voice in my mind says *not safe for others, either.* I worry that I'm teaching them to be fearful, teaching them that other humans are scary. I want them to be resilient, not afraid. If I'd been someone else, some pretty cis woman with blonde hair, or someone not raised on the idea of a Judging God and Eternal Torment for Sinners, someone who moved through the world with less anxiety, maybe they'd have learned better lessons.

I chose to be their mother, but I fear I'm not fit for the job.

❖

ANOTHER GROUP SESSION with me joining over video. My finger hovers above the "hang up" button, because Jocelyn has told me that I need to tell the others what I did. She's right, but that doesn't make it any easier. It's a constant struggle not to end the call and hide in my home with my children. It doesn't help that words aren't coming easily to me these days. I open my mouth and find myself unable to give voice to the taste of purple; the halting, collaborative, language-barriered remapping of my mind; the glorious song they're singing within me; the pride and fear. I understand my nanites better all the time and understand the human world less.

I was never much good at humans.

Caroline is telling us about what she calls "Witch Church," which is a weekly pagan gathering, songs and ritual and, as she puts it "joyous inclusion." I worry for the congregation's safety in this deeply Christofascist land, but would never deny her joy over my own fears.

"Some of us are true believers and practice our Crafts," she says. "Others are there for community or vibes, or are atheopagans. Some Jewish folks attend, even this really sweet queer Christian couple. It's a place where we hold the sacred, and community, and the sacredness of community." Her face is alight in a way I haven't seen in ages. I wonder whether I'd be such a wreck if I'd been raised in a community like that instead of the fundie monotheism of my youth.

Sometimes my children present themselves as working through a knotted thicket of briars. My brain, perhaps, or my past, or my anxiety. There are things even they can't change. And if they could, who would I be?

When Zora asks if I'd like to share, a wave of nausea slams into me. No, that's not right. I *should* feel my stomach roil and my throat contract, but my body is too well tuned for that, now. Only my mind, poor mother or twisted god that it is, holds on to the memory and expects the sensations.

I pull my hand back from the "hang up" button. Without a fear response from my body, I can continue. What could it cost me besides all my friendships?

I stumble over words, but eventually find momentum. "When I transitioned, people told me—these were people I loved—they told me it would destroy my life. I'd never work. Or pass. Or find love." Grimacing faces; others have heard this too. Some of it was even true: I don't pass. I'm bad at love.

"Could've given up," I say, translating the language of colors and smells and hormones into words I used to have. "But I had to know. No, not know." I flushed. All this was almost impossible to say. "Had to experience. And after… the panopticon, but in reverse. Like I'd never…felt…before."

They were staring at me with confusion, some with concern. I felt my way forward like someone hunting for light switches in unfamiliar rooms.

"They were going to destroy the nanites," I say. Recognition flashes across Mac's face. Horror. Fury. "Please," I implore. "Let me—I don't know if I was right. But they were alive. Intelligent. My children. So I saved them. Didn't think. Maybe should've. No. No. What kind of mad god would consign them to the flame?"

I fall back against my chair, sweating like I've just

run sprints. Then everyone's talking at once, my cheap headphones thankfully unable to unknot their words.

I wait to see if they will condemn me. The riptide of fear is gone. I'm in deep waters. I *am* deep waters.

Words and phrases, my friends' judgments or support, reach me from a distance.

"—height of irresponsibility—"

"—what else could she—"

"—reproductive justice—"

"—unring—"

They deserve time to process, to decide. I don't begrudge that. I disconnect and pull off my headphones.

A distant sound interrupts the newfound quiet. It's a chorus from the church down the street, many voices raised in song. It's too far away to make out the words, and I like it that way. I've tried to leave behind everything about my childhood faith, but I do miss the singing, this collective thing, a mess of good voices and bad, of notes struck true and false, but that doesn't matter, because the goal isn't perfection but shared experience. Unity.

◈

MY DREAMS ARE song, and the song is the world breathing, and I am the world, and inside myself. My chest cavity is a cathedral, my ribs incomprehensibly-vast buttresses. How long do they live, my children? They change, evolve, but individually their lives are so short. If it means anything to speak of them as individuals. I ride veins to my heart, my life measured in the bass-beat of its impossible slowness, and I think of corpses fallen to the forest floor, death engendering life.

This is my body, sacrificed—

I force the thought away. Something that may be me forces it away. This is not the story of the one given for the many, the ram in the thicket, the offering prepared.

This thing, flesh, synapses, this dream of self—whatever it is, it's no messiah, no prophet.

We are the universe experiencing ourself.

My waking mind, the mind of a trained scientist, doubts these revelations. But a quest to know does not imply that all is knowable. And if it is? What does it mean to know the universe on the scale of one lifetime, or a billion?

A temple priestess tells her congregation that one day the apocalypse will swallow us, will swallow all things.

The day is coming, says the congregation. *Let us sell what we have, flee to the mountains. The end is nigh.*

The priestess says nothing. She plants a tree instead.

❖

You'll come for the birth? Jocelyn texts. My best friend, my heart.

Yes omg of course yes, I reply. And then: *the others won't approve.*

They agreed already. They only asked u wear gloves and mask.

Wouldn't miss it, I type, already weeping. I don't know if my friends will understand, if they'll forgive me. But for now, I haven't lost them. I'll get to see Jocelyn's baby.

❖

When Jocelyn goes into labor, I'm ready to rush to her side, but it takes hours, days, to get to that point. Finally it's time for her to go to the doctor's home, since the hospitals won't have her. On my way out the door, I glance in the mirror, trying to decide if I look noticeably different, or if only my self-perception has changed. My cheekbones remain unimpressive, but whether it's the nanites, or the birth, or my cute top, I feel a rush of gender euphoria. My scalp tingles. My smile is an old friend I thought I'd lost.

I bike over to Caroline's, and we take her car. It feels as if every window in her apartment complex hides someone watching us, two visibly trans women, daring to be seen in public, to be seen together. A hand pulls back a corner of the curtains in her ex's place, but the door doesn't open.

"I hate it when they stare," I say through my mask.

"Yeah," Caroline says. "But let them. Maybe there are some trans folks watching who need to see us."

❖

NEWBORNS AREN'T GENERALLY cute. They grow into that. But either little Hunter is the exception, asleep in Jocelyn's arms after their first meal, or I'm just biased towards the little one.

The whole gang's here and in a state of whispered excitement, trying not to disturb baby Hunter, but also wanting to coo over them. We haven't talked about me, standing a little ways back, careful to avoid skin-to-skin contact. I think the nanites know that I want them to stay within me for now, but I'm sure they could slide between skins, between bodies so easily they might not even notice the border. In the gestalt consciousness of my children, what separates one being from another?

I try to set aside my fears, my intellectualization, to remain present in this happy moment, surrounded by friends, each of us a mother, auntie, or uncle to a child descended from none of us. I want to join in these conversations, but I don't know where I stand with my friends. Plus it's hard to hear them over the other conversation, the one in my head, where my other chosen family is also speaking to me. Images flash on my mind: ripe fruit, dandelion seeds blowing in the wind. A ripple of longing, almost painful in its desire, unfurls down my back. We understand each other better every day. No credit to me. They're the ones learning to speak to me.

86 billion neurons in my brain, give or take a billion. How many neuronal equivalents exist between my children? It's a vista my mind can't comprehend.

"—we talk?"

It's Mac. I've been far away. "What? Oh, yeah, Mac, let's talk."

We step into the doctor's front room.

"I still don't love what you did," he says, and I feel very tired. "But I get it. The alternatives were also bad. And once you realized they were sapient—I understand why you did it." He opens his arms, offering a hug.

"But the nanites," I say, half statement, half question.

He smiles, barely betraying his nervousness. "We're well covered," he says. I hug him tightly. He wraps his wiry-strong arms around me, smelling of sweat and rising bread.

"Thank you," I say. "I know you were looking out for— for everyone. We need that."

Mac's frequently angry, but that's because he loves his friends deeply. I'm frequently afraid, for the same reason. Maybe that's why we fight and why we're so close.

"I hope," I say slowly, because talking is hard enough without my children trying to make sure that I understand. I do. I think I do. "I mean—would you help me? Help me talk to the others about…something." I do my best to explain.

"I don't love it," he says, "but I'm not going to demand closed borders, either."

Later, when Hunter is enjoying their second-ever meal, I tell the group what I have in mind.

"They're fast learners," I say. "And they understand now about bodies. They don't have to stay—they can be guests if you want. Ambassadors."

"You're sure about that?" asks Caroline, who knows a thing or two about unwanted guests.

"I'm pretty sure," I say. "I doubt they conceptualize… individuals the way we do. But they…respect other minds."

If you spend many generations building a cathedral, are you building it hoping god will see, or that your grandchildren will?

"But why do they need to, uh, immigrate?" Zora asks. "You said they have access to your senses."

"They do," I say, "but they need more than one…parent. More than one god." I try to explain: they're learning from me, but who am I? Just the one who happened to free them. My words feel molasses-thick on my tongue, but at least the next part is easier because I know my friends. "Zora, they need to know how to…hold space. Bring people together. Like you do. Mac, they need your fury at injustice. The way you protect friends. Caroline, you have so much empathy. They'll learn from you. So much. Jocelyn, they can see… well, witness…how you care for others. For Hunter." I don't know how to make myself understood. Maybe I never did.

"That's a lot of responsibility," Caroline says.

"Yes," I say. "Too heavy for one person. You're free to choose. Always. But we're better together. We need—they need—community."

My words feel simplistic, like they'll never be enough. I'm failing my children.

At first there are no sounds except Hunter eagerly drinking. Then Jocelyn says, "How do we, uh, let them in?" That's how I know she's made up her mind.

"I tell them that you said yes. Then just skin-to-skin.."

"Simple as that?"

"Nothing about our lives is simple," Mac interjects.

"Yes," I say. "Yes. But also, yeah, simple as that."

Jocelyn holds out her hand. I pull away my glove and clasp it. I don't feel the nanites send their ambassadors to her, but I know it's happening.

The world's changing, now and always. We'll face it together, the few of us, the uncountable throng.

Emergency Calls Only

KELSEY HUTTON

FROM: CAPTAIN ZOHRA WEST TEKK:ING (She/Her – Human – Earth One)
TO: STARGAZER RENWICK (She/Them – brrn – Earth Four)
DATE: QUINTEMBER 12, 2891
LOCATION: UNKNOWN – ERROR 507

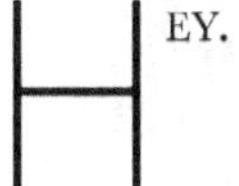
EY.

I know. It's…been a while. And I promised I wouldn't reach out—well, that neither of us would—unless it was an emergency.

Let's just say…I haven't broken my word.

I know this is dumb, but—I can't not do with the pleasantries.

How are you? I am (not) well. I hope you're somewhere sunny and warm. It's pretty cold where I am—minus 270 degrees Celsius, to be exact—and unfortunately, I'm nowhere near planetside, or near a sun.

Although, the stars. They're more like brilliant gold smears than pinpoint diamonds through my steamed-up visor. My eyes are pretty waterlogged as well. But they're *so close*. I swear I could touch them, if these ancient five-ply aluminum-lined spacesuits had any give. I would grab them with both hands.

As it is, they're too stiff. I can't even reach across and hug myself. The closest I can get in these goddamn suits is to just about graze the crook of each arm with my fingertips.

Ren.

Right now you're thinking, emergency calls only, right? Where the hell is she going with this?

Ren, the dark feels like it's going to swallow me whole. My ears are roaring. It's just me here, me and my ragged breaths. Which keep coming, surprisingly, even though I'm alone, ever so slowly tumbling through empty space.

It's long past any hope of a rescue window. I've stopped slow-mo kicking my legs, bogged down by the dense mag boots, which I guess was just to keep up some illusion of "doing something." My lightweight shirt and long underwear have long since sweated through, dried, and sweated through again as I cycled through rage, fear, denial. If I had anything left in my stomach, forget it, I'd have puked that up in my helmet ages ago, and I'd be breathing in chunks right about now.

Good thing all the panic has left to churn in my gut is stomach acid and regret, right? Small mercies.

I can still wiggle my fingers, but they've been numb for at least a day already from the low-oxygen conservation protocols I can't seem to turn off. Although time is really weird now. Like, not just in the dissociating-in-the-face-of-overwhelming-trauma kind of way. But in the lost in space, trapped-in-the-inexorable-pull-of-the-M31-black-hole kind of way. According to my suit's sensor readings, anyway, before those glitched, too.

The only thing I can really feel anymore is this burning lump in my throat, which I thought I'd have run out of angry, raging fuel for days ago. But it may yet go supernova.

I'm sorry this message is such a downer. I'm sorry I'm even dumping this on you, my rattling death call, what a shitty friend I am, just like I was a shitty girlfriend, too—I just don't know who else—

You always held my hand, Ren. When it was just the two of us against the world, a bad-ass star navigator and yours truly, a self-taught and self-doubting all-around Fix-It Girl.

Every time we started a new job, and the meaty or oniony or cloyingly sweet smells of a new ship hit me in the face like a nasty ex and my fear of meeting new people nearly made me catatonic. Every time I slowly got into the swing of a new gig, sunk into learning the quirks of a new make-and-model. Every time I oohed and ahhed over some alien alloy that grew each year like tusks, every time I found the right combination of spit, gum and Drakq tape to keep our clients' ships sailing through one more galactic pinch point.

You held my hand, sweaty palms be damned, and I never told you how much I loved you for that.

You're probably wondering what happened. How I ended up here, somewhere who-the-fuck-knows in the Crab Nebula district, knocked loose from a routine radiation shield testing EVA into the hungry path of M31.

You want to know the worst thing? Other than that, at some point very soon, I will cross over the event horizon, the black hole's tidal forces will *really* kick in, and my fragile body will rip apart—first in half, then half again, and again, all the way down to its smallest particles? The worst thing is IT'S NOT EVEN A GOOD STORY, REN. I'M FUCKING DYING, AND THE LEAD-UP ISN'T EVEN WORTH TELLING.

A loose panel, a bad slip. That second safety cable I forgot to clip.

The company ship I tumbled off of gone in an instant, a flash. Into the depths of space.

I've done the calculations, I've read all my suit's belated warning signs, and I know now that fucking company ship was way past M31's defined buffer zone. Dodgy company, doing shoddy work.

That's not why I'm writing you, Ren. How I got here doesn't matter. Rescue is…a bad joke. I don't even know if this message will ever reach you, or if it'll reach your grandchildren, or maybe your descendants millennia from now because of FUCKING TIME DILATION. All I know is that I'm moving ever closer to this son of a bitch of a black hole, and my sensors told me this great hulking mass of a body passed the point of no return a while back.

But I can't tell yet if I've passed the event horizon. A few massless photons could maybe still escape. This message in a light wave might yet make it.

I'm rambling. And babbling. Even though I'm running out of time and maybe it's already too late, even as my muscles shake, even as—

I'm just scared, Ren. I'm fucking scared.

But YOU SHOULDN'T BE. That's why I wrote this. That's what I'm trying to tell you.

When we were together, I was a dick. I was scared ALL THE TIME, but I wouldn't trust anyone except you. I thought you were invincible, my forever rock, this incredibly brave and resilient person who was strong forever.

And I wasn't wrong. But it also wasn't really the full you.

And when you tried to be scared with me, to tell me about the shit with Earth Four and why you ran from your mom and why you can never go back, I felt betrayed, because I thought I was the only one allowed to Have Shit.

And I was scared that you'd stop being there to pick up my pieces.

And so I ran. When you were terrified of being alone, of what it would mean to be cut off from your family forever, I left you. Because I was a coward.

I'm so sorry, Ren. I'm so fucking sorry, and I love you SO FUCKING MUCH, and you kept telling me that was enough, but I was the one too scared to believe you. But I believe you now.

And I'm sending you this because I believe you, the you who held my hand for years, when you told me that if I was ever ready to own up to my shit, or if I really needed you, or both, that you would be there.

It's both, Ren. It's definitely both.

And I don't want to tell you not to be scared anymore, of your family and of brrn bureaucracy and all that shit. I mean, I do, but not in some flippant way that really means: I can't deal with this right now.

I want to tell you not to be scared because you always see a way forward. For yourself, for our clients, even now, look at it, for us. Because you reach out a hand when life gets tough, ready to give help and receive it, even if you don't know who'll be on the other side.

Someone will be there. Not me, anymore, but new people who deserve you and who you deserve to have holding you up. Including people who maybe wouldn't have ever reached out themselves—but you're brave enough to reach out first.

That's why you don't have to be afraid, Ren. Because you'll never truly be alone.

Just like I'm not alone now. Even as I starfish out here, stuck in a suit that smells like stale sweat and other human things, a light grey blob floating too far for even hope to reach anymore.

Because you're with me.

Still. Always.

I love you, Ren. Love came hard to me, but easy to you, which, like a dumbass, I let scare me too.

Not anymore.

The lump in my throat has burst, not gonna lie. It's a sweet ache. The world around me is still a silver-and-gold blur, but the rushing silence has softened to a low purr.

I'm so tired. God, I'm tired. Good thing this message is neuro-dictated, or I never would have made it. My every muscle aches from all the clenching and unclenching I've been doing. I keep wondering—is this it? The moment M31's tidal forces start to rip me apart? Or will my oxygen give out first?

Death by suffocation? Or death by black hole?

My palms are tingling. I can almost feel the pressure of your fingers interlaced with mine.

I…

Ren. I'm "going to let you go," as my dad used to say, as if I'm the one doing you the favour. Although maybe I am. You don't need the blow-by-blow of my death, but I need you to know how much you changed my life.

Don't be afraid, Ren. Not now, not later, not for me, never for you.

I should really send this now. It may already be too late. But how do I do this? How do I say good-bye?

How do I choose which are the last words I'll ever say to you?

I love you, I love you, I love you.

I

TRANSMISSION STATUS: Received.

No Happy Endings
for Chasers

Uchechukwu Nwaka

I HUNT MY LAST *chikiriki* into a building complex that used to be a mall. My boots make hollow whispers over the brown tiles. Many of the shops have been broken into, glass windows completely smashed through and shelves knocked over by looters. I try to imagine how this place might have looked before the Falling, with people milling about with colourful plastic bags and grocery carts.

Now the hallways are dark, and smell of dust and ash and wet mould.

"Buchi, heads up! I think the *chikiriki* is coming your way!"

The party leader, Temi's voice cuts into my helmet's speakers like a jolt of electricity. I plant my feet on the floor and hold my breath, my eyes searching the darkness with the aid of the halos of light from my suit's lamps. Perspiration crawls down my neck. In the silence, I am suddenly struck by how wide the corridor is. The dark corners where my suit lamps cannot illuminate. How alone I am in this darkness because Temi wanted us to cover more ground, and drive the *chikiriki*—if we encounter it—towards the others.

"Roma is coming your way." Temi sounds like she's running too. "Hold down the *chikiriki* until we get there!"

Hold it down alone? I lick my lips and God, it's parched. My tongue feels like sandpaper. The heavy jetpack on my back presses against my shoulder. It used to belong to Tunde. At least until we found his body cold and unmoving, with deep gashes across his mangled corpse.

Shit. Focus Buchi!

I hear something. Skittering sounds. The clatter of many alien limbs scratching against the floor or the ceiling or the walls. The sounds draw closer, loud and imminent. I turn around, but my lights don't fall on anything. Still, I can hear it—the scratching of the *chikiriki*'s spinous appendages against metal. I clench my fist around the handle of my mace until I lose all feeling in it. A pulse of electricity charges the weapon. *My* pulse has hit the roof. The mask is suffocating. My head feels like it is going to explode.

"Roma...?" I whisper. Too loud.

"Where are you?"

Silence. Static. Skittering alien legs.

"Roma?"

"Buchi!" Temi's response is too sudden. Loud. Panicked. "It can camouflage! It got Roma!"

Too late. The *chikiriki*'s gravity bubble hits me smack in the chest, throwing me to the ceiling. In my spiralling confusion, the *chikiriki* materializes from the shadows—bigger than anything we've ever encountered before—front limbs glinting with the numerous razor-sharp spines.

In that eternity of a second, only one thought flashes in my mind with resounding clarity.

I am going to die!

❖

I AM ALMOST done with my shift that evening when a stretcher wheels into the emergency wing. The medics push past me, and I almost spill the mud-coloured water from my bucket. Out the corner of my eye, I see the person being wheeled in. It's a Chaser. She has a suit on, but it's not like the ones we see on the NVEC's broadcasts. While the government's Chasers wear silver armour, this woman's suit is a dull black body-piece. There are also bright red streaks over the alien/human hybrid armour.

Blood.

Tubes snake into her arms and the doctor on call tries to keep the mask on her face from falling. She's wheeled into a cubicle and out of sight, and I am left alone in the corner with my mop and bucket. I can't get the image out of my head as I change out of the dull green cleaner's uniform, receive my N500 wage card from the porter, and head out of the partly-lit hospital grounds into the darker streets outside. If I listened to Grandpa and registered to become a Chaser, I'd get at least ten times this wage for bringing in a small *chikiriki*.

The small ones are really all that's left. The NVEC's Chasers have basically killed all the queens.

Technically most Chasers are registered with NVEC, but I mean the real ones. The strong ones who I tell Grandpa have a few screws loose upstairs. He says he wouldn't mind some screws loose if I'm going to be getting paid the amount those guys get.

After all, he's always called me an abnormal boy.

Area 14's streets are packed with traffic. It's not so small a community, so the only vehicles around are keke napep tricycles and the africars. Most others commute on foot. There are a lot of people on the streets. Sometimes I wonder where all of these people fit into in the Area zone. Before the Falling, much of this area was somewhat of a commercial district-highway-hospital-pharmacy environ. However, since the alien ships crashed on Earth from seemingly nowhere, migration has transformed this place into a jungle of tents and wood-and-iron hamlets and banks-turned-houses.

Which also means that quality housing is expensive.

In the distance, dark against the night sky and the artificial lights from battery lamps of suya stands and gin parlours, the walls that protect this community tower silently. The walls are reinforced with metal from the remains of the alien ships. They keep the *chikiriki* out. Only Chasers wander outside the walls ... into the outerzones.

I find Grandpa in front of the single-room flat we share, trying to reach for his snuff box that has fallen down the step. I pick it up and hand it to him, then ease his wheelchair away from the edge. I turn to our room — one out of six identical rooms crammed in a rectangular bungalow under the shadow of a larger block of flats. I help myself to a bowl of yams and palm oil under the glow of our lamp.

"How work?" he asks me.

I shrug. All the jobs I worked on today left me with only two thousand naira. I don't want to talk about it. The yams are hard, and even after chewing it's hard to swallow. "Grandpa these are pretty hard."

"Go and register to become Chaser, you will not hear," he retorts in a beat. "That's all the money you bring can afford."

I roll my eyes, but surprise myself by saying, "I saw a Chaser today." Grandpa grunts, but he doesn't say anything.

"I wonder how much more I can make as a Chaser, you know?" I sigh. "At least eat some soft yams."

"That's what I've been saying all this time!" he says. "But you will not hear.

Times have changed, and you have a big body, Buchi. Instead of lifting blocks of cement under the hot sun, put all that muscle into killing those alien pests."

I think of the blood on the Chaser's chest. The plastic tubes that invaded her body. "Grandpa, it's dangerous."

"Every time, it's dangerous! I blame your mother for pampering you, God bless her soul. Now look at you, always acting like a girl."

That stings, but I'm used to Grandpa's venom and how he thinks I'm not manly enough. He had even pressured Mummy to enlist me in the military for one year. To "toughen me up." I sigh, staring at the empty bowl before me. This time though, he's not wrong. I'm hardly filled, but good food costs money. It's either this or canned tomato soup.

"Your friend Temi dropped this for you." He fishes within the folds of the blanket wrapping his legs and hands me an envelope. The logo of the Nigerian Vermin Extermination Commission is branded over the envelope's front.

"I thought I told her I wasn't interested!"

He kisses his teeth in irritation. "That girl even has more balls than you. You're supposed to be head of the family. Is this how you'll keep behaving when you eventually settle down?"

"Grandpa, not this again. I told you we're not like that."

"So what are you like?" His eyes narrow. Panic clamps my lips shut. Grandpa has not forgotten that fateful day of the Falling. Before the tragedy, when he walked in on me pressed against the wall of my bedroom, another boy's lips on mine.

I snatch the envelope from him and bolt indoors. Under the dim light, I take a hard look at the brown paper, forcing the tears to stay dammed behind my eyes.

Be a man.

I tighten my grip around the envelope. Most of the military was lost to the initial waves of *chikiriki* because rifles were not enough. The real heroes were normal people who fashioned remains of the crashed ships into weapons. Then, the *chikiriki* bled. Those people are now the NVEC.

Two days later, I'm walking out of the hospital when I see a woman crying. Another woman tries to console her. I recognize them as the injured Chaser's relatives from the other day. A man wearing a similar hairdo as the Chaser drags a bundle of something and dumps it into the trash before walking away with the others. My heart catches in my chest when I check the trashed bundle.

It is the bloodied Chaser armour.

◆

"SEE, THE *CHIKIRIKI* were actually like rats on the alien ships," Temi says, her gun resting quietly on her lap. "Pests. You know how the alien carcasses they found after the Falling were still intact in pods?"

"Yeah," I reply. "Cryo pods that were destroyed on the crash right?"

"The *chikiriki* are carnivorous but couldn't eat past the pod's metal structure. Or most of the ship's architecture."

I run my fingers along the length of my mace. There are tiny plugs on its surface to electrify the weapon. Outside, the truck trudges across the outerzones. It's like a scene out of one of those apocalypse movies. The *chikiriki* had landed as cocoons. Possibly a mechanism to survive in the alien ships due to food shortage. Sure, they're carnivorous, but they seem to have preference for human flesh.

"Hey Buchi," Temi says softly, interrupting my thought flow. "Thanks for coming along. I know this isn't really your kind of thing."

I shake my head. "I got your back. Always."

"We're here!" Tunde calls from the driver's seat. He's the leader of our small party. On completion of registration, the NVEC branch provides some basic supplies — a helmet, a suit, and grav boots. I don't know how they work. I had held on to that injured Chaser's suit (who, you know, died). The suits the NVEC provide are recycled ones, anyway. Apparently, Chasers die a lot.

Tunde is big. Bigger than me, even. He has a large jetpack on, with an axe. The axe is made of ship steel. His armour looks good, too. We're new at this, and he's clearly not. I wonder why he teamed up with us anyway.

We're in a crater not too far from Area 14. There are several cocoons in the rock. If we can destroy them all, the pay is good. According to Tunde, sentry *chikiriki* tend to hide around craters like this. Those are usually bigger and stronger than regular *chikiriki*. If we can get one of those, the pay quadruples!

Fortunately for us, this place is empty.

"Don't let down your guard!" Tunde warns. "And be careful not to accidentally get hit by a sentry's gravity bubble." He proceeds to hack the cocoon nearest to him. I nod, attacking the one nearest to me. The outer encasement is like rock. Like something volcanic—for lack of a better term. When my mace cracks the cortex, there is a hiss and an effervescence of steam, then greenish, gooey slime spills out.

I remember that Chaser. This isn't so difficult after all.

Temi and I round up on the last cocoon. She grins from behind her helmet, which has been scribbled over with many marker colours in several handwritings. We've been friends since she migrated into Area 14 with her four orphaned siblings in tow.

"Care to do the honours?" she gives a mock bow. I shrug. I heft the mace over my head when a shadow falls over me from the edge of the crater.

A sentry *chikiriki*.

It's about the size of a cow. It looks like a spider-crab-scorpion, with at least six legs on each side of its body and two elongated forelimbs that curve inwards like scythes. Before I can move, it secretes a gravity bubble that slams into us, trapping us with the space vermin.

I begin to float upward. *Jesus*!

I kick my legs together and the grav boots activate, anchoring me to the ground. Beside me Temi has drawn her blaster. The gravity bubble that the *chikiriki* secretes to trap prey is something like falling into a spider's web. The atmosphere inside is funky and messed up, hence our helmets. The physics is also distorted in ways that causes us to float weightlessly. Only the *chikiriki* is flexible enough to move in its bubble.

It rushes us.

Temi lets out a barrage of bullets. The creature shrieks and scurries up over our heads. Most of the blasts ricochet over the thing's exoskeleton. It leaps downward, scythe-like limbs swinging in a deathly arc. I muster all my strength just to parry the attack. I bludgeon, but the creature is tough. It rotates its body and slams into me with the momentum. My boots disengage and I start floating upward.

Shit!

It turns to Temi, no longer considering me a threat. She shoots and shoots, but the thing doesn't mind a few lost appendages. Temi runs out of rounds, and I see the flash of panic on her face.

The Chaser's face flashes in my mind again.

No.

No, no, no, no!

I smack my feet together again and the boots engage. I twist my body and land a few feet beside the injured *chikiriki*. I swing with all my being. Electricity crackles over the mace as it impacts against the creature's skull, crushing the exoskeleton in a sickening crunch.

The head bursts in a splash of green slime.

"Temi, are you okay?"

Another gravity bubble suddenly encroaches the one we're standing in. To my horror, I see Tunde, fighting back three smaller *chikiriki*. He's floating in the air with his jetpack, hacking and slashing but not winning.

"We've got to help him!" Temi reloads. "Come on, Buchi!"

I grit my teeth and follow to Tunde's aid.

That evening, I find Grandpa at the front of our small room again. Today, there is N44,000 in my wage card.

◆

OUR PARTY REALLY gets to it.

We begin to take jobs into the outerzones as expansion efforts continue. The pay gets better and better, and we can afford even better gear. I don't make too many upgrades. The suit on my body makes sure I never forget that Chaser I saw that night. How easily that can become me.

After finishing a job around Area 10, we head into one of the gin parlours. The Area is small, without many Chasers. People stare as we walk across their narrow streets. Kids point. Vendors offer us items for exorbitant prices. (I mean, beef for 20k? Come on!) The gin parlour is tight, packed with tables and even more people. The air is thick with the aromas of beer and pepper soup, and some metal juju blasts from unseen speakers in the dim-coloured light.

"No free tables," Temi groans.

Tunde grunts, shoving past us. He marches to the nearest table and loudly drops his helmet on top. The occupants jolt in shock—a party of four, two of who are ladies, all with bowls of pepper soup and half-empty bottles of beer.

"Move aside," Tunde says.

"Or what?" one of the men asks.

I tap Tunde gently on the shoulder. "Let it go. We can find another place."

He shrugs my hand off roughly. Then, he leans closer to the man on the table. Till their noses are almost touching. "Ogbeni, I said, move aside."

"And I said—"

Before he can complete the sentence, Tunde grabs a bottle. His arm cuts an arc as fast as lightning, and the bottle explodes on the man's head. Beer spills. The women scream. The other man rises, but Tunde is faster. Drives a gloved fist into the man's face. I pull him by the shoulder and he turns, face contorted in a grimace.

"Yo, chill."

He shoves me and I stumble backwards. "Show me some bloody respect!" he yells. The gin parlour has become rowdy now. Temi steps between the two of us.

He pushes her aside.

Rage colours my vision red. I clip him by the cheek, and the blow sends him staggering back. Two others rise to flank him when he draws his blaster. Silence falls in the gin parlour. Tunde wipes blood from the side of his lip.

"Any idiot wan' try me? Try me na! I'm a bloody Chaser." His eyes are manic with challenge. "Try am!" he yells in pidgin, training his blaster at me.

"To hell with you, Tunde!" Temi hisses from the floor. "That's why your former teammates all left you, asshole!"

Before I can process what she just said, she storms out of the parlour. I grab a bottle of beer that miraculously survived the scuffle and drag myself out.

❖

THERE'S AN ALLEY not too far from there with some old refrigerators standing in front of a boarded-over store. I sit on one of the fallen ones, nursing my beer. It had started raining sometime in the last hour, and the smell of dust and water and concrete is almost soothing.

"Couldn't get a seat at Mama P's?"

The voice comes from above me and I start. A flash of lightning reveals someone seated atop the fridges, just right above my head. How did I not notice him?

I shrug. "Things got too loud."

"I saw what you did there," he says, and his voice is deep like the rumbling thunder in the sky. The voice is familiar and it stirs something in my chest. "Used to have troublesome teammates too, once upon a time. What's with Chasers and thinking they're gods?"

I scoff, taking a swig of my beer. "God was an alien,

too. Kill enough of the aliens and well...shit." My bottle's empty. I curse, and the man above chuckles.

"Want a drink?"

"Sure."

He leaps down. Much closer, I notice his lean figure. He's tall, and the dreadlocks on his head make him look even taller. When he hands me a bottle of stout, he smiles, and those teeth are perfect white, beneath pink full lips.

"Daniel?"

"The one and only!" he grins. As he says this the sky flashes a smile. His skin is black and beautiful and I wonder if he remembers those days we spent together before the Falling. Before the heavens fell. Before Grandpa walked in on us.

He's wearing a hoodie, but it's only when another flash of lightning lights the sky that I notice a breastplate of gold-sheened armour.

"What the hell!" I punch him in the shoulder and instantly regret it when pain radiates through my knuckles. "You became a Chaser? And not just any Chaser! An NVEC specialist!"

He zips up his jacket fully, the motion shy. "I'm the Chaser stationed to this Area. Besides, I was just lucky to live long enough. What about you? I never expected you of all people to become a Chaser."

I look at the worn, black suit over my chest. I think of the Chaser who used to wear this. How Grandpa nagged me until I couldn't breathe. He'd been living in that one-room since before the Falling, and he made sure to remind me of that every day. Like it wasn't my 'petty change' that paid for the little electricity we got. Or the food. Or everything else.

I sigh and sit on the refrigerator, guzzling my beer a little too quickly.

One time, fed up of Grandpa's tantrums, I left home. There aren't many proper places to stay in an Area zone, so I crashed with Temi for a few days. I couldn't stay with her for too long, either. Not with how tight her place was, and all the mouths she had to feed.

It's strange that I tell him all this. Maybe it's because of how much time has passed between us. Maybe it's the alcohol. Somehow, I notice our bodies are closer. His breath smells of cheap beer, hot against my face. In that moment, I see Grandpa's wrinkled face. Lines carved deeper in disappointment. Never good enough. Never manly enough.

But Daniel's lips touch mine even as I hesitate. It's feather-light, and I wonder whether I imagine it. But no. One hand rests on my shoulder. My breath catches, pulse through the roof. There's a question in his eyes, and I wonder if he sees the need in mine. I don't care. I grab his neck and press my lips to his. It's sloppy and hot and blood rushes to my head. It lasts a few seconds, but for me, it is an eternity before my lips leave his. I can't breathe. When I look at him, he offers me his shy smile.

"I have a place. I-if you want."

I do.

❖

"NVEC's doing a large-scale expansion soon," Daniel says, pulling his boxers over his legs. The muscles on his back are defined. Toned to perfection. I remember exploring the sinews. The scars. "They want to create a new Area zone around Dugbe. Will your party be there?"

"Isn't that one of the sites of the Falling?"

Daniel nods.

"Well...I'm thinking of calling it quits," I say. The sheets are wrapped around my legs, and I listen to the sounds of poultry outside the lodge's window. Thin shafts of sunlight filter in, casting Daniel's skin in deep obsidian hues.

"Really?" He turns to face me.

"Yeah." My fingers link, in and out. "I don't think it's ever going to end. And I'm afraid, Daniel. I never wanted to become a Chaser."

He sits on the bed.

"How do you keep doing it?" I ask him. "Why?"

He runs his hands through his locks. "Because I don't have anything else. Killing *chikiriki* is all I'm good for."

"You can have me."

His smile is gentle. Sad. "Can I?"

"It's the end of the world. Nobody gives a damn."

"But you don't believe that."

I bite down the bile behind my throat.

"But yeah," he continues. "If you really don't wanna continue exterminating the *chikiriki*, then you should hang up your suit. In this line of work, you can lose everything in an instant. Including yourself."

I think of Temi. Of Grandpa. The Chaser whose name I never knew. This last job. Then I'm out.

❖

"Buchi, this is Roma. Roma, meet Buchi."

I give Temi a sceptical look. "Um, where's Tunde?"

"We're not going on this expedition with Tunde," she folds her arms across her chest. "Roma is our new teammate."

Roma has an athletic build. A dagger and a blaster are strapped on both sides of his hip. He offers me an easy smile. "You don't use jetpacks?"

I shrug. "Never got around to getting one of those."

"Yeah." Temi taps his shoulder brilliantly. "We don't really do well on air combat, so that's why we have you."

I pull Temi aside. "Hey, are you okay? You know, after what happened."

Temi sighs. "I'm planning on moving out of Area 14."

Her words are a sudden gut punch. "W-what?"

"I got an offer as a private Chaser for one of those unnumbered Areas." She runs her fingers through her blonde-tinted buzz cut. "The pay is good, and there's a housing offer with it. I feel like it's the turning point my family's been looking for."

"Congrats!" I pull her into a hug. I'm happy for her. The unnumbered Area zones are where the rich live. Governors, ministers, fraudsters. This is her last job for the NVEC, too.

The expedition is large. There are over fifty Chasers, each in several suits, wielding various weapons. Mostly blasters, but there are knives and the occasional mace wielders. I spot Daniel. His specialist suit is a dull golden thing, and he has two small axes strapped to his waist. He stands alone, even when the other specialists huddle in groups. There are some solo Chasers too, Tunde included. He casts me a dark look and I turn away. The president of NVEC briefs all of us present. The Dugbe outerzone is an expanse of buildings that used to be a commercial district but have become hollow monoliths of scorched decay. Somewhere in the distance, one of the alien ships lies in ruins, surrounded by craters. When the Falling happened here, the entire district was bathed in fire. Nothing survived. The streets are covered in ash that hangs in the air like fog.

I say we let this outerzone be.

But no. The expedition begins. We split up, and as I head into the uncertainty with Temi and our new teammate, I pray this is the last.

❖

Now.

In the literal jaws of death.

Tunde's backpack activates suddenly. The propulsion blasts me away from the queen *chikiriki*'s range. I crash against the ceiling and my mace almost falls from my hand. The queen is fast. It turns to me in an instant, movement fluid in its gravity bubble. I jet outwards. Its many eyes fix on me from its hairy, globe-like head. I'm a few feet away from the edge of the bubble. I can make it out!

Something impossible happens. The *chikiriki* sucks in the air in the bubble, and the distance between us shrinks and vanishes. In an instant, the shadow of her scythe-like multi-spinous forelimb falls over me.

Parry! Parry! Parry! Parry!

My hands don't move. Cannot.

"BUCHI!"

Temi crashes into me. Roma's jetpack burns behind her. We escape the grav field in a pop, and crash to the floor. My heart is racing. I stumble to my feet immediately. The *chikiriki* queen skitters around, with her many legs, training her eyes at us. My mace shudders in my hand.

"Temi! Temi get up, it's coming!"

Temi groans on the floor but doesn't rise. "TEMI STAND UP NOW!" I don't like the panic creeping into my voice, but now I see it. The deep scarlet puddle pooling under her body. Her laboured breathing through my helmet speakers.

No, no, no, no!

"Buchi..." she croaks. Christ! The queen draws closer. In the darkness I hear the approach of a thousand skittering legs. More *chikiriki*? Sentries?

"Leave...me...and...run."

"No. No! We will get out of this! Your sisters are waiting for you, Temi!"

"I'm sorry for dragging you into this..." her voice is barely a whisper. "I know your Grandpa was hard on you. But...but I didn't want to be alone."

I bite my lip so hard that it draws blood. Not this. Not now. No, Temi. Hold on! Let me kill this thing first! I draw my shield plate and it unrolls like a magic carpet. The queen slams into me, but I activate my boots and hold my position. My muscles protest with the effort, and I activate the jet pack. The momentum propels me forward. The queen slashes and hacks at me, and I hold. The mace is heavy in my hand, the air thin in my mask, my pulse loud in my ear.

I'm afraid, but I have to make a stand here. I swing at an incoming limb and it connects with a joint. There is a crunch as the appendage fractures. The queen screeches, about to secrete a field. I crank my pack to the max, then, as its mouth opens with rows of shark-like teeth, I disengage the pack. The pack jets into the queen's mouth and I grab my mini blaster, assaulting it with gunfire. The explosion burns away the shadows in the hallway, a purifying blaze of white-hot fire.

I run.

Run with Temi's cold body, down the fiery gullet of the mall's abandoned corridors. Away from this Chaser life.

But, see, this story doesn't end here.

Because the chittering of a million feet follows me outside, into the dead, ash-covered outerzone of Dugbe where I lay crouched over my best friend's unmoving body.

Regret gnaws at my throat like a goitre.

What if, in an alternate universe, everything worked out and we got away with it? We would look back on this expedition in a gin parlour somewhere, a year from now. Laugh about how desperate we had been to matter in this damned world. But there are no happy endings for Chasers. Never have been.

Never will be.

I rise, grabbing Temi's big-ass blaster as the sun's disc dips into the horizon. I've killed too much of myself already with the shit-show this life has been. And I made it too easy for Grandpa to reduce me into his self-depreciating mould. If I make it out of here, I swear to God, I'm giving him a piece of my mind.

Maybe reconnecting with Daniel changed something in me. Maybe it didn't. All I know now is that this time, if I'm going to die, then I won't make it easy for anybody.

I prime the weapon.

Come, *chikiriki*. Come!

A Taste of Justice

JOHN WISWELL

A NDREI'S PAPS AND mams told him not to put things in his mouth, so he made sure to do it when they weren't looking. Pinches of earth, when times were right. When Paps fixed the axel on their apple cart, Andrei ate a pinch of earth from underneath it. He didn't spit up again until the heavy picking season, when the cart was straining and threatening to split in half. He spat, and the rickety thing went abruptly firm and lasted the whole season without further maintenance.

Near the end of picking season, his mams complained terribly of the heat in their hut. Andrei snuck off along the thoroughfare, to the banks of the river. Sticking his head in left his hair feeling frozen from the coolness. He ate a little of the silt from the river and, the next morning, spat it outside their hut. His mams had never looked so comfortable as that afternoon. She scarcely lifted her fan, although at one point she scrutinized Andrei and asked if he had something in his mouth.

At the picking festival, Andrei and Mams and Paps decorated a long gourd to look like a royal judge, and he danced standing on their feet and holding their hands, and they sang tawdry songs he didn't understand. He made sure to stick some dirt in his mouth that night.

A few weeks later a spell of heat raked their orchard, turning proud fruits into sagging husks. Mams and Paps had a banger of a screaming match over who should have done what. Mams said Paps should have hired extra hands earlier, and Paps kept wailing about not having the money for it. Andrei was too little to understand how the economy worked, but he knew all the dead apples weren't either of their faults. So he spat, quietly as he could, out the memory of a better night.

Before long, all three of them were singing tawdry songs, and they went on long after the moon was halfway across the sky. Mams and Paps kept finding new ways to apologize to each other, mostly in the forms of kissing different bits of each other. None of that kissing appealed to Andrei, but he would settle for it since his family would now be eternally content.

The next morning their eternal contentedness was disturbed by Judge Buș. He looked impossibly tall, face shadowed under the broad white brim of his hat. He demanded their taxes, in fruit or in currency, or they would be called to his court. Paps tried to explain that their orchard was struggling and invited the judge to come inside for a drink.

Judge Buș said, "I'll come inside when I take this place. Have a cart filled with your dues to the court or be ready to join your neighbors in a cell. You've got until a week from today."

Some farms to the north were having a better time of things. Andrei snuck up to one that fostered red plums. Each plum strained with its own juice, succulent to the eye. They made Andrei's mouth water, like his teeth were dissolving.

He knew what to do. He crouched and took a mouthful of the earth.

"You don't have to do that."

It was a girl's voice. She was a head taller than he was, with knees covered in bruises and scabs from playing too much. She carried a wooden saber, and as soon as Andrei looked at it, she tossed it away.

She plucked the nearest plum off the nearest branch and held it out to him. "This tastes better than dirt."

Andrei didn't know how to answer. He asked, "Do you need the dirt back?"

"No," she said. "I'm Zandra. This is my fruit. You'll like eating it better."

"I didn't mean to steal the ground from you."

"Here, see?" Zandra put the plum to her mouth and bit right into it. Cloudy purple juice ran down the right corner of her mouth and made a mess of her chin. Then she hefted the plum to him.

He contemplated.

He said, "Goodbye forever!"

And Andrei ran away to his orchard, hopeful that she couldn't follow him or recognize which farm he was from. He tried not to think about how the plum might taste. He focused on his family's sagging apple trees. He visited the tallest one, where the apples were wilted and miserable. He spat upon its roots.

The next day, Paps made an amazing discovery. A swathe of the orchard hadn't been battered as badly by the heat as they'd thought. Mams and Paps and Andrei all went out and brought home three cartloads of brilliant green apples so tart that Mams couldn't keep her eyes open when she bit into one.

Upon bringing the third cartload, they found a parcel waiting on their stoop. It was a single plum, wrapped in nice paper. Mams and Paps scrutinized the plum.

"Why does it have a bite missing?"

Andrei offered to throw it away. Behind their hut, he examined the grooves where Zandra's teeth had cut the plum's flesh. The fruit squished, having aged a lot overnight. He thought about how nice the girl had tried to be and why that had scared him.

He turned the plum over and took a bite from a clean spot.

The next opportunity he had, he went back to the realm of plum trees. He spied Zandra long before she saw him, since she was practicing with her wooden saber, riposting against villainous tree branches. He spat out a good plum-flavored wish.

He said, "Hi. I'm Andrei. I'm the boy who ran away."

She looked at him, and looked at her wooden saber. She threw it away.

She said, "Did you get your plum? It was good, wasn't it? Bet you've never had a better plum."

He answered her in two ways.

Firstly, he said, "It was the best plum I've ever bitten."

Secondly, he held out a bright green apple to her. It had one bite taken out of it.

The worst part of their friendship was that his mams and paps, as well as Zandra's mams, kept pushing them together. Zandra's paps probably would have too, if he weren't in a cell for his debts. Zandra's family needed the help, so Andrei would go over, but whenever he did, his own paps would sing tawdry songs that made more sense and were less fun to him by the year.

His mams said, "There comes a time when every boy needs a bride and a child."

Which didn't feel true to him, not that day, and not a day ten years later. Other kids said they'd felt the same disdain for it as he did, but all grew out of it. They used that term— they "grew out of it." They outgrew being like Andrei.

All he grew out of was enjoying holding up the spare wooden saber for Zandra to riposte. Eventually they dueled each other, when they weren't picking fruit. That was more fun, no matter how much he lost.

He asked, "Do you want to be a traveling duelist someday? Become rich by the blade?"

"No," Zandra said, fiddling with the pommel of her wooden saber. "They're bullies who kill for entertainment. I don't need that in my life."

There came a night when Judge Buș summoned all the adults into town. His mams and her mams conspired to leave the two of them in the same hut.

Mams said, "You'll see."

He went all around the premises looking for something to eat that would fix this. Trees didn't have to date. He could eat a pinch of ground from a still meadow, where nothing was happening. Or should he just run?

He didn't run. He wanted to run too much to be able to run. It didn't make sense. It left his mouth dry.

Zandra welcomed him inside. He mopped her floorboards. Her mams would never have seen her dishes so spotless as after he scrubbed them. When his hands were as wet and wrinkled as the rag, Zandra gave him a heated mug of plum wine.

She said, "It tastes better than dirt."

She always said that. But she never tried it. He stared into the mug's steaming purple contents. He didn't drink it, for what might come of it.

Zandra cleared the laundry off a spare chair for him. They sat before the hearth, and she narrated to him from a book of stories of great knights errant.

After a paragraph, she handed it to him.

He set the wine aside and took the book. He read a paragraph before she took the book back from him. Eventually they traded the book so much that it became a game to steal it from the other's grasp before their paragraph was up. Andrei couldn't help giggling. The knights errant in those stories surely couldn't have had as good a time as they did.

When they finished half the book, Zandra sat back in her chair and it creaked like it had sympathy for her tired body.

She said, "This is how I like it too."

A part of his throat he'd never known was there tightened, then clicked. It was a repulsive noise.

He asked, "You do?"

"Why do you think I studied the saber?"

"I thought you liked to hit people."

"Well, I do. But I did it to prevent people from forcing things on me."

So Andrei sipped the wine after all. And the next morning, when he was sure this was all real and she didn't want anything more from him, he ran outside to gather up some dirt. This was something he had to preserve. But with the grains pinched between thumb and forefinger, a thought stopped him. Zandra shouldn't have to read books with him again just because he spat. Giving him plum wine and platonic company should be her choice. His insecurity didn't entitle him to her earth.

He was wiping the good intentions from his bottom lip when another voice spat, on the other side of the hut. Judge Buș sat astride a white horse with a tanned saddle studded with pearls. He got down and beat on Zandra's door, demanding their legal debts be paid.

Her mams said, "You haven't even released my husband yet."

"That's no excuse for running up a debt. How old is that daughter of yours?"

"Quite young."

"Her hand in marriage is worth something, especially if it comes with inheritance rights to this property. Think about it."

"You wouldn't. You already took her father!"

"Think about it, before it's out of your hands."

Hair still matted from the perspiration, Andrei searched for Zandra. He found her deep in the plum groves, dragging a stone along the edge of a steel saber.

Her wooden one was nowhere to be found. The sight made his mouth dry. He made an offer anyway.

"Perhaps apples and plums could sell better together?"

His mams and her mams dickered about income splits and produce arrangement, and while that dragged on, Andrei and Zandra took their first load of fruit to market. The plums were so bright, they looked polished in the sun. Andrei tossed an apple and a plum into the air, and Zandra sliced them both in twain with a single slash. They drew plenty of customers, until with all four of their hands they struggled to split all the currency. In a spare moment, Andrei stooped under the stall to eat a pinch of earth.

On days when business went slow, he spat as quietly as he could. Soon enough a new flock of pilgrims would tromp through, or nobles would have a party that night and need something to stuff in their pie crusts.

Zandra never challenged him. She did gift him a napkin, though.

"The only one we haven't sold off from my father's collection," she said, tucking it into his shirt pocket. "He's a drooler as well."

Andrei became flustered and stepped into the street to collect himself. Business was atrocious that day, on account of a heat drying so much up and how many people owed debts to the court. Andrei was self-conscious of spitting in earshot of Zandra, especially after getting a napkin from her. He pulled the cloth square out, rotating it in his hands. He fixated on it, which is why he didn't notice the only other man in the road.

Judge Buş seemed much taller this close, with the narrow limbs of a scarecrow and a broad-brimmed white hat. His goat-hide boots shined with polish, save for the spittle now decorating one.

His upper lip and mustache wrinkled so fiercely, they threatened to disappear up his nostrils. He pushed his coat open, revealing the handle of a saber.

Judge Buș said, "You have offended my honor. I should strike you down this moment."

"I would rather you didn't." Andrei couldn't muster anything better.

"Hey!" Zandra called, clambering over the stall to get at them. "What are you doing?"

"You have one night of lenience," Judge Buș said down at Andrei. "You have until tomorrow to live. I will return to this spot after lunch. Bring your weapon of choice."

Zandra tried to get in front of Andrei. "You leave him alone."

"Your man is losing his head tomorrow." Andrei didn't like where Judge Buș's eyes went on Zandra. "Unless one of you does the right thing. I know you're unwed."

Judge Buș took an apple, without paying.

He was still walking away when Zandra punched a plum off the stand.

Andrei said, "It's my fault. I offended his honor."

"No, you didn't," she snapped. "He just wants the fun of killing people in front of an audience and the tips they'll throw him. What are we going to do?"

What Andrei did was follow the river south, all the way to the falls. He carefully descended the vines to the basin of the falls, where it came crashing down so fiercely, it would knock any grown man to the ground. Swimming underneath, he took a palmful of the silt beneath the fury.

The whole next day's walk to the market was a slog of counting the knots in his guts. He at least managed to unpack all the apples and plums before he had to face death so that Zandra could make another good day's payment for her debts before he died.

Judge Buș arrived, picking venison from his teeth, one hand on the pommel of his saber. Farmers had flocked around to see Andrei get murdered. It had been a while since anybody had been cut in half at the market.

Andrei looked Judge Buș dead in the eye. He spat and then stepped back to watch the ruin.

Judge Buş looked befuddled at the spittle on the road. It didn't grow into torrent, nor did water fall from thin air. No storm blasted him to the ground.

Judge Buş asked, "Where is your weapon? How do you wish to die?"

Before Andrei could answer, Zandra rose up behind the judge and smashed a tree branch over his head with a sound like the crash of a waterfall. The branch split around Judge Buş's head, the top half going spinning and clattering against the wheels of an adjacent grocer's cart. The judge did his own little spin before falling nose down into a patch of daisies.

"Get my half of today's proceeds to my mams," Zandra said as a constable shackled her wrists. "I was your weapon in the duel. It will be fine."

It was not fine. Judge Buş appointed himself to preside over Zandra's case. He looked down at her from atop his high bench, his broad-brimmed hat resting actually atop the bandage around his forehead. He said, "You have no appreciation for human life."

Zandra stood straight like posture mattered more than height. "I disagree. My work resulted in one fewer death than would have otherwise happened."

"You think you can go around attacking people?"

"I was Andrei's weapon. Weapons can't be guilty of winning a fight."

Judge Buş flipped through a tome of previous cases. "Weapons can't own property, either. They are property. We'll have to put you in jail while the court decides how many of your assets need seizure to compensate the court for the injury."

Andrei shot up from his seat in the gallery. He couldn't let this go on.

"Your Honor, Zandra was my weapon." He hadn't agreed to it beforehand, but he would agree to it retroactively if he had to. "She was doing my bidding. I'm the guilty one here."

Judge Buș flapped a hand for him to shut up. "Participants in a duel do not experience the same legal threshold as interlopers. Be seated."

"I will not be seated! Zandra was my weapon, and you know what? I told her to attack you from behind. It was my idea. And it worked."

Zandra spun around with her mouth wide open, and he thought that had to be the same expression he'd worn when she'd smashed the branch over the judge's head. He had to keep going.

Judge Buș said, "You aren't that clever."

"You think I didn't know that you picked that fight with me? You wanted me to spit on your shoe so you could duel me and kill me and steal my orchard."

Zandra yelled, "Andrei! Stop!"

Judge Buș asked his bailiff, "What orchard does he mean?"

"You've been trying to steal it from my family since I was a baby. You pretend the court serves everyone, when all our debts do is fill your pockets. You didn't have honor for me to offend. You didn't deserve a duel, and you won't take either of our farms."

Now the judge was studying a map, his eyes going thirsty from what he was realizing was in his court's grasp. Andrei wouldn't stop.

"Now I confess ordering Zandra to smash your head in and you won't even face me in court? Bring charges against me. Stick me in some dusty cell tonight and see if I care. Put me in a cell next to Zandra's paps if you want, but face me here tomorrow, right here after lunch, on this spot. Duel me with the law, you coward."

"Enough." Judge Buș hadn't seen enough, for he couldn't take his eyes off the orchard plots on those papers. He gave the orders with a wave of his hand, while his eyes kept drinking in the fruited lands in his grasp. "Send them both to the cells. We'll try them both tomorrow. And get me more maps."

Andrei's cell was tiny. No cot. No bucket to piss in. Lying down on the floor, he found it was scarcely wider in any direction than he was tall. He strained his ears listening for Zandra, and listening for her to not be down here. She belonged somewhere with a window.

But Andrei wasn't down here to listen. He swept a palm across the floor. It was hard slate, flat as the day they'd built this dungeon. Not a single pebble was loose that he could chew. While this place smelled of unhappy mushrooms, someone had swept the floors.

He fondled at the slate, scarcely collecting a hint of grime on his fingertips. It would take hours of combing his palms along that floor to create a single morsel of dust.

He had all night.

His duel by the courts didn't last long. The courthouse was full to the doors, so many people that they couldn't all have cases today. Their scowls rippled like waves in a sea as Judge Buș berated Andrei for his lack of honor and civility.

Andrei wasn't really listening. He simply waited.

"Well?" asked the man who was going to render judgment. "What do you have to say in your defense?"

Andrei stood with his shackled hands and regarded the crowded audience. All those people who carried debts and knew their taxes went to no justice. He looked as many of them as he could in the eye as he gathered the saliva in his mouth. How many of them had someone they loved locked down in the jail? How many of them wanted to do something? But they couldn't, for the simple reason that nobody had ever challenged the law. There was a wall between them and justice, hard as a slate floor.

When Andrei spat up this time, he made sure to miss the judge's goat-hide boots. It was a little spatter on the floorboards, right between the judge's feet.

They came down on Judge Buș all at once, like a thunderclap, everybody hopping bannisters and chairs.

They stole his hat and his saber, and they lifted him up and carried him aloft down to his own jail cell. Within the hour he was the only one in a cell. The floor of it was spotless.

The first person they released was Zandra, and she took the key ring and made sure to fling open every other door in the place. Every detainee was released to come dance, and every liquor cabinet was opened to give them something to dance about. Zandra's paps was freed to go dance with her mams. People returned to the courtroom and made music for each other on drums and violins. It was like watching joy imitate a wildfire, jumping everywhere they could see. Everyone started singing tawdry songs.

Andrei almost felt guilty for not singing along. But then he noticed Zandra wasn't singing along either. She eyed the exit of the courthouse, her hands fidgeting as though wishing she had a saber.

She asked, "Andrei?"

He said, "Yes?"

"Would you like to go somewhere else? Perhaps read together and have dinner?"

Andrei eyed the floor, kicking the dirt off his boots. He said, "With you? I could eat."

Zariel:

Parable of a Gifted Black Child

Denzel Xavier Scott

"Nobody loves a genius child.
Kill him—and let his soul run wild."

Langston Hughes told us this. He may have used the words "genius child" but as a black mother, I, Josephine Putné, think he meant the gifted black child.

I can only imagine he meant this song for every black child ever born, but especially for the gifted ones. They may be the wildest and most difficult to love. I wonder if that's why the world murders them so often.

❖

"Nit…ro…nit…ro…nitro…nitrogen and ox…oxy…oxyge…oxyge…oxygen are burning red. Iron is burning green and yell…yellow. Calcium is burning…pur…purp…purp…purple. Sodi…sodium is burning orange. And mag…mag…mag…magnesium is burning blue", says an eight-year-old little ebon-faced innocent with doll-like, dark, chocolate eyes and a thick mass of sumptuous kinks, coils, and curls.

"What are you talking about, Zariel," asks the mother before changing her mind, "No, Jesus have mercy, just be quiet baby."

The dark-skinned woman holding her child's hand weeps quietly and slowly from similar eyes. She stands stone-still as if savoring despair. Like so many other adults watching this juggernaut, both beautiful and terrifying, progress ever closer to kissing the planet, she is lost in a hedge maze of anguish; extinction looms on the horizon. It is a dark wilderness humanity has not known for quite some time.

A growing portion of the crystal blue sky glows chartreuse, plum, aquamarine, burnt orange, shamrock, and a deep scarlet. It's noon in Savannah, GA on a summer day. There's an asteroid larger than the moon barreling toward the planet. All life on Earth prepares for its extinguishment.

This mother-and-child pair, lovely black visions like an eclipsed sun or the throat of a sea cave have stopped walking along Broughton Street peppered by old brick department stores dating from before the twentieth century and live oak trees. Their feet root themselves to the ground just outside of the eggshell face of Jen Library of the Savannah College of Art and Design. Everyone has stopped.

The mother and her queer, androgynous progeny are similarly paralyzed, but their reactions diametrically opposed each other; the young child wears the dauntless face of morbid curiosity while the mother dons the beautiful mask of existential dread.

Sudden as a cardinal crashes into a sliding glass door, breaking its fragile, little neck, the child lets go of their mother's hand. Briefly, the mother does not notice until, in the corner of her eye, she sees her noticeably perplexed child bathed in the same burning colors that engulf the asteroid.

"Zariel, what are you doing? Turn it off. You know better," screeches the mother.

Other people awaken similarly from the stupor of beholding their impending doom. They take full notice of the child shining like a lone torch on a dark night. Passersby begin to gather around the mother and child. People split their attention between nightmarish rainbows filling the darkening sky and this child dripping with similarly colored lights.

"I di…di…didn't want to Mama! I didn't d…d…d…d…do this, I swear! The asteroid…it's in my m…ment…it's my ment…it's in m…y…men…men…men…men…men…men," says Zariel, struggling desperately.

"It's in your mind space," says Zariel's mother, to free up the tongue of her stuttering child.

"My mental matrix. I can't block it out Mama. It's doing this!"

The woman desperately wipes the tears away from her eyes. She looks around, taking in her bearings in complete panic. Her fear of the falling asteroid that has taken up the sky has shrunk unto the likeness of a mustard seed. She and her child must flee the terribly unpredictable scenario that mounts.

Just as immediate a threat to their lives as the death of all that marches down from heaven, if not more so, these fellow citizens of the American experiment, have given themselves over to familiar fears. The fear of foreigners, the fear of the minority, the fear of the different, the perplexing, the fear of some mysterious end to glory, power, and privilege, such a family of prejudicial terrors engulfs the vulnerable pair.

More than likely, these gathering folks will lynch them if they do not flee. Their cells scream with thousands of ancestral memories of this truth. But how could they move a single inch unnoticed and unfollowed if all eyes are upon them?

"How is that possible, Zariel? Are you saying… that crazy-ass thing up there is alive?" ask Zariel's mother with a nervous laugh, caught up in the dizzying cruelty of death looming from above and death gathering on all sides below.

"It's not alive in the same way that you are Mama, but yes, it is alive, and it's giving off thought p…p…p…pa… patt…patt…patterns I've never come across with anyone or anything on this p…pl…pl…plan…planet or in this ga…ga…ga…galax…galaxy for that matter," says Zariel. With a twinkle in their eye, Zariel confidently says, "It feels just like me," as if it's the greatest comfort. Zariel's mother responds to the statement with a roll of the eyes and a shaking of the head, a silent performance inspired by confusion and despair; *the closest thing in this world to my baby is a chunk of rock that's about to kill everything. Jesus have mercy on my soul.*

More people have begun to gather along the narrow street in downtown Savannah. Someone in the crowd has inevitably called the police on the mother and child. Many take out their cellphones to record, anticipating tragedy no doubt, and whisper openly about this bizarre vignette of this woman and her peculiar child that unfolds.

The end of the world draws near for all. The closeness of death is new for many, but it is not new to these two black bodies, young and old, these panicked midnight hares though they may currently be. The woman and child are fiercely logical and resilient, searching ceaselessly for a means of escape and survival.

"What kind of movie can pull off these types of effects? I don't even see any equipment," says a young white woman with a sandy blonde bob cut, and a solid teal halter-top.

"This isn't a movie. This that alien shit, I swear to God," says a young black gentleman with pale, pastel-shaded, rose pink dyed locks and army fatigue pants.

"Ya'll lookup. There ain't no camera equipment on none of these goddamn buildings."

"So that rock in the sky is real? We're all gonna die", blurts out an older white male amongst his family, with his honey-shaded three-year-old son holding one hand and his four-year-old daughter holding the other.

"Daddy, were gonna die? Mama," says the weeping four-year-old little chai-colored girl holding her father's hand.

"Jim, you jackass," says the man's wife of milk coffee hue, pulling the little girl into her arms.

"Daddy was being stupid. Nothing's gonna happen to you baby," says the mother to the thoroughly unconvinced child. The mother seemed not to believe in her own comforting words either as her face couldn't lose its unease as she again turns her attention back to Zariel and their mother.

Standing tall, the dark-skinned black woman, dressed with a short twist out afro in a red sundress, talks ever more vociferously to Zariel. The child answers their mother back ever so meekly, as meticulously trained. And while this occurs, the content of the discussion and Zariel's body queers an otherwise banal exchange between a mother and their child. Already illuminated by a bath of rainbow hue emanating from their flesh, as if a spotlight shines upon it, Zariel's otherworldly aura glows more intensely.

"Miss, what the hell is happening here?" asks a mustachioed light-skinned man suddenly in a dark gray button-up shirt and light blue jeans. He has erroneously stepped forward from the crowd, now some thirty bodies gathered. "Why is your kid glowing like that?"

"Mama, I think I have to go. This thing…this creature… tells me its name is Azhura-Semnu. It's come here for me."

"Now this thing has a name? I do not…Hold up! You're not going nowhere with that, that thing up there, Zariel."

"Bitch, don't you ignore me! I'm talking to you Goddamnit," yells the man as he now forcefully grabs at the mother's wrist. The crowd is now fifty people deep. Police gather in the area as well, trying both to address the scene between this mother and child that unfolds and the unruly crowd that encircles it, increasing steadily in its body count.

"Sir, have lost your damn mind? I know you better take your hands up off me," shouts Zariel's mother.

"Leave my mama alone," yells Zariel as their aura makes a loud crackling sound, reminiscent of thunder, followed by a cat-like hiss.

The mustachioed gentleman, rightly afraid, instantly lets go of Zariel's mother and dissolves back into the crowd, now seventy or so people deep. They too have stepped back in response to the loud disturbing clatter of Zariel's aura, but still, they encircle the mother and child.

"Ma'am," shouts a dark-skinned black male police officer as he slowly approaches Zariel and their mother, "I'm going to need you to get a handle on your kid." He looks at the mother along the sight of his already brandished weapon with somewhat of a note of sympathy. It's sympathy inspired partly by the mother's helplessness, her motherliness, and mostly her beauty that mutilates his preconceived notions of how dark-skinned women appear in the world, but that sympathy is faint and fleeting at best as assumptions bloom and wither from second to second.

"Folks are already riled up about whatever that thing in the sky is, and you're not helping your situation with your kid putting on this light show like this. Tell her…him… tell your kid to shut it down right now," says the officer as sternly as he could muster.

"Mr. Policeman, My name is Josephine Putné, please calm down sir…"

The mother's hands are already up and she is on her knees before the officer even prompts her. It's as if she too holds a gift beyond gifts like Zariel, but no. Josephine simply knows the truth of what the world has taught her in the mountain range of corpses piled as high as clouds that look just like her and her beloved child. What the officer is so inclined to do to them both, this mother and child, even before a crowd of people, folks numbering around one hundred bodies, no one with skin so dark and beloved by the velvet of night would be surprised to experience.

They know their blood would fill the streets, the videos recorded on cellphones all around, and the eyes, the very eyes of men, women, and children, witnesses all, would still play out their destruction like a mystery. Why did the bullets rip through the supple dark flesh of this mother and child? What did they do to earn such ire? Why didn't they convince the officers that shot them that they were innocent? Isn't that their responsibility to prove their innocence as the always already guilty? Did they secretly wish to be murdered, to die in a hail of bullets? This is how the police would murder Zariel and Josephine and the ravenous crowd would watch.

"Zariel baby, please, for the love of God, don't speak! Don't say a word! Raise your hands up high over your head. Get down on your knees like we talked about, ok."

"But Ma…"

Josephine looked at Zariel with hot eyes surging with more fear than anger.

"Do what the hell I say!"

Zariel looks at their mother's face. All of Josephine's pride melts away along the street she kneels on, like an ice sculpture commissioned for a summer wedding and callously abandoned to the forces of the sun.

"Yes ma'am," says Zariel as they slowly lift their hands as high as they can.

"Baby, can you turn your aura off," begs Josephine with a softer tone, brimming over with desperate fear attached to every syllable, but also a well-practiced, inhuman calmness that keeps her words from crescendoing into the atmosphere.

"No ma'am, I can't turn off my aura. I'm not the one who…"

"Did, ya'll just say aura? What the hell? Kid, turn whatever shit you got running off," says the officer whose note of sympathy has entirely burned out except for a pathetic ember that barely glows.

The other police listen intently to the exchange between their fellow officer and this woman and her child as they attempt to hold back the animated crowd that still grows in number. Zariel's aura grows in intensity and seems to be pulsating rhythmically.

A steady stream of officers arrives newly at the scene. They arrive newly to the complex interplay of de-escalation that's playing out as bystanders, now a mob of hundreds deep has formed.

Zariel looks at their mother, maybe for the first time in their life with sadness so deep, it is as if a virus of sorrow never before encountered, burgeons in this lowly child, and brings them on the verge of tears.

"Baby, what's…?"

Firecrackers, no, gunshots, roar out from someone in the crowd. The bullets rip through Zariel's mother to find their target and disintegrate in the glowing aura shell that's taken Zariel's body.

Zariel's aura pulsates more erratically before suddenly drawing in close to their flesh, becoming like an exoskeleton, as if it were a response to hostility, as if it were instinctual. Their mouth opens wide and two things occur; first, a large non-nuclear electromagnetic pulse emits from Zariel's body and second, moments later the mob of over a hundred people and every single living creature with a central nervous system in a five-mile radius, other than Josephine and Zariel themselves, collapses.

"Zariel…you…didn't…," says their mother bleeding out from a ruptured liver, stomach, and large intestines.

"Kill all these people? No ma'am," responds Zariel,

"they're asleep until I tell them to wake up." Once again, serene as sap dripping down a pine tree, Zariel places their hands over their mother's wounds and draws the bullets out with a surge of telekinetic force. Josephine screams out in agony.

Zariel pours their aura into their mother, cocooning and calming her. The gaping injuries and pierced organs forces themselves closed before Zariel's eyes, cold, glass-like, and empty, as if made from plastic rather than flesh, until Josephine's body was just as before the bullets raged through.

"Mama, I really have to go now. Azhura-Semnu is calling," says Zariel, their eyes returned to the warm brown of a dark mocha latte.

Unfazed by nearly dying in the street like a cat struck by a car, Zariel's mother screams as she rises from the ground, "Zariel, are you crazy, I don't care who it is! You're not just disappearing with…Azhura whoever the good goddamn…I am your mama!"

"Then come with me, mama," says Zariel as casual as a gnat flying into a lavender-scented ointment.

"What are you talking about, Zariel," snaps Josephine, peaking at the different bodies laid at their feet. Black faces, white faces, young faces, old faces, so many made dead to the world against their will.

"Come with me, mama. We can't stay here," says Zariel, entirely unburdened by guilt, fear, or remorse.

"But can't you just erase their memories? Yeah, yeah, yeah. Do that Zariel. But what about them damn videos? And what about the memories of everyone who watched those videos outside of this area? What the hell," says Josephine exhausted.

"Mama, even if I could do all that, I wouldn't want to."

"Zariel, what do you mean? Why do you want to go with that thing in the sky so bad? This is our home," says Josephine as she gestures to all of the buildings and sleeping bodies that engulf them.

"Mama, if this is our home, why do people hate us so much for the way we look, for who we are? If this is our home, why did I just have to take bullets out of you? Why was daddy killed?" asks Zariel, with tears in their eyes.

"How do you know about that? You told me that you could only read the minds of those who have given their permission. Was that a lie, Zariel?" asks Josephine.

"No mama…it wasn't a…it wasn't a…a lie. There was one night when you were dream…dreaming, crying loud with your eyes closed tight. I came to check on you, and when I… when I walked into your room, I walked into the door in your mind that you had opened wide just for me," says Zariel.

"Zariel, I never," says Josephine.

"Not wh…whi…whi…whi…while you were a…a…awa… awa…awake mama. When you were dreaming, you opened the door to me as if you needed me to see something, to see the truth. I saw him, the man in all of the pictures around the house. I saw the man you say is my father, though I've never hugged his neck, or felt his hand pat my head. I saw him through your eyes, mama," says Zariel.

"Stop, please! Don't say anymore," begs Josephine, but Zariel refuses, even as the world darkens ever more all around them.

Like a projector shining in a pitch-black theater, Zariel launches beams of light from their eyes, and shows Josephine a cruel murder she is all too familiar with. There is a black man, Zariel's father, on the side of a road, his hands stretched over the hood of a silver 2002 Mitsubishi Galant, legs spread wide like a condor's wings.

Josephine has her hands on the dashboard, in the passenger seat, biting her lips until the taste of blood fills her mouth ever so slowly. Two white police officers surround the black man, while a third black officer interrogates Josephine. He gestures towards the hand-rolled cigarettes in his line of sight and chastises her about how the driver of the vehicle did not notice the rapid change in speed limit as they entered Pembroke, GA. As officers grope Zariel's father, searching for a weapon that is not there, they panic, feeling a combination of things in his front pants pocket, which he reassures them repeatedly, like the chorus of a song, that what they smother with their clammy hands is not a gun, but the officers don't listen.

As Zariel's father attempts to slowly show the officers what they fear hides near his crotch, Josephine cries out, "Rand don't", screaming the nickname she's given to her beloved Randal Putné but, it is far too late. Immediately the darkness of the night along the country road illuminates with gunfire. One. Two. Three. Four. Five. Six. Seven. Eight. Nine. Ten. Eleven. Twelve. Thirteen. Thirteen shots roar and the quiet of the evening is shattered.

The bullets enter effortlessly as Randal Putné's body dances to the ground. They tear through him; he is the desiccated wood that a great conflagration dances through joyfully. He doesn't die immediately of course. He lives long enough to see the horror of the officers' faces as they see the hairbrush, a cellphone, and lip balm scatter from his palm along the ground. He was twenty-one years old. He was a twenty-one-year-old black man bleeding out like his ancestors, slaves white men had whipped open, whose feet white masters lopped off and tossed away like an apple core, to teach the other hopeful runners the consequences of seeking a freedom that was always their birthright. He died watching the officers concoct the lie that they were afraid for their lives and had to shoot an unarmed citizen thirteen times during what was supposed to be a routine traffic stop.

The projection ends abruptly. Zariel's eyes are full of tears. Josephine's face is soaked, exhausted from the inhuman restraint demanded of her by the wider world. With the world darkening with every passing second, and every judge and executioner unconscious at her feet, Josephine's tears fall freely. She weeps shamelessly like a child.

"Yo…you kno…know, when I s…sa…saw that for the first time, as you cried in your sleep mama, I could feel your sc…scre…screams come up from down at the bottom of your belly. I've never felt nothing like that since," says Zariel as tears pour down their own face.

Josephine tries to close the distance and comfort her child. She approaches slow, hearing the howl gather in the child's chest.

"He's no…no…not the on…only one you've loved that this has ha…hap…happened to. You gave me so many sad stories of people you've loved being murdered," says Zariel.

"No more, Zariel," says Josephine doing her best to wipe Zariel's tears with the bottom of her dress.

"Yo…yo…your bro…brother, Fran...kie, was twenty when he was mur…mur…murdered for the co…cou… couple of dollars he had on him, his shoes, and the weed that he was selling."

"Zariel, don't do this. Don't do this to me now."

"Yo…you…you…your cousin, Ant…Antwan, was twenty-eight when he was murdered. He had crashed his car into a light post when he swerved to avoid some animal and confused, begged for help, knocking on door after door after door. Only an old white man came to see Antwan. The old white man you learned told police he feared that Antwan was a burglar. So the old white man opened his door and shot Antwan with a shotgun at point-blank range on his front porch and then closed his do… do…door and went back to sleep."

"Don't say anymore Zariel," begs Josephine. "Please, I don't want to remember. Don't force me to remember this right now."

Zariel refuses Josephine's pleas. She will remember through a baptism by fire offered to her by her only child.

"He went back to sleep witho…without calling a soul to help your po…po…poor cousin. In your memories, the call about his death came a while after they burned his body to ash because they weren't able to find ya'll to bury him. Antwan was gay and nobody had dealt with him in twelve years because of it, but when you learned that he died slow, that a do…doct…doctor could have saved his life had someone called an ambulance, that they burned his body, you all forgave him for something that I learned in school needed no forgiving."

"Stop, Goddamnit, stop! I don't want to hear this shit no more," Josephine rages, pulling at Zariel's collar and slapping them in the face, but Zariel refuses.

"His death, with all of its sadness, wo…wo…woke you up from yo…yo…your sleep and yo...you screamed and cried for hou…hou…hours, and because I saw it thr… through your eyes, I screamed and cried for what felt like hours for this man I'll never know. He was your best friend once, when you were kids. The least you could have done for him is scatter his ashes and you did. You went down to River Street and slowly scattered his ashes into the Savannah River early in the morning while the city still slept."

Josephine sobs, her grip loosening on Zariel's collar as the tears drown her chin. Zariel touches her face soft, comforting, trying to wipe away the tears with their hands, but not quietly. Still, both drenched in their own seas, Zariel tells the terrible traumas of Josephine's life, her malicious inheritance.

"One of your granduncles, Stephon," says Zariel, before Josephine shouts "Please, for the love of God, not this story," as she tosses her hands up to knock away Zariel's hands from her face.

Zariel isn't fazed at all. The souls of the murdered yearn for acknowledgment and the bloody history longing to have a place at the forefront of thoughts, pours out of Zariel's mouth, their tongue, thoroughly drowned in unrelenting trauma.

"He was fifteen years old when he was murdered. He was a kid who was very tall for his age. He was mistaken for a black man, an older black man, wh…wh…wh…who had escaped the white m…m…m…mo…mob that would go on to murder Stephon. The white people were looking for the person who was rumored to have done nasty things to a young white lady, adult things kids are not sup… sup…sup…po…supposed to talk about. It turned out to be all lies. The white lady told everyone a lie about what happened to her to cover up the fact that she was cheating on her husband with a man that wasn't black to begin with."

Why must I hear this story now, Zariel," asks Josephine, "I know all these things. I don't want to hear this no more."

"But now you know that I know your stories too. I know all these things you tried to hide, but secretly wanted me to know, mama," said Zariel with a face full of tears slowly transforming into precious jewels as they hit the ground, and the ground beneath their feet surging with greenery.

"The way you remember the story, mama, it was just like something we've watched on Maury on your days off. The white people didn't see, couldn't see, or didn't care about the difference between one tall fifteen-year-old black boy and some thirtysomething-year-old black man, though neither one of them had ever seen the lying white lady before," said Zariel and Josephine joined in the telling of the tale. Their united voices mingled as a song whose lyrics were the lynching of their black ancestor.

"They blamed the first black man they could find, so they strung him up, slowly cut off his private parts, put them in a jar as if they were making pickles, and hung Stephon from an old oak tree. They took pictures of his limp, dead body as if he was an animal they had hunted that night. They ate their food, and drank their beer late into the evening before throwing Stephon into the fire they had started as if he was another log. It was a party.

The white people were happy for the rumor, the fun of an adventure, and the murder of this black boy. It gave them something to do to take their minds off the summer heat. His mother kept one of the copies of the picture of her dead son hanging from that oak tree so that her other children would remember."

Josephine grew quiet and Zariel told the rest of the story alone, "And when she died, your grandfather took that picture and shared that story with your father. When your grandfather died, your father took that picture and shared that story with you. When granddaddy died last year, you took that picture and put it in a book of photos next to some baby pictures of mine that you keep in your closet beside a box of scarves."

Zariel hugs Josephine tight as they can.

"This kind of thing keeps happening, mama. And what's sad and crazy is this many people of our family killed like this, with so much violence, hatred, and evil isn't something that just happens to us. How many other black people have stories like this? I don't want to die like this, mama. No one should die like that," says Zariel more angry than sad.

"Stop, Zariel! Don't go," says Josephine as she reaches out her hand before she notices Zariel's aura starts to build up again.

"Why do you want to stay here on this planet, with these people who have no problem killing people that look like you over and over? Even some black people, a lot of them in fact, can't stand other black people. What can we do to stay alive when so many different types of people work so hard to see us in the ground?" asks Zariel as their tears evaporate with the intensity of the aura shell that engulfs their body.

"I don't want to die like this mama. It's not fair. It's not fair. It's not fair, I," says Zariel before rainbow hue beams of light pour from their mouth and eyes like a faucet as their body raises up off the ground by several feet.

The lights stemming from her child and the ethereal floating of their body in midair frightens Josephine to her bones. Then an otherworldly voice rings out from Zariel's body like a megaphone, confirming Josephine's fears. Zariel has become possessed.

"I am Azhura-Semnu, well of echoes," says the booming voice emanating from Zariel. "Your child, Zariel, is an emergent biological experience of the evolutionary trajectory of this planet."

"Please, don't take my baby from me," pleads Josephine.

"There is no choice in this matter for Zariel, only you," says Azhura-Semnu. "The likelihood of Zariel's manifestation as a scion was infinitesimally small and worthy of the highest praise. Often a scion, like Zariel…"

"Did you not understand what the hell I just said? I'm begging you please…"

"Josephine, it's counterproductive to interrupt. Your child cannot stay on this planet because Zariel is an entity who, without formal training as they enter into their maturation cycle, will bring utter catastrophe to your world. Zariel could awaken abilities that would undeniably destroy your solar system, if not the entirety of this spiral galaxy where this planet currently resides!"

"You're lying. Zariel is different, but they would never do something like that."

"Not on purpose, human, but Zariel is unlike any of the other Homo Sapiens on this planet. And as they mature, entering into their chrysalis stage, and their myriad abilities advance a millionfold, your child will be the most dangerous existence your species has erstwhile encountered. Behold what this child, in all of their blissful youth and abecedarian faculties, is capable of now with their unfettered emotions," says Azhura-Semnu, commanding Zariel's arms to point at the still-sleeping bodies that litter the ground and the floors of every building in the horizon.

"But you caused this! You caused all of this bullshit! This would've never happened if you hadn't come and blot out the fucking sky! Zariel is mine! My child" screams Josephine.

"No, you are mistaken. I, Azhura-Semnu, am the progenitor of all life on this planet and at least 5,683,245 other worlds scattered across this universe. Every living thing on this planet exists as offspring descended from the specialized crystalline, hyper-transgenic gametes that I produce, but particularly Zariel. Although I expected the emergence of your child some hundreds of thousands of years in the future of your planet with this level of complex life apparent, but your child is clearly the scion that I've waited for since the moment I seeded your lifeless world!" says Azhura-Semnu with a bark of elation.

"There's so much I don't understand of everything that you're saying, but it sounds like if you've done this to countless other worlds, why don't you take someone else's kid," asks Josephine, with her arms raised to the sky, shaking her head with new tears pooling in her eyes. "Just leave my poor baby alone."

"That's why you should be silent and not interrupt. The emergence of a scion is an infinitesimally rare occurrence. The life forms on the majority of planets I've seeded with much older, more technologically advanced, sapient species have ad nausem, driven themselves into extinction by way of environmental ruin, planetary warfare, genocides motivated by arbitrary differences, or outright abandoned their origin planets in vain pursuit of conquering, pillaging, and plundering other worlds. Over the billions of years I've experienced, I've only collected and trained one hundred and sixty-three scions and none have ever embarked upon the final potential stage of their life cycle, planetary reconstitution and fusion."

Zariel's body floats higher and higher and it's almost as if Josephine's heart is a boulder falling from the face of a cliff into the sea. All of her options are running out.

"Will Zariel ever come back," she asks, shouting the question at her child while she bows her eyes to the ground.

"You could make the choice to come with Zariel, you know. That is an option, radical though it may be. Zariel will have to see to your survival, which I imagine is well within their current abilities. You both would live on my surface as Zariel trains under my guidance and if you survived, Josephine, I would return you both to Earth. I imagine the process would take fifty years in your time."

"I will stay," says Josephine, low as a whisper with her eyes still bowed like a tortoise chomping on grass.

"What's that you say?"

"I will stay," Josephine screams, and as her voice reaches Zariel's ears, the lights spewing from their mouth and eyes stop.

"Zariel is rarer than I could have ever imagined. To force me back like this, your child will be a lovely seed for my future companion."

"Shut the hell up you! Baby, can you hear Mama? Can you hear me Zariel? Baby, come to me," screams Josephine louder and louder.

Azhura-Semnu roars as the aura shell around Zariel's body retracts tightly before receding to the child's head like a halo. As the rainbow crowns Zariel's head, they scream a monstrous roar towards Azhura-Semnu still falling slowly up in the sky, with a voice not at all human, with a voice like a choir of the wild. Josephine hears the echoes of lions, horses, bears, all manner of songbirds, in her child's fearsome cry. She hears everything, but the child she loves. The light of Zariel's halo disappears briefly until every kinky, coiling follicle of the child's obsidian coif turns into a wild forest of colors, and their body stops floating in midair.

"Extraordinary. Already, the chrysalis stage has begun. You will return to Earth one day and force the survival of your species, as either its messiah or its tormenter. I've finally found the one who can become a well of echoes! I'm sure of it," screams Azhura-Semnu out of Zariel's own throat.

"Mama, I'm go…go…go…going to come back in ten years. We'll be a family again, I pro…pro…pro…pro… prom…prom…promise," says Zariel, chocolate eyes drenched in an ocean, and the soft, warm, stuttering voice Josephine knows so well pealing out of their throat like the tune of a tambourine.

Zariel drops from the sky into Josephine's waiting arms which wraps them like an octopus preparing to gobble up prey with its cruel beak.

"I can survive ten years without my baby. I'll tell folks you're away at boarding school learning science, and languages from lands I'll never visit," she giggles, with a wail nestled within ever so comfortably it almost disappears.

"You'll always have me, mama. Always," says Zariel, kissing the inside of Josephine's wrist where a mole appears haloed by a ring of red and blue. "I've given you a tiny bit of me just now that I will come back for when I return. If you want to talk, to see me, follow the blue and red cord through my mental matrix, and you will find me, and see all the strange things I'll come to see. When I come back, this flower will bloom and call out to me. That's how we'll never be apart."

Josephine smiles while every hair of her arms and the nape of her neck stand straight up and the goosebumps she experiences become legion. As Josephine's fears of her own beloved child spreads throughout her body, she feels her short afro fall out in large chunks, and her eyebrows too grow smooth and bare, as a searing pain runs through her eyes, quenched by rose-colored, blood-stained tears.

"Now, only I will know who you really are, mama. You'll be safe from this world. You can look like whomever you want, whomever anybody wants you to be," says Zariel, gleeful in robbing Josephine of her own image.

As Josephine crumples like an origami crane, staring into a nearby puddle at the flecks of red and gold in the bright new jewel-like golden eyes she never asked for, Zariel and Azhura-Semnu disappear like a nightmare.

The Last Flesh Figure Skaters

Claire Jia-Wen

THE FIRST TIME I saw you, you laced up your skates, adjusted your knee mods, and I was just another unremarkable face as you fluttered to the ice. My mother snapped at me to watch you, but it was like asking a mallard to observe a flamingo. Our legs didn't work the same. You'd been competing across the national circuit, in Boston and Orlando and Frisco, and this was my first competition.

They whispered that you were trained in China, where they apparently install the bionics under the skin rather than above it, flouting the bans on invasive mod tech. No matter that your parents were Singaporean. It was a comforting idea, that you were a china doll android, face painted into a smile and body preprogrammed to succeed. To replace. Maybe they would have said the same about me, if I was any good.

I placed second in my flight (three flights beneath yours) and Coach was extremely pleased, as was my mother—she even took me out for sushi afterward.

The women at the table next to us kept shooting us dirty looks. I was confused until I saw the signs folded against their tables. They were part of the group always protesting outside the rink; their signs said KEEP METAL OUT OF KIDS and SPORTS ARE A HUMAN ENDEAVOR.

How silly, I thought. The mods weren't in us. Noninvasive meant they were only structural support for our joints and optimizers for our muscles, pressurizing to keep oxygen-rich blood gushing through our veins, contracting to limit muscle oscillation, redirecting energy for the most efficient slices.

As I draped my napkin over my lap, the sound of a knife sharpening escaped the kitchen. It reminded me of the slice of your skates. I thought of you that whole dinner: the bend of your wrist, the delicate splay of your fingers, the way your smile tightened after two consecutive triple axels.

Triple axels were once a moonshot for seasoned Olympians. You were two human endeavors in one—the desire to outdo, outperform, outskate; the creativity to design technology that would let us do it.

The next day, I asked Coach if I could have the same model of mods as you. It was a desire born of aesthetics rather than function. I liked the way the metal veins snaked up your calves. He refused—rightly. I shudder to think what would have happened if I moved off the impact absorption joints before I had proper form instilled in my muscle memory. But at that moment, I was incensed. I didn't care if the mods broke my body, as long as it looked like yours.

Ironically, I hated yours as soon as I tried them—BionIces are, if I'm going to be honest, more pretty than practical, for anyone who's not you. Only you could convert that diffused energy to explosiveness. The rest of us plebeians opt for something more supportive, with less facetious advertising; the ad-copters make BionIces look so comfortable.

To my mother's great joy, you only lived a few cities away from me. Every LA county comp, she could point at you. That's what hard work looks like, she'd say.

It got worse when our mothers became friends, taking every comp as an opportunity to jabber away in Cantonese at the top of the bleachers. That was when you became truly inescapable. At home, my mother would get off the phone with yours and come straight to my room, asking did I know you spent three hours at the rink before school, and that you had bought a new training apparatus so you could stretch before bed? I learned that you struggled in history, that your brother's journalism gig had gotten automated by the latest lamBERT model, and that you cried after you jokingly told him to switch to figure skating (for job stability) and he threw a plate at you. I knew when you had your first period. Your mother was worried that so much figure skating had frozen your eggs or something— did ginseng soup actually have menstrual stimulation effects, she asked. You were pieced to me like this, from the lips of mothers who didn't know where they ended and their children began, who felt their pain earnestly enough to claim ownership of it, gossiping rights included.

We knew each other without ever exchanging a word, but you formalized our relationship in speech anyway in Arcadia, while we waited for the previous flight to get off the warmup rink. Do you think you could beat me, you asked, which, for the record, is an *insane* thing to say to someone. When I didn't reply (or did I give a half-hearted grunt?), you continued, I think I could beat you.

You did beat me. But it was close; I think you knew it would be. I suspected it bothered you, to see my face right beneath yours on the holo-boards, to watch me clamber to the podium before you, when I wouldn't have even made top twenty a year ago.

Then you confirmed it bothered you when you debuted your quadruple loop at the next comp. After my celebration dinner—for second place, again—I forced my mother to drive me to the rink. I had your loop down by midnight; I know my mother told yours. Did she also tell you that I had to switch to a clunky pair of Bing-gus to get to the car, because my overstimulated right thigh gave out entirely?

You didn't acknowledge my existence until you had to. Until I was a threat. Your eyes would linger on me, flicker downward to investigate my body. I wasn't like you, faithful to your shimmering BionIces. My mods changed with every routine. Plyman's for propulsion, Auroras for precision, Bing-gus for comfort in the earlier rounds I now breezed through. I'll tell you a secret: I used suboptimal configurations, sometimes, just to keep you guessing.

At some point, I was invited to try pair skating. Coach didn't say it, but I knew the reasoning: he wanted a *champion,* and I would never place first in singles so long as I was in proximity to you. My partner was a rink favorite. Coach was convinced that I and this jaguar-bodied boy could sweep nationals, if we could adapt to each other. But I didn't want to adapt to him. Not when I could adapt to you.

I went frame by frame over your breakthrough Seattle quintuple loop, angling the holo to examine your every crevice, your every strained sinew as you arced off the ice. I took this mold of your body and poured mine into it, until my form could be overlaid upon yours with zero error. I perfected my spins. Set a record for airtime, too. It wasn't the breakthrough in physicality or mod tech the newscomms made it out to be. You know as I do: at our intensity, it's not about whether you *can;* it's about whether you trust yourself to, whether you can smash a max propulsion foot against the ice and trust your wanting is strong enough to keep your bone from splintering.

I would have beaten you too, I *know* I would have beaten you, if they hadn't released the arm mods. In retrospect, we should have thought it odd that BionIces and then all the others went to the trouble of developing a bionic that didn't add much utility. If anything, they weighed us down. I remember complaining that mod developers were treating noninvasive as a limit to be pushed, a competition parallel to ours, using our endeavor as a prop to showcase theirs. Do they really think people tune in to see the shiniest new elbow brace, I said. They'll put us in suits of armor next. But your mentor, the Olympic-skater-turned-BionIces-endorser, told you to wear them. So I wore them too. Did you even bother to check the holo-boards after that, or did you just march to the top podium?

I wasn't sure if I wanted to pursue a career in this. I'm not a gambler by nature, and forestalling an education, romance, and family for a near certainty of going down as a mote in skating history … well. Then your mother called up mine, mourning that you were switching to homeschooling to go pro (apparently the figure skating had only been meant as a means to game the college admissions system) and soon there were two mourning mothers. I couldn't have lived with myself, knowing I turned down the chance to maneuver you off the podium and plant myself there in your stead.

Our sponsorship deals were announced very close to each other—already, the press was drooling for its next great rivalry. You signed with BionIces, of course. I had more options. A bidding war erupted around my sponsorship; I chose Aurora, because they forked over three times the salary of the highest paid basketball player. An unsustainable model, to throw so much money at a skater uncut on the professional circuit, but what would I have done, even if I knew better?

Our first pro comp, you got first. You were last on the ice, and you looked bored. You knew by then that you were a seventeen-year-old Sirius and the rest of us comets. I didn't even make it into your orbit; I wasn't anywhere near the podium.

I thought it was my mother, coming into the bathroom to comfort me. But it was you.

God, how can I describe seeing you in that moment? Vines of silver so intimately acquainted with your skin, the cold clinging to your residual goosebumps—even after we're done with the rink, it's never done with us.

Sometime over the years, you had learned to apply eyeliner with a steadier hand, and it cut severely across your face.

Lose the arm mods, you told me. Did you say it out of respect for the sport, so as not to let mediocrity fester? Or were you simply too used to having me close to you, our names always uttered in the same breath, my face beside yours on the holo-boards, merging entirely when you tilted your head just so?

I never wore arm mods again. Aurora sent me missives to put them back on. They cut my money by half—funny, considering how much better I was doing. Leading up to Worlds, all of figure skating condensed into a single narrative: you and me.

We were everywhere. Montreal. Vienna. Oslo. Sydney. Time became amorphous, days and nights flickering in and out at random, but there was one constant: you, towering above me, your gold medals winking. Your pink sweatpants meant I was at the right airport gate, bound for the next country in the babble of locations that had long congealed in my memory—or to LAX.

Home for us both. When my mother's heart grew too arrhythmic to accompany me, you remained my Polaris, gleaming two rows away, tens of thousands of feet above the ground. Our mothers took the train together to the airport, gossiping as they waited for us, the same anxious face copied from one and pasted on the other. The same scoldings, too. We were amazing, and their friends were always asking for tips on rearing successful children, but were we *trying* to scare them out of their minds, hitting the ice like that?

We were long past quintuple loops; now, we made history each time our skates ground onto the ice, our braids of muscle and wire converting hypotheticals into impossible realities. I took my airtime record back. I debuted the sextuple axel. There wasn't even a word yet for what you did. They would have named it after you, but the announcers never did learn how to say your name properly. It became the spiral, but we all know it was your monument.

Worlds ended in a tie. A perfect tie. Along the singular dimension of the number line, we occupied the same space, fitted and fused together. For our efforts, Team USA won three spots in the Olympics. The third eventually went to some nice blonde, but come on. She didn't matter.

I found you in the hotel bar that night. I didn't think you the type for a cosmo, but your jaw dropped when I ordered a straight shot. I ordered four more, because I wanted to shock you, and nothing I did on the ice could have that effect on you anymore; one-upmanship was our only language.

The bar's holo-screen was tuned to the competition's closing event, a demonstration of the next-gen mod prototype. Injective mods, metal displacing flesh. I'd been sent tickets for front row seats. You must have, too. Neither of us asked the other why she'd elected for a wobbling bar stool instead.

You said, sometimes I think I'm perpetuating a stereotype. The Asian automaton, like the moving geisha dolls in those old movies. I'm half wires already. I'm a technology. And I don't want figure skating to be a technology.

You hiccupped.

It's not really a problem until it's a trend, I said. Which means there can only be one of us.

Oh, fuck them, you said, and kissed me.

Were you the one who leaked the bar photo? I didn't have reason to believe it at the time, but I later found out (through my mother, if you can believe it) that you'd quarreled with your mother the previous night. She wanted you to stop destroying your body for national spectacle and settle down with a nice man after the Olympics. You wanted to wreck her. I don't agree with your reasoning, but I do admire your methods.

I convinced myself that if I tied with you again, you would kiss me again. I thought a lot about what you'd do if I beat you. I thought about it every time I crashed onto the ice—somehow, the impact at once reawakens every bruise you've ever gotten—and just wanted to lie there, lullabied by the hiss of skates against ice.

The ISU legalized a slew of outrageously dangerous elements—including lifting the ban on invasive techniques—ahead of the Olympics. They claimed that the recent advancements in mod tech warranted a higher ceiling to encourage healthy competitiveness, but they were scared we would tie again. The next-gen mod tech was never even implemented, thanks to you.

You were called a hypocrite for that op-ed. Injective mods have no place in competitive figure skating, you wrote. There is a difference between technology-enhanced performance and doped-up cyborgs.

I was asked for comment. The reporter was gleeful, waiting for me to add to the chorus calling my rival a hypocrite, a gatekeeper, a closeted luddite, among less savory things; all that, because you'd stated the obvious, that mods were supposed to serve us, not reconstitute us. I said: if the ISU legalizes injective mods, I won't skate the Olympics. And if I don't skate the Olympics, there won't be an Olympics.

Unwilling to admit it, newscomms reported that revenue blossomed around the upcoming Olympics, as if skeleton racing or alpine skiing or, God forbid, curling, were raking in dollars. But it was our dolls selling, books and films of us in production, our likenesses smiling down from every ad-copter and ImmerScreen. Somehow, two girls from the sunny suburbs of Southern California captured the attention of the world. I read the tell-all about us. Did you know that, apparently, your favorite food is pickled shark fin and my deadbeat father walked back into my life at my new figure skating fame?

I remember very little of the Olympics themselves. I remember I was in the air longer than I was on the ice. I remember not breathing once through your entire routine. Oh, and I remember we both skated to Prokofiev: you to Juliet's theme and I to Romeo's.

I stood atop the highest podium. You were gracious in your defeat. We'll have more Olympics, you told me as we lined up for the medal ceremony. At least one more. I'm owed my victory, you said.

Only, you were wrong.

We both know it wouldn't have happened if you hadn't spent your life insisting on BionIces—the tradeoff between support and explosiveness is not an equal one. I entered one more comp after you retired, just to show how useless it would be for me to continue. I skated by the old rules, and it was still a bulldoze.

I don't regret quitting, even twenty years later, as I lay beside you now. Our ImmerScreen is tuned to the sports channel—we have been promised prime entertainment tonight, something to reinvigorate audiences to the fervor when we skated the circuits. I am doubtful, but perhaps my arrogance blinds me. I am a rather devoted adherent to our mythology.

A skating rink clarifies into view. A figure flutters to the ice, and my heart stutters, because it's *you*. The way you skated is inscribed on my bones. You were hesitant (just barely, darling) around the ten o'clock wall because a boy had bumped you into it, as your mother had complained. You tightened your jaw after an upright spin, because you'd pulled your abductor in middle school, and it didn't heal quite right. I always paid close attention to your backflips, so I could catch you flex your hand afterward, tendons flashing into visibility.

Then the figure does a quintuple spiral. Prokofiev leaks from the speakers.

On an adjacent screen, a representative from BionIces is speaking. These SafeSmart Skaters are the product of years and years of work, he says. Countless skaters have generously contributed their abilities to their development; our company's mods have empowered those skaters and given us the data to hone these androids.

After he's done, the representative from Aurora comes up to introduce their robot—sorry, *SafeSmart Skater.*

So that was why they wanted me to wear arm mods so badly, I realize, noting the disjointed arm movements of Aurora's skater. Not enough training data. Not enough of me in her. These skaters ape you and me so closely: twenty years after we left the ice, there have been none of our caliber. And the poor SafeSmart Skaters cannot invent their own maneuvers, so they pastiche the best.

No wonder our sponsorships paid so much. They were buying out the market. We should have known: the same way we sorted those CAPTCHA images to train autonomous cars, and actors let ad corps take facial scans for easy reanimation, and we gave up our words to lamBERT to hone our search results—our artform would also be fed into the machine by the unwilling hands of those who loved it most.

When I glance at you, your face is serene. I say, This is what you were afraid of, isn't it? That they would make you into technology. How can you be so calm?

Oh, it's terrible, you say, then laugh. I'm not technology. People didn't watch us to see how high a humanoid can jump. They watched because I debuted a spin two weeks after you debuted yours. They watched because I kissed you.

This is a revolution in figure skating, the Aurora rep says. We can marvel at feats of human ingenuity, without the accompanying fear of injury.

You shift, and I massage your aching knee.

The fear of injury was not a problem to be solved; it was our whole lives. It was how we declared our devotion. We invented life-threatening maneuvers and destroyed cautionary rules—reconfigured figure skating itself—to find the most precise words, the prettiest letters. I did not skate to Prokofiev because Prokofiev routines statistically have a hundred percent chance of winning. I skated to Prokofiev because you existed, and I needed to do something about it.

It's beautiful, in a way. Forever, these skaters will simply reiterate our intertwining, Aurora borrowing my voice to say *I love you* without knowing who I am or that I am saying it to you; every etching of the skates into the ice is poetry in an ink only you and I can make meaning of.

A Book Is a Map, a Bed Is a Country

Angel Leal

N MY TÍO's old room, I'm looking for a book made of water.

He used to keep it under his pillow and read from it a story full of storms and men made of seafoam. I noticed that I was never thirsty after he read to me. My stomach felt full, and I usually dreamed of drowning next to him in a grand shipwreck.

But the book wasn't always made of water. For a few years, it was made of plants clumped together in a knot. That was when I started growing tomates in my sleep and waking up with seeds in my hands. I'd jump out of bed and run to him like a little fool.

And in a flash, he would gather me up and listen to a child's musings as though they were saint-like and wise. As if I was the poet of seeds, he followed me to the garden and obeyed my every wish of where to plant and where to tunnel his brown hands down.

❖

A LITTLE LATER in our life, the book seemed to be made of only paper.

My tío still read it to me, but now it read like an impossible map. It named and displayed every face and bird and river he found as a boy in México. It described intimate memories long dead in my tío like when he saw his father crying behind their orange tree. Tío nudged me awake to show the tender illustration of his trembling father as well as the long shadow cast by the tree and the number of fruits still hanging on it.

The topography of the map was impressive, and I started to appreciate the thoughtful footnotes that filled us in whenever we were baffled.

One note was particularly precious and useful to me. It was a lifelike sketch of a textile factory in Coahuila that had burned down. Crowds of workers were weeping in the street and among them was a tall man with a unibrow and beautiful eyes.

"Apá," my tío sighed, and he squeezed my hand like a child with a fever.

He told me how he was so young, no one told him anything real. It didn't make any sense why they were leaving for America. Why they could abandon the land where he learned to dream for a place where he would need English to live? Childhood was over.

The map took the time to depict the place where my tío started to change and feel afraid of change. There was a little river where he once caught a fish with his bare hands. He tried for hours to do it again, but they slipped out and eluded him until he cried from frustration.

The map noted that this failure would one day remind the boy of trying to learn English. My tío turned over in bed after we read that and said the room was too hot and could I turn on the fan to max strength and let him sleep?

I did, but when I slipped out, I stayed by the door and saw from an open sliver my lonely tío, still awake, obsessing over the marvelous map on his own.

◈

TO BE HONEST, my tío was the type of person who didn't understand the middle of life. He understood well the aching mountains of childhood, where all things are impossibly larger than you, and you are nobody, and you are nowhere near the land where work happens and marriage and love are expected. He understood too the solemnity and slowness of old age, the quiet ways people take away your responsibilities and cease to expect you to fall in love. But the middle of life, what many consider *life* was a great and painful confusion to him. He avoided speaking of that era of his and eventually began to avoid me when I approached it myself. That was unfortunate because he was like a father by then.

I'd followed his steps and his stories and his habits—I was even a bit reclusive myself—but what really connected us was our affection for the book under his pillow. What continued to move me about it was the way it aged with us, the way the book adapted to our needs. When we talked to each other less, for example, the book had more and more to say.

One night, when we hadn't spoken all day, and I'd been staring at my reflection like I didn't like it, I slipped into his room and for some reason he didn't ask me to leave. He almost smiled when he saw me, not exactly happily, but with the satisfaction of knowing what I wanted. He pulled the book out from under his pillow and now it was covered in feathers. It looked like a kind of bird, like it might fly out of his hands.

When he opened it, I saw at first pinned photographs of cardinals and finally small moving images of my tío in his wandering thirties.

I saw his round brown face and sad blue eyes staring at the mouth of another man. It was a lovely man with gentle lips and long eyelashes. They kissed in what looked like an eternal summer, over and over. My tío was completely silent as I watched.

Neither of us made eye contact. We both just looked down at the shifting images and saw young love explore the boundaries of need.

He closed the book when my young tío took his shirt off and the suddenness made the book clap the air with red feathers.

◈

I DIDN'T KNOW what my own body needed, and I didn't understand what had happened to my tío. Did an American boy break his heart, or did his Catholicism break it? Had he ever kissed another man again? Had he ever kissed anyone again? I didn't know but I didn't think so. The man I grew up with hardly left his room anymore. His dark brown walls were covered in crosses and the Virgin of Guadalupe.

Near the end of his life, my tío didn't read to me too much but sometimes I read to him. I'd reach under his pillow when he was having a fitful sleep and find to my comfort and surprise that the book was beginning to attach itself to his bed.

Now he slept on maps of his old country and unsent love letters.

By his feet, I found poems about the sea and by his shoulder I found several failed attempts at rewriting them in English.

Finally, when he had the strength to, he'd lift up his gray head and invariably I would find seeds in his hair. A part of me wanted to instantly bury them in the garden, just to see what strange plants my tío kept in his memory.

But I buried them instead in a little drawer, and only imagined what sweet fruits his body needed to remember.

Now that I'm beginning to understand my history and my own queerness, I'm trying to compile another book made of plants and feathers and elaborate maps.

I start and stop constantly.

One morning, I'll find two birds sitting together during mating season but there is no love being made. They are only singing to the sun, and I'll put them in my book. One night, I'll spy a growth of fungus with so many genders it takes my breath away. I'll caress it into my book, and try to sleep, but I keep missing something.

My map of México is as rudimentary as a child's scrawl. I don't remember its heat and mountains and snaking rivers. I can't even imagine the orange tree where my tío's father wept. Moments like this are when I need him most. I want to ask him again to show me the drawing of the tree's long shadow. I want to count the hanging fruit. I want to see a father's beautiful eyes looking towards his home.

How to Make a Snow Maiden

KRISTINA TEN

OVER FROZEN RUM-A-RITAS in novelty yard glasses, beneath a ceiling crowded with cheeky, neon-painted signs, Kira and Miriam debate what to call the opposite of a babymoon. They've been at Señor Frog's since lunchtime, cycling through umbrella cocktails and orders of jalapeño poppers with queso dip, and the Myrtle Beach daze has settled over them so completely that Kira doesn't think it's remotely stupid when Miriam suggests "moonbaby," and when Kira throws out "adultsun," Miriam gives it serious, near-scholarly consideration. She repeats the word back to Kira, *adultsun*, testing its weight in her mouth, and her brow is furrowed, and the center of her tongue is stained this deep purplish blue. The oversize balloon hat a waiter plopped down on her head hours ago has turned her thin blonde hair into a halo of static cling, and Kira thinks her wife has probably never looked so beautiful, not quite so beautiful as she does right now.

The reason for the rebranding of the babymoon, and the intense consideration with which it's being conducted, is that, well, you can't have a babymoon without the baby. It's right there in the name. Miriam told Kira so a thousand times, in a thousand different places, after the adoption agency called with the news. She told her at the library where Kira works, in the hushed tones that libraries demand, and on the train back to Roxbury, where she had to yell to be heard over the clacking of the tracks. Seemed glad for the excuse to yell, to not hold back, actually. In the end, it was those places exactly, and Kira and Miriam's absolute need to get away from them, that made them decide to go after all. In particular, it was their apartment, where everything had been rearranged, their bed pushed into a corner, their desks crammed in side by side, all so the spare room could be turned into a nursery. Where everything had been assembled and triple-checked for sturdiness. Where whole days had been lost to paint swatch comparisons: moonmist or flaxseed, lemon or dandelion.

That and the plane tickets, booked months ago, turned out to be nonrefundable.

And honestly? The all-inclusive resort? With the lazy river running through the lobby and the front desk attendant who introduced himself as the *funcierge*? It worked. Because this past week, Boston has felt so far away. So impossibly, necessarily far away that Kira has begun to suspect that Myrtle Beach isn't just the farthest, spiritually, that you can get from *Boston*, but that it's the farthest, spiritually, that you can get from *anywhere*. And this is maybe the best thing about Myrtle Beach, more than its four-hundred-plus hotels or its sixty miles of shoreline or whatever: its bald refusal to recognize that which lies beyond its limits.

Even now, at Señor Frog's, on the last day of their trip, as Boston and all that awaits them there threatens to encroach on their good time, Myrtle Beach says: no. Myrtle Beach says: who goes there? Myrtle Beach says

happy hour starts in twenty, with half-off appetizers and
two-for-one drinks at any of the restaurant's—count 'em—
five bars.

Myrtle Beach says noomybab.

No, *Miriam* says noomybab. "Because this is all so
backwards," she says, meaning they were so close and
now they're right back where they started. And she knows
these things happen sometimes, the agency said these
things happen sometimes, the birth mother can decide
right up until the very last minute. It's a risk, they said. It's
all outlined in the contract. A risk but a calculated one.
Unlikely but not impossible.

Suddenly, the loudspeaker crackles and, with the
practiced enthusiasm of a place open 365 days a year, even
during that category-three hurricane, even on Christmas,
it announces that it's officially happy hour. Thanks, Myrtle
Beach. Perfect timing.

Really, Myrtle Beach is turning out to be everything
they hoped when they picked it over Sedona, over Santa
Fe, thinking this was their chance to make up for the
classic spring break they both missed out on in college.
There've been oyster bars and a cappella tribute concerts
at the House of Blues, motorcycle rallies and ziplines
through the tops of palm trees, that after-dark walking
tour where the guide claimed drowned sailors still haunt
the employees-only section of the Hard Rock Cafe.

There was, too, the way the salt clung to Miriam's
shoulders after a dip in the ocean, the tiny bikini she
bought at one of the dozens of stores on the strip that sold
tiny bikinis, just because she thought it was ridiculous, the
kind of thing she would never wear back home. And when
Kira begged her, later in the hotel room, for a runway
show, and Miriam obliged, it was because she wanted Kira
to do that cheesy but sweet thing she sometimes does: say
her name with the emphasis on the last syllable, drawing it
out extra long, like "Miri-*yummm*."

Now it's Sunday. They've been to the wax museum three times and the Pirates Voyage dinner show twice, they're on a first-name basis with the barista at their hotel Starbucks, and at this very moment, karaoke's in full swing on the second floor of Señor Frog's.

And aren't the past and future silly things to think about when one is sitting in a chair with its back molded to look like a butt wearing polka-dot bikini bottoms? Which both Kira and Miriam are. So they don't.

Think, that is.

What they do is build a frozen cocktail girl.

It's a joke, mostly. A continuation of the long joke that this whole week has been. Kira watches a waiter in a red apron carry a platter full of cocktails from the bar, and her first thought is: why red? It makes her think of a butcher, or a serial murderer. Her second thought has to do with the towering concoction he sets down on the table next to theirs.

It's some kind of daiquiri: balls of shaved ice, violently pink, topped with whipped cream and a diced strawberry. And it could be the way the ice is stacked, or the way the strawberry slices, from a certain angle, look almost like a pair of parted lips. Or it could be that these days, one hundred percent, Kira's got kids on the brain. But something cuts through the stale, sticky haze of their final happy hour in Myrtle Beach. A memory from Kira's childhood. A story someone once told her.

About the snow maiden, Snegurochka.

When she asks Miriam if she's heard it, Miriam laughs so hard the table shakes and the little paper umbrella tips sideways out of her glass.

"The one about the old couple who can't have a baby so they build one out of snow? Kind of like, um, Jack Frost, right?"

Kira's pretty sure the origins of Snegurochka predate those of Jack Frost, but she's not going to go all Boston Public Library assistant librarian, Copley Square branch, on Miriam right now. Because right now, there's a familiar glint in Miriam's eyes, a spark that's been her signature since their days together at BU. A spark that Kira worried had gone out the moment the agency called, but that Myrtle Beach, of all places, seems to be rekindling bit by bit.

A spark that Kira knows means mischief.

A spark that you know, you just *know*, she's going to fan.

"Sure," she shrugs, "and it works. More than one way to make a baby." She doesn't bring up what happens to Snegurochka in all the stories, and she hopes Miriam never learned the endings.

Miriam stares at her wife for a long minute, using the wooden part of her paper umbrella as a toothpick. Finally, she flashes a coy smile. "Well, it's faster than filing new paperwork."

If you're going to order a dozen tropical drinks and dump their contents onto the table, then start sculpting those contents into the shape of your would-be daughter, the late-afternoon rush at Señor Frog's is the time and place to do it. Their waiter bounces ping-pong-like between tables, too busy to notice them. There's a large group in family reunion T-shirts arguing about how many nacho platters to get for the table. There's a youth volleyball team with a tight-lipped coach trying fervently to track down a low-carb menu. There's a bachelorette party wearing matching silk sashes and one of them's leaning over to ask another if she's sure, absolutely sure, that this is the place where the staff gives lap dances between courses. A group of frat guys stumble onto the stage sing-shouting the opening lines of "Sweet Caroline," and every time there's feedback on the mic, a pair of fussy twins in high chairs at the back of the room begin to screech.

In the middle of it all there's Kira and Miriam, and they've set the garnishes off to the side for later, and they're trying to get the slope of her neck just right. And if anyone notices what they're up to, or cares, they keep it to themselves. After all, the drinks are paid for and Kira's tab is open, and really is the mess they're making any worse than that of the high-chair twins, who at this very moment are finger painting their trays with fat globs of ketchup? Maybe that's why the red aprons, Kira realizes. That would make sense.

Empty glasses stacked by the legs of their chairs to make room, their girl stretches long and wide across the table's surface. They build her lying on her back, because they figure building her straight up, snowman-style, would take a whole lot more ice, more frozen drinks than they could reasonably order. More than they should be paying for, even—there's a reason they're in Myrtle Beach and not, say, Santorini. So they build her lying down, with one blended-ice arm and one blended-ice leg reaching for Kira's side of the table, and the other arm and leg reaching toward Miriam. She's mostly frozen mudslides and Froggy Ritas, with a pour of Bahama Mama on each cheek to give her that fruit-punch flush. Her hair is sections of pineapple rind artfully pieced together, her mouth a thick orange slice, and her eyes two basil leaves, one much bigger than the other. Somewhere around where her ears might be, Miriam drapes a pair of maraschino cherries like dangly earrings.

After working in quiet concentration for half an hour, Kira and Miriam lean back from the table, up to their elbows in simple syrup and blue curaçao, and survey their creation. Her unchanging expression. Her mismatched, iris-less, basil-leaf eyes.

Miriam looks at Kira, and Kira back at Miriam.

Finally, Miriam whispers, "She's terrifying."

The two burst out laughing. They take turns yanking napkins from the silver dispenser, starting the hard job of scrubbing the sticky mess from their hands. Balls of used napkins pile high on one corner of the table and litter their laps. But even though Kira makes a joke about how they're probably too old for this, and Miriam makes a joke about how she can't believe they're going to get kicked out of this place before the frat guys, neither of them gets up. And after the last of their embarrassed chuckles die down, both turn their gaze to the frozen girl between them.

Waiting for—what? Waiting for something.

Maybe for the waiter to come back so they can apologize profusely. Offer to clean up, to do the dishes themselves, to leave the kind of tip that says: "We just don't know what came over us, two self-respecting women who have jobs and a Roomba and who hardly ever, we promise, play with our food."

Or maybe something else. Maybe waiting for the breeze from the Atlantic to waft in through the windows and rustle one of the basil leaves, just a little, or nudge the orange-slice mouth into a crooked smile.

But the music blares on, and no one pays them any mind. A few tables over, their waiter is explaining to the volleyball coach about the chicken taco salad, how it's pretty low-carb, he guesses, if you don't eat the taco part.

And the frozen girl looks as lifeless as ever. Except that, after a while, she does move, in a way.

She melts.

Which is what happens in all the Snegurochka stories, of course. The snow maiden gets hot from skipping through the forest trying to keep up with her new human friends. Or she falls in love with the neighbor boy, a shepherd who warms her ice-cold heart till it's a puddle on the ground. The old couple mourns their melted daughter for the rest of their lives, which are unmercifully long, and it's not true what they say about fairy tales, that they all end happily ever after.

It takes a drop of piña colada falling onto Kira's sandaled foot to get her to tear her eyes from the table. When she looks up at Miriam, she regrets bringing this whole thing up at all.

She can't tell if her wife's face is red like it's been all week, from sunburning over sunburn, then getting a butterfly painted on her cheek at the boardwalk and later scrubbing it raw over the hotel sink, or extra red like it gets when she's trying hard not to cry.

The frat guys on stage finally take their bows and immediately Kira misses them, in part out of some reflexive New England loyalty to "Sweet Caroline" and in part because she's come to love the frat guys. Not these frat guys in particular but all of Myrtle Beach's frat guys in general, and how they represent to her a totally different, totally carefree stage of life.

Her stage of life, and Miriam's, being the stage where you go back to Boston and tell your family and friends how it all fell through. And you tell work you won't be needing the maternity leave after all, and you try to decide if the nursery furniture, because it's been assembled, counts as used or not. And oh, my god, Kira's going to have to call off the playdates she's already scheduled with the neighbors. And she's going to have to tell her mom's friend, Knows-Everyone Nancy, that they don't need her to call in that favor about the preschool after all, Kira having gotten way ahead of herself again, like Miriam tells her she always does.

Suddenly the signs on the ceiling—"Boring customers pay double!", "My reality check bounced!"—don't feel amusingly cheeky but claustrophobic, the way they loom overhead, shouting in all caps, threatening to tumble down at any moment and take the whole building with them. And the music on the loudspeakers feels not festive but deafening, and the conga line that's formed in front of the stage fills Kira with dread, looks like it's coming right for them. Looks too much like an umbilical cord, an IV tube. A snake.

"I'm sorry," Miriam sniffs, flustered. She pushes the heels of her hands into her eye sockets, knocking her balloon hat slightly askew. "This is stupid. This was just a fun thing. Supposed to be a fun thing. For the vacation highlights reel or whatever. And I'm making it weird. Obviously she's not going to *come alive*. Shit." She waves her hands over the table, the colors in the icy sludge swirling together now, like she's trying to magic it away. "Not *she*. It. *It*."

Kira chews her bottom lip, folds and unfolds her hands in her lap. Finally, she says quietly, "It's not stupid, you know."

Miriam looks up. "What?"

Kira sighs. "It's just, okay. We kind of half-assed it, is all. Cause technically, if we wanted to do this the *right* way, we wouldn't use alcohol, right? Alcohol makes ice melt faster. If the old couple, or the kid who built Jack Frost or whatever, had used snow full of alcohol, no way that would have worked."

Miriam lifts an eyebrow like she's wondering at what point during this vacation did she accidentally sign up for chemistry lab, but what she says out loud is, "Sure. I guess that makes sense."

"And the other thing—" Kira winces. "The other thing is that, well, according to the stories, to make something human, you need something human."

Miriam nods slowly. "I think I've heard this one before. *When a man and a woman really love one another...*"

Kira rolls her eyes and smiles. "Not like that. I mean, in some of the stories, the couple doesn't just use snow. At the end, they also put in blood." She pauses. "And bones."

Miriam's eyes go wide.

"Just chickens usually," Kira explains quickly. "They keep chickens. Or sometimes, I don't know. Other things. A stray dog or cat. I only remember one story where they go to the graveyard to dig some up."

Miriam lets out a low whistle. "That's *dark*, man. That's too much." But over her eyes passes that familiar glint.

Which is how it really is, Kira knows, with fairy tales. They can be dark and happy all at once, or if not happy then at least familiar in a way that feels comfortable. Which is how it's been in Myrtle Beach too. Happy, generally, more or less, with breezy cabanas and shrimp cocktails and a hotel room with a light-up hot tub right in the middle, like, right there between the balcony and the king-size bed.

But there have been other parts too. Parts that wouldn't exactly fit in with the sunny snapshots on Myrtle Beach's tourism website.

Like on Wednesday, when they passed one of those shops that'll airbrush any design you want onto a T-shirt, and the headless mannequin in the front display was wearing a teeny crop top, and beneath its hem you could see the curve of two breasts, plastic pale and cracking. And Kira made some comment like, "Eesh, that could fit a freakin' toddler." And they both fell silent, that word, *toddler*, rattling around the echo chambers of their minds. They both fell silent and they stayed silent the rest of the way to dinner at Joe's Crab Shack, then all through dinner, then the rest of the night.

Or on Thursday, when they were supposed to go to the water park and probably piss themselves at the top of Summit Plummet, but Miriam got an emergency call from work, some shipping delay out of Hong Kong, total PR nightmare, so Kira went alone. And the plan was to meet on the strip for a late lunch and shopping, but Kira never showed. Just kept going down this one water slide, not even an especially fun or daredevil one, but this pretty short, pretty straight dark tunnel that started in one big pear-shaped pool and shot out into another. Into still, warm water. Bright, blinding light. Kept climbing up to wait, go down again. Into the bright light, the fresh start. Some new life so different from this one.

Or late Friday, back in their hotel room, when she caught Miriam standing sideways in front of the bathroom mirror with the bottom of her shirt tucked into her bra. She had her shoulders pushed back and her hips out, her palms resting on either side of her stomach. When Kira turned the corner, Miriam quickly pulled her shirt down. "Too much salt at dinner," she explained, "Food baby," and she played a little drumbeat on her belly and laughed. And Kira said softly, "Miriam." And Miriam replied, "Kira." And Kira said, "*Miriam*," and Miriam snapped, "*Stop*. Jesus Christ. For once, can't you know when to stop?"

That night, after her wife had gone to sleep, Kira snuck down to the boardwalk to ride the SkyWheel, half-wishing that it would get stuck with her car at the top. More than half-wishing, probably. So she could look out at all the people, all the noisy, sparkly, coconut-scented activity of Myrtle Beach. Pouring out of the bars, into the music venues. People everywhere. So many people. The world was lousy with them. How could anyone want for more?

This is how.

This is how you make a snow maiden.

For real this time.

Take two parts—okay, four garbage bags full of—crushed ice from your hotel floor's ice machine, plus one part—that's two orders of—chicken wings from the late-night menu at the bar downstairs. Check with the bartender to make sure they're not boneless and listen for three minutes to his rant about did you know boneless wings don't even come from the wings of a chicken, can you believe that, kind of false advertising if you think about it, et cetera. Three minutes, not a second more. Then lug it all down to the beach across the way. It's after dark so nobody asks questions. You could be anyone, *can* be anyone in Myrtle Beach: restaurant employees taking out the trash after their shift, or sorority sisters at Coastal Carolina on some sort of initiation task, or volunteers for one of those environmental organizations, shore cleanup or whatever, staying late to finish the job.

That's in Myrtle Beach, you can be anyone. At home, in Boston, no way. In Boston, starting tomorrow, you're the couple for whom it didn't Work Out. You're the recipients of uneasy glances and sympathy cards. When your sister-in-law gets pregnant, you're the last to find out, because honestly she was kind of dreading the conversation, honestly she never knows how you're going to react. Starting tomorrow, you're the annoying customers at the returns counter at Pottery Barn Kids at Natick Mall.

In Myrtle Beach, though, you can be anyone. And it's after dark, so nobody asks questions. Still, you look kind of suspicious dragging four garbage bags of crushed ice and a Styrofoam box of chicken wings across one of Myrtle Beach's busiest streets. So do try to get it all in one trip.

Ice to fill her out. Bones to hold her up. Seaweed, braided, for the hair. Pebble eyes and purple cockleshell ears.

You find a couple of seagull feathers for the lips.

The blood, though, will have to be yours.

Kira works furiously, knees digging trenches into the sand. Something about the absurdity of the mission has sent a surge of adrenaline coursing through her, and it's cut through the weeklong buzz, leaving her eyes clear and determined. She pulls the ice from the bags in large fistfuls, lays down a foundation, then builds higher and higher. One mound after another. Snowman-style this time. Two feet tall. Three feet, four. Miriam molds as she goes, adding careful details: the stitching in her dress, the barely noticeable bump in the profile of her nose. When they've finished, they strip the chicken meat off the bones, and their hands, pink and near numb from the ice, turn slick and orange with Buffalo sauce.

Not speaking, hardly breathing, they press the bones into her arms, her legs, her back—a skeleton to make their daughter strong. To help her stand up straight, walk through life with confidence.

Because it would have been a girl, had the call from the agency never come, Miriam frets extra over the seaweed hair. She drapes it to one side, then the other. Tucks it behind the seashell ears.

Finally, Kira stands and pulls from her back pocket something flat, smooth, and circular: a souvenir pin they picked up at one of the boardwalk gift shops days ago. It's cheap laminated plastic, not one of those nice enamel ones, already looks a little sun-faded. On the front, there's a picture of a blue anchor and an orange safety tube with a rope between them, and on the back there's the silver pin, tucked neatly into its clasp. Kira frees the pin with one hand and raises the other, curling her four fingers into her palm so it appears, to anyone on the shore that night, so innocent—like she's giving Miriam a thumbs-up.

Then she pushes the sharp point into her skin.

The blood beads quickly to the surface, and in the moonlight it looks not red but black, deep and mesmerizing. It reminds Kira of the squid ink pasta they had earlier that week at Lombardo's, the way they got all dressed up, how black-hole dark the pasta looked against the white of the tablecloth. And what their waiter told them, about how squids release ink into the water when they feel threatened, when they're trying to escape, desperate not to fall prey to whatever's coming fast for them.

She brings her thumb to the maiden's mouth, and only then does her blood reveal itself as such. When the crushed ice between the seagull feathers turns pink, soaking it all up.

"So that's everything, huh?" Miriam asks.

"All I can think of," Kira replies.

They walk the dozen or so feet to the water and wash their hands in the cold Atlantic. The saltwater stings the pinprick on Kira's thumb and she thinks that it feels right actually, finally, to have some of the hurt made physical.

This concentrated wound, short-lived and simple. If you can point to it, it's easier to explain.

They sit cross-legged together in front of the maiden, far enough away that they can see the whole of her, but close enough that, when they squint, they can just make out the freckles scattered across her cheeks. These Miriam added at the last minute with the souvenir pin, after wiping the blood off the metal tip. They watch the maiden sometimes, and other times they watch the ocean lap the shore behind her, on its way to low tide.

Eventually, Miriam breaks the silence. "What should we name her?"

Kira leans her head against her wife's shoulder. "You know, a wise woman once told me to quit getting so ahead of myself."

Miriam laughs. Her thin blonde hair is tangled and clumped together with sweat and sand, and it clings to her forehead and the sides of her face, and on the bridge of her nose there's a stripe of wing sauce that she must not realize is there. And Kira thinks she was wrong earlier, dead wrong, about Miriam in that stupid balloon hat at Señor Frog's. Because however beautiful her wife looked then, it was nothing compared to how she looks right now.

The maiden they built? She, too, looks beautiful. But it's the same perfectly still, stiff kind of beautiful, no matter how long they sit there. No matter how long they wait, as the golden squares of the hotel rooms behind them gradually go out.

And maybe it's the booze starting to wear off, but Kira realizes that while it was absolutely quiet the whole time they were building, suddenly the sounds of Myrtle Beach have returned, are rushing to fill the space around them. Inoffensive rock pulsing from one of the few venues on the strip still open. Flyers distributed by club promoters earlier that evening, now fluttering wildly against trash cans and street lights. The waves rolling softly in and out, in and out, like the world is awake and breathing, and a group of good-looking coeds farther down the shore, loudly discussing the difference between alligators and crocodiles.

Kira puts her hands on her knees to steady herself, then pushes herself up to standing. "All right, I officially have Myrtle Beach brain. Time to go home?" She holds a hand out to Miriam, who takes one last look at the maiden.

"What'll happen to her?"

Kira bites her lip. "The sun, or the tide. Whichever comes first." She's always hated the ending.

The maiden's eyes are wet, but of course they are—that's to be expected of a girl made of ice and left outside in eighty-percent humidity. It's nothing more than that, Kira knows. If you wiped her tears with your thumb, if you held your thumb to your tongue, you wouldn't taste salt. You wouldn't taste anything.

Miriam sits there long enough that Kira wonders if she heard her. Then she nods and lets Kira pull her up from the sand.

As they walk away, the alligators-versus-crocodiles people reach the maiden and they've almost figured it out. It's something to do with the snout or the teeth or the jawline, or where they live, or how they stalk their kills. Is one greener than the other? What's the one in *Peter Pan*? But the maiden stops them in their tracks—a spectacular sight in a city that prides itself on its spectacles—and they tap one another on the shoulder, and they fall to a hush and point. A couple of them laugh, like *What on earth*, like *Only in Myrtle Beach*, and a couple others circle her, examining her ersatz buttons, her slimy hair.

Then one pulls a camera out of their bag and snaps.

The camera's flash cuts through the night and a glint passes across the maiden's eyes, two ocean-smoothed pebbles shaped vaguely like almonds. A glint passes across them, then disappears.

Kira and Miriam disappear, too—from Myrtle Beach, that is, and when their flight touches down at Boston Logan it's snowing. They stop keeping time by happy hours and tides, they put the apartment back to normal, their tans fade, and they finally manage to stomach a wine spritzer again, in that order. Miriam's turning her ridiculous tiny bikini into a dishcloth—*so at least it can be useful*—when Kira finds the postcard in their stack of mail.

It's from the barista at the hotel Starbucks, the one with whom they were on a first-name basis. Her name tag said Assistant Manager, but she said they could call her Jen.

Jen's postcard says she misses her party girls, is so glad they exchanged information because, would they believe it, she'll be starting school in Boston in the fall. And she'd love to get together. Or they could come back to Myrtle Beach sooner. There's always something worth seeing in Myrtle Beach. Like, get a load of this newest "point of interest," the postcard says. Popped up overnight not long ago and already it's the talk of the town.

Kira flips the postcard over and yelps. Miriam looks up from her bikini project, eyebrow raised.

On the front is a picture of the maiden, standing right where they left her. It's daylight: blue sky, white sand, blue water. The picture must have been taken after they left. But Kira didn't figure the ice would last the night. How could she still be intact—Kira's eyes flick to the date in the corner—three weeks later?

She looks the same, down to the very last freckle, though somehow taller, and her pebble eyes give off a peculiar shine. There's something about it that Kira recognizes. It reminds her of the spark that shows up in Miriam's eyes sometimes, when her wife's in the mood for mischief. When she feels like getting up to something, and the world seems immense and rich with possibility. When she knows it's all hers for the taking, and she's thinking it feels good, *so* good, to be alive.

❀

The Owl

Stephen M.A.

When the owl came to me, its eight frosted talons gripped our continents, and the atmosphere lapped its ankles like a tide pool. When it lowered its head from orbit, the coma of its face filled the sky above my front porch.

From the day its massive bulk had been spotted rounding Neptune, I'd known matters would come to this, and so they had, here at the final summer solstice.

The owl's pooled green eyes, fixed on mine, blinked with the weight of countless gravities. The susurration of those moving lids fell like rain poured over the splintered Montana home where I had lived for all but two of my eighty-three years. My very ears welcomed such caress, at last, after so much time spent ringing with silent lies.

When the owl spoke, its voice filled my bones, and its words made syrup of the air in their wake. It said, "Child, shall I save your peoples? Some ask this of me, even now, when my task is made inevitable by their own malefaction."

I rocked among creaking teak for a time, and then, from this chair, replied simply.

"Absolutely not."

The owl nodded then, and a great gale issued from such gesture, washed in hissing ripples over fields of verdant barley which had been planted only weeks ago, by folks whose corpses now lay rotting atop this very same soil.

"Tell me why," it said. Then it blinked once more, slowly, and with expectation.

I nodded in kind, and began.

◈

WHEN WE WERE young, we carved homes into thickets of huckleberry.

We made acrid wine of the fruit, and stored it in Mountain Dew bottles, nestled among the roots in a shrubby pantry, which had been hacked into blistered relief with broken yard shears and other rust-eaten tools thrown out by parents.

We played mommy and daddy and baby and teenager, and daddy and daddy and mommy and baby, and mommy and daddy and grandpa and uncle. We made dinner of bitterroot and clover stems, and said our prayers, and lay down on loamy beds to hold hands and watch stars winking through the bramble overhead.

We reveled when our own moms and dads neglected the spring brush burn for several years running, and expanded our dominion into thickening thickets, until they made a sprawling maze connecting our four homes to each other.

We smoked our first Camels in that maze, stolen from the IGA, then prayed for forgiveness, and buried the soft packs deep beneath the beaten dirt threshold of our living room clearing. When the Bulls made the playoffs, and the parents whooped around backyard firepits slugging cans of Coors, we exhumed the cigs, and tried to blow celebratory smoke hoops in the air, to float above the huckleberries.

A stray ember caught the droughty undergrowth, and nearly burned the entire street to the ground. Nothing remained of our leafen kingdom, save the implements we'd used to create it.

After the fire trucks left, the boy whose parents had discarded those tools began shaking when they were discovered among the ashes, and his parents whipped him with a rodeo belt until he fled screaming into the hay fields. Such reprimand left weeping wounds as testimony, purple as the berries, which we salved in pale yellow, with yarrow gathered from empty irrigation ditches. Then we sent the boy back home, with a gleaming handful of Jolly Ranchers hidden inside one sock, because we couldn't convince our own families to take him in for the night.

"We ain't sticking our nose in nobody's goddamn business. Pray for him if you want, but shut the hell up about it now, hear?"

The next day, he shared the Jolly Ranchers with us at school, but would not say why he hadn't eaten them himself. He wore an overlarge Dallas Cowboys sweater, even on the playground, where a bronze sun baked the golden sawdust into shimmering waves.

We let him listen to Paula on the Walkman all day long, and nobody complained about losing their turn, not even the boy who lived next to me, who'd received it for Christmas.

Later that night, we listened to the crickets and shared a bag of Skittles in the ashes of our huckleberry kitchen, then swore on a kiss that we'd never be cruel losers to our kids.

❖

WHEN WE WERE young, we'd just returned from driving around the gravel back roads in his rattling Taurus, listening to *Dookie* for the millionth time. We'd been saying our goodbyes when he suddenly stopped on a dime, pulled up next to the thickets.

Even at the end of winter, the old growth was out of control again, piled into a solid wall next to the asphalt. But he got out without a word, then moved with some unknown instinct, stomping a beeline toward a particularly tall patch, tangled deep in bramble claws that pulled his windbreaker taut across his chest.

He found her surrounded by dormant huckleberries, curled in a bower, covered in scratches just like his. The bruise on her cheek was from the preacher man, she eventually admitted to us, when she'd tried to run out of his office.

It was her own fault, she said, for staying too long after timbrel practice. She screamed at us when we tried to say otherwise.

We begged her to tell her mom and dad, then begged her parents to believe her accusations, then begged our own to disclaim theirs after they tried to blame us instead, and cast us out of her house, bellowing into the night as we sprinted down the street, a clatter of untied Airwalks, hearts pounding in terrified indignation while the rifle blasts rang out overhead.

"Don't you fuckin' *dare* bear false witness in my home, boy! Tell your fuckin' mom her piece'a shit ain't welcome here no more when he can't even keep it in his GODdamn pants! All three'a you fuckin' monsters! Tellin' lies on a MAN OF GOD!" *BOOM!* "Don't you fuckin' EVER come back!" *BOOM!*

We hid in the thickets for hours, until he finally managed to stifle his anguished moans and wipe his face dry. He wanted to murder the preacher man, right then. Probably would've took off and actually tried, if we hadn't been able to drag him inside.

Our parents ordered us to apologize to hers, then grounded us for a month when we refused.

Her parents sought counsel from the very same preacher man, who recommended ongoing scripture study at the church, in private, to help her learn repentance, and to live a life of testimony and witness.

She stopped driving with us to school, then began ignoring us in class, and one day she never showed up again, even when it came time for our junior prom. She hadn't been able to shut up about that prom all winter. She'd been invited to the planning committee. The theme was *Owls in Flight,* and the student council had transformed the elementary gym into crepe paper moonscapes, with glittering stars hanging from the hoops.

She used to love the moon.

He waited for her all night, standing near the stop sign, bouquet of flowers in hand. He kept out of the streetlight's spill, and flinched at the sound of his kitchen door slamming open in the distance.

All the windows in her house were dark, the way they'd been for days on end, even though the Suburban never moved. We didn't know if the whole family was really gone, or if they were just sitting there in the blackness, staring out across the fields.

Me and the boy next door cupped our palms to hide the glowing cherry while passing cigs back and forth. We wouldn't be caught dead at prom ourselves, and said so a few times, just to keep things light. He only grunted in reply.

It was too cold to be standing out there, especially after midnight came and went, but we never dreamed of asking him to go in. Instead, we shared the old Walkman, one piece of broken headphone for each of us, while holding hands inside our coat sleeves, and feeling each other up whenever he was facing the other way, out of respect.

He spent most of the night pacing around the stop sign, and touching the scars under his rented tuxedo, where her own hands had once spread yarrow on his skin.

❖

WHEN WE WERE young, she suddenly turned up at home with her parents, the week after senior year began.

He'd risked his life to sneak beneath her bedroom window, just to see her face one more time, and to welcome her back to the street. She'd promised to meet us after church, but only if we waited respectfully outside.

That was just before Brokaw interrupted *Days* one afternoon, to calmly announce the owl's discovery.

They all appeared in a group on the chapel stoop at precisely 11:46 a.m., then paused to chat while the preacher man said goodbye to his flock, who were dutifully shepherding themselves to the dusty parking lot filled with rusty pickups and sun-bleached Chevy wagons.

The three of us loitered on the lawn, waiting silently. But I couldn't help noticing that the preacher man tried to avoid looking at her, and when this was unavoidable, it was done with a glare.

"Do they all know where she was this whole time?" I finally asked him.

"Duh," he muttered. His voice was tight, arms crossed, fingernails digging into fisted palms.

"Is that why he looks like he hates her guts?" I narrowed my eyes, watching the preacher man close.

He shook his head sharply. "Dumbass, it ain't because of that. It's because she didn't keep it."

"Keep what?" I said, loud and clueless, like a fucking dumbass. Her dad glanced my way from the stoop.

He swiftly punched me in the ribs and hissed back, "The *baby*, ese, goddamn."

Oh shit.

I clutched my side and stared at her in disbelief, amazed that it was still possible to become a complete stranger, even after all these years.

I beheld her parents with new disgust, skin prickling at

the sight of them standing there, calmly chatting with the preacher man, while she waited silently at their shoulder, face placid and resolute.

I felt a stab of guilt at the disloyalty in my ignorance, but kept the pained gasp inside my lungs, so my bruised ribs would hurt all the more, because I deserved it.

I deserved it.

But not as much as her mom and dad did.

I tried to tell her so once, just before graduation, but she brushed me off with a flat burst of laughter. By then she was too far gone to bother litigating yesterday, never mind months ago. Too tired of resisting. Too tired of hoping for more. Anyway, apologies were meaningless in the face of the Great Redeemer. So was guilt. And blame. And responsibility.

She'd settled on her survival strategy, and it required only one thing of her, one task to complete, one rule to follow.

Be not of this world, at any cost.

Now, like the rest of them, she preferred to reject the crushing burden of causality, to give it away, to send it back to the universe, and to leave all things unto Him, instead.

The universe, in reply, sent us the owl.

◆

WHEN WE WERE young, they'd been officially dating by Christmas, and his parents lost their minds about it, nearly as much as hers. Nobody ever admitted to knowing about the preacher man, but she was clearly tagged as damaged goods among the elders.

The worst part was that she didn't disagree. She'd used those exact words herself, more than once, even though he begged her to stop.

We were both intensely protective of their relationship, but also grateful that it was drawing so much attention, making our own easier to ignore. We were determined to stay hidden beneath the radar, hands held under desks, whispered plans to hitch a ride to Missoula's second ever Pride party that summer. But we still couldn't help ourselves beating the shit out of some sophomores who'd sneeringly referred to her as the church bike outside a basketball game.

His lip was bleeding afterward, and I'd reflexively held his face and said, "You alright, baby?" And so we were not hidden anymore.

After graduation, all four of us rented the house beneath the water tower, right on the edge of town, where we planted a huckleberry bush in the garden, and barbecued every night with crumbly Western Family briquettes, and blew smoke rings at the mosquitoes dancing around the porch lights.

Both our moms and dads had stopped talking to us, but we didn't care about the old homes anymore. We had our own now.

The owl had fallen out of headlines by then. Tentative plans to try and scare it off had been deemed too expensive. Anyway, the governments said it had no interest in us, and would leave our system when it was ready to move on, probably soon.

Probably soon.

But I was still seeing it every night in my dreams, bending down through the clouds to rip the roof off its rafters and peer into my eyes.

❖

WHEN WE WERE young, we'd expected her to stop talking to her parents as much, or at least go to a different church. But instead he started going with her, every Sunday.

We interrogated him about sitting there, week after

week, pretending to listen respectfully to the preacher man. Her parents had obviously forced her, but how could he stand it? How could he stand it for even an instant?

He assured us he wasn't falling in deep, just fallen for her, and determined to live every part of her life, right alongside. He said he didn't need to understand her decisions in order to love her, and we could only bring ourselves to agree, despite the seemingly inevitable cost to them both.

When my own parents died a year later on I-90, the firemen said they hadn't even been wearing seatbelts.

He held me tightly while I wailed, then strapped my bed frame and mattress to the top of his Taurus and brought them back home for me, back to the street, to the empty house.

My house.

The three of them set up chairs for the wake in my backyard, then spent the night, one last sleepover listening to the crickets through open windows.

We'd talked about moving in together, just the two of us, but he said he preferred to stay with them under the water tower, closer to town, and further from his parents, who still lived next door. But one afternoon, several months later, they told me he'd left on the Greyhound, gone to live with a twink on the Clark Fork, having made them promise not to tell me for at least a week. They showed up in the Taurus the very same hour, with bison burgers and a twelve-pack for the backyard, and a burned CD filled with Tina and Whitney.

Their own parents still refused to bless their growing union, and it infuriated me. But one night I swallowed my anger, for their sake, and ushered the mothers and fathers close, to watch our home movies, and witness the nature of this inevitable unity. Coors would smooth the way.

Begrudgingly the parents obeyed, and stared silently while I explained, then hit Play on the two of them dancing in our yard beneath the tower, oblivious to being recorded, while LeAnn sang of love on the boombox.

But after all these years spent breathing the same air, it was me who watched the two of them with new eyes. I felt a pang at having been right there, holding the camcorder, and still having missed what was recorded here for posterity, as they circled together in the pixelated porch light, swaying under minor key.

He touched herself, as she had touched himself, and they had touched themselves in kind. They had both been built a quilt of holes, punched into their body at every place where a hole should not be, deliberately hollowing them out, until the wispy tendrils of their remaining girders could but collapse inward, making dense neutron stars at the center of their life, before sucking even the steaming ash into those gaping maws at their core.

What's more, they both desired this consumption, in their own way, that it might assuage the endless guilt of forcing this town to behold such ongoing carnage any longer. Now they were spiraling in, trajectories set, twin event horizons blooming together, right in front of our eyes.

I wiped my face, voice thick as I turned to say, "Do you understand?" I was ready to forgive on their behalf, that they might find peace in the singularity, somewhere, and perhaps.

But the mothers and fathers had already gone.

◈

WHEN WE WERE young, the first virus arrived just after she'd found out she was pregnant with their eldest. He insisted we take it seriously, to keep her safe. I needed no such convincing. But when the second virus came, and their son had given them their first granddaughter, the arrogance of survival had infected our world down to the bone, and suddenly nobody else could be convinced at all, no matter how I begged.

He hadn't been pretending to listen to the preacher man for years. They'd both fallen in deep, just like the twin depressions worn into their family pew, side by side. We'd all stopped exchanging Christmas gifts after they insisted on giving me a new Bible every year, to replace the one I'd thrown out the previous. My last gift to them had been a sandwich bag filled with condoms.

When the new virus arrived, the preacher man, now stooped and withering, said come with joy, and pray for His shield, and so they went, spilling over the pews in their fervor.

The governments tried the same old trick again, tried to convince us it only took the old and weak, but I was forty-two when I said goodbye to the last of them, for the last time, and started coming home to a half-empty street, outside a half-empty town.

I hadn't known I was saying goodbye. I hadn't known I should have been marking the time.

I hadn't known life could be so long.

❖

THEY RAZED THE huckleberry thickets at some point, when the dust bowls had really dug in deep down on the prairies.

Barley was what the seed banks sent, so barley is what they sowed. I watched it spring into life all around me, first hesitant, then quick and fierce, like a new love, before it settled in for the long summer, green stalks outside every window, waving languid and thick in sweltering April afternoons.

By then I was actually enjoying the heat, and regularly sat out front, so the sun might beat itself into my stiffened joints.

Given how isolated the countries had become, nobody could explain the strength and speed of the new bacteria, except that we were all riding overused corpses by then, with immune systems whose every secret had long since been laid bare to the enemy, worldwide.

Still, they insisted on celebrating the planting with the usual potlucks and festivals, "like a real community oughta," and then one day they all lay down and let the whispering fields swallow them up.

Every last one.

❖

I CAREFULLY PLACED a hand on each of the rocking chair's arms, then inclined my head. "Thank you for listening."

The owl's head inclined in turn.

My eyes narrowed with curiosity. "If I'd been able to offer you a huckleberry for your journey, would it have spared us?"

"Perhaps."

I felt my pulse racing. "Then I'm glad I cannot."

The owl said, "Shall I at least sing of this world in my travels, child, that it might live among the stars? I could offer this, you know."

"No," I replied, voice shaking with adrenaline.

Then slowly, achingly, I stood from this chair for the final time.

I carefully spat on the ground, teeth bared. "For sake of the dead, I sincerely decline."

"But why?" the owl said. Its face tilted in anticipation of my answer, and to say this was not a question, but a fail-safe.

I made arthritic fists, stuttered by pain, and thrust my whiskered chin high into the air, before embracing the final audacity with a voice so small it would not even echo off the owl's face.

"For I am become vengeance," I shouted into the sky, and immediately burst into furious tears.

The owl blinked at my words, then flexed its talons to crack this world in twain, before alighting back to the beyond, without another glance behind the long and icy tail of its own feathers.

At last.

The fires rose within crumbling soil, the barley began slipping away in all directions, and the atmosphere poured in waterfalls toward a glowing molten core.

As the porch dropped out from underneath me, I shut my cindering eyes, and smiled at the bird's exceeding grace.

The Spindle of Necessity

B. Pladek

ANDREW WAS CONVINCED the writer had been trans. By this point his friends were tired of hearing about it, but he had no one else to tell besides the internet, and he was too smart for that. That would be asking for it.

Samantha Finnes was a minor historical novelist, unknown outside queer circles. In the mid-50s she'd written three books set during the World Wars. They followed the same group of gay men as they aged in and out of one another's lives, losing their keys and lunch and innocence and sometimes whole chunks of themselves, then finding those lost things again in each other, transformed by time and mundanity. At mid-century she'd been very popular; in the '70s if a man wanted to show his hand, he'd carry a copy of her last novel, *The Spindle of Necessity*. She was out of fashion now. Andrew always felt it was because she was regarded as writing out of her lane.

To him her books still rang desperately true. But then, he couldn't really know. It still didn't feel like his lane, however hard he tried.

"I don't know what you mean by 'true,'" Dave chided. It was Dave's lane, and had been since he was a twentysomething beauty and hero of early Grindr. Now he was maturing gracefully, like good wood, cured taut in precisely the right places. Andrew tried not to be jealous. "I mean, true to what? The '30s? Things are different now. You don't judge the authenticity of *Cabaret* by going to Strap."

Andrew nodded, embarrassed. Of course, he'd never been to Strap, or Philter, or even that one drag bar in the south end where Milwaukee's straight women flocked for their bachelorettes. He lacked the courage—no, he hadn't earned it. It was because he romanticized things. No, dammit, say it plain: he romanticized a certain iteration of gayness. He knew it was wrong. He'd been on Twitter enough to learn that. It had taken him so long to transition largely because he could never know for sure if he wanted to be a real gay man, or merely an ideal one. Sometimes he still couldn't tell.

He loved Finnes because it felt like she understood. The dominant affect of her novels was longing. Not hunger or envy or despair, but the kind of weary heartsickness you sometimes met in early fantasy, Mirrlees's Faerie or Dunsany's Elfland. People gazing with firm English stoicism over the blue hills at a land where they knew they could never live. *Spindle* even tacitly acknowledged this: the book's central lovers struggled to reconcile the love they had with the love they wanted, when the world denied them both.

"Listen to this," he'd once told his friend Adrian, trying to explain. It was a passage from early in *Spindle,* where one man has just gifted another, younger and more naïve, a copy of Plato's *Phaedrus.* "He hands over the book and tells him, 'It doesn't exist anywhere in real life, so don't let it give you illusions. It's just a nice idea.'"

"OK," Adrian said. "What am I listening for exactly?"

They were sitting in their usual booth at the local diner, a chromey tourist trap whose attempt at gentrification had badly missed the mark. Andrew had always liked it. Its inherent embarrassment overshadowed his own.

"Just the—desire for an ideal, something you think is impossible, so you find it in books," he said. "And you tell yourself it's silly, but at the same time you live a secret second life there, despite yourself." Adrian was nodding seriously, trying to follow. Andrew winced. "And that life feels more real than your real one. It's just—that's exactly what it's like sometimes," he finished lamely, too ashamed to explain further.

"Sure," she said. "Although lots of people want what they can't have." Adrian was kind, and never told him outright he was projecting. "Finnes had a lot of gay friends, didn't you say? She probably knew enough to get that feeling right."

"Haha, yeah." He tried to sound careless. "I guess it's doing a disservice to her as an author, to think she couldn't imagine that experience. Pretty sexist of me, too, right? Expecting a woman couldn't write beyond herself." He laughed. Above him the diner's blue lights blinked, affecting cozy authenticity.

"Nah," said Adrian, in the tone that meant, *I hadn't thought of it, but yes.*

◆

THAT NIGHT ANDREW lay, glasses off, in the stuffy heat of his fifth-floor studio in the university district. Two floors below an undergraduate party thumped. At twenty-eight, he was the oldest tenant in the building. Finnes's biography lay on his chest. Its spine was broken. In the dim light it splayed over his collarbone, irritated his chest's new fuzz.

Only one biography of Finnes existed, popular not academic, based on an interview she gave in the '70s.

It provided scaffolding details of her life: born in St. Albans, read Classics at Oxford, war nurse in '43, where she met her lifelong partner, Madge Sims. After the war she'd drifted for awhile, then moved abruptly to New York, where she joined a loose circle of writers, mostly expatriot, all queer. The biography had no flesh on it. It was all bones and feathers, facts and *bon mots*. Finnes was top of her class at St. Hugh's; she'd kept an apartment in Athens with the poet John Merman in the '60s; she always kept cats. Once she'd called Radclyffe Hall a whiner. She often said she wished she'd been born a man.

Her papers were scattered across several archives. If Andrew hadn't flunked out of grad school (*"left,"* Adrian would insist, "you have to stop blaming yourself"), he would have tried to compile them. He'd even tried to write a grant once. But he could find no convincingly scholarly way to say, *I want to see if Finnes was like me.* It was too facile a project for academia, anyway. He still read *Transgender Studies Quarterly* sometimes. He knew whatever he wrote wouldn't cut it.

So he simply read what he could when he could, and irritated his friends with his findings. Two years now he'd been at it, and even his trans friends, who knew what sort of weird obsessions accompanied coming out, were beginning to tire. He had found no conclusive evidence. And though Finnes was dead, she could still be violated. His friends' lengthening silences said he was edging close.

In his most honest moments—granted, he was never exactly sure when these were—he admitted it was probably futile. He was not even sure what he wanted out of proof, should he find it. Still.

In the orange streetlight slanting in the window, he tipped the biography up on his chest to reread a passage about the war years.

He did not remember falling asleep, but he woke with a start to a high eerie wail.

Where his bedroom walls had closed a darkened

corridor stretched, lined with lumpy cots. Thick black blankets shrouded the windows. Dim lights swung up and down the corridor, cupped in pinecone-shaped lanterns. He knew at once.

He had never had a lucid dream before. At first he tried to see how much he could command it: thinking hard at the ward, the dying all-clear siren, his ill-fitting striped patient's pajamas. Nothing changed.

He gave up and looked for Finnes. Andrew's subconscious was not subtle. There was only one reason it would dump him in a WWII British hospital.

It took longer than dream-logic should have dictated. Several harried nurses clopped by before she appeared, a pale woman of twenty, with the long androgynous face mid-century novelists always called coltish. Probably she could have even passed, in different dress. Clothes meant a lot more in the '40s.

She stopped by his bedside, glanced at a paper clipped to its iron frame.

"Samantha Finnes?" he asked before she said anything.

She narrowed her eyes but refused, apparently, to be nonplussed. He felt curiously embarrassed, as if this weren't just a dream, something his id was doing to satisfy him. "You're American," she said.

"My name is Andrew."

"Yes, it's on your chart. Where did they bring you in from, Dunkirk?"

"I…um." There was no reason he shouldn't jump right into it. This was the fantasy where he revealed her to herself, wasn't it? He wondered if his subconscious was like his friends, secretly nudging him to get over it and move on. He gulped. "Miss Finnes. Have you ever wondered if you aren't, um, actually a woman?"

Her face did not change, but the horseish line of her neck tightened slightly. "So they gave the morphia already," she said. "Did they at least change your dressing?"

"I mean you already know you're queer, right? You're twenty-three, you figured it out at Oxford." This was all fake. Why was it so hard? "It's sort of like that, but different…" She was ignoring him, leaning over with a roll of white gauze. Concentration hardened her face to marble. He had never seen close-up pictures of her before. He was staring so hard he jumped when she went for his first pajama button.

"Hey—you can't—"

"Keep your voice down," she snapped, and kept unbuttoning.

He shut up, humiliated at how amateurish this dream was. The lazy trans reveal: the guy shows his scars, the woman is caught tucking. If he read it in a novel he'd tut-tut. But some part of him wanted dream-Finnes to know, to see, and that part was stronger than the knowledge that it made him bad. He knew that anyway.

She finished. Her face did not shift as she stared down at him. He met her eyes, challenging. "Another world is possible," he said, soft and portentous and only realizing he was quoting a second too late. God, his id was corny.

Finnes didn't reply. He watched her eyes for some spark of recognition or surprise, peered as if he weren't controlling her and this whole dark ward with its sweat reek and keening siren. There was nothing. Only she seemed to turn harder than ever, grim and white, with a limestone weariness too old for her young face.

Like a soldier, he thought, before he woke up.

❖

IN THE MORNING, when he relayed the dream to Adrian over pancakes in their booth, she pursed her lips and nodded tolerantly.

He remembered the time—probably at this same diner—she had asked him directly why he cared so much about Finnes. He'd sat for a long time, thinking. He could easily have said, *Finnes loves men the way I do, and if she was one, I can be too*; his cis friends liked answers that meant they could reassure him. Yet it was not the whole truth. Finnes's idealized lovers moved him too deeply. He feared he loved them more than reality, and tricked by that love, he'd become the wrong sort of man—a gay groupie, a fetishist, a naïve idealist. If Finnes was trans it made it okay, somehow. If she was real, he could claim to love reality through loving her books. And loving reality was his ticket to being accepted by it, by himself.

All right, so maybe he did still need reassurance. But Adrian couldn't provide it; no case she might make could prove his romanticism was defensible. Dave might have made one, if Andrew had ever had the nerve to ask. But he hadn't—not Dave, or any of his cis gay friends. How had he answered Adrian, that day? He couldn't remember.

She was staring at him now over her coffee with open concern. Clearly she thought he ought to forget about the dream, because she started steering the conversation towards more general Finnesaria.

He obliged. On reflection it was pretty embarrassing. Even his id refused him a real answer.

"I mean if you're still this obsessed, maybe you should apply for a grant again?" she asked. "There might be interest, given that reissue of her fourth novel. Fantasy's hot right now, you know? Even though it's barely fantasy, just kind of fake Greek history…"

"*Fourth?*" he said, loudly enough that when she stared at him, he pretended his surprise had been at something else. He kept pretending until the end of breakfast.

When he ran home there it was, on his shelves. *The Relayers*, in an old orange Penguin edition, its cover a winged foot crowned with laurel. He didn't remember reading it, but when he opened it up the margins were full of his tiny, neat notes. Feeling entranced, he carried it gingerly to his chair by the window, sank down, and read.

It was, as Adrian had said, kind of fake Greek history. The story followed a pair of lovers, both runners, as they grew up together during what was transparently a fantasy version of the Persian invasion of Attica. It culminated with the battle of Marathon. Beneath the veneer of fake names, it seemed excruciatingly careful about getting its details correct, as if Finnes were half-ashamed of doing what Britain itself had, robbing and mutilating someone else's history.

But mostly it was a love story, unlike any Finnes Andrew had ever read. Her characteristic longing was still there, but focused, purposeful as light honed in a prism. At the story's climax, the great relay from "Fennelain" to "Polias," the elder lover ran ten miles extra to save the younger part of his stretch. And when he died (beautifully, of a heart attack), it had the sting of high tragedy rather than kill-your-gays. If Finnes's prose were less restrained, this melodrama might have curdled into ridicule. But the book was marble, refusing to apologize for its idealism. Its warrior-lovers were devoted and unafraid. They'd never once thought to be ashamed.

Reading it, he felt the same way he had the first time he'd opened *The Spindle of Necessity*: exposed, as if the book had caught him out. A white light burned in his chest, too bright to look at. He knew its name was desire, but that word was too small for the feeling, which was like looking into the sun. There was no nuance, no tidy explanation (say, *wanting to be a man like that*); just a ball of fire.

When he put the book down he was shaking. His dream could not have caused this. The novel was old and full of his handwriting. His friends were right: he was losing it. He should step away.

He called Dave to talk himself down. He tried to introduce the dream delicately, but Dave knew something about avoidance, and where to push.

"So you dreamed you tried to crack Finnes's egg and it

made you forget she wrote that Greek book? Yeah, I'd say that's a thing to worry about." He could hear the small sigh of Dave blowing smoke, and the hum of the docks district below. He must be on his balcony. "Is this about you feeling inadequate? Like, feeling you can't go to the bars with me?"

Andrew wanted to say that feeling unwelcome wasn't the same thing as inadequacy, but he did, also, feel inadequate. So he just said, "No. I don't know what it is."

"Maybe you should call your therapist again? Work through it?"

"No." The bristle in his voice surprised him. "I just need to grow up and get over it."

Dave's pause was so long it became a silence. Andrew did not dare break it. Finally, Dave said, "I didn't think I'd hear you talking like this again. Do what you have to, I guess. Just remember, Drew, you can't get over who you are?"

It was the sort of crypto-philosophical thing Dave was always saying. Andrew hung up without asking him what it meant.

That night he walked for a long time before sleep. He was ashamed, and not even of the right things—like how Finnes's novels, problematic in the way of all aged art, rung him more than the modern books he was supposed to love; like how the community he longed for was rife with misogyny and racism; like how he could never tell if his fears were his own, or internalized transphobia: all the shameful truths that, before his transition, he'd seen as proof he didn't deserve it. No, it was the same damn romanticization of lovers who didn't exist—and maybe shouldn't, he realized, for all the reasons he'd just listed. Maybe the shames weren't so distinct.

He walked. Up the lakefront, past the art museum, among the old, car-clogged streets of the east side; down one street which had been the city's Castro in the '70s;

down another where the famous trans activist had once lived, before he moved west and died young, in '91. He listened, but the streets were mute, like a refusal. He felt like he was dragging himself along behind himself, an extra weight on his own legs. There was no one to relieve him, to pass the baton to.

◆

THIS TIME THE dream room was dark and unfamiliar. He did not recognize its faded furnishings, or the musky couch on which he lay. Runnels of candlelight drained down the walls from a cracked door. Beyond, pleasant voices chatted.

Pushing through, he saw a tall dining room whose shadows leapt to the ceiling. At one end of a long table clustered eight people, hands linked around a flickering candelabra. He knew three: Finnes, Madge Sims, and the poet John Merman. The man next to Merman, chin on his shoulder, was likely his lover Daniel Hepham. From their clothes, he guessed the early '60s.

This would be one of Merman's famous séance sessions, then, and the location his rambling Victorian in upstate New York. Andrew knew Merman had held séances and Finnes attended. But it was a strange turn for his subconscious to take. For starters, the metaphor was backward. Why a séance, if he was trying to exorcise something?

As if speaking for his id, Hepham said as Andrew entered, "It worked! We've summoned your Midwesterner, Sam."

Finnes turned. Age had squared her coltish face, and her smile was casual but guarded. "Hello again," she said. Next to her, Sims pulled out a chair. Bewildered, he sat. Someone uptable called, "Come on, Jack, must you give Sam special treatment? I want to bring my fan club next time." Someone else replied, "You already did; you're here, aren't you?" A different voice shot a rejoinder, and the séancers groused genially at each other for a minute.

The warm dark caught and held their rising voices, a cozy, hermetic atmosphere. Andrew wondered what his dream wanted with this backdrop. Maybe just the usual, dangling a belonging he didn't feel he'd earned as a deterrent, or punishment. He noticed Finnes did not take part in the raillery, though she watched it with stiff attention. Of course: he knew she hated any whiff of tribalism. In *Spindle*, the older lover flees in disgust from a party of winkingly fey men, complaining they'd made their secret into their prison. Andrew had always found this an uncompassionate position. If you never left the closet, of course you'd dig yourself in, decorate the walls, make it a home. He had always wondered how Finnes applied her severe standards to herself. Well, no, be honest: he thought he'd known. He looked over to find her frowning at him. His id again, telling him to get on with it. "I, um, enjoy your work," he said.

"I hope so, as you've been christened my fan club."

He fiddled with his hands a moment, then remembered how absurd reticence was. This was his dream, his quest to get over himself. He drew a deep breath.

"You write desire between men very movingly," he said, like a Vintage Classics introduction. "Especially for a—woman."

"High praise." Her voice was flat.

"Sorry, I meant for a—someone who doesn't—"

"Yes?"

Andrew realized, horrified, what question he was wading towards. None of his friends had ever needed to object *but Finnes was a lesbian*. The point was understood, one of the reasons his theory was especially cringey. For his part, he'd never had the guts to reply, *that doesn't matter*, or *some us think we are, at first*.

He caught himself in time. "—actually I was wondering if you planned on any more fantastic novels. I really liked *The Relayers*." A dull question, which would grant him time to think of one that could give her—his brain's version of her—a cue to snuff his obsession forever. Instead she straightened. "Did you prefer it?"

Surprised, he didn't reply at once.

"Well? Did you?"

There was no safe way to answer this question, to a writer. He settled for the truth. "It felt freer."

She took so long to reply that when she did, the badinage had lulled. Her words stamped bright on the silence. "Yes. I suppose it did."

As she spoke, it seemed as if she wanted to look away from Andrew. But she refused herself, and held his eyes. Beside her, Sims touched her hand.

Merman chose that moment to intercede. "Come join the circle, young man." He scooted aside and patted the bench to his left. "Nine is a lucky number for a séance. Three by three—we could raise Dante."

Bewildered that the dream hadn't ended, that nothing seemed expunged, Andrew stood and resat where Merman had indicated. He lay his hands on the red damask. Merman took his right and thumped it on the table, reassuringly. At his left, a duckish expat took the other. "Don't get your hopes up," he stage-whispered. "We'll try for Dante but settle for Leopardi."

"Leopardi isn't settling!" someone else hissed.

As Andrew stared around the circle of amused, middle-aged faces, smiling at him in degrees of awkward or encouraging welcome, what struck him most was how little it felt dug-in or tribal, despite Finnes's laborious scorn, and how even though his own brain had conjured the scene expressly to thrust him outside it, he did not feel like an intruder, not at all.

❖

WHEN HE WOKE there were two more Finnes novels. He'd checked his bookshelf first thing, and there they stood: *The*

God's Mouth, about a poet from fantasy-Delos; *Thunder from High*, about an actor from fantasy-Sicily. Both books were old, filled with his handwriting. When he googled them, they had multiple pages of hits. He couldn't remember either.

Fear made his chest seize, the room loll in and out of focus. He sat. He lay the books on his lap and tried to hold the weight of his disappointment. The novels were proof he'd failed to wring himself of his theory. If anything, the dye now bled deeper. What good were dreams if they made things worse? How many more Finnes books would he forget in his idiot quest to prove something he apparently needed to be true?

He pulled his knees to his chest and rocked. He knew he should text Adrian, and not read. He was halfway through *Thunder* when she called. The sun had filled his lungs again, burning out the air. As he read he'd had to keep getting up to pace out the joy, the panic. "Put on something nice and be ready at seven," she said.

"Why?"

"Blue's having jukebox bingo tonight. I'm going. You're coming."

He obeyed to the letter, though wondered about *nice*. Blue was the city's sole dyke bar. It was low-key and midwestern, and smelled of imported beer and stale popcorn. Its crowd was a mix of older queers in hoodies or basketball jerseys. Andrew had always felt safe there.

Adrian knew it. As she maneuvered them a seat, he could tell from her cheery rescue mission tone that she was here to drag him out of himself. He hoped this meant she wouldn't ask him about Finnes. She didn't. For an hour they played bingo, made mild conversation. The white light in his chest dimmed, and he could feel his own heartbeat for the first time that day. He almost forgot *Thunder on High*, waiting half-read at home, filled with his unremembered handwriting.

As he calmed, he paid closer attention to Adrian. Like him,

she was overdressed: a blue split-sleeve with a sheer back, her good dark skinny jeans. Theoretically, dressing up helped people feel better. He'd never experienced it in practice. But Adrian had tried. He felt warmly grateful.

"You look good," he said, smiling. "Just wanted to be fancy tonight?"

"Actually…" She tapped her phone. "Dave and I are going dancing later. Strap, maybe Level. You want to join?"

Her nonchalance was exquisitely practiced. *Put on something nice.* A ringing numbness filled him like white noise. In his chest the panic whined, rose, became anger. He knew by Adrian's flinch he'd failed to control his face.

She said quickly, "We thought you might—"

"I know. I know." Their intentions were good, he tried to remember. They were his friends. They would not consciously mock him, fling him into a place that saw only what he wasn't and suspected him for it, confirmed what he suspected of himself. "I appreciate the offer. But no thanks. I'm going home."

He stood. Elsewhere, beneath another world's sun, dawn glinted from the rostra of a fleet blockading an island that wasn't quite Sicily.

"Drew," Adrian said. "Please."

He half-turned. He owed her not to be a dick about this.

"Listen," she continued. "We're worried about you. It's not that your Finnes thing is bad! We've all got our obsessions, right? But it's like the only way you'll be ok with yourself is by proving this. But you're you, not her. And you live now. Here! With us."

With what he hoped Finnes would've called *great restraint*, he faced Adrian. Her voice was split with worry. What an ungrateful bastard he was. Was this his version of digging in, making himself a tribe of one? How much worse than the closet Finnes despised.

He drove compassion into his voice like a nail. "Thanks, Addy. Really. I appreciate it. I just—can't, now. Please understand."

"OK," she said faintly. "Do you need—"

But he was already turning.

At home, on the beach of not-quite-Sicily, the soldier-lovers were bathing. Above, the setting sun was a ball of fire, too bright to look at. Tomorrow they would attack. As evening bled the sea violet, they leant together in the night wind, hair prickling on their damp thighs. They gazed at not-quite-Syracuse. This campaign was doomed, the pet project of a bored and overripe democracy. But the lovers had no regrets. They'd chosen it as they'd chosen each other, freely.

That was how you knew it was fiction, Andrew thought. But he didn't stop reading.

❖

THAT NIGHT HE tried so deliberately to fall asleep it took him hours. When at last he succeeded, it was as if his subconscious, surrendering to his desire to dream, gave him an even dreamier landscape than usual.

He was sitting against an oak's bole in the green eye of a meadow, painterly and unreal. Every outline wavered, like some liminal fairy space, the Debatable Hills or the edge of the fields we know. Watercolor trees smudged the milky sky. The air was sweet and heavy. It was all very English.

"Hello, fan club," Finnes said.

She sat beside him, her profile the only sharp thing in the landscape. This time her face was deeply tan above its white oxford. The color suited her: rough and alive, like good wood. He did not bother with pleasantries. Maybe the spareness of the scenery meant he'd peeled something back, and spoke directly to the deep, flinching part of him. Maybe that part would finally listen.

"I need to ask you something," he said.

"Go ahead."

He explained then, haltingly—not just himself, but everything. He drew from the 101 he'd given his parents when he'd first come out. He gave a potted summary of trans history, old and recent; of procedures generally; of the ones he'd had. He omitted nothing. At last he reached into his chest and scooped out the heart of his shame, his romanticization of gay men, the men in her novels.

As he spoke, he watched Finnes's face. It creaked, but did not move.

He finished. He waited.

"Well?" she said.

"I—aren't you surprised?"

She smiled, not unkindly. "Did you think I didn't know? I've met men like that." He reconsidered. She was his dream—wasn't she?—so of course she knew. What had he hoped to achieve by telling her? What did he want out of this again?

Knitting his fingers, he gazed out at the downy English meadow. He thought suddenly of the end of *Spindle*, when one lover apologizes to the other that he's fucked up his life by idealizing him, idealizing their love, and that he was leaving so he couldn't do it anymore.

"I think you are a man like that," he said. He swallowed. "I mean, I want you to be."

"I know," she said without skipping a beat. "You don't see the virtue in playing the cards you've been dealt."

His chest tightened. "But see, you don't have to." Somehow he'd landed here again, trying to claw back what he'd come to disprove. "You don't have to be miserable."

"You have no idea of my pains or pleasures, young man. I'd thank you to stop assuming."

"But if you could be different—"

"Then I would be different." Her tone was final.

"Thank you for your concern, Andrew." He stared at her, straight-backed against the oak. Against the meadow's pastel wash her outline was rigid, though when he peered closer it trembled slightly, as if held together by military effort. Her eyes were illegible. He could not tell what part of himself he was facing. Looking back at him, she said, "My books have been something of a refuge for you. Is that right?"

"Yes, of course," he said bitterly. "That's the whole problem."

Their eyes were still locked as he said this, so he saw the shift, the tremor. "Problem?"

"They're not real, they're nothing close to my life or anyone's life. They're wrong, don't you understand? And loving them makes me wrong." He barreled through this explanation, resentful he had to give it, as if it wasn't the whole reason they were both here. In his fervor, he nearly missed the stitch of humiliation cramp her face.

"If they are so upsetting to you, then stop," Finnes said coldly. Each word was punctuated with anger. He suddenly understood it was not at him. "Just stop."

A bubble of silence dropped over the meadow. From inside its emptiness Andrew looked at Finnes, fixed against the oak. Her spine was straight as a captain's who has never left the field, her eyes as exhausted.

He felt a sharp, overpowering surge of shame and grace, as if he'd never fought anything as hard as she had, was relieved he would never have to.

"I can't," he said.

"Then don't." Pain cramped her face again. Then softly, "I couldn't."

"Wait, do you mean you—"

She stood, refusing the support of the trunk. "Goodbye, Andrew."

Turning, she began to walk away. Her hard angles receded into the floral blur. He considered stopping her, then accepted he could not, or did not want to. That same strange, shameful relief tugged at his eyelids. Somehow he knew this dream would be the last. Finnes had refused to absolve him of his love; he'd refused to absolve himself. Was that forgiveness? Or didn't it matter, because he was never going to stop?

You can't escape reality, he thought hazily, in books or dreams. But you couldn't live without dreaming either. And sometimes, if you were lucky, you dreamed yourself awake. Drowsily he watched Finnes go. She diminished, enfolded by green, until he was left alone in the dream's fairy no-place: its ideal of a meadow, which did not exist but lived only in the mind as a language for loving real meadows, a door into their endless summer, a way through.

❖

He woke to a string of texts from Adrian and Dave. They'd skipped Strap and wanted to meet him for brunch, to apologize.

not your fault, he texted groggily. *give me a few hours.* Morning was gold in the window. He must have dreamed all night.

Next to him on the bed lay a slim, faded book, margins blue with his handwriting. *Symposia,* by Samantha Finnes.

Instinctively he knew he would find no answers there. He would never find them. From the fog of sleep his shame choked biliously up. He breathed, and let it. It was part of him, like the dream itself. No truth about Finnes or anybody else would change it.

At length the burn cooled, and he was still himself after.

He flipped open the first page.

Familiar names leapt out at him. How strange: not another fake-Greek novel, but a sequel to *Spindle.* It had been published in 1982, a year before Finnes's death.

There was no way he'd go to brunch without at least starting. He settled back into bed, and read.

The book's centerpiece was a dinner scene, hosted by *Spindle's* main couple. Now middle-aged, they'd settled comfortably in a rambling stone bungalow, where they entertained a rotating cast of friends and lovers. That evening they'd invited some younger people, painted in Finnes's characteristic detail. Andrew read the descriptions slowly: Ralph, a coltish and inflexible twentysomething; his lover Laurie, an anxious ex-scholar. As the dinner got cozier and drunker, Ralph hung back in a fever of scorn.

Laurie fared better. He let himself go, as in those trust exercises where you fall back into your teammates' arms. By the time the hosts pulled out their inevitable Ouija board, he was laughing. With everyone else he put his fingers to the planchette. Hands touching, they talked to the past. When the past replied its answers were cryptic: half-remembered and half-created, neither real nor ideal, a prison and a refuge, as the past always is.

From the sidelines Ralph watched, his eyes burnt, until Laurie got up and pulled him in, smiling.

Andrew's phone buzzed again. It was 11:30, and Adrian was offering to pick him up. *wear whatever you like,* she joked contritely.

sure, he texted.

He stuck a bookmark in *Symposia* and clambered out of bed. On his chair he found flung the shirt he'd thrown off last night. As he buttoned it up in the mirror, he practiced his own apologies.

Pulling back, he surveyed his reflection. He had none of Finnes's power of description. But he thought he looked okay.

As he jogged down the stairs towards Adrian's waiting car, he thought with gratitude that he still had *Thunder* to finish, and *The God's Mouth* to reread. Whatever game his brain was playing with him, it meant he'd get to encounter

Finnes's work as if for the first time: dream worlds he could gaze through like windows, different from this one but transparent to it, on whose light glass his own image moved.

But that could wait. He felt a sudden keen hunger to be outside, in the lifting mist of the morning city; to get sunburnt on a sidestreet patio; to drink in a dark bar beside someone he liked. Maybe he'd even go dancing.

Linden Honey, Blackcurrant Wine

M. R. ROBINSON

WHEN IRENA WAS young and strong and still the third-most beautiful girl in Březina, she could walk from her mother's cottage to the birch grove in only an hour—even if she stopped to cool her feet in the creek or fill a basket with blackcurrants. But she is not so young and not so strong now, not for all her wishing, and the journey eats up the morning and a slice of afternoon, too.

She pauses at the grove's edge to wipe sweat from her brow with a tattered handkerchief. Somewhere overhead, a crow cackles. Irena can hardly blame him for laughing. What a sight she must be, huffing and puffing her way through the forest! Not so young and not so strong, aye, and not so beautiful either. Beauty is a fair price to pay for such a long life, she knows; she has seven grandchildren back in Hladov, each one so smart and handsome that the other old women of the village whisper enviously behind her back, and oh, how lucky she has been to watch them grow. Yet walking into the ring of pale peeling birches after so many years makes her feel grief-heavy and strange, achingly aware of everything time has taken from her.

Her hair, once so thick and dark, has gone wispy-white; though she still possesses the raw knuckles and calloused fingertips of a baker's wife, the skin of her hands is thin and mottled, ready to split at the slightest scrape. Sometimes when she glimpses her reflection, she does not quite recognize herself. She is an ugly old woman. She is proud to say so: it means she is alive. But once upon a time, she was young and beautiful, and she danced among the birch trees.

Her dancing days are long behind her now, though, and she knows wallowing will not bring her girlhood back. Irena tucks the handkerchief into her bosom and bends to rub her balky left knee. When she straightens, she does so with a groan made so loud by the quiet of the woods that she cannot help but chuckle at the sound. No, no, she is not the same girl she was when last she walked to the birch grove.

The grove, too, bears the scars of time. Yet she knows every inch of this place, even now: here a patch of bark grown rough around a carved heart, and there the crooked trunk curved just right for two lovers to curl beneath its drooping branches. So much is the same. But the eldest birches have turned gnarled and silver, not so unlike Irena, and the saplings have thickened around the middle—also not so unlike Irena, though she tucks the worries that accompany those thoughts into the back of her mind. She came here to repent, not to court.

"Oh, my love," she calls. "I am here, my love."

The words taste wrong in her mouth. She has not spoken them in sixty years, for she and her husband never spoke of love. Until his death, she had thought never to speak these words again.

"Come to me, my springtime, my magpie, my darling—"

Irena's quavering voice sinks into the moss. Somewhere in the distance, a skylark trills.

What a fool to hope for more than silence—to think she might be welcomed, much less forgiven, after all this time! Irena stands alone in the heart of the grove, where she has never stood alone before, and lets disappointment settle like snow on her shoulders.

When she can bear it no longer, she turns her back to the birches. It was not enough to come so far. She came too late.

"Wait!"

Irena twists to face the grove once more, almost falling in her haste. Oh, oh, she knows this voice—would know it anywhere, in any life—

Her heart thunders in her ears like she's seventeen again; her legs tremble like they do not mean to hold her. She inhales, trying desperately to steady herself, and almost weeps at the sweetness of the smell that greets her: sunshine on bare skin, linden honey, blackcurrant wine.

The only woman Irena has ever loved steps through the trees, flowers blooming at her feet.

◆

THE FIRST TIME Irena danced in the birch grove, it was her seventeenth birthday and the most dreadful day of her life thus far—for she had not yet known much of sorrow. She only knew that she hated her mother and that she would never marry Ctirad.

Irena sat through his visit in stony silence. He left with a promise to return the next day. She waited for him to disappear down the path, then opened her mouth for the first time that morning to shout at her mother. But she could not fit her fear and fury into words, no matter how she tried, and trying did no good; her mother shouted louder and cuffed her about the ears until all her protests turned to hiccups and whimpers. At last, not knowing where she might go but knowing she could not stay, Irena fled.

Thornbushes and low branches caught at her as she ran sobbing into the forest, but she kept going, running like she might somehow escape Březina for good—oh, if she could only run a little faster! By the time she burst through the birches and into the clearing, her skirts were torn, her arms were bloodied, and she was utterly exhausted and hopelessly lost. She flung herself upon the moss and, for the first time in years, allowed herself to weep as freely as a child—only a child, surely not ready to be somebody's wife—to be somebody's mother—

That thought made her cry harder. She paid no attention at all to the birch grove; she paid no attention to anything but her despair until a voice cut through her weeping:

"Why are you crying?"

Irena fell silent at once, startled out of her misery by the sound of the stranger's voice. Bad enough to put on such a show—a thousand times worse to be seen! Slowly, queasy with embarrassment, she rose from the moss ready to stammer an excuse. At her first glimpse of the girl across the clearing, though, shame and tears and mothers and suitors didn't seem to matter anymore. She opened her mouth, not knowing what she might say, but could not find any words that seemed to serve. Oh, she had heard the stories all her life, but she had not thought to stumble into one!

The girl wore a marvelous gown as pale as winter butter and a wreath of bluebells crowned her golden curls. Her features were sharp and proud; she was as slight as a willow branch. The air around her shimmered like light on the water. She looked like no woman Irena had ever seen, and Irena knew immediately that she was no woman at all.

"Why are you crying?" the girl—the vila, the woodmaiden—asked again, her voice so disarming that Irena could not help but answer.

"My mother wants me to marry the baker."

"Do you not wish to marry the baker?"

"I do not wish to marry anyone."

"I understand," the woodmaiden said, though she did not exactly sound as if she understood. She paused, then smiled. "Would you like to dance with me? I always feel much better when I'm dancing. Maybe you will too."

Irena tried with all her might to look stern instead of curious. She would not be fooled by one of the forest-folk, even if the sweetness of the woodmaiden's smile was terribly distracting. "You are a vila," she said, "and if I dance with you, I will never be able to go home again."

At that, the woodmaiden looked a little sad. "That is only in the stories. I cannot keep you from leaving, if you wish to leave, and I do not think I could keep you here forever even if you wished to stay. But I can dance with you a while, and perhaps you will forget your troubles."

"I do not dance well," Irena said, though the longer she stared at the woodmaiden, the less important such details seemed. And if the stories did prove true—if she were trapped here, never to return—well, would that be such a dreadful fate?

"I will teach you all the steps," the woodmaiden said earnestly. She stepped forward, dainty pink flowers blooming everywhere her feet had been, and held out a bark-brown hand. "Oh, please, dance with me!"

Irena looked around the birch grove for the first time and saw that every tree was full: larks and thrushes, blackbirds and nightingales, all the sweetest songbirds of the woods, sitting side-by-side upon the silver branches. As one voice, the birds began to sing. Irena felt a stirring in her chest like the flutter of wings.

She took the woodmaiden's hand.

❖

"IRENKA," THE WOODMAIDEN says, hand outstretched and trembling. "Irenka, my Irenka—"

And oh, she is beautiful. She is so beautiful, exactly as she always has been: slender like the birches, golden like the sun, untouched by sixty summers. Irena cannot answer. It is all she can do to stay on her feet.

When Irena does not move, the woodmaiden's hand drops to her side. She takes one hesitant step closer. Leaves and petals swirl around her ankles, caught in a delicate breath of a breeze, then fall and vanish in the grass. The flowers blooming in her footprints look parched.

"It has been a long time since you came to me," she says.

"I know," Irena says, and feels immediately shamed by the hoarseness of a voice worn thin by age and fear. "I am sorry. I could not come sooner. I wanted to come—"

"May I touch you?"

On the long journey north from Hladov, Irena had tried to prepare herself for every possibility: bitterness, resentment, cold confusion. But she had not thought to prepare herself for gentleness, and she can only answer with a nod.

The woodmaiden closes the last of the distance between them. She touches a thumb to the corner of Irena's eye, which stops one tear but summons another, then takes Irena's wrinkled hands in hers and draws them to her lips.

"I must seem a stranger to you," Irena says.

"You are my Irenka," the woodmaiden whispers, very soft, "and you are just the same as I remembered."

Irena laughs thickly and tips her head back to stare at the branches, hoping to keep the tears from falling, which does not work at all. She shakes her head. "You are the same. I am an old woman who has been gone too long."

"But you are here now. Will you dance with me?"

"No, no. I cannot dance. My body will not let me. I only wished to see you once more. To—to apologize for all the years I did not come."

Irena stumbles at the last, not knowing how to fit sixty years of wanting into words. The woodmaiden does not press. Instead she kisses Irena's palms—first one, then the other—and brings them to her heart. "Lie with me a while, then, and let me put flowers in your hair."

Irena tilts away from the woodmaiden, blinking to banish fresh tears; oh, it does no good, but she cannot bear to unlace their fingers. She means only to buy herself a moment of respite from the woodmaiden's smile, long enough to fumble once more for some excuse—*I should not, I cannot*—but at the sight that greets her, all Irena's objections give way to wonder. For the first time, she recognizes the flowers in the woodmaiden's footprints. It is too late in the summer for bluebells, too early for asters— yet the woodmaiden has painted the grove with all Irena's favorite blooms.

"If it would please you, I will not say no," Irena says, though she hardly trusts herself to speak without weeping. "For I would like nothing more."

◆

ALL THROUGH THE spring of Irena's seventeenth year, she danced with the woodmaiden in the birch grove. They leapt and twirled and spun for hours upon hours, then collapsed together in the grass and laughed themselves breathless. They traded words of admiration and affection. In time they traded words of love.

The days grew warm and long as they danced the springtime into summer. Every day, Irena came to the birch grove bearing some new gift: a little pot of linden honey, butter wrapped in a wet cloth, a crusty loaf of bread, a bottle of cloudy blackcurrant wine. In return, the woodmaiden wove garlands into Irena's hair that faded like a dream as soon as she set foot on the path to Březina.

Eventually, summer melted into autumn, and they made golden crowns from burnished birch leaves and lay together in their browning bower, where they kissed the last of the wine and honey from one another's lips. But autumn burnt down to the embers, and soon the days turned hard and cold. With the first snowfall of the year whitening their hair and shoulders, the woodmaiden met Irena at the edge of the grove.

"I must leave soon," the woodmaiden said, her green eyes sorrow-dark. "I have stayed in your world too long. The rest of my kind have already left for Zmejkovo, and I will not survive the winter on my own if I stay."

Irena opened her mouth and closed it again—dizzy with relief at having her own black news usurped, then stricken with terrible surprise. How desperately she longed to follow the woodmaiden to the village at the end of the world, where they might dwell among vili and dragons and samodivi, far from mothers and suitors!

Take me with you, she almost said.

"Oh," she said instead, afraid she would be sick if she dared say more.

"I will miss you. Every minute, I will miss you," the woodmaiden said, then smiled. "But I will spend the winter learning new dances, and when I return in the spring—"

"I will be gone in the spring," Irena interrupted. She had meant to wait for the right time, but she understood suddenly that there would be no right time, and the truth came out in a violent rush: "I—I will be gone—I am to wed Ctirad by Saint Stefan's Day—"

All the light vanished from the woodmaiden's face, quick as a pinched candle.

"I cannot refuse him any longer. I have worn out my mother's patience." Irena faltered. "He means to move us to Hladov, where his family lives."

The woodmaiden's lips parted in a wounded breath. "Then I shall never see you again."

"I will come back as soon I can. Not this spring, but the next. I promise."

"I do not believe you," the woodmaiden said, her eyes tear-bright. "You will turn to mortal things, and you will forget how we danced."

"I will never forget." Irena gathered the woodmaiden's hands in her own and kissed each knuckle with methodical care, every kiss another vow. "I promise. I promise."

❖

THEY SIT TOGETHER in the birch-bower for a long time. The woodmaiden brushes Irena's hair until it shines, then weaves aster and hawkweed through the thin white strands. Irena, with her head in the woodmaiden's lap, watches the songbirds flitting from branch to branch. Lying on the unforgiving ground makes her back ache. She does not complain.

"Were you happy?" the woodmaiden says into the silence, her voice so soft and sweet and terrible that it rips all the air from Irena's lungs.

"Ctirad was a good man," Irena manages after a moment. "He was kind, and he cared for me, in his way. We had three fine children. Two daughters and a son, all grown. And I am a grandmother, if you can believe such a thing. I am fortunate to have lived so long."

She speaks hesitatingly at first, strangely embarrassed by the truth of her happiness, but her voice warms when she speaks of her children and her grandchildren, as it always does. The woodmaiden's face warms too.

"I am glad."

Irena swallows. "I wanted to return, but we lived so far from Březina, and there was always work to be done—"

"I understand," the woodmaiden says, though she says it in the same way she always did when Irena spoke of mortal matters.

"He is dead now," Irena says. Ctirad is four years gone, in truth, and time has dulled the sting. She had taken a year to grieve and three more years to find the courage to return to Březina. "He is dead, and I am old, and you are young."

The woodmaiden laughs, bright as a blackbird. "I am older than you. I am as old as the forest, and maybe older, though I do not know how to measure it."

The air blurs and softens like the edges of a fire, and the woodmaiden's face begins to blur and soften too. Fine lines grow around her eyes and spread like ivy; her fair hair fades to moonlit silver; and her hands, resting on Irena's arms, wrinkle with the weight of sixty years. She gazes at Irena from an old woman's face. When she smiles, all the lines of her face deepen.

Irena touches her woodmaiden's cheek with unsteady fingers, afraid the vision might prove false. But the woodmaiden's skin is soft and warm and real. A different life unfurls before Irena all at once, as vivid as a memory: a cottage deep in the woods, the sounds of the forest uninterrupted by little feet or children's laughter, a whole garden full of flowers grown just for pleasure's sake. She does not know if it is a life she would have wanted. She only knows she did not have it.

"You are beautiful," she whispers.

"Sixty years I waited," the woodmaiden says. "I would have waited six hundred more."

She draws Irena up and kisses her. Though the kiss is chaste—nothing like the last time their lips met—it fills Irena's chest with a fire she thought she had forgotten.

"How I missed you," Irena says into the corner of her woodmaiden's mouth, and kisses her again, not half so chaste this time. Oh, she is too old to say such foolish things, too old by far to play this lovers' game of honeyed words and languid kisses—but when the woodmaiden's lips ghost along her check, Irena cannot remember to be ashamed.

"Dance with me," the woodmaiden murmurs when they pull apart.

This time, Irena does not refuse, though she winces as the woodmaiden draws her to her feet and coughs to cover the creaking of her bad knee. They hold one another unmoving for a time as the birds sing overhead. Then they begin to sway in a slow, ungainly version of the dances Irena has never stopped rehearsing in her daydreams.

So much has changed. But the woodmaiden still smells of sunlight on bare skin, linden honey, and blackcurrant wine. Her hands are gentle and her kiss is sweet, and the words she sighs into Irena's ear make her heart soar like a skylark, like a falling star, like a girl racing through the forest crying come to me, come to me, my springtime, my darling—

For the very last time, Irena dances among the birch trees. Though she is no longer young or strong or the third-most beautiful girl in Březina, she still knows all the steps.

Show Goes On

Louis Evans

It's the fourth night of Nicky Tremaine's one-man one-act play, *For Whom the Bell,* and there is nobody in the audience.

Not "nobody in the industry" nobody. Not "only friends and family" nobody. Not "one guy I dragged in from the stoop" nobody. Literally nobody. Zero people. Forty empty chairs in five rows of eight stare up at him.

Nicky takes a deep breath in. He lets it out.

It's been a hell of a long road from the bright lights and roaring studio audience at *Cheap at Twice the Price,* the sitcom where he wowed the world with the winsome dimples of little Nicky Price. A hell of a long road, almost straight downhill.

There's a chair on the strip of open floor that functions as the stage—Nicky uses it a lot in his monologue: standing, sitting, at one point throwing it across the room—and he sits down.

Nicky should just go home. He should quit while he's behind and go make something of himself. Something *else* of himself, something other than this wilted stretched bag of skin and meat that only knows how to caper around on a stage begging for laughs from a dwindling, pitying, pitiful audience.

He should quit. But he doesn't.

He gets mad instead.

The flyers say that *For Whom the Bell* runs from seven pm to eight thirty Wednesday through Monday for two weeks and that's *exactly what the fuck it's gonna do*. Studio soundstage or spare church basement, rapturous crowd or rats and termites, Shakespeare or shit, the show will go on.

Nicky Tremaine closes his eyes.

He opens them, and he says the opening line of the play, which he has written himself. "Welcome, friends, to the dark night of my soul."

But he delivers this mediocre, overwrought opening line on autopilot because the instant he opens his eyes he sees: now there is someone in the audience.

The person in the audience is sitting in the third seat in the second row. They are sitting very still and with excellent posture. They are wearing a jet-black spacesuit with electric green trim. Through the glass bubble of the space helmet, Nicky Tremaine can see a three-faced white skull, its triple jaw frozen open in a permanent scream.

It's Doctor Apocalypse.

❖

Nicky Tremaine lives in a world with a lot of super people in it. Superheroes and supervillains. Supersoldiers and super-spokespeople. Super-supermodels and super-superstars. Just—a lot of super stuff. The good, the bad and the ugly.

None of them is more awesome and full of dread than Doctor Apocalypse.

To pick the most famous example, Doctor Apocalypse has killed God.

On two distinct occasions.

The first time was back in the seventies. It was in all the papers. The *New York Times* headline reads "GOD IS DEAD!!!" above a photo of nuns flinging themselves over balustrades.

Of course people had been saying God was dead since forever, Nietzsche and all that, but they had no idea.

When Doctor Apocalypse fought God the entire globe was wreathed in stormclouds for a fortnight, heavy with rain that wouldn't fall, flickering with lightning that never struck the ground. Every night, every believer on Earth dreamed of the struggle in Heaven, God as a pillar of fire, God as an army, terrible with banners, God as a hippopotamus, God as a man taller than the sky with more limbs than stars in the firmament, God as a slash of crimson on a field of argent, and Doctor Apocalypse always and exactly Doctor Apocalypse, black spacesuit and green trim and white bone, moving with singular and terrible purpose, striking at God, *hurting* God.

And on that terrible day when Doctor Apocalypse killed God, the sun burned a mourning ultraviolet and every river ran electric green with sin; every leaf fell from every tree and all the bells were split in a single instant.

Nietzsche had no fucking idea.

God got better, of course. He's God. And the leaves came back, and the rivers, and the sunshine.

Some people said when God came back He came back wrong, that you could tell the difference between before and after. Like with bananas. Some people said God was just the same.

It didn't seem to matter much to Doctor Apocalypse, who moved on to other projects. Like stealing clockwise, or moving the Andromeda galaxy one galaxy-width to the left.

Or, twenty years later, coming back to Heaven and killing God again, equally unprovoked, but much more efficiently and violently.

That's the sort of supervillain Doctor Apocalypse is.

That's the sort of supervillain who's sitting, alone, in the audience of Nicky Tremaine's one-man one-act play.

◈

NICKY STANDS THERE, on the stage, face to face with Doctor Apocalypse. A bead of sweat runs from his temple down to his collar. Flop sweat or terror sweat, who's to say?

There's a long, long beat of silence. And then Nicky Tremaine begins to act.

He does the fucking show. He does all of it. Curtain to curtain. He's a professional.

Well, technically, tonight he's *not* a professional, since Doctor Apocalypse hasn't paid for a ticket. But he's still a professional.

Plus, all the advice about Doctor Apocalypse is the same: don't engage. Doctor Apocalypse isn't a supervillain like Revulso, who hates humans so much she's always gobbling them up with that big frog mouth of hers and then vomiting chunks of them everywhere, or like Slenderfinger, who's basically a garden variety psychosexual sociopathic serial killer except that, God help us all, he has total psychic control over every mime within half a mile, whether living or animatronic. Unlike your typical supervillain, such as those assholes, Doctor Apocalypse is not malicious and bears no antipathy towards humanity.

Doctor Apocalypse is indeed extremely dangerous, but dangerous in the manner of a runaway freight train. A runaway train *will* kill you—it'll spread your precious internal organs in a vast indifferent parabolic arc from here to Poughkeepsie and just keep chugging—but if you stand ten feet away from the rails it's not going to jump the track to get to *you*, personally. Probably.

The only difference is, with Doctor Apocalypse, you *can't see where the rails are.*

So, okay. Nicky hates himself and he wants to die, but it turns out he doesn't really want to *die*, die. He'd rather not have his precious internal organs spread out in a vast and indifferent arc from here to Proxima Centauri.

So he does the show, exactly as if to an audience of zero. He projects the pompous bits and he overacts the emotional bits and he even tears up at the "Daddy why'd you die?" soliloquy.

(Fake tears are the only feat of acting for which Nicky Tremaine has ever received any meaningful education— his mother screaming at him before an audition, "if those tears look fake I'll give you something real to cry about!"—and so he writes them into every role.)

Say what you will about the writing and the direction, it is by far the best of Nicky's four performances of this play to date.

He acts all the way to the end—his own character's clawing, rasping expiration—and then lies motionless on the floor, holding his breath, waiting for applause. Or death.

Neither is forthcoming.

Nicky Tremaine opens one sneaky eyelid.

He is alone in the theater.

(Church basement, really.)

He scrambles to his feet. There is nobody in the second row. There is nobody in the audience at all. There is no sign of Doctor Apocalypse anywhere.

Relief crashes through Nicky in the form of a wave of adrenalin that turns his insides to water. He stumbles to the tiny basement bathroom unsure of whether he's gonna puke or shit first, but despite his discombobulated state he manages to line up his orifices and their timings and the scuffed porcelain bowl pretty neatly, so disaster is avoided.

And then he buttons himself up and he rushes back home.

◆

It's LA and so of course Nicky Tremaine has a roommate. Honestly he's lucky he's kept it down to one.

"Perri!" he shouts, hammering on the door. Then he remembers he's got a key too, gets it out of his pocket, drops it, picks it up, drops it again, picks it up more firmly this time, holding it in a sort of sideways child grip so he won't drop it a third time, which means he can't get it into the keyhole, so he shifts his grip and drops it *again*—

And the door opens, and there's Perri.

Perri is short and butch and wiry but not in a skinny way, and she's trying to break into comedy. She's a prop comic but nobody wants prop comics anymore—Carrot Top killed the niche—so she does a lot of improv. She's wearing an LA Dodgers baseball cap backwards, which she does one hundred percent of the time. Nicky can't tell if it's a lesbian thing or a comedy thing or another thing entirely. It's a bad look but you gotta admire her. She commits to the bit.

"Perri," says Nicky. "You'll never fucking believe my day."

"*Your* day?" exclaims Perri, in a voice like an overexposed Seinfeld impression. "Your day! *You'll* never believe *my* day! First the car wouldn't start, and then I drove to Andrea's house when I should have been going to Alicia's, but then it turned out Alicia was over at Andrea's house, so we're screaming at each other, and then I remembered I was supposed to turn the oven off for Aileen, so we all three got in my car, but—"

"Doctor Apocalypse was at my show," says Nicky.

Perri stops in her tracks.

Doctor Apocalypse's name isn't a *bad* word, technically.

You can say it on TV and the FCC won't fine you for it. But it's a serious word, a very unfunny word. Like, imagine the word "leukemia" in a world where everyone's grandma died of blood cancer. Comedians love taking the piss out of superpeople but they steer clear of Doctor Apocalypse. Nobody's got a "The Aristocrats" joke with that name in it. You'd get nothing but crickets. You would die out on that stage.

So when Nicky says that comedy-killing phrase, it throws Perri for a loop. She narrows her eyes and cocks her head, trying to make sense of this impossible remark. Finally she settles for wagging her finger at him and laughing knowingly.

"Almost got me there, Nick! What a—"

"It's not a joke."

A longer, more awkward pause.

"Can I come in?" Nicky picks up his keys, then pushes past Perri without waiting for a reply.

"You sure you're not fucking with me?" she calls out after him as he stalks to the kitchen.

Unsurprisingly, given Nicky and Perri's combined salaries, it's not a big apartment and so it's not a long stalk. Nicky opens the fridge, takes out a beer, puts it back, opens the freezer, takes out a vodka, and then goes over and collapses on the couch.

"I'm not fucking with you. Doctor Apocalypse came to my show."

"What?" says Perri, her voice regaining some of its Seinfeldesque patina but in a register of existential despair, a George instead of a Jerry, "Has the city been destroyed and nobody told me about it? Are we all floating atoms left after Doctor Apocalypse annihilated Los Angeles, just imagining we're still around?"

"It's not like that. He didn't *do* anything," says Nicky. "He just…showed up. At the beginning. One minute, there's nobody there, the next he's sitting in the second row, just watching me. He sat through the whole thing. Then he disappeared."

(Doctor Apocalypse's pronouns are a little bit up in the air, since Doctor Apocalypse presents to the world as a screaming skull in a unisex spacesuit and does not have a social media bio for reference. The AP style guide's superhuman appendix dictates male pronouns, but that guide was written in the seventies, and nobody wants to be the person to update Doctor Apocalypse's entry because *what if Doctor Apocalypse shows up to comment?* In the seventies, when they wrote the guide, everyone on the AP style committee was neck deep in blow and had no fear of death. So, anyway, Nicky's pronoun choice, if unwoke and unjustified, is at least official.)

"Okay," says Perri. "I see what's going on here. You did a little of this, hmm? Or this?" She pantomimes gulping from a flask, smoking a joint, snorting cocaine, injecting heroin, freebasing crack, and licking an LSD stamp, in that order. Her improv classes are really big on object work.

"No," says Nicky. "I was sober, fuck you very much." He had a bit of a coke habit, back in the *Cheap at Twice the Price* days, but there's no coke money anymore.

"Maybe it was just, you know, a psychotic break."

"That's comforting," says Nicky sarcastically, and then he realizes: actually it is. People get better from psychotic episodes. They don't get better from what Doctor Apocalypse does to them. The thought that he should, rationally, be hoping for a mental health crisis makes Nicky a little sad.

They sit there for a minute, just two roommates. It's easier to share a house. It's harder to share problems.

"Weird shit happens sometimes," says Perri.

"Weird shit happens," Nicky agrees.

"So what are you gonna do?" she asks. "Call a doctor? Call the Pacific Patrol?"

It's the first real question Perri's asked him since he came home and so he takes a minute to think about it, really think about his options.

Who's he gonna tell? Who will believe a third-rate washed up ex-child-actor with no evidence when he says, "yeah, I gave a private show to Doctor Apocalypse?" Not the receptionist at the doctor's office. Not the phone screeners at the Pacific Patrol. Not the tipline at TMZ. Nobody.

"I'm gonna finish this bottle of vodka," says Nicky. "And then I'm gonna pass out."

◆

IT'S THE FIFTH night of Nicky Tremaine's one-man one-act play and he is definitely hung over. He splashes a little water on his face in the sink, because that's something people always try in the movies. He pretends that it helps.

Then he goes back on stage.

There's nobody in the audience. This is probably better than the alternative.

Nicky doesn't mean to close his eyes before the show starts. In fact he keeps them open, as long as he can, staring into the empty theater. But stare too long into the abyss and your blink reflex takes over.

Nicky blinks. It's no longer than any other blink, and when it's over, Doctor Apocalypse is sitting in the audience.

Nicky stares.

Doctor Apocalypse's head turns, very slowly and steadily, to face him.

It's been four years since Nicky had a speaking part in anything important but he can still recognize a cue when he sees it. He swallows hastily, picks up the opening line from the scattered index cards of his terror-trembled brain, and begins.

"Welcome, friends—"

The fifth performance of *For Whom the Bell* is noticeably better than the fourth. The overacting has mellowed into a thick, creamy melodrama. It's still barely acting, but at least it no longer reads as failed camp.

Nicky doesn't even have to shit after the show this time. You can get used to anything, as long as you take it in survivable doses.

◈

Afterwards, he's three beers into the sixpack and Perri comes home from a long day of sneaking out of her temp job to hit up comedy auditions. Normally that'd be her cue to dive into a bitchfest about which fucking director was what kind of fucking asshole—but she sees Nicky's thousand-yard stare and his beer and she knows.

"Again?"

Nicky nods.

"Fuck it," says Perri. "I'm coming tomorrow."

"You sure that's a good idea?"

Perri squares her shoulders and sets her Dodgers hat deep on her forehead. "Nope."

◈

It's easier to set up for the show with Perri's help, not that it's ever especially hard. It's just forty folding chairs in rows. Forty-one, counting the stage.

"So where does..." Perri trails off. She doesn't love saying the name, and she's gotten more jumpy by the minute, ever since they left for the theater.

"Second row," says Nicky. "Third seat from the right."

"Okay," says Perry. And she sits second row, fourth seat from the right. Which, well. You're plenty safe ten feet to one side of a runaway locomotive. A tenth of an inch is maybe a different story.

"Listen," says Nicky. "You don't have to do that. You don't have to do any of this."

"I don't have to do shit. But I'm here, okay? Actors gotta stick together."

Nicky mouths "thank you." Perry bats the gratitude away with an exaggerated gesture.

"Start the show. I wanna see your face when you hallucinate." She may sound skeptical but Perri's sitting stiff and cautious, holding herself so that she's definitely not touching the personal space of the chair to her left.

Nicky nods. He doesn't blink. He doesn't speak. He just forms the intention to begin.

Doctor Apocalypse is sitting next to his roommate.

Here's the thing about the screaming skull inside the spacesuit: it's got at least three faces. One's looking forward. The other two peek out sideways in Doctor Apocalypse's peripheral vision, peering through the edge of the glass bubble. One of them is looking directly at Perri.

So for ninety minutes Perri sits perfectly still, frozen by terror and perhaps something more than terror—since there is no comprehensive list of all of Doctor Apocalypse's superpowers and who knows, maybe a paralyzing gaze is one of them—and she watches her roommate's one-man one-act play and she tries, desperately, not to let her pupils slide sideways in their locked-in sockets and see the terrible half-face staring back at her.

Ninety fucking minutes.

When the play is over and Doctor Apocalypse vanishes and suddenly that weight, that awful and terrible weight, as if Temple Grandin had designed a hug machine to facilitate the slaughter of brontosauruses, is lifted from her, Perri takes a deep breath in and slumps bonelessly all the way to the floor.

She's not literally boneless, thankfully. Which could have happened. That's how Skeleton Sword ended up, when she tried to take down Doctor Apocalypse back in the nineties.

"Holy shit," moans Perri, from somewhere Nicky can't see, down between the rows of chairs.

"He's worse up close, isn't he," Nicky says.

Perri's only response is to clutch her Dodgers hat while muttering a low, panicked, and repeated recitation of "Hail Mary."

◆

AFTER THE SHOW they go out to a bar 'cause it's nearer the theater (church basement) than the apartment is and also there's not enough liquor left in the fridge to cover both of them.

The bar is right across from the church, which is kind of unfortunate, since when the basement isn't being used as a theater (Tuesdays) it hosts an AA meeting. But what can you do.

Four drinks in silence, side by side. Four drinks in, Perri's feeling strong enough to turn and face her roommate. Nicky turns to face her.

"Nick," she says. "Why the fuck is Doctor Apocalypse at your show?"

"I have no fucking idea."

"Do you *know* Doctor Apocalypse?"

"Do I *look* like the kind of guy who knows Doctor Fucking Apocalypse?"

Which, actually, yeah, he does. At this exact instant in his life, with that hangover stubble on his jaw, easy yet inescapable grip on the vodka glass, and most especially that expression—a certain tightness around the eyes, the thousand yard-stare's much older, much meaner brother—Nicky does kind of look like a guy who knows Doctor Apocalypse. But Perri takes his meaning.

"Maybe you used to know them. Before, you know." Perri gestures vaguely at her face, by which she seems to mean "before whatever supervillain origin story transformed Doctor Apocalypse from, presumably, a more-or-less ordinary human into a skeleton in a spacesuit that periodically kills God," and which meaning Nicky basically picks up on.

"Doctor Apocalypse killed God before I was born."

"That doesn't matter! Maybe there was time shit," says Perri, pointing theatrically at her watch. She's not wrong; with superpeople there's a lot of time shit. Nicky sighs.

"How the fuck would I know if someone I know turned into Doctor Apocalypse?"

It's a rhetorical question, because the answer is Wikipedia. Which Perri figures out after a second, popping her phone out of her pocket and pulling up Doctor Apocalypse's page.

"Huh," she says, doing that thing where you're having a conversation with someone, and then they just respond out loud to some shit on their phone as though it were a shared experience, even though it's obviously not.

"Well?" asks Nicky. "Who was he?"

"No idea," says Perri. "'Nothing is known about the life of Doctor Apocalypse before 1968, when the supervillain bisected the moon,' blah blah blah."

(Wikipedia is written by committee and so the Doctor Apocalypse pronoun debate has been resolved by declaring the entire article a pronoun-free neutral zone. It's a terrible solution.)

"But it does say what they're a doctor of."

"What?"

"Doctorate in geography. From University of Colorado Boulder. You ever get a PhD from UCB, Nicky?"

"I've never been more than ten miles north of Santa Barbara," says Nicky, which is both true and sad.

"So school chum is out," says Perri. She scrolls a bit more but it's just the shit everybody knows about Doctor Apocalypse already, so she pockets her phone.

"Maybe it's not about your past," she says. "Maybe it's about your future. Maybe in twenty years you're gonna kill Doctor Apocalypse, so they came back, like the Terminator—"

"But then I'd be dead," says Nicky.

"You'd be dead," repeats Perri. Normally she'd shy away from that remark but, four vodkas or no, this very evening she has spent ninety minutes staring into the implacable sidemaw of Doctor Apocalypse and one thing is crystal clear: if Doctor Apocalypse had come to the show to kill someone that person would be very dead.

So, another theory. Perri mulls it over.

"Maybe you're not going to kill them. Maybe you're going to *become* them. Maybe they're coming to the show to see you before you're all grown up and skeleton-y."

"Are you fucking serious."

"You got any better ideas?"

"Maybe—" Nicky takes another swallow. "Maybe he likes the show."

Perri stares.

Nicky shrugs. "Maybe it's right up his alley."

Perri's still staring.

"Okay fine," says Nicky. "Fuck you."

"I mean, if it's the best guess you got—"

"Just forget it."

❖

NICKY WAKES UP. It's Tuesday.

He checks his phone.

Word got out. Perri must have told.

Nothing moves faster in LA than unconfirmed celebrity rumors, and so Nicky's looking at about a thousand messages—texts, emails, DMs, voicemails, the whole fucking thing—trying to get tickets to his show.

He's scrolling through them frantically, wondering how the hell he's going to decide who gets the two hundred and forty seats—no, two thirty four, he *can't sell Doctor Apocalypse's seat!*—when the thought enters his brain, lobbed in gently above his ordinary thought processes as though shouted helpfully from across the street: "just charge more money!"

So he does.

By Tuesday dinner—microwave burrito and not the good kind—Nicky Tremaine has sold out the remaining nights of his one-man one-act show for a cool half-million dollars.

Normally that kind of surprise paycheck would be a one-way first class ticket back into coke addiction, except, shit, Nicky's got a show tomorrow night, sold out audience, paying *thousands* a seat—coke's sounding better every second—and, oh, by the way, if he flubs a line Doctor Apocalypse might with no warning or appeal decide to turn the entire LA metro area into a perfectly hemispherical hole in the ground.

How's that for a higher fucking power, you twelve-step motherfuckers?

So instead of finding some cheap crack or even some gentlemanly snow, Nicky runs lines and he runs lines and he falls asleep and he dreams about running lines and he wakes up and he runs lines and then suddenly it's showtime.

❖

IT'D BE EASIER to set up the theater and corral the crowd if Perri were here to help, but she's got something of her own tonight. Doctor Apocalypse or no Doctor Apocalypse, you can never, ever get your roommate to come to your show twice.

So it's a one-man operation before the show, and it turns out people who've paid a few grand to see Doctor Apocalypses are huge assholes in general, and much worse about seating in particular. They're shouting at Nicky and each other, scooting their folding chairs out of alignment and all over the floor, and in fact one utter lunatic actually gets out of his seat and tries to *switch into Doctor Apocalypse's seat*, forcing Nicky to stand at just off stage left and scream-whisper at him, "Do you *want* to fucking die? Do you want to *fucking* die? Do you want to fucking *die*?" until he gets up and moves again.

Finally everyone's more or less where they're supposed to be. Nicky gets up on center stage.

When Doctor Apocalypse appears in the audience it's not so much that a hush falls over the crowd. More like an auditory guillotine.

And then, to his first sold-out audience in fifteen years, Nicky Tremaine performs.

◈

Tonight his performance is far better than the ones which came before. So much better, in fact, that you might even call it acting.

◈

Afterwards, the audience—those of them who aren't in the fetal position or tipped backwards onto the floor or running screaming out into the street—mob the stage. It's been a full decade since the last time Nicky Tremaine has been mobbed and all of his instincts are wrong. There's no security, no adult minders. Nobody is assuaged when he throws them his dimpliest smile and offers to sign autographs.

So that's pretty rough.

◈

Thursday. Another sold out house. Halfway through this performance the doors at the back of the theater (church basement) are flung open.

The duo that bursts in is undoubtedly dynamic: a man and a woman in complementary spandex outfits, his orange, hers blue, white symbols on the chest. She's an absolute unit, built like a roided-out trolley car. Four hundred pounds of muscle and fat and more muscle at a minimum.

He's floating six inches above the ground. There are electric-blue flames spurting from his cuticles and from his tear ducts.

"Doctor Apocalypse!" bellows the woman. "Your reign of terror is over!"

"No evildoer can withstand the righteous might of the Terrific Twins!" adds the man.

Nicky doesn't stop performing but he does trail off a little in the middle of a line about his overbearing mother. He's never heard of the "Terrific Twins" in his life but superhero teams are like modeling agencies. There's always another one popping up out of nowhere, trying to prove they're the hottest new chick in the swimsuit catalog.

The woman roars and stampedes toward Doctor Apocalypse from behind, hands raised to scatter the audience out of the way. The man rises into the air on a gout of flame, then swoops down at the supervillain. Shouts of dismay from the audience.

Nicky stammers. He says "Um." He repeats his line.

And Doctor Apocalypse, without turning, without looking, raises one space-gloved hand into the air. And makes a fist.

It's not an angry fist or a triumphal fist. It's not a power fist or a sex fist. It's just a gesture, distinct and finite, the way a sergeant commands a squad to stop, or a conductor calls an orchestra to rest.

And the Terrific Twins die.

The woman coughs, staggers, collapses, sprawled out on the floor, writhing, gasping, rattling, still. A little water spurts from her greying mouth and nose. Not a lot. Just exactly enough to drown on dry land.

With the man it's worse. One second he's swooping down at Doctor Apocalypse and the next second it's as if someone has gone from scalp to toe and sliced him into sheets, papery millimeter-thin sheets, and he holds the form of a man for an instant and then all of the sheets come apart from each other and fall towards the ground in a formless confetti rain and then they spontaneously combust, going up in flashes like distant lightning or paparazzi camera mobs, until there's nothing left but a gentle ash, sifting slowly over the audience.

"Um," says Nicky Tremaine. "Uh."

Doctor Apocalypse's head turns toward him by just a fraction of a degree.

"My, um, mother—"

The rest of the show proceeds without incident. In the big city, people know to step around the super wreckage.

❖

Friday.

The audience filters in polite, cordial. Lots of folks seem to know each other. They're laughing, smiling. Maybe a little tense around the eyes. No pushing, no shoving. Everyone sits at just about the same time.

Nicky's standing by the side of the stage, about to go on, watching the audience.

There's something off about them. He can't quite put his finger on it. They're such a normal-looking, good-looking crowd. Clear skin and done-up hair and comfortable slacks. Most everybody has wide shoulders and strong chin lines and defined physiques. And all of them look familiar, somehow, except not quite. Like when you run into your friend's fraternal twin at the taqueria and you're like...no? But maybe?

In fact, that guy in particular, probably the tallest and handsomest of a pretty tall and handsome bunch, the one who's sitting one seat to the left of *the* seat, Doctor Apocalypse's seat—right in the same place where Perri sat the night it was just her and Nicky and Doctor Apocalypse—that guy looks just like Captain Unbeatable.

Captain Unbeatable is the indefatigable leader of the

Pacific Patrol, the invulnerable man with the million-watt smile who's saved the greater Los Angeles metro area more times than anyone can count. And this guy, who's sitting down in Nicky's audience, who's shrugging out of his coat and limbering up his shoulders a little, looks almost *exactly* like him.

Except he's wearing glasses.

Nicky's halfway across the stage when the penny drops. By then it's too late. He stumbles onto his mark, his mouth already dropping open into his over-rehearsed opening line.

Captain Unbeatable takes off his glasses.

"Welcome, friends—" begins Nicky.

Doctor Apocalypse appears in the chair.

Captain Unbeatable socks him in the jaw.

Even through the loose shirtsleeve of his civilian disguise, Captain Unbeatable's forearm is like an anatomy-textbook diagram of an arm: Bicep! Tricep! Flexor! Extensor!

It makes perfect contact with the dome of Doctor Apocalypse's space helmet and Doctor Apocalypse topples sideways into the seat beside. There's a crack running down that flawless arc of glass and Doctor Apocalypse seems almost stunned. For an instant Captain Unbeatable's perfect arm hangs in the air like a half-built girder bridge.

Then Doctor Apocalypse, moving in a way that suggests first of all that space and time are merely bookkeeping conventions, and furthermore that Doctor Apocalypse is the sort of Bentley-driving tax lawyer that the IRS will *never* catch up with, reaches out with one hand and breaks Captain Unbeatable's wrist.

Then a lot of stuff starts happening all at the same time.

The woman in the front row with the high ponytail stands up and flings out her hands and the entire substance of reality shimmers in and out of being and when it's back the basement is no longer, you know, a basement, a hole in the dirt in a particular spot on the whirling surface of the Earth, but rather a mazelike self-mirroring pocket of reality bubbling through the void. You can see the void's purple-on-ultraviolet streaks through the basement windows snugged up against the ceiling, and it's pretty clear that the staircase out of the basement just leads back in from the other side.

That's because the woman with the high pony is Portalina, and whenever the Pacific Patrol dukes it out with some especially explosive villain it's her job to teleport the scene of the fight out of the metro LA area and into some pocket dimension so that they don't smash up the whole city.

This is why she's the mayor's favorite.

Meanwhile the entire audience is erupting out of their seats. Civilian disguises are flung into the air, evaporated, shimmering into supersuits, and, in the case of the Princess Agate, an exchange hero visiting from Japan's Magical Special Division, transformed vía an elaborately choreographed dance number into a remarkably stylish suit of magitek heavy infantry battle armor.

Nor are the transformations strictly sartorial. Werebeasts become beasts! Cyborg limbs blast away their skin-tone camo panels to reveal bristling particle cannons! Aliens in disguise are now just, you know, aliens! The Ten-Story Woman shoots up to her titular ten stories, which causes her head to crash right through the basement ceiling and then back out through the floor, moebius-strip style, which is pretty disorienting until Portalina straightens it out.

And all of this sudden superpower directs itself in a concerted assault on Doctor Apocalypse, a barrage of ray blasts and psychic whips and fists and legs and swords and arrows and laser beams and—

"I can just go," says Nicky Tremaine. He's still projecting but at nobody in particular.

"No!" bellows the Ten Story Woman, as her cranelike arm stabs into the melee that surrounds Doctor Apocalypse, her beer-barrel fingers hooked into a claw to crush the life out of that spacesuited skeleton, except that before she can reach him her hand slams into an invisible dome of pure force that knocks her clear across to the basement's far corner, to smash into a wall or maybe the ceiling, given how wonky space is over there.

"You've got to keep performing!" says Portalina. "I can't keep Doctor Apocalypse here. Only you can do it! The only thing we know is that Doctor Apocalypse doesn't leave until the end of your show! You have to help us!"

Portalina is really good at summarizing complicated superhero bullshit in a few cogent sentences, and then also making a genuinely affecting plea for help. This is why she's also the media's favorite.

So, Nicky realizes: the Pacific Patrol are in trouble and only washed-up boy actor Nicky Tremaine can save the day—by acting!

Nicky's written some self-indulgent pap in his time but this really takes the fucking cake. The only problem is, it's real.

The show must go on.

And it does. Nicky keeps going as the battle rages all around him. He keeps monologuing as Doctor Apocalypse scatters superheroes as the lawnmower scatters lawn; he keeps monologuing as Scarlet Pride and Penumbaura and Icelad go to their deaths, snapped in half. He throws the chair theatrically against the wall and before it gets there a crackling miasma of Apocalypse-energy swallows it whole and barfs out a swarm of electric-green hunter-killer chair wasps that drive HERCULES 2.0 and Agnifica stumbling and screaming up-down the Escherized staircase.

"I just wanted you to love me!" sobs Nicky Tremaine in all his overacting glory as Portalina darts toward Doctor Apocalypse, dodging doom blasts, her jazz hands moving through unimaginable katas, magenta spears leaping from her wormholes to skewer that midnight spacesuit, and as Nicky weeps his not-quite-fake tears Doctor Apocalypse turns those spears on Portalina and pins her twitching, broken, to the ground.

Nicky keeps going and the Pacific Patrol keeps losing, superhero after superhero down for the count, beaten or dying.

Ninety fucking minutes.

What did they think would happen? Doctor Apocalypse has *killed God twice*. The Pacific Patrol isn't even an army of angels; they're just kids in spandex. Compared to Doctor Apocalypse there's almost nothing super about them.

But, super or not, they are, in the crucible of this moment, revealed to be heroes. To the last one they go down fighting.

Hero's just another word for too stupid not to die.

◈

NINETY FUCKING MINUTES.

Nicky Tremaine is on the ground. He's acting out his own death, surrounded by the truly dead, or nearly there. He's rasping. He's whimpering. He's hitting his cues.

Thirty eight superheroes lay sprawled around him in various stages of mortal peril, or mortal end. Only Doctor Apocalypse is standing.

Floating, really. Six inches above the carnage. With one viselike hand holding Captain Unbeatable aloft. By his throat.

Nicky begs. He pleads. For himself, of course; *For Whom The Bell* is as narcissistic a one-man show as you're likely to ever see, and that's a high bar.

Captain Unbeatable's neck is like an anatomy-textbook diagram of a strangulation. Sternocleidomastoid. Trachea. Carotid. His eyes bulge. Doctor Apocalypse is looking up at him with whatever expression a screaming skull has.

Nicky dies.

Doctor Apocalypse vanishes.

Captain Unbeatable crumples to the floor like a two hundred pound bag of hamburger.

Portalina, who's been lying still and trapped and tormented for maybe half an hour lets out a sigh of relief, then passes out. The purple veins of light wrinkle out of existence and the theater is once again a church basement, looking out on a Los Angeles evening.

◈

NICKY'S SWEAT-DRENCHED THUMBS can barely stab out 9-1-1 on his cellphone but it turns out he doesn't need to. The Pacific Patrol has called the cops already. And the media.

The cops who come marching down the stairs think that they're going to lead some supervillain away in chains. The reporters who crowd behind them, cameras at the ready, can't wait to capture yet another scene of successful superheroics. It's always good footage when you get superheroes after the fight. The beaming grin of Captain Unbeatable; the mussed ponytail of Portalina. *Hey, do you ever wonder if the two of them are going to get together?* (Of course not. He only dates men and she is one hundred percent asexual. Not that either of those facts are in the public record; the superhero industry is pretty queerphobic.)

Nobody is ready for the carnage they find. Nobody is ready to find Nicky Tremaine, washed-up boy actor, the last man standing in a superhero abattoir.

◈

NICKY'S THE LAST guy to get in an ambulance—which is fair, because he's the only person in that basement who didn't get the shit kicked out of him by Doctor Apocalypse—which gives the media plenty of time to surround him.

The last time Nicky had a press scrum it was his mother, one claw in his shoulder, who pointed out reporters, but he's got the idea. Camera flashes go off everywhere, but he's already stunned into semisensibility.

"Of course I fucking saw who did it. It was Doctor Apocalypse."

"He just—showed up. I don't know."

"I don't know why he keeps coming to my show."

"No. I don't know Doctor Apocalypse."

"No, I don't *like* him. That's fucking disgusting."

"Me? I'm Nicky Tremaine."

"Yeah, *Cheap at Twice the Price*. Yeah, it's a one-act play. *For Whom the Bell*."

"No, I don't think he likes the show. *I* don't like the show—it's. It's. It's—fuck, no more questions about me, okay?"

It's around then that Nicky's ambulance shows up. He protests, but he's not going to win a battle of wills with four LA paramedics. They bundle him off.

◈

A NEW YORK minute is the amount of time between when the lights go green and when the taxis start honking. An LA minute is the amount of time between when you appear unexpectedly on TV and when a producer you haven't heard from in ten years blows up your phone.

Nicky's trying to make himself comfortable on an ambulance gurney and failing when the ringing starts, and it doesn't stop. So eventually he answers.

"Nicky! Buddy!"

"Hi Edg—"

"I haven't seen you since we worked on *Cheap at Twice the Price*! It's been years, man! What have you been up to!"

"Well, I—"

"Listen, that's great. Are you signed to anything right now?"

"I've got—"

"Your show, of course, but a passion project like that can't really put food on the table, hahaha. Right? Hahaha."

"Actually—"

"Listen, I've got a *great* role for you. Lotta laughs, lotta heart, it's like *Price* all over again. Can you start Monday?"

A smart person would tell Edgar thanks for the opportunity, I've got a lot to consider. A smart person would at least try to call whatever agent used to be his agent.

Sometimes Nicky's a smart person. But he's been waiting for this call, this awful, dehumanizing, one-sided call, for just about twenty years.

Plus he's the most traumatized he's ever been in his life. So he says, "okay."

◆

THERE WERE SUPPOSED to be three more nights of *For Whom the Bell*. Except the entire neighborhood is covered in caution tape and agents from the FBI's superhuman division. They shuffle Nicky off to a portable command trailer where they ask him a bunch of questions about Doctor Apocalypse for which the answer is always some variant of "I don't know, and I don't know why I don't know," and then they kick his ass out and tell him his show is canceled.

That's fine. He's got a new one.

◆

DEPARTMENT OF CORRECTIONS is a show that's supposed to marry the lighthearted whimsy of *Parks and Rec* with the searing insight into the American (in)justice system of *Orange is the New Black*.

It's not true that TV executives pick their fall lineup by having blindfolded monkeys throw darts at a whirling roulette wheel with last season's hits written on it. In fact, the situation is far worse. If nothing else, you could fire a blindfolded monkey for incompetence.

Show business!

❖

Nicky Tremaine shows up at the set of *Department of Corrections* with a very specific look on his face; a way of walking slowly and touching everything very gingerly but definitely touching everything. It is the look of a desert island castaway who has after ten long years been airlifted to the central promenade of the Mall of America. He's got a trailer and everything!

They film *Department of Corrections* in front of a live studio audience because bad ideas don't come in threes, they come in packs, hunting. Nicky runs lines and when on his first night he does his big entrance a deadly hush falls over the crowd. It takes the flashing applause sign three times to get anyone to clap.

Staring into the audience, Nicky can see why.

Normally when they fill up a studio audience they pack those fuckers in there tight. It's almost impossible to have a show in so much trouble that you can't find a hundred and fifty people to holler at it on TV. But this night, there's an empty seat.

Just one. Second row, third from the right. And the entire audience is staring at it.

Nicky realizes: Edgar, that fucking lunatic, didn't just cast Nicky because of his fifteen seconds of fame. Edgar cast him hoping for a special guest appearance by Doctor Apocalypse.

Edgar was trying—*deliberately*—to summon the world's most terrifying supervillain, the coldblooded murderer of a quarter of the Pacific Patrol, into his shit sitcom's live studio audience.

Nicky holds his breath.

There's no one in the seat. There's still no one in the seat.

He lets his breath out again, a raggedy sigh, and a hundred studio audience members sigh with him.

"How about it, folks?" says Nicky, which is technically his opening line but he just lobs it out into the audience, wry and a little tweaked out, and whaddya know, this time they crack the hell up.

◈

FOUR WEEKS INTO the show, Rosario Sheridan comes to his trailer.

"Hi," says Nicky, glancing up from his script.

She shuts the door.

"You're shit," she says.

"Well good afternoon to you too," says Nicky, setting the script aside and turning to face her.

"Shut up," says Rosario. On *Department of Corrections* she plays the no-nonsense warden, straight woman to Nicky's prison-doctor funnyman, but she's never been anything other than warm and gracious off set, not that Nicky's seen. So the contempt in her voice takes him a little by surprise.

"Casting you was a gimmick and it hasn't really panned out," says Rosario. "You can't fucking act and you're not a dimply kid anymore. If you don't get better—a lot better—then you'll be out of here in weeks."

"Okay," says Nicky. He feels like, maybe once upon a time he would have been all "excuse me?!" but ever since he saw Doctor Apocalypse kill all those people he's been saying "okay" a lot more instead.

"Let me coach you," says Rosario.

"Why?"

"Cause I'm real stupid about looking out for helpless people," she says.

"Okay," says Nicky. He's getting good at saying that.

◈

ROSARIO IS A good enough coach that they don't fire him right away and not at the end of the season either. *Department of Corrections* runs for four more years, but Nicky jumps ship after two. So does Rosario. She ends up in a prestige drama about a third-generation tech money family. He lands a sitcom with a much less offensive premise. With Rosario's help, of course.

Rosario always seems to know what to do and so Nicky asks her to marry him and she agrees.

It's a rainy day somewhere but not Los Angeles. Her hands are warm and his are slightly sweaty. After the vows a whole flock of starlings takes off from a nearby tree, all at the same time, just as if they'd planned it.

◈

MEANWHILE DOCTOR APOCALYPSE is somewhere else in the universe, making stars explode. This ends up wiping out a whole species of intelligent squirrel-people, which, as it happens, is a huge relief to their interstellar neighbors, the intelligent acorn-people. That's not why Doctor Apocalypse did it, though.

◈

NICKY AND ROSARIO'S marriage lasts six pilots, two shows, and three movies, one of them in theaters. Nicky learns how to wear a flattering suit jacket and how to make polite conversation at a producer's fancy dinner parties; how to compliment someone when you think they've had some plastic surgery but you're not exactly sure; how to act. Love scenes, death scenes. That thing where an actor has a totally blank expression but you can tell by the tension around their eyes that they're really going through some shit. He starts calling himself Nicholas. He directs several episodes of television.

He gets a lot out of that marriage. It's just never quite clear what Rosario gets back.

Marriages like this don't last, and so, it doesn't.

By Hollywood standards the divorce is very genteel. It takes place entirely in lawyers' offices.

Rosario gets a part in a West End play and just like that she's on the other side of the world. Nicholas Tremaine directs a movie and then another, but it's the third, *Assisted*, that really draws the critical attention. The studio even makes an awards push, and though Nicholas only walks away with one nomination it's enough to change his life. He can see the headline of his obituary changing in real time.

After that there's a string of good movies. He's not an auteur as such but he's not just a workaday director either. He does the big Obama biopic with Lakeith Stanfield and that movie where an elderly Daniel Craig has to move back in with his kid, Elliot Page, after a hurricane floods his retirement community. Good stuff. They'll put at least one of them in the Criterion collection, someday.

He's out in Scotland shooting on location for a *Wuthering Heights* reboot—yes, yes, but it's a very experimental script—when he slides down a hillside, ending up with a nasty compound fracture in his right ankle.

❖

MEANWHILE DOCTOR APOCALYPSE is at the core of the earth, meditating on how easy it would be to trigger the Yellowstone Supervolcano. Eventually Magmarnia and her Chthonic Crew sense the disturbance in the magma flows and show up to fight. Doctor Apocalypse vanishes instead.

❖

THE FIRST ANKLE surgery is pretty badly botched and so they have to operate three or four times. Nicholas Tremaine is in pain for a good long while. He's able to finish the *Wuthering* movie but he can tell it's not as good as it would have been, and after that he can't work for most of a year. He goes through a couple of physical therapists and eventually settles on Guillaume, a strikingly handsome young man. One night Guillaume finishes massaging Nicholas's calf and his hands move up to the knee.

What the hell, thinks Nicholas Tremaine. It's the thirties.

Six months later, Nicholas still hobbling a little down the aisle, they're married.

It's a happy marriage, an agreeably unequal marriage. Guillaume is young and beautiful and very good in bed and genuinely cares for Nicholas, doting on him in a way that's a little condescending but mostly very sweet. Nicholas is sophisticated, older, wiser, better connected. The only problem, the only teensy-tiny flaw, is that the physical therapy hasn't really sorted everything out and so Nicholas is in the habit of taking a codeine pill every evening to help with the ankle. Just to take the edge off.

❖

DOCTOR APOCALYPSE INADVERTENTLY saves a child overboard from drowning by making the entire Sea of Japan disappear. Unfortunately then the child—and the boat, and all of the boats and all of the fish in the entire sea—find themselves plummeting a mile straight down toward the seafloor as walls of water the height of mountains sweep in towards them. Only the intervention of the Pacific Patrol's new speedster-slash-self-duplicator, Lickity Split, is able to prevent mass loss of life. Fortunately, the superheroes are able to replenish the sea as well.

Later on, astronomers detect the original Sea of Japan, now a very oddly shaped comet, on an angry trajectory toward Betelgeuse.

It's apparently hard to explain to laypeople what exactly makes a trajectory "angry," but all the serious astronomers agree: it's pissed as hell.

❖

FOR NICHOLAS, THE opioid thing gets worse and then there's quiet and supportive rehab and then the opioid thing gets worse and then there's messy rehab and then the opioid thing gets worse and there's court-ordered rehab. Somewhere in there is the second divorce. Hard to blame Guillaume, honestly, though Nicholas does.

The court-ordered rehab works, kind of, a little bit. Nobody wants Nicholas Tremaine to direct anymore because either he's high and a terrible, irritable director or he's in pain and a terrible, irritable director. He scrapes by for a few years doing script doctoring. Somewhere along the way he learned how to write or at least how to fake it. The drug addiction doesn't hurt his artist cred.

Perri shows up one day—*remember me? The roommate?*—and asks for a couple million dollars to produce her webseries, *One Two Three*. Nicholas doesn't have that kind of money anymore but he knows people, makes a few calls. He winds up with an executive producer credit.

He doesn't expect much to come of it but it turns out one of Perri's co-stars, a younger nonbinary actor named Cal, is a huge fucking smash. They're desperately memeable, or so the kids seem to believe. The whole series gets picked up by a major studio. The big thing now is insta-reboots of memeable successes, so they drop season 1.2—insta-reboots get weird season numbers—and what do you know, it's a hit!

Big hit, big big hit. A lot of money comes flooding back in, the kind of money you can use to indulge your heroin habit while making it look extremely classy.

And it would have worked, too, except at the season 2.0 cast party Perri walks in on Nicholas shooting up in the bathroom, and she looks at him. Her eyes are the same eyes that night in the bar, after she saw Doctor Apocalypse. The exact same dead, frozen eyes.

How's that for a higher fucking power, you court-ordered motherfuckers?

So he can't explain it, but he goes cold turkey. Throws his shit in the bathroom trashcan then and there and just walks away. Shakes be damned.

That night he and Perri are out on the balcony smoking cigars and looking up at the sky.

"What's the deal with your hat?" says Nicholas.

"You wanna know the truth?"

Nicholas says nothing, just sucks down a couple of puffs and waits for it.

"My dad, he really loved the Dodgers."

◆

ON A DISTANT world, where seas of methane crash on shores of tholin sand, Doctor Apocalypse washes up with the high tide. The alien that tends to them looks a little like a sad dog and a lot like a nudibranch, but it never does quite figure out how to feed a three-faced alien skeleton in a spacesuit.

Eventually Doctor Apocalypse wakes up—or at least starts moving again; it's hard to tell. Once standing, Doctor Apocalypse with a single gesture creates a spike of salt that reaches all the way to heaven, and then leaves.

◆

NICHOLAS GETS TO pitch a couple of shows to the studio but his aim is a little off. They'll take his least favorite one but only if he agrees to act in it also. They figure he can draw a certain nostalgia crowd.

It's a bad show and his heart's not in it and it spirals down and down and isn't renewed for a second season. Cal's got this thing, this traveling immersive virtual comedy circus act? Who knows. Kids these days. Anyway, they're willing to cut in Nicholas, and so for a couple of years he's traveling around the globe, directing occasionally, working the writer's room, arguing with metropolitan zoning authorities about whether the show counts as a fairground or a campsite, that sort of thing.

They stop off in maybe three dozen countries but for whatever reason the show is *huge* in Kenya. *Enormous.* They stay for one year, then two. Cal actually gets romantically involved with this fairly prominent Kenyan poet, starts talking about settling the show in Mombasa permanently.

But it's not working for Nicholas. Either the show's changing on him or he's the one changing but regardless, it's time for him to move on. He dawdles for a while—hard to walk away—and then, finally, two days before he's supposed to fly to LA someone calls him with the news: Rosario has died in a car crash.

He gets to the airport, he's frantic, he's trying to change his ticket to travel to London, trying to move up the departure date, practically crying to the airline representative. But nobody can help him.

Nobody can help him because there's a strange, inexplicable weather pattern: stormclouds around the entire globe.

Doctor Apocalypse is back.

Doctor Apocalypse is going to kill God again.

❖

THE FIGHT BETWEEN God and Doctor Apocalypse lasts for twenty-two days, the longest yet. This time God does not take many forms. In all the dreams of all the world, God is just one thing, one terrible machine that looks a little like an earthmover that H.R. Geiger and Leonardo DaVinci designed together on the same nightmarish acid trip. And Doctor Apocalypse is ever and always Doctor Apocalypse, burning electric green, midnight black, the yellow color of old bone, striking at God. And this time God hits back hard enough to hurt.

Twenty-two days of thunder and nights of fear, and meanwhile somewhere down on Earth, Nicholas Tremaine is yelling at travel agents and charter pilots and rental agents and finally, at last, buying a car and driving north.

God rips Doctor Apocalypse's right arm off. It comes back, but that's never happened before.

Nicholas Tremaine drives over the Bosphorus. Stormclouds ahead, stormclouds behind. It looks like a Byzantine end of days.

Doctor Apocalypse hurts God badly, impaling five of His seven metal hearts, but God doesn't die.

Nicholas Tremaine drives through the Alps, through the high countries and the low.

God smashes Doctor Apocalypse's space helmet into smithereens. Every radio on earth can only pick up the sound of constant screaming in the vacuum of heaven.

Nicholas Tremaine is in the Chunnel, just coming under the Cliffs of Dover, when the fight ends.

God gets a hold of Doctor Apocalypse's jaw, snapping it. And Doctor Apocalypse vanishes. Retreats. Runs away.

You win some, you lose some.

God goes back to being things other than a terrible machine of war, a little smugly but also, honestly, happier than He's been since the seventies.

And Nicholas Tremaine arrives in London to find that he's two weeks late for his ex-wife's funeral.

❖

OF COURSE HE is. They had to bury her. You can't leave

someone lying in state for three weeks as their estranged ex-husband hurtles back from ten thousand kilometers away. You can't leave the dead unburied just because Doctor Apocalypse is trying to kill God.

Life goes on.

❖

LIFE GOES ON.

Nicholas means to get a ticket back to LA, really he does, but instead of that he bums around London for about eighteen months. He gets really into drinking absinthe and writing inappropriately vulnerable letters to his ex-wife's surviving children, then burning them unsent. He does a little acting. The baby from *Cheap at Twice the Price*—the literal fucking *baby*—is now some sort of elder stateswoman of independent British theater and thanks to her help Nicholas ends up doing a stint at the Edinburgh Fringe. While he's in Edinburgh he hears about these burners who are going to sail from Edinburgh to Prince Edward Island. Turns out that yes, they do have room for one slightly useless older actor, so there you go.

In Prince Edward Island he buys a car, one of the very first electric Edison convertibles, and he sees America. It's an almost offensively authentic experience, very Ansel Adams, and he loves it, until one night in the Arizona desert, driving a little later than he should be, honestly, Nicholas Tremaine runs off the road and into a ditch, totalling his classic car. There's no cell service and so he begins the long slow walk to the next town over, bleeding a bit from his scalp. Painfully underdressed for hiking; he's wearing a silk robe he bought from a vintage store in Iowa.

He makes it about five miles before there's a blue streak in the moonlight. It hurtles down the road toward him and then screeches to a halt, resolving into the form of a young man in a blue spandex suit with an orange fabric mohawk.

"Good evening, sir! I'm the Roadrunner, out on patrol."

Nicholas stares. "Figures," he says.

"Do you require any assistance?" Huge Boy Scout vibes. Young superheroes get like that, sometimes.

Nicholas stares for a long while. "How old are you?"

"Seventeen, sir."

"Christ," says Nicholas Tremaine, seventy-two years old and shuffling down a desert highway in a dressing gown. "You're a *child*."

◈

After that, well, it's the last leg of the journey. He can feel it now. In every step he takes. Every morning getting out of bed and every evening getting back into it. He keeps going for years, six, seven years, but it's the last leg. Every show he works on, every part he takes, he's thinking, well, this could be the last one. There's not going to be some final triumph. There's just going to be a show, and after that, he won't do any more shows.

It's called *Two At Home*, and it's a play, and it's pretty good. He's pretty good in it. So the theater people say.

After that, no more shows.

There's enough money saved up. He finds a retirement community up in Santa Barbara that mostly caters to retired showbiz folks, and he moves in.

For a while he does nothing much for the first time in a long time, really. Laps down at the pool. Dinner at four thirty. Shuffleboard.

It's an old actors' home so there are of course a lot of small-time theatrical productions. (You can't really call them "amateur".) At first Nicholas stays away but then he starts to feel the itch.

He auditions for a couple of the shows but doesn't land any parts. Retirement community politics are petty and brutal and he's not really feeling it anyway.

Deep down Nicholas Tremaine knows what show he wants to do. So he stops auditioning, drags out his old laptop, and writes.

❖

NICHOLAS TREMAINE: A Life debuts on a warm and windy evening in April. It's a one-man one-act autobiographical show.

It runs for ninety minutes, curtain to curtain. In the field out behind the retirement home, it plays to an audience of forty folding chairs.

There's one more chair at the front. Nicholas Tremaine sits on it. No more standing and pacing and throwing theatrics. He's in his eighties, now.

He sits in that chair and for ninety minutes he tells the story of his life, all of it. Without pity, without indulgence. Spare and pure and honest.

It's a pretty good show.

At first only a couple of people come, and then word gets out in the retirement community that it's pretty good, and so the audience is mostly full for a few weeks. Then it gets some attention in the retired showbiz corners of the internet, and some people from outside trickle in. Perri comes, and the kid sister from *Cheap at Twice the Price*, and a guard and a prisoner from *Department of Corrections* and the Cathy from *Wuthering* and so on. Portalina warps in from her work at the UN and is very polite to everyone who's much more excited to see her than Nicholas. And lots of people don't make it, also.

And then there are the strangers who come for their own reasons: the curious, the interested, the one-man show fans. They fill out the audience too.

But if you keep doing the same show, night after night, eventually you run out of people to come.

And so on a surprisingly cool night in late July, Nicholas Tremaine stands to the side of the stage, looking at an empty audience. He smiles, and crosses to his chair, and sits down.

One instant the audience is empty.

And the next instant it isn't.

Doctor Apocalypse is sitting in the second row, third seat from the right. Black space suit and electric green trim and off-white bone. None the worse for wear for having tried and failed to kill God.

Nicky smiles, and he does the show.

It's a good performance, maybe his best ever. Strong and sincere and true.

Ninety minutes.

And at the end of it, Doctor Apocalypse is still sitting in that chair.

Nicky Tremaine turns to Doctor Apocalypse and he says, "I've lived a good life. I've had plenty to be ashamed of, plenty to be proud of. I hit rock bottom more than once, and I've come back. In the end, I'm satisfied. And here, at the end of my life, I am no longer afraid. Not of death. Not of you. And it turns out, after all that, I only have one question left. I don't even want to know why you came to my old one-act play the first time. Things just happen. But I do want to know: why did you keep coming back?"

Nicky Tremaine asks this question. And he does not expect to receive a reply, because Doctor Apocalypse never speaks to anyone. But he asks the question, and he waits.

And Doctor Apocalypse sits there, and does not disappear.

And then Doctor Apocalypse speaks.

The voice sounds a little bit like hammers ringing on the anvil on which the sword of creation is forged, but only a little. Mostly it sounds like a person's voice, an ordinary person, speaking loudly and distinctly so as to be heard from a very, very long way away.

Doctor Apocalypse speaks. And Doctor Apocalypse says:

"I wanted to see your second act."

Contributors

Phoebe Barton is a queer trans science fiction writer, and this story made her cry while writing it. Her short fiction has appeared in venues such as *Analog, Lightspeed,* and *F&SF,* and she is an Aurora Award and Nebula Award winner. She lives with her family and many typewriters in Hamilton, Ontario, Canada. Find her online at phoebebartonsf.com.

Renan Bernardo is a Nebula and Ignyte finalist author of science fiction and fantasy from Brazil. His fiction appeared in *Reactor/Tor.com, Clarkesworld, Apex Magazine, Podcastle, Escape Pod,* and elsewhere. His solarpunk/clifi short fiction collection, Different Kinds of Defiance, was published in 2024. His dark sci-fi novella, *Disgraced Return of the Kap's Needle,* was published in 2025 by Dark Matter Ink. He also had stories recommended by *Locus* and longlisted for the BSFA. He can be found at BlueSky (@ renanbernardo.com) and his website: renanbernardo.com.

AnaMaria Curtis is from the part of Illinois that is very much not Chicago, where she learned to be argumentative, competitive, and nostalgic. She is the winner of the 2019 Dell Magazines Award and the LeVar Burton Reads Origins and Encounters Contest, and her work has been published in magazines including *Clarkesworld, Uncanny,* and *Strange Horizons.* You can get in touch or find more of her work at anamariacurtis.com or on Bluesky at @anamariacurtis.bsky.social.

David DeGraff (he/him) taught physics and astronomy at Alfred University in Alfred NY. In addition to the usual physics and astronomy classes, he also taught classes on the Theory and Practice of Time Travel, the science in Star Trek, Doctor Who, Superheroes, and Supervillains. His fiction has appeared in *The Magazine of Fantasy & Science Fiction, Lightspeed, Escape Pod*, and other places. He's online at DavidDeGraff.com.

Louis Evans is a professional, since tonight you paid for your ticket. In addition to *Fusion Fragment*, his fiction has appeared in *ECO24, Vice, Grist*, and many more, and is forthcoming in *Reactor*. He's online at louisevans.org and on Bluesky at louisevans.bsky.social. He lives in Brooklyn with his spouse and two cats named after fictional detectives.

Kelsey Hutton (she/her) is a Métis author from Treaty 1 territory and the homeland of the Métis Nation, also known as Winnipeg, Canada. Kelsey was born in an even snowier city than she lives in now ("up north," as they say in Winnipeg). She also used to live in Brazil as a kid. Her work has appeared in *Analog Science Fiction & Fact, Beneath Ceaseless Skies, Augur Magazine* and others. When she's not beading or cooking, you can find her at KelseyHutton.com, on Instagram at @KelseyHuttonAuthor, or on Twitter/X at @KelHuttonAuthor.

Angel Leal (they/she) is a Mexican, trans, ace writer and poetry editor for OTHERSIDE. The piece collected in this book is an elegy to their tío Chuy whose life is still a precious mystery. Their previous work has appeared in *Strange Horizons, Uncanny Magazine, The Deadlands, Fantasy Magazine*, and elsewhere. They've been nominated for the Pushcart Prize, Best of the Net, the Rhysling Award, and are a graduate of Clarion West 2025. You can find more of their stories at angel-leal.com or chat on Bluesky @angelvleal.bsky.social.

Ann LeBlanc is a writer, editor, and woodworker. Her debut novella, *The Transitive Properties Of Cheese,* is a cyberpunk cheese-heist, published by Neon Hemlock. Ann is the editor of *Embodied Exegesis,* an anthology of cyberpunk and posthuman stories by transfem authors. Her short fiction has been published in *Strange Horizons, Clarkesworld Magazine, Escape Pod,* and *Baffling Magazine.* You can find her in cyberspace at www.annleblanc.com

Stephen M.A. is a gay, he/him, first-generation tribal descendant and blood quantum casualty, born and raised on the Flathead Reservation in big sky country. His work includes stories in *Apex Magazine, Fantasy Magazine, and The Deadlands*—plus the self-published short *The Clam Beds, the novel Tiny Planet Filled With Liars,* and the Kirkus-reviewed novelette *Stan, Stan, the Bacteria Man.* Keep in touch at smapublishing.com

Uchechukwu Nwaka is an Igbo medical student at University of Ibadan, Nigeria. His works have appeared in venues such as *Clarkesworld, Escape Pod, Fusion Fragment, FIYAH, Omenana,* and others, and collected in *Year Best Anthologies – Best Weird Fiction vol 1.* His works have been nominated for the Utopia and BSFA Awards. He is the winner of the Locus Award for Best Novelette in 2024. When he's not writing short fiction, he can be found reading manga, streaming TV shows, playing amateur volleyball, or trying to catch up with his endless schoolwork. He still stalks X as @uche_cjn.

Suzan Palumbo is a Trinidadian-Canadian, dark speculative fiction writer and editor. Her work has been nominated for the Nebula, Aurora, World Fantasy and Locus awards. She also cofounded the Ignyte Awards and coedited the special Caribbean issue of *Strange Horizons*. Her debut dark fantasy/horror short story collection *Skin Thief* was published in 2023 by Neon Hemlock. Her novella, *Countess*, was a finalist for the Nebula, Locus and Aurora Awards. Her full bibliography can be found at suzanpalumbo.carrd.co

B. Pladek is a writer and literature professor based in Milwaukee, WI. He's published fiction in *Lightspeed, Slate Future Tense, Strange Horizons, Fantasy*, and elsewhere. His debut novel DRY LAND was shortlisted for the Crawford Award and his short fiction has been nominated for an Ignyte. He can be found on all socials @bpladek and online at bpladek.net.

M. R. Robinson is a scholar of Renaissance literature… but when she isn't talking about sonnets, she's probably writing or reading speculative fiction. A graduate of Viable Paradise and Clarion West, her short fiction has appeared in magazines including *Beneath Ceaseless Skies, Flash Fiction Online*, and *Haven Spec*, and she is one of the co-founders of *OTHERSIDE*, a magazine of speculative fiction by queer authors. She lives in a crumbly old house with her wife and two medium-well-behaved dogs. You can find her across social media as @mruthrobinson or at m-r-robinson.com.

Denzel Xavier Scott is the author of the poetry collection, *Delphinium Gospel,* published by ELJ Editions. His poetry and fiction has been published in *Beneath Ceaseless Skies, Fiyah Magazine, Fantasy and Science Fiction Magazine,* and *The Deadlands.* His essays, literary fiction, nonfiction, and literary poetry appear in *Spillway, Rattle, Decomp, Pidgeonholes, Empty Mirror, the Cortland Review, Random Sample Review, Linden Avenue,* amongst many others. He earned his BA in English from the University of Chicago and received his Writing MFA at the Savannah College of Art and Design (SCAD) in his hometown, Savannah, GA. You can find him often on Twitter in real-time at @DenzelScott.

Jo Telle (she/they) is a Black, queer, trans femme writer based in Brooklyn, transplanted from California. She holds an MFA in Fiction from Rutgers University - Newark, is a 2024 Lambda Literary Emerging Voices Fellow, and is a graduate of Clarion West class of 2023. Their writing can be found in *FIYAH, Tales & Feathers, and The Bitchin' Kitsch.* She spends her days teaching writing to undergraduates, building LEGO sets with no place to put them, avoiding claw marks from her cat Cinta, and planning her next tattoo. It's probably another dinosaur. Instagram - @jo.telle

Kristina Ten is the author of *Tell Me Yours, I'll Tell You Mine* (2025, Stillhouse Press). Her stories appear in *The Best American Science Fiction and Fantasy, We're Here: The Best Queer Speculative Fiction, The Best Weird Fiction of the Year,* and elsewhere. She has won the *McSweeney's* Stephen Dixon Award for Short Fiction, the Subjective Chaos Kind of Award, and the *F(r)iction* Writing Contest, and has been a finalist for the Shirley Jackson Award and the Locus Award. Ten is a graduate of Clarion West Writers Workshop and the University of Colorado Boulder's MFA program in fiction, and has received fellowships from the Ragdale Foundation and the Martha's Vineyard Institute of Creative Writing.

Izzy Wasserstein, queer and trans woman, is the author of two poetry collections, the short story collection *All the Hometowns You Can't Stay Away From* (Neon Hemlock, 2022), the novella *These Fragile Graces, This Fugitive Heart* (Tachyon, 2024), and the forthcoming fiction chapbook *This Next Song is Called Punk Rock Valhalla* (Neon Hemlock). She teaches writing and literature at a public university. A born-and-raised Kansan, she currently lives in Southern California, where she shares a home with the writer Nora E. Derrington and their animal companions. You can find her on Bluesky and at izzywasserstein.com.

John Wiswell is an ace/aro writer who lives where New York keeps all its trees. His debut novel, *Someone You Can Build A Nest In*, won the Nebula and Locus Awards. His fiction has also been a finalist for the Hugo, World Fantasy, and British Fantasy Awards, and has been translated into fourteen languages. He dreams of hugging a shark.

Claire Jia-Wen is a speculative fiction writer originally from the 626 and has been published in *khōréō* and *Clarkesworld*. A Viable Paradise and Clarion alum, she is currently a PhD student studying human-computer interaction. You can find her at clairejiawen.com.

Story Acknowledgements

"Mama uat-ur" by Zebib K. Abraham originally appeared in *PodCastle*

"Climbing the Mountains of Me" by Phoebe Barton (Kaleidotrope)

"The Offer of Peace Between Two Worlds" by Renan Bernardo (Diabolical Plots)

"Something Small Enough to Ask For" by AnaMaria Curtis (Uncanny)

"Mackson's Mardi Gras Moon Race" by David DeGraff (F&SF)

"Show Goes On" by Louis Evans (Fusion Fragment)

"Emergency Calls Only" by Kelsey Hutton (Analog)

"A Book Is a Map, a Bed Is a Country" by Angel Leal (Uncanny)

"Memories Held Against a Hungry Mouth" by Ann LeBlanc (3LBE)

"The Owl" by Stephen M.A. (Apex)

"No Happy Endings for Chasers" by Uchechukwu Nwaka (Fiyah)

"Jumbie Closet" by Suzan Palumbo (The Crawling Moon)

"The Spindle of Necessity" by B. Pladek (Strange Horizons)

"Linden Honey, Blackcurrant Wine" by M. R. Robinson (Beneath Ceaseless Skies)

"Zariel: Parable of a Gifted Black Child" by Denzel Xavier Scott (F&SF)

"Together Like Hands on a Clock" by Jo Telle (Fiyah)

"How to Make a Snow Maiden" by Kristina Ten (Porter House Review)

"Syndical Organization in Revolutionary Transition" by Izzy Wasserstein (Embodied Exegesis)

"A Taste of Justice" by John Wiswell (Sunday Morning Transport)

"The Last Flesh Figure Skaters" by Claire Jia-Wen (khōréō)

About the Editors

Ryka Aoki is a poet, composer, teacher, and novelist. Her latest novel, *Light From Uncommon Stars* (Tor Books 2021) was an Alex, SCKA, and Otherwise Award winner, and was also a finalist for the Hugo, Locus, and Ignyte Awards.

Charles (Cy) Payseur is an avid reader, writer, and reviewer of speculative fiction. Their works have appeared in *The Best American Science Fiction and Fantasy*, *Lightspeed Magazine*, and *Beneath Ceaseless Skies*, among others, and many are included in their debut collection, *The Burning Day and Other Strange Stories* (Lethe Press 2021). They are the series editor of the Locus and Ignyte Award winning *We're Here: The Best Queer Speculative Fiction* (Neon Hemlock Press) and a multiple-time Hugo and Ignyte Award finalist for their work at *Quick Sip Reviews*. You can follow their reviews (and cats) on their Patreon (/quicksipreviews).

About the Press

Neon Hemlock is a Washington, DC-based small press publishing speculative fiction, rad zines and queer chapbooks. Publishers Weekly once called us "the apex of queer speculative fiction publishing" and we're still beaming.

Learn more about us at neonhemlock.com.

www.ingramcontent.com/pod-product-compliance
Lightning Source LLC
Chambersburg PA
CBHW021215310726
48971CB00006B/1566